THE GREAT HI

~

COPYRIGHT 2017 DAVID OLIVER
ALL RIGHTS RESERVED

~

FOR ME, BECAUSE I HAVE ALWAYS WANTED TO WALK IN THE FOOTSTEPS OF THE GREATS.

~

Map of the central Andurran Empire
wrought by Scribemaster Dali
Forgoth
Lagos
Rossen
Anderal
Melioth
Missen

Map of the Central Empire my arse!
Completely useless. I've added some more
useful content - maybe you'll crack a smile
when you finally think straight.
CD

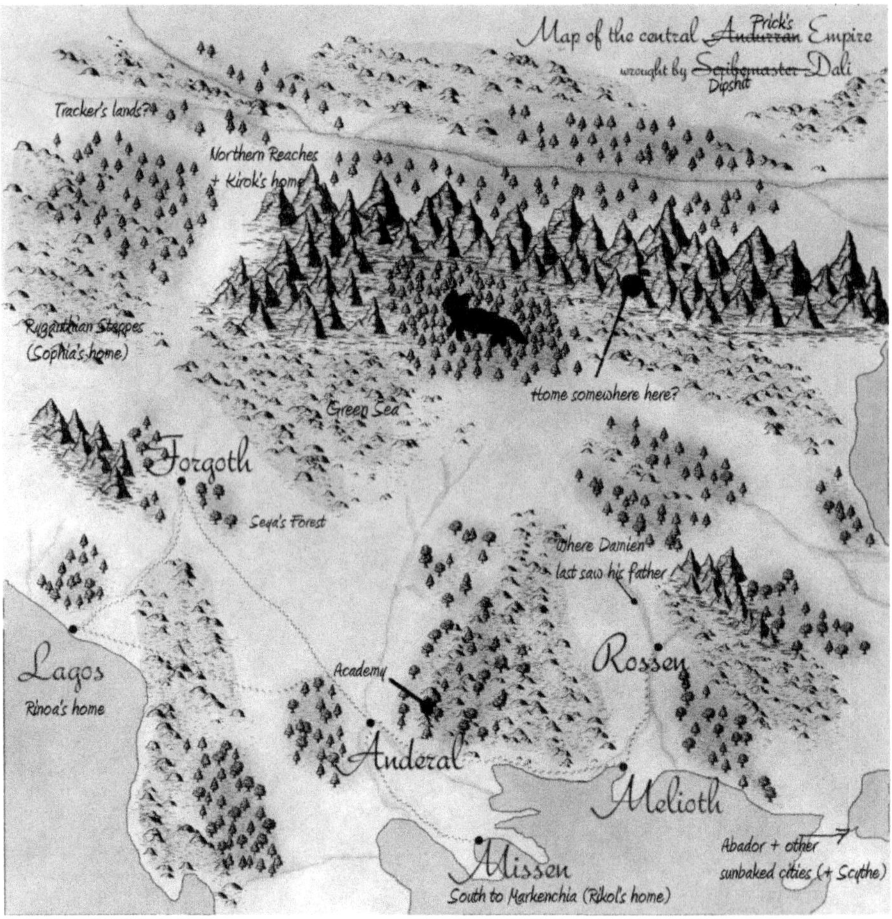
Map of the central ~~Anduran~~ Prick's Empire
wrought by ~~Scribemaster~~ Dipshit Dali
Tracker's lands?
Northern Reaches
+ Kirok's home
Steppes
(Sophia's home)
Home somewhere here?
Green Sea
Forgoth
Seya's Forest
Where Damien
last saw his father
Lagos
Rinoa's home
Academy
Rossen
Anderal
Melioth
Abador + other
sunbaked cities (+ Scythe)
Missen
South to Markenchia (Rikol's home)

PROLOGUE

~

A moonlit night
Screams
Blood
Fire
Hunger

The crack of a broken branch shook me from my reverie, the sound carrying far in the frozen woods where I stalked my prey. Somewhere to my south east ran a desperate man. A hard working father, loyal husband and model employee. A man who fled because he knew what I know. That underneath the facade he was a monster of hate and sadism, a monster who unbeknownst to his wife owned a small property on the edge of town which reeked of blood, murder and children's bones.

But mainly he ran because he was prey. The fiend knew that an alpha predator had come to upset his little game, and like any displaced predator he understood that the tables had turned and that escape was the only option. More amusing is that he, like all the others before, knew that escape was impossible, and yet still he tried. Still scrambled and scraped his way through the forest in a terror induced panic. Still splashed through ice cold rivers and dark gullies with his heart beating so quickly, so sweetly. Still held onto the faint hope that he had a chance of escape.

Unfortunately for him, I was not alone.

I casually strolled to the fire that lit up the frozen, forested landscape. A large figure sat silhouetted by the flames, firelight dancing across his polished armour. Nearing eight feet tall, Cassius was a hulking monstrosity, my one true friend and utterly, completely, insane.

Clapping Cassius on the shoulder I sat down by the fire and basked in its warm glow, sipping the mug of brandy enriched coffee that I had carried while sedately meandering through the woods after our fugitive. Unlike him, I found no need to sprint through the forest at night, preferring to stroll in a leisurely fashion that held just a hint of menace...we killers all like our little games.

After a few more sips of coffee my eyes slide upward to where the prey hung, swinging by a rope just above the fire. His hands and mouth were bound; his legs very much broken. It appeared that Cassius had stopped the man's night-time jog through these lovely woods with a sweeping blow from the flat of his blade. An easy enough blow to dodge in a normal fight perhaps, but from a man the size and strength of my brother in arms, a man who wields a greatsword as a hand and a half weapon, I'm surprised he had any legs left at all. As it was his legs looked as though they had suddenly stopped and everything from the knees upwards had kept moving.

I reached up and removed the gag from the swaying man's mouth. He spluttered and whimpered, no doubt in sweet, agonising pain. Hanging bound by your feet when your shins are now behind your calves must have been excruciatingly painful and yet the man didn't dare raise his cries to above a murmur. Either he was still in shock, or he had become fully aware of who was chasing him. I decided to test the theory and poked him with a fiery stick. He screamed at the top of his lungs...looked like the latter.

"Do you know who I am?" I asked. He mumbled something incoherent. I stepped forward and took hold of his ear; quick as a flash my belt knife sliced up and separated it from his taciturn head. Relishing the sound of his screams I held his ear against mine and said, "Sorry...I didn't ear that." Little games, like I said.

After unnecessarily cauterising the man's ear hole I waited for him to regain consciousness before asking again, "Do you know who I am?"

"Imperator!" he cried.

"And do you know what being an Imperator means?" I asked sweetly.

"You, you are the Emperor's right arm, his voice in the wild!" the man exclaimed.

"Exactly," I replied. "His voice in the wild. Wild. What that means is I have better things to be doing than travelling to your shithole of a town to investigate some missing children. You are a complete and utter waste of my time. Worse - you're an inept killer. Can't hide children's bodies effectively and can't keep Cassius entertained for even a second with a good fight." I glowered at the man and he cringed, seeing the bloodlust in my eyes.

"You know what being an Imperator means, but do you know what we are? What the Emperor makes out of us?" I asked, studying the broken man.

"Killers," he replied.

"True enough," I sighed, grabbing my knife. "But he doesn't just make killers…What the Emperor makes," I thrust my blade deep into the man's throat and stood underneath him eye to bloodshot eye. "…What the Emperor makes is monsters."

I cleansed my face of the incompetent murderer's blood and walked over to Cassius. He hadn't moved an inch during my pleasant conversation with the man he captured.

"Now that that irritating diversion is taken care of, are you ready to continue?" I asked. Cassius stood, towering over my lean six foot two inch frame and began to glide off silently into the woods; an impressive feat when wearing plate armour. "Excellent!" I replied, "Off we trot!" That's the problem with being brothers with a silent lunatic, the conversation is somewhat one sided.

We left the corpse swaying in the wind as we walked away.

My name is Calidan Darkheart. I am what the Emperor made me. Monster.

PART I
SHADOW & FLAME

~

CHAPTER ONE
BIRTH

~

I WASN'T ALWAYS A KILLER. In fact, I didn't kill until I was eleven years old. Cassius, though he may look and act like a hulking violent brute at times, managed to avoid killing until he was fourteen. He always was a slow learner.

Cassius and I were born in a small village, nestled high in the mountains. One of my few recollections of the place is the feeling of perpetual cold, but with that cold came a stark beauty, particularly when the sunlight glanced off the small lake beneath the village. My parents were, if memory serves, adequate at fulfilling the role. There was affection in our relationship, I was kept warm, well fed and likely had a happy childhood.

Cassius was the boy next door. My best friend from a very young age, Cassius was bold, bright, and full of laughter. His natural charisma made everyone adore him. Most people were more reserved toward me, feeling that I was at times quite cold and calculating. I attribute this to the tendency I had to make the adults around me feel a little slow when talking with me. I learnt fast and had an inexhaustible curiosity about everything - an uncommon trait in a boy from a remote mountain village. Cassius and I were inseparable and filled with mischief, managing to elude our eagle eyed guardians on multiple occasions and embarking on grand, child-sized adventures.

It was during one of these great escapes when we were eleven years old that our lives took a turn for the worse. We were hunting for trolls and demons, staging mock battles and enjoying the vivid imaginations of our youth. We were engrossed in a particularly glorious stick fight when Cassius stiffened, eyes sliding past me to focus on the lakeside. I took the opportunity to deftly slide past his open defence and skewer my friend through the heart.

"Ow! Calidan!" he exclaimed rubbing his chest.

I adopted a kingly voice, "Calidan triumphs over his mighty foe! All shall bow before him..."

"Calidan shush," Cassius said, gripping my shoulder and interrupting my victory dance. "I'm sure I saw something at that side of the lake."

Sensing his seriousness I joined Cassius in peering across the lake, looking for anything out of place. "What did you see?" I asked.

"I'm not entirely sure, I thought perhaps people," he answered quietly.

"That doesn't seem that unusual," I replied, my mind still filled with the euphoria of sweet victory and not yet working at full capacity.

"I don't think any hunting parties have left the village today," he countered, "no one should be outside."

My brain switched on.

Cassius was right. We had snuck out in the early morning light. The night before there had been a feast, the adults had been up late drinking their foul smelling, sweet liquid and most had not arisen when we crept out. The likelihood of anyone from the village being out with us was relatively slim.

"Let's head back," I began to say, before noticing the hair on the back of my neck start to rise and the wide, panicked look in Cassius's eyes. Something moved in the corner of my vision.

I bolted.

Cassius was right beside me as I sprinted like a startled hare through the forest towards the village. Or at least he was until his foot caught a tree root and he fell heavily. A heavy set, bearded man landed on his back and cruelly bound his hands together before throwing him over his shoulder.

I kept running.

I abandoned my best friend.

Not my finest moment perhaps, but even at age eleven I was well aware that my mighty stick sword would not fare well against one made of iron, and that my chances in a duel against Cassius's kidnapper were non-existent. So I listened to my brain and not my heart and ran. I ran as far and as fast as I could, dodging through the trees and the undergrowth until the sounds of pursuit faded.

Even in my mad rush my feet followed the paths that Cassius and I had run many times, I knew that I was near the village and vowed to get help to rescue Cassius.

Slowing my frightened sprint to a walk I began to creep along the forest trail, knowing full well that Cassius's survival depended on me not being discovered before I got back to the village. There was a strange smell in my nostrils, metallic. Similar to when the hunters came back with a fresh kill. I shook my head, trying to remove the smell and that's when I heard the first scream.

Looking at it now, with a professional's eye, the mastermind behind the attack on the village did an excellent job. His or her men had obviously scouted the village, ascertained the day on which there would be a feast, silenced the guards and enjoyed the advantage offered by sober troops versus drunken families. The professional in me admires the skill with which it was done, the hurt child in me still swears revenge.

CHAPTER TWO
SHADOW

~

MEN ROAMED THROUGH THE VILLAGE, killing all who resisted, corralling those who surrendered. I watched from the trees as my father was cut down in front of my family home, his body dragged off to a growing pile in the middle of the village square. I saw my mother dragged from the house and raped by three men before being thrown in with the captives. Most of the women experienced similar, and screams and sobs filled the air. Nor were they the only ones violated; several of the men were treated as the women were until the screams of the village chorused in horrific harmony.

Turning my eyes from the sight, I saw that Cassius had been deposited with the rest of the children, kept in a cage that the village used to protect food from opportunist scavengers. He, thankfully, looked to be unharmed and was bravely trying to console the others. I hoped that he didn't think less of me for leaving him.

Eventually the screams began to quiet and only sobbing remained. A tall, wiry man covered in what looked to be tattoos approached the subdued captives. He was the only one who did not partake in the killing and rape, seemingly preferring to sit back and watch. When he talked he did not yell, but still his voice carried. Reverberating.

"Cattle," he began. "You are all cattle. Fit for breeding and for eating." He smiled wolfishly, "So be glad that you will be part of something greater, for my master comes and he is ever so hungry."

With that he left the villagers and walked over to his men. He raised one finger and spoke in a guttural language that I had never before heard, before entering the chieftain's lodge, the largest building in the village. The previous occupant lay across the veranda, filleted from shoulder to gut.

My younger self never forgot the words that the leader spoke, even though I didn't yet know their meaning. These days I do. A forgotten offshoot of Deinrani, the language was Dethranik and has been considered a dead language for nine hundred generations.

"Kurkekk dein inderk", "You may enjoy one."

I watched through the day as the savages, as I then thought of them, forced the broken men and women to dig a pit in the earth, before making a large fire in the town square. Rocks from the lakeside were gathered and placed in the fire, heating until they glowed. In the afternoon the captives were lined up whilst one of the savages prowled up and down, as if he were a trader inspecting his wares.

Eventually, after enjoying the terrible silence that had fallen at his predatory pacing, the savage pointed at the sole pregnant woman of the village, Silania, whose young husband was one of those broken by the men earlier in the day. Her husband, Dilanius, bravely stood and reached for her, screaming, losing an arm for his efforts. The prowling savage clapped his hand on the screaming man's shoulder, almost as though consoling him, before unleashing a brutal kick to his chest - driving him back into the pile of captives. He then walked Silania over to the pit, now filled with the hot rocks from the fire and grinned at her husband wickedly before ordering her to strip. Holding that same grin he locked eyes with Dilanius as he slashed her throat with a dagger and pushed her into the pit. Dilanius howled, a heartbreaking wail, but no longer had the strength to stand and was held down easily as one of the villagers bandaged what was left of his arm. His cries faded into nothingness as he fainted into what I can only hope was sweet oblivion.

The savages piled more hot rocks on top of Silania's body before covering it with the earth from the dug pit. I had seen this before - for large celebrations the village would often do something similar...the savages had built an oven and Silania was the meal.

As daylight faded distressingly sweet aromas started emanating from the pit oven. But it was only when the sun had long since set and the moon was in the sky that the savages opened the pit and brought out their main course. Poor baked Silania. Even now, as an older, more calloused man who has seen and done many terrible things, I can still remember the sight and the terrible conflict of emotions as I watched the savages tear into Silania, and the horror I felt at myself for my salivating taste buds. You can't blame your body's reaction to this situation however, as it has been conditioned to like this smell... a roasted human body smells strangely similar to roast pork.

Whilst Silania was cooking the savages had busied themselves with creating larger cages, much like the one in which Cassius was housed. They lashed together strong branches with thick twine and before the meal was eaten had completed several. The surviving villagers were then frog marched into these pens. From what I could see, this meant that the savages could have fewer guards watching the villagers and more to join in with the meal. I decided that I could use this to my advantage.

Moving stealthily I crept along the treeline, testing each foot placement before allowing my weight to settle. The crack of a branch now would have given me away as easily as if I was holding a fire brand. Several hours passed before I reached the closest point to Cassius's cage, and the dawn light was just starting to soften the darkness. The guards loosely patrolled the village, focusing primarily on the adults' holding cells. The children were obviously not considered a threat.

Dropping down to slide on my belly, I slithered up to the cage and gently poked Cassius awake. He started and flung his head round with terror filled eyes, only to relax slightly as he recognised me.

"Calidan," he whispered, "you're alive!"

"For now," I whispered back, "but shush, I need to focus and figure out how to get you out of here."

He nodded and looked at me with hope in his eyes. I looked around me, taking in anything nearby that could be used to free my friend. The only thing I could see was the rusted, blunt blade of an axe; the shaft having broken off the previous winter. Hopefully it would still cut through the twine that lashed the cage together.

I slowly dragged the blade against the twine fastening the cage. It made a low grating sound, but didn't leave any noticeable mark in the fibres. Cassius kept watch as I sat down and quickly as I dared, drew the blade up and down. By the time it was too light to avoid detection, I had made a frayed divot in the knot. I gripped Cassius by the shoulder before returning to my hiding place in the woods, making a small den in some ferns and sinking into an exhausted slumber.

When I awoke it was twilight. Exhausted and hungry, I considered approaching the village stores, but I was too afraid of the guards to make the attempt. From my vantage point I could see that something had changed. Several of the adults had disappeared from the cages, and there were fresh, red, swirling patterns across the village square. The patterns made my eyes water and my head throb with a dull, pulsing pain. I turned away and waited for full dark. Whatever these patterns were, they could wait until I had saved Cassius.

Darkness fell. I once again slithered my way to Cassius's cage. His face lit up when he saw me, though his eyes were sad and dark. In muted whispers we conversed and he told me about the missing villagers. Four people had been taken into the village chieftain's house, the building that had seemingly become the residence of the savages' leader, and each time one had entered, a bucket of red liquid had been returned to be painted on the ground. He told me that one of those people was his father. I could guess what that red liquid was, and judging from Cassius's haunted eyes, he knew it too. I gripped him by the shoulder, offering what little comfort I had to give.

As the guards seemed to be converging on the painted swirls I attacked the twine again with gusto. Slowly but surely the axe blade did its work, and the twine began to fray. With each stroke the wooden pole that trapped Cassius loosened.

My focus was pinpointed entirely on the twine, and I relied on Cassius to keep watch. I started as he put a hand on my shoulder and a finger to his lips. He turned my head towards the village square. Three of the villagers had been released from their cages and now stood in the square, each one in the centre of a whorl of patterns. The tattooed man stood upon the dais, reading from a scroll. The moon was full and the man appeared to almost bathe in the moonlight, drinking it in. Shadows, unnatural swirling clouds of black, formed around him and the swirled lines on the floor began glowing a deep red. One shadow, larger than the others, began to form before the chanting man. Three tendrils from the deep central void lashed out to the three villagers, who screamed as if struck by a blade. Their bodies twisted and convulsed. Their screams reaching fever pitch as they disintegrated before my terrified eyes.

A form, darker than the deepest black, began to take shape in the large central shadow. Three more villagers were plucked from the cages. These three did not go willingly.

One was my mother.

She screamed as she was dragged towards the swirls by two men, and this time the tendrils of shadow did not hesitate. As soon as her feet touched the whorl one of them whipped towards her, spearing her through the stomach and doing to her what it did to the others. The only solace I could take was in watching one of the guards, too slow to let go, also be reeled in by the shadow. Their screams... her screams, echoed through the night. Tears blinding my eyes, I turned my head away from the horrific display and feverishly tore at the twine. I didn't understand what was happening, but I had just lost my entire family and so I focussed on trying to save the one person I had left. I cut and cut, hoping that the screams would drown out the noise of my blade.

Slicing. Cutting. Hacking.

Sweat and tears mingled with the blood now dripping from my hands. An inherent problem when using tools not suited to the purpose. Or lacking handles.

A roar freezes my harried scrabbling, a monstrous sound that turns my limbs and guts to jelly. Turning my gaze to the square I could see that the red pulsing swirls had darkened, and the shadows had disappeared. In their place stood...something. Something inhuman. Terrifying. Monstrous. Dark, shadow clad scales that seemed to absorb the moonlight. Two large arms, with biceps bigger by far than the strongest man in the village, lead to six inch claws. A thick, long tail trailed along the floor, curling around clawed feet. The beast's head was crowned with what looked to be four horns, and its eyes glowed a dark red that emanated a frightening intelligence.

It stood on the dais, looking down at the tattooed man who appeared to be in the throes of orgasmic pleasure. The beast towered above the man, easily nine feet tall. It opened its mouth and spoke, the sound paralysing me.

"DOTHRENIK KYULL OKREYNEYEK MAK"

(Bring forward my offerings)

It spoke the same unknown language as the tattooed man. With haste he gestured to his guards and they approached the caged villagers. Once the door was open, the first two 'offerings' tried to run. The guards anticipated the attempt and with swift blows cut deeply into their legs, slicing through bone, tendon and sinew, causing them to drop to the floor in agony. The guards dragged the crippled villagers before the beast. The monster's head swung down and swiftly cut off the agonised screams. The remaining captives started backing further into the cage, fighting with each other to not be next; anything to live that little bit longer.

The creature became increasingly impatient as the guards wrestled with the villagers. Faster than a horse it leapt forward, sprinting towards the cage. It plowed through the cage door and into the wrestling occupants, its vicious claws dispatching everyone nearby, guards included. It roared its delight as it crouched down to feast.

My eyes returned to the twine. I could hear crunching emanating from the remains of the adults' cage. Cassius had just lost his mother. His eyes, seen in the few terror filled moments when I looked up were unforgettable, the image seared into my brain, silently screaming. With a final hack at the fibre the twine finally snaps. I grabbed the branch and started to heave.

Nothing happened.

Fool! I realised now that the stake was wedged firmly into the ground. I squatted down and started feverishly attacking the dirt around the branch in an effort to loosen it.

More screams rose from the square. The beast had found the second cage of adults. Only the children remained.

I kept my head down and continued digging. I was determined not to lose him.

Another roar. Don't look, keep digging.

A heavy footstep. Keep digging. Keep focussed.

A child's scream. I looked up, unable to stop myself. Iola, a four year old girl, was suspended in the air. A viciously clawed hand had broken through the bars and a large red eye inspected what it had caught.

"RYKILIK. NORGATH. TENGEK."

Young. Sweet. Tender.

Crunch

My hands found the top of the bar and desperately pulled.

A guard noticed the motion as the red eye, finished with its meal, swivelled back to the cage.

"CASSIUS!" I screamed as the clawed hand found Tobias, a young child from four houses down. Cassius whipped around and slammed his shoulder into the bar. The bottom shifted slightly before finally coming free from the dirt. My friend threw his body against the bar as I pulled and finally, the gap was made. His momentum carried him through the opening and he landed on top of me. Freedom.

We had no time to pause, the guard was yelling and pointing in our direction. The satisfied crunching from the monster had ceased and I could sense its attention on us. A deep growling, pitched lower than anything I had ever heard reverberated behind us. I dragged Cassius to his feet and we sprinted into the forest.

The beast didn't give chase. Afterall, it still had two more morsels in the children's cage. One, Tidus, tried for the same gap, but the beast was a quick learner and snapped him up in its jaws.

Cassius and I fled into the forest. Three men sprinted in pursuit.

CHAPTER THREE
PURSUIT

~

AS DISCOVERED SO RECENTLY BY the child murderer I hunted, sprinting through a forest, especially at night, is no easy feat. For Cassius and I though, there was a trade off. We had thoroughly explored the forest surrounding the village over the years, and were both fleet of foot. However as eleven year olds we didn't have the stamina of the grown men pursuing us. But, for the immediate chase we managed to make good use of the full moon's light, and gained a considerable lead.

By the time we stopped running, we were completely lost, and much deeper into the woods than either of us had ever gone. Confident that we had shaken our pursuers, Cassius and I found a rotten, hollowed out log and squeezed inside. Small stature has its benefits when hiding in the woods. A long and exhausting night followed, where every bird call was a footfall, every animal noise was the monster.

I awoke, unaware of where I was, Cassius's hand over my mouth. Just before I unconsciously began to struggle, my brain fired up and I realised why Cassius had woken me. Voices murmured softly somewhere nearby. The language was not one I understood, nor was it the same as the language spoken by the beast and the tattooed man. Peering out of a small gap in the rotten wood I caught a glimpse of one of the men, standing only a short distance away. He was small compared to the other savages I had seen, carrying a bow and speaking softly. In fact he looked much like the best hunter in our village, a tracker renowned for finding prey when no others could. I processed that thought again. Tracker. At eleven years old I didn't yet know any particularly good curses, but what went through my mind had much the same gist.

I slowly began to crawl out of the log, trusting in my small size and slow movement to hide me. I knew that if we stayed where we were we would be caught, and if caught, we were dead. Once free of the log I motioned to Cassius to do the same, and together we slid on our bellies out of the men's line of sight, behind a small rise in the ground. From there we painstakingly crawled until once more lost in the undergrowth.

Rising to his feet Cassius extended his hand and helped me up. He didn't let go once I stood upright. I looked at him questioningly, raising an eyebrow.

"Thank you," he said. "Even if we're caught, you've given me a chance, and that is a lot more than I had." Not used to such emotion I gave him an embarrassed grin and a quick squeeze of his hand.

"Let's get out of here," I replied, somewhat more confidently than I felt.

Together we slipped through the forest, attempting to hide our trails as we went. Looking back now our attempts were laughable, but at the time we felt that they would throw anyone off our trail. Running back and forth across our own tracks, leaping from stone to stone, and even rolling down a hill. Amazing how a child's mind can set aside trauma and still be whole enough to make a game of being hunted.

We had three major problems; no food, no water, and pursuit by men who likely wanted to feed us to a monster. I wrote off the third as being as fact of our new lives and focussed on the first two. Together Cassius and I managed to find some eggs which we consumed raw, leaving behind an empty nest for the mother to return to. To that bird, we were probably just like the shadow beast, for we would have likely eaten her too had she been there. Aside from that and a few berries that looked fairly recognisable, we hadn't eaten in two days. Hungry doesn't quite cover it.

As for water, living in a forested area on the side of a mountain meant that we were rather well stocked with cold, clear streams. However we had no vessels with which to carry any water, so if we needed some and couldn't find one we would be out of luck. I remembered my father once telling me that a boy could last nearly a week without food, but barely a day without water. So far we had been lucky, if having your village wiped out could be counted as that, but our luck could soon run out. I knew I had to change the dynamics of our current situation.

On the third day we came across a small lake, brimming with fresh, clear mountain water. Cassius and I stood by the lake for a while, discussing how best to proceed. Could we fool the Tracker in some way by swimming across? Looking around I noticed that there were several tracks in the mud besides ours, and realised that this was likely a local watering hole for the wildlife in the area. My blood chilled as I remembered the stories my father had told me of the predatory animals that prowled the area. Panthers, great boars and bears to name but a few.

Some of the hoof prints looked very large and deep in the mud. I figured that they could only belong to a great boar. My father had told me that they stood nearly the height of a man at the shoulder, and had tusks longer than a grown man's arm.

Just like that, a plan formed.

Cassius paled as I explained my plan to him. And well he should. It was highly likely that it would fail in any number of ways, but to my mind, we either faced starvation and death whilst being hunted, or potential starvation and death whilst adopting a more leisurely pace through the woods. I have always been a lazy soul.

CHAPTER FOUR
HUNT

~

FOLIAGE SHIFTED SILENTLY AS THE Tracker knelt by the footprints. The two men with him ambled around with no thought to the spoor they left behind. I did not see or hear the Tracker before he slid out of the bushes, but the two men I heard coming a mile off. It is likely thanks to them that Cassius and I had stayed alive for so long; knowing that your enemy is close is a beautiful advantage.

"Come on," I whispered from my vantage point on a small hillock. "Take the bait." The Tracker looked like he was undecided about whether to follow, but after a short argument with lots of gesturing from the other two, he capitulated.

The three men followed the muddy tracks into some dense brush, the Tracker looking increasingly concerned as he periodically stopped and peered at the tracks that Cassius and I had left for him. The two men grew increasingly irritated at the Tracker's slow progress, doubtless bored with tracking two young children and missing out on the wanton cannibalism and destruction of our village. Eventually, after what sounded like an angry tirade, the two men shouldered their packs and walked on ahead of the third.

Cassius gave me a thumbs up from further along the hillock where he had his eyes on the action that was about to unfold. The two men wandered off along the track, paying no attention to the huffing noises occurring with increasing regularity. Nor did they pause to consider why there would be a wide track through the brush leading directly to the watering spot. A worried shout came from the Tracker and my gaze snapped back to him. He had seen something he didn't like, something that confirmed his suspicions. He took his bow off his shoulder and flexed it, shouting again - more loudly this time.

An angry shout came back from the two men, followed by a guttural, roaring squeal and cries of shock and pain. One of the men reappeared from the brush, arm hanging loosely, running for his life. A loud thudding rapidly approached, and a pair of tusks pierced his chest, lifting him high in the air. As the blood dripped down the great boar's massive tusks, the boar snorted and flung his body away. The man's crumpled corpse hit the ground and rolled limply, blood soaking into the ground around it. The animal grunted angrily and I noticed the sword piercing the massive creature's side, where one of the two men had scored a lucky hit.

Thunk

An arrow launched from the large bow hit the boar in the throat. It squealed in rage and agony, trampling the foliage around it in its throes of fury. Two more arrows followed in quick succession, one piercing the boar's chest, the other following the trajectory of the first and piercing its throat a second time. I gasped, awestruck; no one in our village had ever been able to let off three arrows that rapidly! Forgetting myself, I raised my head, only to immediately duck, an arrow whistling past my ear. It appeared the Tracker was a formidable foe, holding multiple arrows in his left hand rather than the quiver, in a style of bowmanship that I had never before encountered. In hindsight, this wasn't too surprising. Being eleven years of age and living in a small mountain village, one is unlikely to encounter a master of bowmanship.

The near miss did me one favour however. It made me adamant to try to never react unconsciously to surprising or distressing situations, a vow that has served me very well over the years. By reacting to my error however, the Tracker himself erred. He took his eye off the wounded beast, which bent its head and charged, one last, poignant time. The Tracker's aim snapped back to the boar.

Thunk

Thunk

Snap

Two arrows, phenomenal shots both, hit the boar's two eyes almost simultaneously. However the body of the majestic beast took a while to register that its brain was dead, and as it crashed to the ground in its death throes, one of the hooves caught the Tracker's leg as he dived out of the way, breaking it with an audible snap.

The man groaned in pain, lying on top of his snapped bow, leg cruelly broken. It saddened me to realise that the Tracker was just a man - a man with such a talent, and yet with a capability to commit such depraved acts, to eat human flesh and summon beings even fouler than he. I guess if you had to pinpoint a moment, it was this realisation that started to form my current dispassionate view towards, as the priests would say, *'the human spirit'*.

Cassius and I approached the groaning man. He knew we were coming but could not summon the energy to move away. Cassius held out one of the dead men's swords. We found it in the brush next to the filleted corpse of the first man to come upon the startled boar. As we walked slowly towards the Tracker, Cassius holding the sword out in front of him, barely able to keep it aloft, the man eyed us and started laughing, a thick, cruel laugh.

He coughed and spoke in that unintelligible language. When we didn't respond he switched to a second, and then a third. At the fourth attempt, Cassius's ears perked up.

"I recognise some of those words," he said to me, "aren't they similar to those spoken by the trader who visited last summer?"

"I think you're right," I replied, nodding slowly.

The man, sensing our recognition, tried the fourth language again. In time I would come to know it as Low Gothic, the popular language used by the masses in the Andurran Empire; generally just referred to as 'the Empire' (to be said with adequate fear and foreboding by the peons). While training as an Imperator I learned that the language Cassius, myself and the now extinct villagers spoke was a highland language called Tarr, a derivative of Khurdush; the language spoken by an invading Empire two thousand years ago, who took the mountain passes but was prevented from travelling further into the heartland by snow and infighting.

Our fathers hadn't learnt much of the trader's language, aside from that which is necessary in bartering, such as "what", "want", "now" and "how much." As such our own vocabulary was...limited. However, between us we managed to decipher two words that the broken man repeated; "What now?"

A pretty good question.

We could scavenge anything left by the dead men worth taking, salvage what boar meat we could and continue on our merry way, but that left an extremely dangerous man to our rear. Someone who could be found by the others, fixed up and continue in his hunt for us. If he could be removed from the equation, then…

I glanced at Cassius and he met my gaze, steadfast. "I'm not killing a defenceless man," he stated, the tip of the savage's sword buried in the earth by his side. Cassius always was the embodiment of morality, bravery and all things good and decent - even when left an orphan. I had known what he would say before he said it, loved him for it, and knew that he would not condone me to kill the Tracker, if even I could.

"Okay, so if we can't kill him, then what?" I asked. "We're lost in the middle of the forest, with no equipment, food, or weapons. At the very least, we need his things."

"Even with his leg so badly broken, I wouldn't want to go near him to strip him of his gear. We could just take as much as we can carry and leave him here," he replied, still holding me with his reproachful gaze. He knew that I planned the man harm.

We discussed it some more, the crippled man looking at us, expression scornful throughout. Eventually, we came to reason that if other men were going to come they probably would have by now, and decided to stay and try to salvage some meat before scavengers or other predators arrived.

To this end, I squatted down in front of the man, pointed at him, and mimed hunger and our intent to eat the boar. Although his eyes were still murderous, he slowly nods, once. He in turn mimed something else. Fire. He pointed at us to go and gather branches, and on our return he pulled a round piece of glass from his jerkin. Glass was a very rare commodity in the village, only available from the infrequent traders who passed through, so to us, owning a round piece of glass meant wealth beyond compare.

He then pulled out some small, dried pieces of brush and fur. Tinder, which even at my young age I recognised the value of when lighting a fire. Reaching out to the nearest sunbeam, that mottled through the forest trees, the Tracker showed us how the glass focussed and concentrated the light. A short time later we sat in front of the dead great boar, crackling fire right behind us, clumsily using the swords to hack away bloody chunks of meat. I kept the glass disc.

That meal was one of the best of my life. Juicy, dripping, and above all, *fatty* boar steaks, barely cooked over an open fire. I say barely as we were both too hungry to let the steaks cook for long. By the time we were satisfied, Cassius and I were both liberally smeared with boar blood, but for the first time in days, the horrors of the past were shoved to one side and we only thought of eating.

Sated, I tossed a steak to the Tracker, who grabbed it, nodded once and began eating. Say what you want about me, but I honour my agreements. Tired and content that the Tracker couldn't reach us, I closed my eyes.

Growling

Hunger

Fear

BEAST

My eyes snapped open and I leapt up, heart pounding in terror. Something had woken me, something reminiscent of that awful creature and its growling. After looking around myself wildly, heart racing, I started to calm down, blaming my over-stimulated imagination. Cassius and the Tracker were both sound asleep still, and hadn't reacted to my late night imaginings. Idly I tossed a branch onto the fire that had started to die down, causing sparks to fly in the air. The sparks danced around against what was visible of the night sky, and I followed their beautiful meandering through the air. I rubbed my eyes. Two of what I had thought to be floating embers hadn't moved or disappeared. Deep orange, they hung motionless. My mind became blank as I realised what they were; not embers, but eyes. Magnificent, beautiful eyes.

I carefully placed another branch on the fire, hoping that whatever was behind those eyes would be deterred from joining us in our makeshift camp. I noticed that the Tracker was awake - he looked at me and placed a finger against his lips before looking back at the eyes with something like awe on his face. Taking the initiative I slowly, silently, sliced a large part of the boar free and threw it into the night,

I WOKE LATE IN THE morning. Rolling over I found that Cassius had gone, presumably to find water and not currently lying in the belly of a strange, massively proportioned beast with orange eyes.

Sitting up I saw that the Tracker was awake and eyeing me with fierce interest. No longer was his face twisted in perpetual scorn when he looked at me. When he realised I was awake and watching him, he grinned, thumped his chest with a clenched fist and spoke two words in his language. He laughed at the confusion in my face and repeated the same two words to himself, shaking his head in amusement.

I shrugged, and focused my attention on finding Cassius. I followed his tracks back to the lake, where I spotted my friend filling a flask with water. After I quenched my thirst, I asked him what he was up to.

"If you and I are both parched, I can only imagine what the Tracker feels like," he answered. Of course. Cassius the Compassionate. "I found the flask next to one of the dead men, the other was broken and I don't know how to ask the Tracker if he has his."

"Let me," I said, surprising myself. "For some reason he seems to have taken a liking to me." With that I tell Cassius about the large orange eyes in the night around the campfire. "I've never seen anything like it," I muttered. "Whatever it was it had beautiful eyes."

"There are many things living in this forest Calidan," Cassius replied. "You must remember our fathers telling us about the bears, snakes and wolves that roam here. Could it have been one of them?"

"I don't think a bear would have cared too much about a small fire," I mused, "and it would be rare for a wolf to be away from its pack. Nor do I think a wolf would be big enough - those eyes were huge, the same goes for the snake."

Cassius paused thoughtfully before replying, "The storyteller in the village, he used to talk about the old creatures of the forest, how some animals lived to great ages, growing to much bigger sizes...even possessing intelligence and reasoning. He never claimed to have seen one, but thoroughly believed they existed...maybe it was one of those?"

The thought of a giant, intelligent animal watching me was frightening, though upon reflection, I hadn't detected any malice in those eyes, unlike the eyes of the savages or the beast.

Cassius and I returned to the Tracker, where I gave him the flask of water. He took it wordlessly, sniffed it once and then tossed it back, draining the flask swiftly. He nodded appreciatively to me, scowled at Cassius and removed a similar flask from his waist. Throwing it to me he mimed drinking, doubtless asking for more.

After obliging I turned to Cassius, "We need to think about moving," I said, "this boar will attract many unwelcome guests, and a fire may not keep all of them at bay."

"What about him?" Cassius replied, jerking his thumb at the Tracker. "We cannot...I **will** not leave him here for animals to find." Cassius obviously still believed I meant the Tracker harm. Which was true - it turned out that forgiveness for the massacre of my village was not easily forthcoming. However the man knew something about those eyes, knowledge I needed. Plus, he could prove useful...vengeance should never take precedence over pragmatism.

The man's leg was well and truly broken. I knew from my limited medical knowledge that dislocations could be "popped" back in by squeezing hard. Unfortunately that wouldn't do much with a leg broken in what appeared to be three places, including the ankle. Still...the sadistic part of my brain would have liked to try. I grinned ruefully to myself, ignoring the thought and went with Cassius to find the biggest branch we could. If we could find something for the Tracker to use as a crutch, we figured he could walk with us.

We swiftly came back to the fire, which we had kept going even in the day time to try and deter predators, with a forked branch the rough size of a man. The Tracker looked at it, and us, with something akin to surprise on his face, before accepting it with a rough nod. He lay down fully and placed the branch next to him with his shoulder in the crux. The branch was a little too long, extending past his foot. He sat up and pulling out a knife from his boot, deftly carved off the offending extra few inches of branch. When he looked up Cassius's sword was aimed at his face, albeit held by two shaking hands and a boy struggling for breath. The man gave him a savage grin and then smoothly cast the blade between Cassius's feet. When he jumped from fright the Tracker burst into cruelly satisfied laughter.

His peals of laughter died away when I picked up the knife. He eyed me as I marvelled at the blade, made out of black stone of some kind, cunningly fixed to a handle made of bone. Finger grips were carved into the bone handle, and the four inch blade was exquisitely sharp. None of the men in the village had had a knife like this. The Tracker reached back into his boot and removed the small sheathe that had kept the knife hidden. He tossed it to me languidly, and nodded as if bequeathing me the knife.

Fair is fair I suppose - he murdered my family and village along with raising some demon shadow beast, but in exchange he gave me his knife. The scales balance.

Cassius and I cooked some strips of boar meat on the fire before wrapping them up in one of the dead men's shirts - freshly washed in the lake of course. Sadly there wasn't much more we could salvage from the corpses. Both were full grown men so, aside from having tusk holes and bloodstains, their clothes were much too big for us to wear. I took a belt which, after adding a few more holes, fit relatively snugly and more importantly had a loop for a water flask. Cassius had the dead man's sword and its corresponding sheath, but it was too long for him to walk with it around his waist. So we fixed up the sheath as a belt around his shoulder, allowing him to carry the sword awkwardly across his back. There would be no quick drawing of the sword, but seeing as he could barely lift it anyway, I decided to put more faith in my newly acquired knife if we suddenly had need of sharp implements.

Together we set out. Cassius and I had discussed where to go but our geography was limited to the immediate surroundings of the village. Consequently we decided to follow rivers down the mountain, reasoning that there must be something at the bottom. If nothing else it took us away further away from the village and the cannibal savages. Well, all except one. I had half expected the man to attempt to hobble away when we got him on his feet, and I hadn't quite figured out what to do about it if he did, but he did nothing of the sort. Only looked at me, murmured those same two words, spat on the floor and then began to hobble in our direction.

For three nights we walked, following streams that meandered in and out of existence, winding slowly down the mountainside. Granted we could have just relied on gravity and our senses to tell us our direction, but having spent days being chased by three men, thirsty beyond comprehension, I was intent on staying as close to water sources as possible.

Every night we made a large fire and kept it built up, for there were still many predators in the woods. Every night I looked out into the blackness, both hoping for, and terrified of, seeing those orange orbs looking back at me.

The Tracker started teaching me some words in Low Gothic, a language he wasn't particularly well versed in himself, but he managed to get across the meaning of words for 'tree', 'water', 'food'. Not too surprising to find that the vocabulary of a man who spent most of his time in nature was indeed nature based. I say that he started teaching me, not both me and Cassius, because it's true. He would only speak directly to me, treating Cassius as though he didn't exist and scowling at him every time he spoke. I still didn't know what had caused this shift in the man's attitude but was positive it had to do with the orange eyes. Just one more reason to keep looking out at night, even though I had no idea what I would do if I saw them again.

And see them again I did.

On the fourth day it rained. And rained. And rained some more. It rained so thickly that we could barely see the ground before us and the Tracker began to slip more and more with his makeshift crutch. Eventually Cassius spotted a small overhanging cliff that would allow us some shelter from the rain. A tiny space, the recess under the cliff barely provided enough room for the three of us to sit down without still getting wet. Thoroughly drenched, we spent a miserable afternoon waiting for the rain to pass.

Towards the evening the rain petered out, leaving behind a deeply humid forest filled with bird noise, insects and wolves. Extremely aggressive wolves. Cassius and I were out in the dusk, failing to find any dry wood for a fire when we both heard the howls. Eerie sounds that made the hair on our necks stand on end. Distant at first, but slowly the sounds came closer. The pack might not have been hunting us, yet, but they were certainly moving in our direction. I thought, hard and quickly. A fire wouldn't help us now, if we could even get one lit, and there was no chance of outrunning a pack of hungry wolves. I bade Cassius grab all the long sturdy branches he could find, and after doing the same, joined him in sprinting back to the cliff.

Using the knife and sword we swiftly made stakes of the branches and jammed them into the mud surrounding the recess in the wall. We kept two of the longer, sturdier branches as spears. One for me, the other for the Tracker, who was grimly regarding the encroaching darkness. Cassius preferred to hold his sword, keeping the pointy end between him and the outside world whilst we worked. Finally, we could do no more. The swiftly erected defences looked shabby and inadequate in the fading light, but I could think of nothing else to do. Our weapons were meagre; sticks, a sword, a knife, and no fire. It's amazing how something as common and natural as rain can screw everything up.

Unwelcome darkness fell, and a faint moonlight began to paint everything in soft, silvery colours. The howling we had heard earlier had vanished; weighty silence reigned. Each of us waited with baited, clipped breath, hoping that the wolves were not hungry, begging whatever deity we each believed in that they would pass us by. It was not to be.

A silvery flowing flash streamed across the periphery of my vision. I turned to look, but lost whatever it was I had seen. My father's voice came to me, reminding me that at night it is best to avoid looking directly at what you want to see. The Tracker twitched - he had seen something too. Slowly he raised the head of his spear. I followed suit, while Cassius kept the point of his sword resting on the ground; a smart move, given that he couldn't keep it aloft for long. My eyes caught something again, three, no, four shapes slinking across the ground towards us. My grip tightened on the spear. Part of me wondered why I didn't seem to be afraid; my palms were dry around the spear, my heart rate just a touch north of normal. Perhaps the past week had made me lose my response to fear, or just accept that death is inevitable. Either way I silenced that part of myself, and concentrated on the task at hand. Survival.

The wolves paused just shy of our perimeter of stakes. Low growls began permeating the air. My pulse soared and fluttered at the first growl but soon recovered - it was nothing like the terrifying, impossibly deep noise the beast had made. Eyes shining with malice surrounded us, glinting in the moonlight. These wolves were hungry, and they intended to feast. The growls advanced into snarls, chorusing in the night until one of the wolves broke from the pack and sprinted towards us. It deftly weaved through our defences, dodging around the various stakes in its way and ran straight for the Tracker, as if it had determined that he was injured, and weak. A fatal error it appeared, as while injured he may have been, he certainly wasn't weak. The Tracker thrust with his spear and his aim was true. The sharpened tip entered the wolf's chest, killing it instantly. Unfortunately we had no time to remove the wolf from his spear - the rest of the wolves, as if emboldened by the first, were streaming towards us.

The first to reach us dived for Cassius, attempting to seize his leg. He lashed out with his sword, scoring a gash down the wolf's side and it danced away, snarling. I was attempting to keep the other two wolves at bay, covering the Tracker and myself with the spear. Jabbing out every time they came near. I heard a scream from Cassius and whipped my head around, seeing nothing but the wolf atop my friend. The distraction gave the waiting wolves the chance they needed. One leapt past my spear and landed on my chest, snapping at my throat. I screamed, dropping the spear, and flailed, trying to keep the jaws away from my face. The dog suddenly grunted and paused in its attempts to savage my neck, which gave me a chance to grab my dagger. Screaming wordlessly I stabbed it in the neck over and over until its eyes went glassy and the struggles ceased. No time to rest. Fresh screams were coming from my right, the Tracker bellowing in agony as the fourth wolf dragged him from the hollow by his broken leg.

Two more wolves arrived to assist - we obviously hadn't met the whole pack yet. That's when I noticed the spear, my spear, sticking out of the wolf I had just slain. The Tracker had used it on the one attacking me, instead of defending himself.

Without thinking I rolled out from under the wolf and leapt to the Tracker's defence, slashing at the faces of the wolves dragging his leg and screaming. Two backed away, while the other held its ground, squaring itself to face off against me. I lashed out with the knife and it dodged, aiming to launch itself at my throat, but my wild slashing hit an outstretched paw and it retreated. Panting, I screeched at the world, a wordless and primal cry. As the two of us faced each other again, I saw the wolf's ear twitch and heard a deep rumbling. The wolf's tail lowered and it whimpered. Chancing a glance above me, I was privy to a sight that I still remember to this day with perfect clarity.

Perched on the cliff overlooking our battle site, silhouetted against the moonlit sky, was a gigantic cat. This cat was larger than the giant boar that we had feasted on, larger than any panther that the village men had killed and taken for skins. It was monstrous... and beautiful. It was then that I saw its eyes, so large and orange - it was my friend from beyond the flames. It roared in anger as I was struck from the side, letting me learn another lesson; never take one's eyes off an angry wolf, or indeed, any opponent. My head struck the ground, and everything went black.

I awoke to a strange sensation. My entire body was vibrating, like there was an earthquake in my skin, and there was something wet and raspy dragging across my face. As I opened my eyes I realised that the raspy feeling was a very large, immensely wet tongue, and the vibrating was emanating from the giant cat that was now curled around me. As if it sensed my waking, the licking stopped, and the massive head of the creature blotted out the sky, two enormous orange eyes filling my vision. There was an expression or emotion in those beautiful, splendid eyes...was it concern?

Feeling no fear I reached up and stroked the sleek fur over the cat's cheek. "Thank you," I whispered. The concern vanished from the eyes to be replaced by something more akin to joy. A big lick drenched my face once again. I laughed and then grew sombre as my thoughts caught up with me. Cassius. Panicked I bolted upright and saw him sitting with the Tracker a few metres away, both staring at me in awe.

The Tracker touched his brow and bowed his head deeply to the giant cat. He appeared to almost revere the great beast. His eyes turned to me.

"Elkona Melkhuk," he intoned loudly, almost as if daring anyone to challenge him. He reached forward and touched my chest near my heart, "Elkona Melkhuk," he said again more softly. Elkona Melkhuk, the same two words he had been repeating since we first saw the orange eyes in the blackness beyond the flames. I drew back, unsure of my feelings towards being touched with an almost religious fervour by a man who had committed such atrocities against my kin. I looked at Cassius and asked what happened to him. I had to repeat the question three times before he registered my words, and snapped out of staring at the cat, now purring contentedly, vibrations buzzing through my spine.

"I managed to graze the wolf with my first swing and I think I just pissed it off," Cassius began, laughing ruefully. "It obviously decided that the direct approach was best and jumped straight for me, but as it knocked me backwards I kept hold of the sword and it was impaled through its gut. It stayed alive for a few seconds more on top of me - terrifying having that thing snapping at you - but it couldn't reach my face without impaling itself further...and after awhile it just kinda keeled over and lay there." He took a breath, his shudder barely visible. "When I managed to get out from under the wolf I saw you facing off against three of them, protecting the Tracker. Then there was a great rumbling like a quake and you all looked up, including the wolves. All except the one that you had just cut. It jumped at you and knocked you down but before it could do anything this great black cat of yours leapt down, dark as the night, and just...swatted it out of the way. It seemed so angry! It savaged the wolf, almost as if making a statement, and then ate it. Two bites Calidan. Two bites is all it took to eat an entire wolf!" Cassius's eyes were getting wider and his voice started to be tinged with hysteria. "After that it eyed the other wolves and roared, a massive sound that felt like it went right through me. They ran like the wind! Then it just started licking your face and purring. What is it Calidan? Why is it protecting you?!"

"Cassius, lower your voice," I replied. "The last thing we want is for you to anger or startle the cat." Cassius immediately shut up. I felt a little bad, as the cat wasn't expressing anything other than a contented joy. My brain clicked into gear...joy? Why did I keep thinking I knew what the cat was feeling? I looked back at the mighty creature and found it staring at me, bemused, like it knew what was going through my mind. Then the damn thing winked.

Conceding that I had no idea what was going on I turned back to Cassius. "Cassius, meet orange eyes, the ones I was telling you about whilst at the lake." I held up a hand as he started to splutter, "As for what is going on...I haven't got a clue." There - that cleared everything up.

Turning to the Tracker I pointed at his leg and asked him in Low Gothic, "good?" He shook his head and mimed teeth biting. In the moonlight I could see several dark lines running down his broken leg. For the first time I felt a little sorry for the man, no matter who you are having three wolves gnaw on your thrice broken leg is not going to be a pleasant experience. The scales seem to balance a little more.

I closed my eyes and a suggestive image seemingly floated into my head, the three of us sleeping in the hollow, with the cat keeping watch. At this point I'm more bemused than shocked. Whatever was going on, there seemed to be some pretty interesting side effects...and having a giant cat pet - I felt a jolt of anger which subsided to warmth when I instead thought giant cat friend - can't be a bad thing. I decided to trust in my new friend and together with Cassius pulled the Tracker back to the tiny cave. I gave the injured man my canteen of water and he took it, drinking some and using some more to try and wash out his wounds before handing it back with a nod. With the cat on purring guard duty outside, we each slipped into an exhausted sleep.

CHAPTER SIX
BONDS

~

MY FIRST EXPERIENCE OF SLEEPING whilst bonded with the watching beast was not dissimilar to the first time Cassius and I experienced psychedelics - much later in life and a story for another time. My dreams were filled with colour, and lights streamed across the usually blank canvas of my unconscious mind. At least, I believe I was unconscious. At times the sensations cleared and solidified into what I can only presume was the vision of the cat. I caught flashes of the night-time world, flickering in and out. Visions of my sleeping companions and, most disturbingly myself, along with the local fauna and flora all outlined in perfect detail in the dark night. Along with the visions came a sense of understanding the world around me, in terms of smell, hearing and detecting minute changes in the outside environment...all combined with almost tangible feelings of emotion and an overwhelming sense of power.

I woke with an errant sunbeam shining directly in my eyes. Rubbing my face I left the others to sleep and slid from the shelter of the hollow. Standing up I prepared myself, expecting aches and pains to explode throughout my body from the antics of last night. Surprisingly, I felt fresh and strong. Tentatively I patted my head and frowned in surprise at the lack of a lump from my successful attempt at getting a rat's perspective of the ground.

"Another thing to ponder," I mutter to myself as I start my search for our night-time guardian. A cursory glance showed me no giant cat, but a feeling in my chest made me think that she was close. I paused and wondered why I thought the cat was female; after all it's not like I could see this during the night, but the flood of warmth that accompanied the thought rendered it more than likely to be true. Trialling something I paused and closed my eyes.

Darkness.

I opened them again.

I could feel something akin to laughter in my chest.

I tried again, trying to clear my thoughts. An image flickered - I'm paused with one massive paw in the air, mid-step, watching a tiny human standing with his eyes shut. My tail swishes through the grass, playfully. Astonishment makes the vision fade.

I quickly scanned the landscape. Surely a cat larger than a horse can't be that hard to spot! Failing, I tried a third time - emptying my thoughts and focussing on the warmth in my body. My blank vision flickered and suddenly the darkness was replaced with a flood of sensations, light, noise, smell. I'm crouched down low to the ground, hidden in a large patch of brush, amused that the tiny human had let me get so close before figuring out the trick.

Sensing that the game was up, I burst out of my hiding spot only six metres from the boy and playfully pounce.

Opening my eyes, my human eyes, I turned in time to see a magnificent black panther soaring through the air towards me. Larger than a horse, larger than two horses, it flowed through the air, landed just before me and cuffed me playfully on the head before sprinting off, vanishing before I could blink. Whilst the panther might not have been on the scale of a domestic cat, she certainly hadn't lost any sense of amusement from making fun of humans.

I could feel a sense of challenge from the cat. My turn to hunt her.

Game on, panther.

Half an hour later I'm sitting in the same position in which I started. Frustrated. It turns out that a gigantic cat has all the advantages when playing a game of hide and seek. Every time I moved an inch the cat let me know it had heard me via a sense of laughter in my chest. The furthest I managed was three feet, and that was because I had jumped. Even then I sensed that the cat knew I had jumped due to the vibrations the disturbance to the air made on her whiskers. As it was she certainly heard me land! The only way I could figure out to beat her was not to move at all, however that was also losing the game...though I suspected that she could hear my breath and heartbeat anyway.

The game ended when a yawning Cassius scrambled out from under the cliff, turning to extend a hand to the Tracker, helping him to stand before reaching down and handing him his crutch.

"Morning!" Cassius said brightly. "What are you up to?"

"Playing hide and seek," I replied. Cassius's face showed confusion for a second and then he looked about himself warily, the events of the night and our dark, feline saviour flooding back to him.

"So...where is the big beast? I need to thank it for saving our lives," he said, eyes darting all over the forest.

I closed my eyes briefly. "Do you really want to know?" I asked, a grin lifting my cheeks. He nodded emphatically. "Then you might want to look up."

A strange mix of terror and consternation filled his face. Slowly his eyes slid upwards and then locked in place as they met the piercing, highly amused gaze of the giant black panther comically lounging with her legs hanging over the fork of a massive tree. Cassius's colour blanched as the cat opened her mouth wide, and in a cruel display of affection lithely descended from the tree in one leap, pinning Cassius to the ground and licking his dirty, pale face. I burst out laughing, unable to contain my amusement at his expression. It felt alien to laugh - humour had been a stranger of late.

Cassius emerged from under the cat's tongue, soaked with saliva. At first he looked undecided as to whether to cry or laugh, but when he heard my howling laughter he joined in, releasing the trauma of the recent past in a mixture of pealing laughter and stroking of the cat's lush, black fur. The panther furthered the playful mood by rolling on her back and playfully swatting at Cassius, who bravely dodged her mighty swipes and played the ultimate game of dare by stroking the cat's smooth belly. Mighty purring filled the air as the cat lost herself in sweet bliss. I felt a euphoria rise in my chest; the cat's emotion was incredibly strong.

After several long minutes of petting heaven the cat rolled over and affectionately nuzzled Cassius, an amazing sight as her head was as near as large as Cassius himself. She then turned to the Tracker who stood in apparent respectful awe. He caught her gaze and dropped to one knee, seemingly not affected by the pain that must have caused, and touched his head with his hand.

"Amatuk Elkona," he said in a reverent whisper. The cat adopted an almost regal stance and gave a courtly nod to the Tracker. Then moved behind him, grabbed the back of his jerkin delicately with her teeth and slowly lifted him back to his feet. He gasped, then clenched his fist against his chest and bowed as deeply as one can on a crutch.

A touch of annoyance crossed my mind. The man must know exactly what I was dealing with here, but I was unable to communicate properly with him. I couldn't even figure out two words like Amatuk Elkona! The cat looked at me, knowing my thoughts. An image formed in my mind of a heart that slowly grew bigger. I looked at her again; was there nothing she couldn't do? "Big heart?" I asked. She shook her head. "Growing heart?" Again, a head shake. "Great heart?" A happy nod. "Great Heart, that's what you are?" More excited nodding. "Amazing," I muttered. "How about Elkona Melkhuk?" The Great Heart looked at me, as if weighing me with her eyes then an image formed, a heart clad in shadow.

"Dark heart," I said, feeling out the word. The cat nodded emphatically. "Dark heart...I like it."

With the cat once again standing guard, the three of us set about skinning the wolves. Or at least Cassius and I did; whilst my feelings towards the Tracker had started to soften, I still didn't want to give him back his knife. An obviously experienced huntsman and skinner, he pointed out the best way to complete the task, guiding our hands as they moved across the wolves' bodies. Whilst both Cassius and I were relatively experienced at skinning the kills brought back by the village hunters, it was a different matter when doing it for survival as opposed amongst friends and family.

Once the skinning was complete, the sun much higher in the sky, we placed the skins on branches to dry. My reasoning behind skinning the beasts was twofold; firstly, waste not. A mantra all members of the village are raised with. Secondly, I figured that we could use the wolf pelts for warmth if necessary; even though it was spring the nights could still be chilly, or to trade for goods if we encountered another village. As evening encroached the Great Heart came back and dumped a small deer on the ground. She had suggested to me through images that we both go hunting whilst the others built up a large cooking fire. I had managed to talk her out of it by suggesting that skinning the animals was more important, and though this time she acquiesced...I felt that next time I wouldn't have much say in the matter.

The deer was quickly filleted and skinned. Cassius, the Tracker and myself took the lower haunches, enough food to sate us all for the evening and still leave some to cook for jerky. The rest we gave to the Great Heart, who accepted it like a royal gift and daintily swallowed it in one bite.

After dinner the panther began nudging me with her head. I knew what she wanted, I could feel it deep inside my chest. Much like domestic cats who bring home their prey as a gift of food to their humans who lack hunting skills, the Great Heart believed, through a series of mewling kitten images, that I was as useless. And with that she picked me up with her mouth, taking care not to hurt me, and carried me away from the fire whilst the others looked on bemused. With as much dignity as I could muster, which perhaps unsurprisingly isn't that much when in a wet cat's mouth, I dryly told the others that the wild was calling and I would be back soon. That left them as clueless as I as to what was about to happen.

The panther deposited me in a forest glade. An open patch of ground clear of vegetation, about the size of the village square and lit solely by the moonlight. Through a series of mental images I understood what the panther wanted me to do. A surprisingly simple task at first glance, but one that would take me a long time to master. I was to listen.

Listen. Sounds easy enough? We do it all the time! Unfortunately a human's listening ability is many times worse than most predators, and even when we have the ability to listen we, as the cat was suggesting, rarely could do it properly because we could not calm ourselves. As far as I could understand, being able to listen, to truly *listen*, required your entire being to be calm, still and peaceful, both physically and mentally. A tall order for an eleven year old with an overactive mind.

And so the training began. I was to remain seated in the middle of the glade, the only easily achievable task, and describe to the Great

Heart what I could hear. An hour into the game and all I had successfully identified was the rustle of wind in the trees and an owl who hooted nearby. I began to get frustrated at what seemed like a pointless and impossible mission. Opening my eyes I jumped in fright, for those beautiful orange eyes were right in front of me. I had had no idea that the panther was nearby, and with the panther fuelling a grim emotion in my chest, my lesson was learnt - I had to be able to know what was around me, food, water, friends or enemies. And so I settled back down and set to it with a will.

Two hours later I walked back to camp with the Great Heart, exhausted (who knew listening was such hard work!) but content. I had managed to hear the calls of deer and even guess at the direction, which pleased the panther no end. But I could tell she expected more from me. For some reason, she thought I would be able to see the world as she does. I doubted this myself, seeing as I didn't possess the giant ears or eyes of the great cat, but then acknowledged that as I had some kind of bond with the Great Heart, maybe such things would also be possible. I vowed to do what I could to learn from the majestic creature, then giggled as the grand cat's tongue washed over my face. She loved it when I thought of her in this way. Majestic. I wiped the saliva from my face and grinned, nodded to the Tracker who was on sentry duty, and fell immediately into another colour filled sleep.

This routine continued for nearly a week. The Tracker had worried that his mauled leg would become infected, so with the help of the panther's nose and her image translation skills, Cassius and I managed to find him several plants which he used to prevent any infection. We stayed in the same place, sleeping around the fire and huddling under the outcropping when it rained. I would like to say that we stayed to ensure that the Tracker's leg healed, but for me at least, I wanted to learn as much as possible from the Great Heart before we moved on. Call me selfish, but it's not every day that you develop some kind of magic bond with a beast straight from the village stories. I could tell that Cassius felt a bit excluded, and so started bringing him on the multiple training sessions that the cat ran daily. She approved. Another human to play tricks on.

And so together we practiced stealth techniques, attempting to get close to the deer that grazed in the area, as well as moving quickly but silently through the forest, both during the day and at night. The cat also had us play its version of hide and seek, one where we had to find her and the other where she had to find us. She always won. Some might call it an impossible or unfair challenge; I called it practice for the day when I would hunt down the beast that destroyed my village. For the day when it would open its eyes and be surprised to see me, and even more astonished to find that its throat has already been slit. And so we trained. And through it all we practiced *listening*.

A week turned into a month, which turned into six months that we stayed on the side of the mountain. Once the Tracker's wounds had healed, Cassius and I had discussed where we should go, but as we didn't know the geography, we decided to continue with our plan of following the mountain to its base, and going from there. However we weren't certain if the Great Heart would follow me forever, or if she was to stay with the mountain, nor did I have the courage to ask her that at the time. I had just found my friend, my feline mentor, and I had no desire to think about the possibility of her leaving. And so we decided to spend as long as possible training with the panther and then leave before the snows came in late autumn. The Tracker seemed only too happy to stay with us, and over the months we learnt some more of each other's languages as well as how to make our own equipment; clothes from skins, bows, arrows and knives. Between us we found a cave and created a sturdy home from a wooden lean to with animal skins and willow branches keeping out the worst of the weather. It is one of the most interesting and happy times that I remember.

But all good things must come to an end. Although I wished to stay and learn more, we knew that the winters on the mountain were extremely harsh and our chances of surviving it alone, even with the Great Heart, were low. So when the leaves had fully began to depart the trees and there was a noticeable chill in the air, we decided to embark on the next stage of our journey.

CHAPTER SEVEN
PATHS

~

THE TRACKER PAUSED AT THE crest of the next rise and looked around, scanning the surroundings. He still carried a crutch, a better version now, carved smooth and polished with animal fat, for his leg was a twisted and mangled thing, healed wrongly and paining his every step. He swivelled his head, as if trying to spot something, but after a short period gave up, frustration evident in the way he continued to descend the rise.

And frustrated he should be, since for the last two weeks the Tracker had been the subject of an insidious game, a game he had been sorely losing.

I should feel bad for the man, I thought to myself as I stalked him through the long grass, but practice makes perfect. I knew that Cassius was far to my left, stealthily moving behind a ridge in the undulating ground. I could hear his footfalls and his breathing. If I concentrated, I could even hear his heartbeat. I knew enough to recognise that even constant practice couldn't enhance a normal human's abilities to this extent...something about the bond between myself and the Great Heart was triggering...changes. But this was not the time for such thoughts. Following three feet behind a man without him hearing was no mean feat. Or at least it shouldn't be. I had now been following him for two minutes, right within his shadow, with my thoughts elsewhere. Either the Tracker was getting worse at this game, which was unlikely (his watchfulness was astounding) or my new skills meant no normal person could hear me if I did not want them to.

Growing bored I reached out to Seylantha, otherwise known as the Great Heart. As my understanding of the Tracker's language deepened, the panther and I broadened our understanding of each other. She, somehow, knew the Tracker's language, and thus we started to be able to converse in language as well as emotions. She told me that her name was Seylantha, (I promptly nicknamed her Seya) which meant 'eyes of the deepest sun'. My orange eyes. The name came not from Low Gothic, the Tracker's language, but from another, much older one. She told me that the tongue had largely died out, but was once spoken by the great denizens of the past. I knew little of what she spoke, my village education not covering ancient history, and so presumed that she meant an old empire of man.

I found that Seya was doing much the same as myself. It was becoming more and more obvious that we were starting to share mannerisms. Yet instead of stalking the prey, Seya was stalking the stalker...Cassius. Having been on the receiving end of her silent approach many times, I could easily empathise with Cassius. He was blindly concentrating on reaching the Tracker unheard, unaware that I was already there, for as young boys do we had made this a competition between us. The first to touch the Tracker without him knowing he was there, won. It was hard to silence my mirth, as in my mind's eye I could see the panther playfully pausing with each step, imitating Cassius, and feel in my chest her great amusement with our game. We conversed silently and she agreed to join my fun.

And so when Cassius approached the edge of the ridge, preparing for a silent dash towards his target, the Tracker, he instead saw me and froze in surprised annoyance, before raising a hand and giving me the finger. I motioned for him to turn around and he did, just in time to be bowled over by Seylantha's pounce. She rolled him over and gave him a voracious licking. All in deadly silence. Or at least it was, up until the first laugh escaped my lips. I couldn't help it. Cassius's look of impotent rage as he was treated like a newborn kitten was far too funny. As soon as the sound passed my lips I realised my mistake, for the Tracker whirled and hit me with the crutch - a surprisingly effective weapon. He wore a victorious grin as I rubbed my head ruefully, and then he too burst into peals of laughter when he took in Cassius's predicament. With that the game was done for the day. Neither of us won, but it was a surprisingly effective training method, and certainly a more entertaining way of travelling.

~

When there were more leaves on the ground then on the trees, we came to the base of the mountains. The air was much warmer than I had expected, a welcome surprise given the approaching winter. The late autumnal temperature seemed almost balmy to Cassius and myself. The trees thinned until we faced a large expanse of space, a vast emptiness as far as the eye could see. From conversing with Seya I learnt that we were on the steppes of a massive grassland, known in her ancient language as the Green Sea. I hadn't seen a sea before, but knowing it was meant to be made of water, I expected that green wasn't its usual colour.

Crossing a vast grassland is probably not as arduous as a desert, but it is close. Whilst you have nice lovely grass to lay in, you also have the plethora of resident bugs, spiders and snakes who make it their mission to irritate you. Furthermore, aside from the herds of animals who roam the expanse, there is little in the way of food, and less again in the way of water.

Little surprise then that according to the Tracker, who had yet to share with me his name, the Empire classed this as its second line of defence against attack from the North, the first being the mountains where Cassius and I were born. An army that managed to cross the mountains would then have to deal with the relative scarcity of supplies when crossing the Green Sea. I asked the Tracker why this would be such a problem and he laughed, explaining that an army marches on its stomach, and that whilst we can just tighten our belts and carry on, an army's regular soldiers, conscripts or volunteers, would likely start deserting, foiling a campaign before it could properly begin. The man spoke with impressive knowledge of military activities, and it occurred to me that although I knew him as the Tracker, I had no knowledge of his past.

It appeared that Cassius had the same thought and he spoke up, asking what the Tracker used to do. The man paused in thought for a long time, and then softly spoke in a mixture of his language and ours. "I was the lead scout for a platoon of men." And stopped talking. Expecting more Cassius and I held our tongues, until we couldn't wait any longer. "Who for? What happened? Were they the same men as at the village?"

"No!" the Tracker snarled. "Not the men from the village." He gazed wistfully away, lost in thoughts known only to him. "Good men... Dead men." And with that he spoke no more on the subject.

For the first time Cassius and I wondered whether the Tracker was actually part of the attack on the village. He seemed to be vehemently against the idea that his 'good' men were of the same group as of the village massacre. Neither of us had seen him take part as the others raped, killed and ate their way through the population of the village. Perhaps he wasn't as bad as we originally thought. These thoughts bounced around my head and I realised that even before this bit of enlightening news, I no longer hated the Tracker. The scales still may not be balanced, indeed they might never be, but my feelings towards the man were now amicable. He had done nothing since our first meeting to indicate that he was anything other than interested in staying with the group, and he had proven time and time again that he was a useful addition to our team. I resolved to be nicer to the man, no matter his role in the village attack. We all have our dark sides.

Our training continued on our journey across the Green Sea, with Seylantha upping the stakes. Instead of trailing the Tracker, we now had to hunt and slay the great herds that roamed the plains. Armed with our bows, which we had been instructed in the making and use of by the Tracker over the past six months, Cassius and I stalked the herds. Easily startled, the massive cows would take flight if they heard, sensed or smelt our approach. Furthermore, if we didn't kill one cleanly we were then faced with an angry and injured cow, who was probably supported by bigger, angrier bulls. Seya refused to catch a cow for us, suggesting it was part of our training to be able to fend for ourselves. By the end of the first week we had been successful once, creeping close to the rear of the herd and killing an adolescent cow. Cassius had taken the shot, his skill with the bow outclassing my own by a large margin, and the arrow had taken the cow in the eye, killing it instantly and allowing us to butcher and dry it in the sun while waiting to be joined by the Tracker and Seya. Another downside of the Green Sea; no wood for fires.

Near the end of the second week, we decided that another hunt was in order. Moving stealthily we crept to within range of the herd, and paused to eye up the cattle to see which would be the best choice. As we paused, I realised that something felt off. I focussed my senses and *listened*. Smiling I touched Cassius and held up a hand, preventing him from taking a shot at the herd. I motioned for him to wait and watch. No more than a few minutes later the long grass exploded with motion and a fleet of lions raced into the herd, quickly taking down one of the beasts. One of the lions emerged from the grass only ten feet away. I thanked Seya profusely through our connection, feeling the warmth of her acknowledgement. Without her training we wouldn't have been able to move quietly enough for the lions to not notice us. It turns out that when you have been hunted by one large cat for months on end, you quickly learn to move with stealth...not that either one of us could hide from Seya.

After scavenging some meat from the remaining cow carcass we continued our journey, traversing a series of hills looming from the grass. Nearly three weeks it took us to cross that great sea of green grass but we managed it without incident, which was refreshing for myself and Cassius. It would probably look, from the outside, as though our lives had become one big series of unfortunate events. However, eating of raw meat aside, I was having the time of my life. Cassius, always having been that annoying, buoyant type of personality, had long been proclaiming that the past six months had been a grand adventure. I couldn't help but agree. Despite the traumatic events that preceded our journey, I felt more alive than I ever had before. Cassius and I were closer than ever, and I had my seemingly unbreakable bond with Seya. Life was good. And then as we made it to the top of those hills, everything changed.

In the distance, rising from the ground like a termite mound, was a city. Neither Cassius or I had ever seen a city before and our brains struggled to absorb the sheer size of it. Farmland extended on either side, and there looked to be a line, hundreds strong, of people passing the stone walls through a series of massive, towering gates. Awestruck doesn't quite do our feelings justice. The Tracker merely laughed, clapping us on the shoulders and pushing us forwards down the hill. Seya decided to keep her distance and hunt, and that I should call her if needed. I agreed; I had no idea what to make of these people but suspected some might react badly to a giant black panther strolling through their city, alongside some ragged boys and a crippled man.

Several hours later we wandered the streets of what I assumed was the seat of power in the Empire. Cassius and I marvelled at the structures, the vast stone walls and strong buildings within. The road was cobbled and carts clattered along uneven pathways, their drivers bellowing at passersby to get out of their way. Soldiers marched through the streets, tramping to wherever their commander shouted. Scantily clad women adorned the doors and windows of certain shops, and at times I had to pull the Tracker away to make sure he didn't lose us. I didn't yet know of the allure that women could hold.

We received some odd looks, gawking at the city sights, wearing our wolf hide clothes, but we were left to ourselves. Perhaps people unconsciously observed the almost sinuous way that Cassius and I carried ourselves, or, perhaps more likely, they noted the dark looks that the Tracker gave to anyone showing too much interest in our party.

We walked to the main square, where a gallows had been erected. I had never seen one before; life in the mountains ensured that the selfish actions of the few affected the many, so acts of violence and theft were few. Three achingly small figures dangled from the ropes. Children, like Cassius and myself. I remember being surprised that people were just walking past, going about their lives. This was my first introduction to the Empire's laws, indeed any laws, and the brutality of the punishment and indifference of the citizens of the city shocked me to my core. Did they not see the corpses? Or did they just not care? In my backwater raised mind killing someone was still sacrilege, and I couldn't understand what appeared to be the public murder of children.

Looking back, I was terribly naive.

CHAPTER EIGHT
CITIZENS

~

THE PROBLEM, OR BENEFIT, OF travelling long distances in the wild, is that money is useless. What did I learn about living in a city in the Empire? Money is everything.

I sold my bow. My handcrafted bow, carved from yew and lovingly polished with animal fat. I sold it because we had nothing else to sell. Cassius was going to sell his, but I talked him out of it - if we had to leave the city then his bow would help keep us safe and fed. The sword and knife we declined to sell as well, as too many emotions were connected with those weapons. Surprisingly, according to the Tracker, the bow fetched a good price. His fumbling grasp of the Empire's language was the only method we had of buying anything. The Tracker then, through a process of trial and error, took us to a dilapidated building that offered rooms to sleep in - my first encounter with an inn. For a small copper coin with a strange face printed on it he got us a room with straw bedding on the floor. With my wolf pelt spread over the straw it was surprisingly comfortable. That said, I think you can sleep on anything when you've spent six months living rough and sleeping on the ground.

"So, what now?" asked Cassius.

"I have no idea," I returned somewhat despondently. I had imagined that a grand plan would form in my head when entering the city, but so far I was still waiting.

"This is a strange place, massive, busy and we don't speak the language...we have no concept of how people live their lives here."

The Tracker followed our conversation, nodding with each of my points. He cut in, "Busy yes, strange no. City all the same. Whores, pubs, merchants, military," he said ticking them off on his hand. "Which one you want to choose?"

"Choose?" Cassius asked.

"To be!" chuckled the Tracker, slapping his thigh in amusement. "You are young, get strong, live well."

"You forget what happened Tracker," I replied darkly, my eyes turning cold. "We are not here to make new lives and forget the past."

"Past no forget," he replied gravely, eyes turning inward. "Past never forget." He thought deeply for a moment before turning back to us, "Why not grow here, learn, then chase past?"

Cassius and I looked at each other. Maybe he was onto something.

"He has a point," said Cassius. "We know what killed our village, and we know that we have to do something about it. But, Calidan, we're eleven years old! We need to learn what we can, much like we have with Seya. Learn so we can beat that damn creature and its men when next we meet!"

I liked his fire. "You're right," I said, addressing both of them. "So, considering that we want to be able to fight...I guess we're joining the military?"

They both looked at me and nodded. Decision made.

Finding a military establishment in a city is not difficult. Generally if you hear lots of shouting and marching feet, and see flags waving, you're probably not far.

And so it was that after a few hours of wandering around the city we came across the military barracks. Hard looking men stood outside, their gazes taking in our dishevelled, wolf clad attire. As we walked forward, one stepped in front to bar our way and ordered us to stop. We did so, and the Tracker attempted to answer a few questions about our intent. Whatever he said we were smartly marched down to an office where a weary looking man sat at a desk filled with papers. He motioned for us to wait whilst he finished signing a document, before sighing and looking at the three people before him.

"I am Major General Kyle," he said, "I hear you have turned up out of the blue and asked to join the military. For what reason do you wish to do this?"

Blank faces met his inquisitive look.

I turned to Cassius and the Tracker. "Did you understand that?" both shook their heads. "No," the Tracker replied in his language.

"Korketh nia magnar?" the military man asked the Tracker, whose face lit up as he nodded and started speaking rapidly, Major General Kyle interrupting periodically with fluent grasp of the Tracker's language, Korketh, and looking at us with increasing interest. After a short time he stopped the Tracker and left the office for a few minutes, before coming back with some official looking forms. He spoke briefly again to the Tracker who turned to us and attempted to explain the situation.

"I have explained I am mercenary. Tracker. If I prove skill I can train men here. For you, Kyle - the man - has sent for person who speak your language. Here shortly. I not talk about what happened at village. Might not be safe." With that he turned back to Major General Kyle and continued the conversation. Looking at the way the Tracker stood, his stance relaxed, it was obvious that he was relishing conversing with someone fluent in his language.

Some time later, the door opened and a man in long grey robes entered, bowing to the Major General. He conversed briefly with both Kyle and the Tracker, flawlessly switching between Korketh and the language of the Empire. He then turned to Cassius and myself and tried a language that had some similar pronoun citations and syntax to ours, but we were unable to comprehend his meaning. Smiling, he switched to another language, but was met with the same problem. His smile grew broader as he switched to a third which had some very obvious similarities to our own. Seeing our ears perk up, he tried one more.

"It has been a very long time since I have spoken any language that is a derivative of Khurdush. Tarr is extremely entertaining to speak. Ah! I see you understand me! Excellent." He practically glowed with happiness, seemingly a man who truly relished the opportunity to converse with native speakers of other languages.

"I am Brother Gelman from the order of scribes. As you may have guessed, the Major General over there has brought me here to ask you a few questions so he can figure out what to do with you. Is that okay?" After sharing a quick glance, both Cassius and I turned back to Brother Gelman and nodded.

"Brilliant! So firstly, I believe your names are Calidan and Cassius, correct?" Again we nodded.

"Where are you from?"

"We come from a small village at the very top of a set of mountains north of here," Cassius replied.

"Does this village have a name?"

"No, to everyone there it was just the village. There were very few visitors, the odd trader passed through every now and then, maybe they have a name for it?" I hazarded.

"Hmmm, no problem," replied Brother Gelman, "there aren't that many villages in the Tordstein mountains, I'm sure I can narrow it down." Tordstein mountains… my first time hearing the Empire's name for the mountain range of my home. The place where one day I would return to seek my revenge.

"Calidan? Calidan?" My gaze snapped back into focus, as Brother Gelman looked at me with slight concern. "Are you okay Calidan? You went blank on me for a moment there."

"I'm fine," I replied, embarrassed at both my lapse of attention and the concern in Brother Gelman's voice. "Sorry, talk of home just sent my mind wandering." Cassius clapped me knowingly on the shoulder, reassuring me that I wasn't alone in my thoughts. I brightened up, "Please continue Brother Gelman, I'm fine."

We spoke for nearly an hour. Cassius and I told Brother Gelman that our village was attacked, and that we were the only survivors. The Tracker was a man who found us in the forest, and helped us stay alive. We made no mention of Seylantha or the Beast, thinking it best to keep that information to ourselves. The Brother continuously wrote on a piece of parchment with a beautifully engraved pen, his face becoming more sombre as the joviality of sharing a rare language was marred by the sad story we had to tell. Eventually he ran out of questions, thanked us with sad eyes and turned to the Major General. He presented the parchment and spoke to him quietly, before gesturing to us to follow him and leading us from the room.

"We're going to get you some food," he said, the words sounding like peals of joy in my mind. When you have been as hungry as I have, any opportunity for food is a welcome one.

Later, sated, Brother Gelman led Cassius and I back to the Major General's office. The Tracker was still there, though an empty plate on the desk next to him suggested that he too had eaten. Through Brother Gelman, Major General Kyle explained that the military didn't allow anyone under the age of fifteen to join as a full member of the army. However under exceptional circumstances he had the power to take on wards, and be personally responsible for keeping them safe, schooled and if they so wished it, trained. This meant that when they came of age they could join the army as exemplars of army potential.

It was a stunning offer. Cassius and I had thought that we would be little more than servants in the army if we could not be one of the soldiers. Something about our story must have impressed the kind hearted Major General.

"What about the Tracker?" I asked.

"We are going to test his skills, but I imagine that if he was part of the unit that he tells me he was then the test will pose no challenge. If...when, he passes he will be offered a place here to teach his scouting skills. We have very few who possess these kinds of skills, and such a talent would not be allowed to go to waste."

Cassius and I nodded, before sharing a look. We knew exactly how good the Tracker was, having been hunting him for the past few months, but what did that make us? We both knew that the Tracker could no longer decipher where we were, hear us or see us unless we wanted him to, thanks to Seya's training.

"Everyone should have a giant panther trainer really, so useful!" I thought to myself...I felt a wry grin of amusement pass through my chest from Seylantha at that.

"So what happens now?" Cassius asked.

"If you accept then I will firstly take you to the bath house where you can remove the stink and grime of your journey," replied Major General Kyle. He wasn't wrong. It was a musk that becomes almost commonplace after a while, and six months of living and travelling cross country had certainly imbued us with a rather fragrant odour. "Then," he continued, "I will direct you to your accommodation which will be attached to my abode. Tomorrow, once you are well rested, fed and watered, I will meet with you to discuss your studies, likely using Brother Gelman here, to help you learn Andurran. We will also discuss what you would like to focus on over the next few years before you join the army proper."

If it seems like Major General Kyle is an excellent person, that is because he simply is. Over the years I have kept tabs on Kyle and looked into his record. The man had a soft spot for children, likely as his only son died at a young age. His military record was impeccable, and he was considered to be extremely bright and competent. Indeed, having seen some of the missives that were passed between Kyle and other members of the military up the chain of command, I know that he helped us not just out of the kindness of his heart, but as a stepping stone for some of his own plans. He believed that if he could train us at an early age we would become exemplary soldiers or officers, and he could use this success to help instigate the creation of a cadet school for young children. A fine plan, and I have helped him where I can over the years, with some subtle and not so subtle assistance. A story for another time.

So Cassius and I accepted Kyle's offer. He insisted that we call him Kyle until we were officially enrolled the military at age fifteen. He took us to the military baths where our wolf pelts were taken to be washed, and we scrubbed ourselves for what seemed like hours to remove the many layers of dirt. After this mammoth task, he took us to his home where a room had been arranged for us with a bunk bed at one end. We met his lovely wife, an extremely pretty, diminutive lady with a ready smile. I have many fond memories of Lana. She did everything she could to be our surrogate mother, and whilst Cassius and I weren't looking for replacement parents, the times we had there were some of the best that we can remember. Or at least, I can. I don't honestly know if Cassius remembers anything of those happy days.

Through my link with Seya I relayed everything that had happened and the new plan. She had no problems with staying near Forgoth, as she had found a forest filled with game, and had no concerns about going hungry. She was delighted at the idea of me learning more and growing stronger, relentlessly invading my mind with images of me as a small panther cub. It could be worse, at least I was no longer a mewling kitten. I resolved to make time to visit her whenever I could.

Cassius and I began to take lessons in Andurran with Brother Gelman, who was no less enthusiastic about teaching a language than he was about speaking it. Kyle gave us some books to read, and told us that he would proceed with our lessons personally once we could read and understand them. It was a somewhat demanding task; the first book was titled Andurran military history, and the second was a treatise on advances in military tactics. Not your average book for an eleven year old, but then again, what do you expect from the Major General of the military? Indeed, it made perfect sense; how else to better learn the military lingo and adopt it into our language studies?

One of the first things that Gelman bade me understand was that the city we were in was not, as I had thought, the centre of the Empire. It was the northernmost city and treated more as a backwater outpost. The city was named Forgoth, and the Forgothian people were often regarded as dour, uncouth and ill educated, something that Kyle wanted to fix with better education and youth programmes. Whereas citizens of Anderal, the capital city and seat of the Empire, were regarded as the best and brightest. I, for one, never agreed with this assessment. The people of Forgoth were, for the most part, warm and welcoming to myself, Cassius and the Tracker. I say for the most part, as there was a strong criminal element in the city, roving gangs of thieves and cutthroats, many of whom children of a similar age to Cassius and I. Children who didn't like the fact that we were benefitting from the Major General whilst they weren't. I say this because whether right or wrong, I killed for the first time in that city.

Brother Gelman's lessons took place in the hall of scribes, a grand building that housed the main library in Forgoth, as well as many little interesting nooks and crannies that Cassius and I had great fun exploring. The hall was some distance from the military compound, and required a short half hour walk along the main high street. This wasn't a problem for us; in fact we delighted in the freedom we had when walking to and from our lessons. Exploring the market shops became a fascination for both of us, having previously seen only the wares peddled by travelling traders, or the practical items made by people of the village themselves. This was completely different! The clothes! Wide brimmed hats, leather jerkins, fur moccasins, finely tooled belts and boots, adorned with shining metals. I had never seen such styles and colours. There were stalls that sold spices and herbs in mounds of vivid colour and scent. In fact I soon learned to not open all of my senses whilst near the stores, my sense of smell being too acute. Weapon shops, an obvious object of fascination for young boys, held gleaming blades of various shapes and sizes. Armour as well, all of the pieces glinting and polished to a high sheen, hung in the store windows. Sadly though, not much armour is made for eleven year olds. I should know. We checked.

All in all it was a delightful place, one that kept Cassius and I occupied every time we strolled through. That didn't stop us from keeping our wits about us however; we had been warned by both Kyle and Brother Gelman that pickpockets were rife in the area, as well as of the dangers of going down the many side alleys that extended off the main high street. Alleys that twisted, turned and became a maze like warren, making it very easy to get lost. And so it was when brave, forthright Cassius saw the purse snatched off the hip of a pretty young flower girl, he grabbed me by the arm, and promptly ignoring all of the warnings dragged me after the thief, straight into the maze.

We sprinted into the alley, close on the heels of the thief, who looked to be about ten years old and was running like his life depended on it. The echoes of our footsteps slapping the cobbles echoed around us, making it difficult to keep *listening*.

"Cassius!" I shouted, trying to grab his attention. "We have to slow down, we can track him."

"No!" he roared back, "we nearly have him, just around this corn-"

Thwack

A thick wooden board caught Cassius across the shins, a trick that we both used to good advantage in years to come, and he tumbled into a heap on the floor.

Crack

The board whistled down a second time and landed on my raised arm, splintering as I covered Cassius from the blow. In an instant I realised we were in trouble. Six people, one breathing heavily - the thief - the others amped and ready for a fight. I could hear their hearts racing. Cassius was moaning in pain but aware. His shins didn't look broken, but were already starting to turn black. Not a great situation.

I looked up. Around us were a mix of children, girls and boys, younger and older. The oldest and biggest, the one with the now broken board, sneered cruelly and tossed it away.

"What have we got here eh?" he said, spitting out his words. " A couple of fancy lads who don't take too kindly to purse snatching!" He chuckled menacingly. "Should have stayed where you were laddies; this is no place for you."

"Give us back the purse!" Cassius exclaimed from the ground. "You have no right to it."

"Right? Who needs right? I took it, so it's mine now." He gestured. "These little ones do what I say, jump to my orders and take what I want." He punctuated his statement by kicking me in the chest, hurling me back against the wall of the alley. "Now you have chased after something of mine and come into my alley. That means you're also mine."

Speech done, he stomped on Cassius's stomach, causing him to retch and throw up. Vomit splattered the cobbles and the boot of the towering teenager. His gaze darkened. Fury erupted in his eyes.

"You son of a bitch! You'll pay for that you little shit stain!" he roared, punctuating each word with a kick to Cassius, who had curled into a protective ball, screaming with the pain of each blow.

"Stop it Regie! You'll kill him!" came a cry from one of the others, the thief I think. I didn't have time to check, I was too busy running at the man sized youth, intent on stopping him from hurting Cassius. He saw me coming, ducked my wild haymaker, swivelled his hip and threw a left hook into my kidney. Pain exploded in my back as the second punch connected with my jaw, flattening me to the ground. He kicked me in the ribs then knelt on top of me, throwing more punches to my face. Through the battering I could see Cassius stagger to his feet. How he could even stand I will never know. He threw his shoulder into the side of Regie's head, buying me some time to slowly, unsteadily, get up. Through blurry eyes I saw Cassius swinging, a lucky punch catching Regie under the jaw and startling him. But the experience and power of the older boy quickly began to tell and he soon slipped one of Cassius's punches, knocking him back to the ground. Regie then reached down to the floor and picked something up. Something black and shiny. My obsidian belt knife.

"Regie don't!" came the cry again. The boy didn't listen. He was going to kill Cassius. Murder him. Eat him. In my mind's eye Regie was no longer the teenage thug; he was the monster in the dark, the destroyer of my village. I could feel strength flow through me, as if Seya was somehow helping. I screamed, a howl of rage and torment. The monster would not take Cassius from me again. I burst into motion, moving faster than I would ever have thought possible. I slid under the downward strike of the blade, my forearm raising up to catch Regie's strike and preventing it from touching Cassius. I then kicked out at Regie's ankle, intending to sweep his leg. Instead the bone shattered, his leg crumpling with the nonexistent support. As he fell I moved behind him and screamed.

"Calidan! Calidan!"

A voice intruded into the rage of my thoughts.

"Calidan, it's over! Stop!" Cassius's voice. My eyes opened and I screamed, not in rage but in horror. The shattered mess of Regie's skull was in my hands. Blood on the cobbles from where I had smashed his face into the floor, over and over. Cassius was by my side, one eye swollen shut, face puffy, the other eye filled with concern. "Calidan, it's okay, it's okay," he whispered as he pulled me into a hug.

"Okay?!" I screamed as I stared into my hands, horrified by the blood and bone. "How is this okay?" I turned and vomited onto the cobbles. A pain in my side cut deeper as I bent to vomit and I patted down my chest to find a familiar bone handle sticking out of my torso. "Oh, so that's where that went," I said, sitting down heavily. The last thing I saw before blackness claimed me was Cassius, sweet Cassius, cradling my head with horror in his haunted eyes.

CHAPTER NINE
NEW BEGINNINGS

~

I WOKE IN MY BED. A strange place to be when presumably dead. I opened my eyes and came face to face with a young girl who squeaked in fright and scampered out the room. A confused chuckle broke from my dry lips. Death had its humour after all.

Cassius sprinted into the room, "He's awake!" he called behind him, before excitedly coming to sit beside me on the bed.

"How's it going Calidan? You feeling okay? You thirsty?" he asked in a rush of questions. I nodded wearily and he helped me take a sip of water as Kyle, Lana, the Tracker and Brother Gelman appeared, ushering along a new man, who I presumed to be a doctor judging by his attire and bag of instruments.

"Give him some space son," said Brother Gelman, and Kyle gently pulled Cassius away from my side.

"Are you okay?" I asked Cassius as the doctor probed my side. His face looked yellow and purple, and he was moving with a limp when he rushed into the room.

"I'm fine Calidan, just a few cuts and bruises which are healing nicely. I have you to thank that it's not worse," he said quietly looking me in the eyes. "I mean it. I saw the knife and couldn't have got away in time, then all of a sudden you were there…" he drifted off, eyes glazing over in memory then shook his head. "Next time you save my life just try to not nearly die in the process alright?"

I chuckled and smiled at my friend, "Deal."

The doctor was saying something to Kyle and Lana, something important by the expressions on their faces. Kyle hid it well but Lana was completely astonished.

Brother Gelman came forward, "Calidan, it's been five days since you've been stabbed. The doctor, as you might imagine for a military doctor, is very experienced with stab wounds. He was expecting you to be bedridden for a minimum of three months. Instead he is saying you could probably get up tomorrow! He has never seen anything like it." He looked at me intently as though he could divine whatever secrets I was holding by the power of sight. I stared back blankly. In truth whilst I had some inkling of what might be helping me,(my bond with

Seylantha) I had no idea how it worked or what the extent of the bond's power might be.

Brother Gelman looked a little disappointed when I didn't divulge any information. However he brightened up considerably when Kyle spoke up, stating that for the immediate future, Brother Gelman would be coming to provide lessons at the compound, rather than Cassius and I walking to the Hall of Scribes. Outwardly I smiled whilst inwardly I groaned. Whilst the military compound was a great place for Cassius and I to live and learn, it wasn't the kind of place where we could be, for want of a better term, free. The military by necessity has to follow strict rules and be *just so*. For children the age of Cassius and myself it can be a little stifling, and so the trips to the market had been a release of sorts. An opportunity to let the inner child free and embrace the wonder of new experiences. Just our luck that Cassius' latest experience was to try and be a hero, and mine was knowing what it is like to hold a crumpled skull in my hands. My mind darkened and the memories rushed back. The rage at seeing Cassius on the floor with a knife descending towards him, the crushed ankle of Regie... the young thief who called for Regie to stop. The blood. I flailed for a bin, failed to find one and threw up. The memory was much too real, etched into my mind.

Me. Killer.

Once I stopped throwing up all over myself I looked over at Cassius as Lana fussed over me. "The young girl who sprinted out of here when I woke up; she is the same girl who stole the money at the market?" Cassius's face lit up.

"Ella!" he exclaimed. "Yes, she stayed behind and helped me carry you to the market where we managed to get help. I convinced her to stay until Kyle arrived with the doctor and he immediately offered her a place here as a thank you for helping." His eyes glazed over as he spoke; I think Cassius was a little infatuated.

I held up a hand to stop further recounting. "I thought so. Thanks Cassius, I'm sure that we will get introduced soon enough," I said as I smiled and awkwardly thanked Lana for her attempts to tidy me up. She beamed warmly at me before leading the doctor out of the room.

Kyle came forward. He clapped me softly on the shoulder and spoke to me through Brother Gelman.

"Calidan, it's great to see that you're doing better. Exceeding all expectations according to the doctor...by a long, long way." A slight furrow crossed his forehead as he said this. "I'm not going to pry into how you're able to heal so quickly, but rest assured if there is anything you want to talk about you can talk to me in complete confidence." He paused and knelt by the bed before gesturing at the remains of the vomit, "Regarding what happened...killing is never easy. I know that you probably feel like you never want to talk about it, but when you change your mind I will be here to listen. One man who has killed to another." He cleared his throat and looked almost embarrassed, "I want you to know that I am immensely proud of you." He looked over at Cassius, "Both of you. You stood up for what you believed in, fought for it and what's more, you survived. There aren't many people who would do what you two did...Forgoth is lucky to count you among its citizens." With that he stood up, brushed something from his eye, surely dust not tears, then left taking Brother Gelman with him.

That left the Tracker, Cassius and me.

The Tracker nodded warmly and spoke in halting Tarr, "Glad you're alive." That's about as emotional as the Tracker gets. He made Major General Kyle look like a cry baby. He pointed at my nearly healed wound, "You truly are Elkona Melkhuk. You heal like one of the old ones."

"Old ones?" I asked.

He tosses his hands in the air, "Legends, myths...truths. Old ones part of great ones. Great ones part of old ones. You have true bond with Seya, she keeps you alive if hurt, you keep her alive if hurt."

"Keep me alive? How? Is she here? Is she okay?" The questions tumbled out of me, but the Tracker just shook his head and said two words, "Ask her."

"Seya?" No answer. "Seya?!" A deep rumble in my chest, not dissimilar to a grumbling, mighty beast who had been woken rudely.

"It is not nice to wake someone when they're tired from saving your life," Seya said, her tone a mixture of annoyance tinged with smugness.

"Are you okay?" I asked, and felt warmth and gratitude flood through me at the question.

"I am fine, just a little tired. Healing one such as you does not take much of a toll, but it still takes a price."

"Price? What do you mean, can you tell me what is going on?" I fired back.

"Our bond, THE bond. It makes us more than the sum of our parts. My power, size and longevity is an inheritance from a time long past. It is designed to assist the bonded. Bleed over into them, make them stronger, faster, better. In this case you." I held my mental breath, this was more information than she had ever shared before. "When you are hurt I feel it, I can send more energy to assist. It just takes a while to recover."

"What if you are hurt?" I ask, "Can I help you?"

'No!" she replied, shame, anger and sadness coursing through my body at her thoughts. "You are small, I am much bigger. If I am hurt and you tried to provide energy I could take it all without knowing. You would be lost."

She refused to talk more, just sending a wave of happiness that I was okay and a reassurance that she was fine.

"How is she?" Cassius asked when I opened my eyes.

"Fine," I replied. "She explained a few things about our bond. How she can use it to heal me, but I should never use it to heal her...something about me being small and her being all big and mighty." I was feeling a little petulant and aggrieved that I could not help my friend if she needed it.

"Well that sucks!" Cassius replied angrily. "Seya is our friend, if she got hurt then it's only right that we help her." I loved Cassius for this, not just for his concern over Seya but the fact that he included himself in helping her through my bond. Probably not possible, but I loved him for it all the same.

"It's okay, I can't imagine Seya getting hurt anytime soon, can you?" I countered, "I mean what could possibly hurt her?" In due time I would come to regret those words.

I was up and out of bed the very next day, my wound completely healed, with only a silvery scar to show for my brush with my own mortality. Cassius was keen to introduce me to Ella and led me on a merry hunt around the compound, but in vain. We would catch glimpses of her but each time she saw us she bolted in the other direction. Cassius was somewhat put out, and assumed that she didn't want to see him. I surmised differently. I was the different factor in their relationship. It seemed more than likely that she didn't want to meet the person who had chased her down and then crushed someone's skull into the cobbled floor. The thoughts came back, but this time I was able to prevent vomiting. I was still in horror at what had occurred; the nightmares I had experienced the night before cementing the fact that my mind was not at peace with what I had done.

As we walked around the compound however I noticed something odd. The soldiers who had up to this point taken relatively little notice of the two of us were nudging each other and pointing in our direction. We heard snippets of conversation as we walked past on our hunt for Ella.

"Hear what he did?"

"Brains all over the cobbles..."

"Bare hands!"

Growing increasingly uncomfortable, Cassius and I began drifting back to Kyle's residence but were intercepted by a group of recent recruits, all, to our eyes, much bigger, stronger and infinitely older, but otherwise just a group of sixteen year olds. They crowded around us and began asking questions in Andurran. It didn't take much to work out that they were wondering how I did it, how it felt to kill someone and how great it must have been. I felt like I couldn't breathe. The questions came thick and fast, weighing the air down around me until I felt like I could take no more. My breath came in short gasps, hands clenched so tightly into fists that I could feel blood dripping. I dropped to one knee and the subject of the diatribe changed.

"What's wrong with him?"

"Why doesn't he speak?"

Cassius, realising my panic was rising was vainly trying to get the recruits to step back and give me space. A forlorn hope, a rock was more likely to listen and obey than a rabble of boisterous, glory hungry teenagers.

Tears began to stream down my face, and the questions became more like pointed accusations, questioning my sexuality, sanity and whatever air of friendliness there had been quickly dissipated.

"Attention!"

The bellow felt like it shook the ground.

In my panicked daze I looked up and saw that the recruits had snapped to attention, falling into place in front of the company sword master.

"Would anyone care to explain what is going on here?" he exploded, his angry gaze holding each and every recruit seemingly accountable for all the problems in his life. One recruit raised a trembling hand and the sword master's gaze fell upon him like a raging bull. "Yes recruit Severil?" he asked sweetly, all trace of anger gone from his voice.

"Sorry sir, we saw that boy, you know, the one who killed someone by crushing their head, and we wanted to ask about it, we didn't think it would-"

"Didn't think?" the sword master said softly before raising his voice and once again exploding into a raging vehement fire. "Didn't think?! In this army we do not want or need troopers who do not think! Do you understand?" his voice had dropped again, soft and dangerous. The recruits nodded, petrified. "Well then, get out of my sight!" he snarled. The troopers ran as if the ghosts of their ancestors were chasing them.

The sword master turned to me, a soft look in his eyes. "On behalf of the Andurran military I apologise for those incompetent ingrates. With times being what they are we take what we can get." He smiled wryly, "Why don't both of you come and find me tomorrow morning at dawn. I have my morning practice sessions then, and perhaps I can help ensure that next time the knife enters your opponent, not you." He winked before turning smartly on his heel and sauntering off. One would almost think that he enjoyed scaring new recruits. I turned to Cassius.

"Did you understand what he said?" I asked.

"I think he was apologising, but I could be mistaken," Cassius replied. We shrugged and moved on, heading back to Kyle's residence, filing away the encounter to the back of our minds.

What we didn't count on however was the sword master's tenacity, or his close relationship with Kyle. And so the next day as the dawn light crept over the walls of the city, Cassius and I were woken by Kyle and our sleepy selves dragged to the training ground where the sword master waited. After a series of gruelling sprints across the freshly swept arena to warm us up we began following a series of slow combat forms that the sword master, Tyrgan, led. He made the movements seem effortless and apparently loved teaching how to perform them, never once complaining about the myriad of times he had to repeat a certain move or sequence. His body moved in perfect synchronicity, a fluid motion that belied the power his body was capable of generating. He called this system Kaschan.

Unbeknownst to either Cassius or myself was that being instructed in Kaschan was a great honour. The combat system had been developed by the protectors of Andurran royalty. Redesigned and refined over generations, the system taught how to fight effectively with weapons as well as empty handed.

Kyle explained that Tyrgan had once been a member of the Emperor's elite bodyguards, and that Kaschan was the system that they employed. Annoyingly he didn't have any further information on the subject, or if he did then he chose not to divulge it. In the years since however, I researched Tyrgan's background using the Imperator's unrestricted access to Andurran records, which confirmed that he had been a member of the Emperor's guard. An impressive position to have held, and an unusual situation to have been allowed to leave. Usually one does not exit employment in the Emperor's guard, unless by death. To have left and not be hunted by Imperators suggested that Tyrgan had done something significant and been released from duty - but even the original information in the archives had been redacted. An irritating and delicious mystery that I longed to solve. But back to Kaschan.

Tyrgan did not teach Kaschan to the regular soldiers. He taught the regimented style of fighting that made the Andurran war machine so effective. The army was taught to fight as a single organism, each protecting the man next to him and moving in cohesion. This doesn't work for bodyguards. Any combat system for the Emperor's defenders had to involve fast movements and quick, precise striking. Precise being key; many of the moves made by the guards would be to prevent harm coming to the Emperor, deflecting blows at the last second. However, just because the guards needed a different system than the military, it doesn't mean that they lost their cohesion. If one practitioner of Kaschan is a force to be reckoned with, two is a deadly fluidity of movement and four is an overwhelming maelstrom of death. The fluid movements of the system are meant to account for different weapon styles, the spinning use of a greatsword moving in sync with the more delicate moves of a dual blade wielder for instance. Much like dancing, the system works better with a partner, steps moving in sync, bodies moving as one; enemies falling like wheat to the scythe.

Cassius and I loved it.

At first we were unaware of the quality of the fighting system that we were learning, or at this stage, being subjected to. To the minds of young eleven year olds, waking up with the dawn to exercise around a training yard before performing slow, flowing motions was not congruent with learning how to fight. It seems that Tyrgan understood this perfectly and so on the third day of our training, he bade us watch as he and Kyle fought. The two of them moved across the even surface of the training ground like water, moving from block to punch to kick in a seamless dance. Kyle's foot swept low, frustration evident as he hit nothing but air. He continued the movement before deftly flicking his other leg toward Tyrgan, using his momentum to propel his leg at the older man. The bout ended when Tyrgan stepped into the high kick, used a leg of his own and swept Kyle down onto the floor hard. Laughing, he stepped back, moving lightly on his feet and still not taking his eyes off his opponent. Kyle grimaced in pain as he dusted himself off and stood up. He eyed Tyrgan and cracked a grin as the older man retrieved two swords from the training rack. He proffered one to Kyle with a knowing smile on his face.

Kyle accepted it graciously, before asking lightly, "Are you sure Tyrgan? I am the city champion after all…" Tyrgan just nodded, his grin never leaving his face, but retreating from his eyes.

Kyle moved forward confidently, obviously more comfortable with a blade between him and Tyrgan. He continued to move in the flowing style of Kaschan but this time as he moved, the blade moved with him, creating a whirl of silver as he launched his attack. His blade flashed towards Tyrgan's neck, missing it by inches as the instructor stepped away. Swift as a viper the blade reversed and Kyle stepped through, the blade seeking his opponent's chest.

It never made it.

Again Tyrgan had moved away from the lightning fast attack, his body never in one place for long. He struck Kyle's leg casually as he spun by, putting no weight behind the blow - almost as if toying with the Major General. Kyle spun, striking low then high, aiming for Tyrgan's legs in an attempt to hinder his escape. His speed was astounding. We watched open mouthed as his blade flashed with the dawn sun, as though it was afire. The two circled around the arena, Kyle hunting, Tyrgan escaping. He hadn't yet deflected a blow. Kyle swung in, aiming to rotate before following through with his sword and found himself face first on the ground, Tyrgan laughing uproariously. The anger quickly left Kyle's face as he sat up and shook his head.

"I still don't understand how nothing I do hits you!" he said, "I know I'm fast enough to do it."

Tyrgan looked at him calmly, barely breathing hard, "Speed is important, but what use is having speed when your opponent knows what you are going to do before you do it?" Kyle looked at him curiously, silently asking him to elaborate. Tyrgan walked him back over to us as he continued, "In Kaschan we move quickly, continuously, not for show or distraction but so we can move where we want to be, and lead the opponent to where we want them to be." He touched his eyes and ears, "In order to master it, you must truly *see* your opponent, the way their muscles move, the minute glances of their eyes. You must *listen* to their footsteps, the sound of the blade cutting the air. If you do this, you can be where their weapon is not."

He looked at us, sitting, trying to grasp the meaning of the still unintelligible words we had just heard and he laughed. The next day Brother Gelman was at the training ground.

And so the days continued. Cassius and I trained with Kyle, Tyrgan and Brother Gelman (who soon warmed to the idea of free weapons training from two masters) first thing in the morning, before eating breakfast together and continuing our language lessons. It was here that Ella could not escape me, though she looked like she was constantly one step away from sprinting out the door. Kyle had offered her a place to stay at his home but on the condition that she learn along with us. As it was her grasp of Andurran was fluent, if a little incorrect in her use of proper terminology, and so Brother Gelman started instructing her in Tarr, reasoning that it might be nice to have a relatively private language for use in the household. As the lessons continued Brother Gelman let us take the lead more and more, using our broken knowledge of each other's languages to try and teach the other. A fun if sometimes irritating game, but certainly a good way to learn. Nothing is more of a motivator than trying to speak to someone who can't understand you.

Language wasn't the only lesson Kyle offered to Ella. Weapons training was also included. Kyle reasoned that although women weren't allowed in the Andurran military, something that the Tracker scoffed at and a rule Kyle was trying to change, everyone should know how to defend themselves. Another reason why even today I still remember Kyle fondly; he was extremely forward thinking.

As it was Ella refused point blank to go anywhere near the training square whilst I was there; obviously the thought of seeing me with a weapon in my hand or fighting was too vivid a reminder of what I had done. Consequently she received her training in the evening, once Tyrgan had finished with the recruits. From our broken discussions we discovered that Tyrgan was teaching us ever so slightly different versions of Kaschan; if possible Ella's version was seemingly even more flowing.

When questioned on this Tyrgan grinned and with Brother Gelman translating said, "Ah so you've caught on already have you? Yes, there are two types of Kaschan. Whilst women aren't allowed in the Andurran military they make for fine body guards. But as men and women are different physically, the styles have to be different. Many men might be able to wield a greatsword but few women could. This is unavoidable. And so the women learn a faster, lighter version of Kaschan, no less effective but designed for use with lighter weapons. In fact the best two guards in the Emperor's employ are known as the Twins. Twins who have practiced the Kaschan from birth, one male, one female. The man, Andros, wields a spear whilst the woman, Geryna, wields dual sabres. Together they are nigh unstoppable, protecting each other and moving in perfect unison. Andros prevents the opponent from moving, whilst Geryna moves in for the kill." He paused and looked at the three of us before continuing, "Eventually you three will have to learn to fight together." He noticed Ella's scowl. "So put aside your differences, whatever they are, and focus on Kaschan, I expect you three to start to challenge me before long!" With that he gave us all a big grin and departed.

CHAPTER TEN
PROGRESS

~

IT WAS NINE MONTHS BEFORE we managed to touch Tyrgan. Nine months of training twice a day. Tyrgan had stopped accepting Ella's dislike of me as a reason to keep us separate and merged the two classes. Except instead of making it just the one class, he decided it would be much more fun and not remotely sadistic at all to keep both classes, and make everyone come to each. For some time Ella still kept her distance from me, fear evident in her eyes whenever I approached. But after the first time she knocked me on my back, I was pleased to see that fear seemingly begin to recede. From that point on she trained just as hard as Cassius and I. To me, she was still an enigma, receiving little in the way of direct conversation from her, but she happily talked with Cassius and everyone, including me, smiled to see them roaming the grounds chatting excitedly together. Whilst we had both matured to the ripe old age of twelve, I don't think Cassius or I yet understood the appeal of girls. Yet talking with Ella seemed to make him happy, and for me, seeing my best friend happy after the tragedy of the year gone past was a moment long past due.

Together we began to thrive under our ruthless training schedule. We became stronger, faster, and our stamina increased to the point where we could all dance like Tyrgan without collapsing after five minutes. Ella was extremely quick, her talents as a pickpocket gifting her with the fastest hands amongst us. Whilst her size and strength were lacking compared to mine, and especially to Cassius, she more than made up for it with lightning fast blows.

Whilst a fraction slower than Ella, Cassius's bladework was flawless. He moved as though he were one with his sword and thrived on trialling any weapon that Tyrgan threw at him, picking up the different quirks and mannerisms of each tool much faster than either myself or Ella.

As for me, I had taken Tyrgan's suggestions of *listen* to heart. Using the skills Seya taught me, combined with my enhanced hearing, I could understand where the others were going to be almost before they did. When Cassius and I practiced by ourselves he could not touch me; in our training sessions however I had to tone down my abilities, else Tyrgan and Kyle would have become even more suspicious than they already were, given that they had witnessed me heal from a stab wound in a matter of days. Plus it was unfair on the others. So I performed with my senses largely closed and as a result was regularly thrashed by the other two. But I consoled myself with the thought that if I could perform well without relying on my bond with Seya, then with it I would be orders of magnitude better.

Tyrgan began changing our routines as we progressed in Kaschan. From the end of the first month we were sparring with empty hands, braving the cold of the winter, which was still surprisingly warm to Cassius and I. At first the thought of hitting Ella seemed immoral, but she soon rid us of that notion when she kicked me in the crotch and hit Cassius in the throat; moves that left us on the floor and Tyrgan gasping for breath laughing.

"In Kaschan, nothing is off limits," he gasped between peals of laughter, "you best get used to hitting girls because not everyone wanting to kill you is a guy." And so when we next fought, it was no holds barred.

By the end of the second month of training with Tyrgan our routine was changed again, beginning weapons training and open handed sparring with a twist. Sometimes it would be two on one, other times one of us would have an arm or leg hobbled with rope. Tyrgan obviously believed in preparing for all eventualities and for continued fighting, no matter the odds.

Eventually we began working weapons play into this, so that by the end of seven months we were proficient with multiple weapons, and how to use them in combat against multiple opponents or as Kaschan is designed, how to use them with friends. In his ever sadistic way, Tyrgan had started ensuring that our sparring matches involved Brother Gelman, who had continued his training alongside us, and Kyle. Their size and strength presented a formidable obstacle to overcome. Brother Gelman was as much a novice to fighting as we were and so whilst one on one was difficult, each of us could beat him. Kyle on the other hand, was a different beast. A master swordsman in his own right before starting Kaschan, (he wasn't lying about being the city champion) he resoundingly defeated the three of us in single combat, and two on one. It was only in three on one that we managed to score a hit, earning a grin of fierce pride from Kyle and slaps on the back from Tyrgan and Gelman.

After Kyle, Tyrgan became more involved in our sessions. He ensured that each training session ended with sparring with him, always three on one, because as he put it, "The young pups couldn't hit me if my arms were tied behind my back."

It's true. We tried.

For two months, twice a day, we would finish our training sessions by sparring with Tyrgan, and for two months we failed. Until one day, I got sick of him dancing effortlessly out of the way and opened my senses. As we attacked I could hear the way his muscles stretched and contracted, I could see the minute twitches of his eyes and feet, and as we began our assault I began moving just a little more, tiny changes in direction that forced Tyrgan to alter his course slightly. His eyes narrowed and the grin disappeared from his eyes.

The game was on.

We began to move faster and faster, Cassius and Ella forgotten as I matched Tyrgan at his game. My blade became a blur, my feet sliding across the ground in perfect unison with my body, each step allowing me to hunt the hunter. For the first time Tyrgan was forced to use his sword in defence, unable to move out of the way of my heart-seeking sword in time. I let my wrist roll with the blow, flicking the point of my sword back at my opponent, stepping in to where his body was going to move. Tyrgan changed his direction mid stride, using impressive core strength to deftly move his body out of the way, sliding out of the danger zone and right into my waiting blade.

Silence rolled across the courtyard.

Cassius and Ella stood close by, their mouths open in astonishment. Cassius had known what I could do, but I knew he had only ever seen me move that fast once before - when I saved his life. The look in Ella's eyes was haunting. The fear had returned. Guilt clenched my heart at what I had done, this was intended to have been kept a secret. Something used only if necessary, yet instead I had revealed it out of frustration and pride, and now my secret was out. I could only hope that it wasn't too damaging to the relationships that I had built. I looked around and saw both Kyle and Brother Gelman also staring at me, obviously judging me. I daren't look at Tyrgan. I dropped my sword and began to walk away, ashamed.

"Calidan," Tyrgan's voice. I kept walking.

"Calidan!" Tyrgan's parade ground voice. I stopped in my tracks and turned. He tossed me my dropped sword. "Good. Again."

In the evening Kyle, Tyrgan and Brother Gelman joined us for dinner. They feigned a casual mood but from the way they picked at their meals and sent furtive glances my way I knew that they only wanted one thing; my story. Ella had ensured that she was sitting as far from me as possible.

Cassius just looked bemused by it all. He leaned over, "I would say that the cat is out of the bag, but in your case it would have to be a very large bag wouldn't it!" He grinned and chuckled at his own joke before patting me on the shoulder. "Come on mate, I think we can both be sure that these people in this room are our friends. They aren't going to hurt Seya."

I sighed heavily. "I hope you're right," I said as I tapped my mug on the table.

"Cassius and I have told you all the circumstances of how we came to end up in Forgoth," I said in Andurran - it, like my martial skills, having flourished over the past few months. "But we left something out, something very important, but we left it out with good reason, to protect someone very important to us. To me." I took a deep breath and continued, "During our time in the forests on the mountains I befriended a giant black panther called Seylantha. And when I mean giant, I truly mean it; Kyle she makes your warhorse look small." Kyle looked astonished at the thought of such a creature. Tyrgan just waited expectantly, an amused smile on his face. Brother Gelman was mouthing my next words as I said them, "She is what is known as a Great Heart." A look of beatific pleasure spread across Brother Gelman's face.

"A Great Heart!" he cried. "I can only imagine the sight! I thought they were all extinct!" He paused. "Ah that explains it," he said knowingly. "So the legends are true after all." At the confused looks on everyone's faces he continued, "You've bonded with it haven't you?"

"She, not it." I replied. "Best not call her an it if you meet her. And yes, we have some kind of bond. I can't explain it well but the bond has made me stronger, faster and able to sense things that normal people could not." I looked at Tyrgan, "It was this that allowed me to beat you today. I'm sorry." I looked at the table.

"Sorry?" he barked. "The only thing you should be sorry about is hiding it! You're not the first bonded person I've met, nor I doubt the last. I could have made your training much more suited to your abilities if I had known earlier."

"Tyrgan," said Kyle slowly. "You mean to say that you have known of creatures like this Great Heart and the powers of this bond? And you didn't tell me?"

"Of course," replied Tyrgan, offering no apology. "Having been in the Emperor's employ you see and hear things. Great Hearts and their bonded are prized amongst the Emperor's inner circle, but aside from training several in Kaschan I do not know what role they truly play."

Kyle sat back heavily. I had not seen him look so out of his depth before. Obviously the information about the Great Hearts and that the Emperor had known about them for some time had upset his otherwise balanced understanding of things. "I cannot believe that giant creatures, larger than my warhorse you say, exist, and that we don't actively know about it!" he said in exasperation.

"I think they are very secretive," I replied. "Seya is aware of others but she has told me that their numbers have dwindled over time; Brother Gelman probably knows more than I do on the subject, he seems aware of the term Great Heart," sparking a splutter from Brother Gelman as he took a swig of cider.

"Yes, I've heard of them. My master, Scholar Jacobs and I have made a study of them in fact," he replied. "Great Hearts have been a matter of myth and legend for thousands of years. However they appear in so many different cultures that we reasoned that there must be a fragment of truth in it. To know that they truly exist! This is a marvel beyond comprehension. Scholar Jacobs will be ecstatic when he-"

"No!" I interjected, pausing his enthusiastic tirade. "You cannot tell him," I looked at them all, "you cannot tell anyone!"

Kyle nodded. "Calidan is correct. If what Tyrgan has told us is true, and I trust him completely, then the Emperor keeps the knowledge of these Great Hearts secret for a reason. If word were to reach the capital that young Calidan here has one, who knows what will happen?" Silence echoed around the table. "So all here are not to speak of this outside of this room, are we clear?" Kyle looked gravely at each person at the table, until one by one they all nodded. "Excellent." He indicated Brother Gelman, "Please continue Brother."

"Ah, yes of course." Brother Gelman said, still looking perturbed at the thought of not being able to share his discovery. "Records of giant creatures, land, air and sea based are in practically every culture's histories. Indeed if you think about the children stories you may have heard as an Andurran child, Kyle, you will doubtless remember the myth of the great bird who carried Tianin the folk hero." Kyle nodded, his eyes glazed over in recollection. "You could pass off one or two tales like this as just storytelling, but they exist in every culture. Giant birds, dragons, squid," he indicated me, "dogs and cats." He paused again to collect his thoughts.

"What really prompted our research into this area was the discovery of an almost complete skeleton in the desert of Turpal. This skeleton was said to be of a giant snake, nearly fifty strides in length and almost completely intact except for a large hole in the skull. What really piqued our interest was the suggestion that there was a human skeleton next to it. Lying with its back against the snake as if its companion, and missing a leg. We sent out a librarian; those of our order who travel seeking new information; but he said that whilst the locals all verified it was true, the remains of both the beast and man had vanished. 'Removed' was his best guess."

"Removed?" I interjected. "Who would want to take a skeleton?"

"What interests me more," interjected Kyle, "is who has the resources to move a skeleton from the desert of Turpal? If this person or persons wants to hide the evidence of Great Hearts, then they must have a lot of people or power at their disposal."

"That's what Scholar Jacobs and I thought," said Brother Gelman. "Since then we have kept our ears to the ground for mentions of Great Hearts, but the few rumours we've investigated have turned up nothing."

I inwardly breathed a sigh of relief. This meant that Seya was safe for the time being, no rumour had spread of her in her chosen hunting grounds.

We continued the conversation late into the night. I was questioned on Great Hearts, how I bonded with Seya, and the way we communicate. For most of the questions I couldn't give a particularly accurate answer. Things between Seya and I just 'were'; I had no idea how we had actually bonded, nor did I know the science behind how we communicated. Once everyone had begun yawning Kyle finally sent us to bed, but not before getting me to promise that we would go and visit Seya when time allowed. I grudgingly agreed. Whilst I might not like it, I'm sure Seya would appreciate more people to fawn over her. I did feel like I had left her alone too much in the past year. Aside from a few fleeting visits from myself and Cassius, which had been tricky to arrange as since my stabbing it had been much more difficult to leave the compound, let alone the city; only the Tracker had seen her on a relatively frequent basis and that was because he intentionally led his new scout recruits towards her forest. I think he enjoyed trying to track her through the trees. And she certainly loved pouncing on him when he was separated from his men; every time she did I could feel the laughter in my chest.

The next morning I woke to find Tyrgan standing above me. It was earlier than usual, the dawn light not yet piercing the moonless dark; we must have only slept a few hours. Cassius was still, rightfully, asleep. Tyrgan had brought no candle and must have felt his way in here through the inky black. I, however, could see him perfectly, outlined in an orange hue. He must have known that this would be the case as he extended his finger and curled it in an unmistakable 'come with me' gesture.

Sighing inwardly - outwardly would not have ended well if Tyrgan had heard - I quickly dressed and followed him out the door, leaving Cassius to (hopefully) dream sweetly. I followed Tyrgan to the training yard where he picked two gleaming swords out of his sheathes. They looked to be twins of each other, both around two feet in length, razor sharp and seemingly burning with an inner fire. Tyrgan reverently grasped the hilt of both blades and I gasped as I saw markings appear on the metal, glowing as though red hot. The markings were replicated in what I had assumed was a tattoo that circled Tyrgan's wrists. They too glowed as if afire, though Tyrgan gave no suggestion of pain.

Instead he was running at me with murder in his eyes.

I had no weapon. I had no idea what Tyrgan was doing; before this he had always had warmth in his eyes when sparring. Even when he had had to focus to fight me the day before, his eyes hadn't held the cold blooded aggression I saw in them now. I realised that this was Tyrgan's true fighting form, that of the man who had fought and killed for the Emperor. But what I had done to warrant those eyes turning on me I did not know. Before my mind stopped considering the situation and began to recognise that Tyrgan had crossed the distance between us far faster than he should have been able to, my body acted of its own accord and twisted out of the way of the gleaming blade that would have sheared me in two.

I felt no terror as I slid between his expert blows. My mind had fallen into an almost empty state - I could *feel* where the blows were going to land, I could *hear* where the blade whistled through the air - and my body just reacted. Tyrgan kept coming at me, his swords a gleaming blur through the air, moving faster than anyone I had ever seen. Inhumanly fast. Faster than anyone, except apparently, me. He moved forward in perfect Kaschan form, sliding from one stance to the next, cutting with each step.

Moving from the sweeping downward strike of 'the water's edge' to the crossed upward strike of 'the scorpion's kiss', he melded the unarmed and armed styles together, merging kick after blade cut, sweep after thrust. Tyrgan flipped over my head, my reflexes flinging me forward as the two blades skimmed above where my neck had been. He landed smoothly, his swords sweeping downward to slice at my legs causing me to twist out of the way. I felt the strength in my arms and pushed off the ground, aiming to fling myself like he had done, but out of the way. Instead I rose about twenty feet off the floor. I instantly knew I had made a mistake. Whilst flips and somersaults are involved in Kaschan, they are dangerous because the practitioner's power and movement comes from their lower body. If you remove that source, like I had just done, there wasn't too much you could do, except in my case watch your inevitable demise get closer as I began to fall back to my waiting death.

I fell and attempted to twist before landing, aiming to get clear of those deadly swords. Instead I found myself face first on the floor with an aching back and stomach where Tyrgan had unleashed a devastating sidekick, flinging me thirty feet into a wall. I raised my eyes and froze. Tyrgan was on his heels in front of me, the smile of his eyes back in its usual place. The two swords were in their sheaths and laid in front of him on the ground. I groaned and sat up. In truth I didn't really hurt that much; the ache had immediately died down and I was certain that I could move quickly again if needed. I began to tense, ready to move.

"Relax," said Tyrgan, as though he could read my mind. "The fight is over...you lost."

Content that I wasn't going to be sliced in two in the immediate future I sat up and frowned at him, "What was all that about Tyrgan? You looked like you were trying to kill me!"

"I was," he replied. "If I hadn't been trying then I wouldn't have been a match for you - even with Kyra and Ryken here," he said, gesturing at the two swords.

"Kyra and Ryken?" I asked. "Those are not normal swords. Even you can't move that quickly Tyrgan, not unless you're bonded to a Great Heart like me."

"You're right. These are not normal swords." Tyrgan showed me his wrist indicating his tattoos. "They are bonded to me, just as you are bonded to your Great Heart. If anyone else were to use them, they would just find them to be well made swords. But when they are in my hands they increase my power, speed and reflexes, as well as a few other bonuses that will remain secret."

"How do you have such a thing? How is such a thing possible?" I asked, the questions pouring off my tongue.

"Do you really think that the Emperor, knowing that there were people bonded to Great Hearts who were stronger, faster and better than his guards, would not take steps to improve his safety?" he replied, a chuckle in his throat. "As for how it's possible, I have no idea. But there are many strange things in this world Calidan; an enhanced sword is probably the least of them."

He had a point. After all, somewhere out there lurked a shadow demon.

"So what was the purpose of all that?" I asked, waving my hand at the training ground.

"Your training!" he replied. "I told you I could have done knowing about your abilities sooner. As it is, we will now meet here an hour before daybreak every day to spar, and then you will continue with the others with your abilities reigned in, as you have been doing so far." I was about to argue when he put his hand up, forestalling my outburst. "There are different methods to fighting when you are enhanced Calidan. You need to understand your powers, explore your strengths and weaknesses, and adapt the Kaschan to suit you. As you saw, there are inherent problems with just relying on your powers to save you. If I wasn't such a nice person," he grinned evilly, "then it would have been a sword in your chest just now rather than a boot." He paused and looked me in the eye, "Do you understand? For your own safety you need to learn how to be Calidan 'Darkheart' as the Tracker has taken to calling you - understanding all the strengths and all the weaknesses of being bonded. But enough talk; we've got a good half hour until the others get here. Feel up to another bout?"

I felt my ribs. Everything seemed to be in order and the aches had completely disappeared.

"Only if you can handle it old man!" I replied, a menacing grin on my face. With the vibrant anger of youth I was positive that next time I would put Tyrgan on his ass. I was proven wrong, time and time again.

Two weeks later, I was woken as per usual by Tyrgan, but this time he was with Kyle, dressed for riding, and it wasn't just me he woke, but Cassius too. Brother Gelman then came to the door with a sleepy eyed Ella in tow.

"What's going on?" she asked in a groggy voice.

"We're going on a ride to visit Seylantha, Calidan's Great Heart," replied Kyle. "Now hush, no more questions for the time being, get dressed quickly and quietly, we want to avoid as much attention as possible. I will answer any questions you have when we are on the road out of the city. You have ten minutes." With that he turned and walked out the room, followed by Brother Gelman who ushered Ella back to her room to get changed.

"Well..." Cassius said, locking eyes with me. "Did you know about this?"

"Not in the slightest," I replied. "Seems a little odd, all this cloak and dagger stuff, but we have no time to question it now. We best dress quickly," and began pulling on my clothes. With a nod Cassius followed suit and we were soon outside the Major General's residence where three horses stood, being saddled by Kyle and Tyrgan. No stable hands were in view and the compound seemed lifeless. In hushed voices, Tyrgan and Kyle directed us onto the horses, sitting behind Kyle, Tyrgan and Brother Gelman. Neither Cassius, Ella nor I had ridden a horse before. Kyle had suggested we would learn once we were a little bigger. I could understand why; these horses were huge! Not the size of Kyle's warhorse but certainly of excellent stock.

With cloth wrapped hooves the horses slowly navigated the dark, cobbled streets. The noise of their hooves, usually an echoing clatter, was instead a series of muffled thuds. In a short space of time we had exited the city, having encountered only a few drunks, a baker and a pair of guardsmen at the gate. Once we were a mile out Kyle motioned us to stop, dismounted and began removing the cloth on the horses' hooves. I took this time to question the secrecy surrounding the trip.

"From what Brother Gelman told us the other night," Kyle said, "Great Hearts are mysterious, almost mythical creatures. But ones that you have confirmed to us exist. If the Emperor is aware of their existence so potentially are other groups. Not all may wish the Great Hearts well. I would not want us to potentially lead trouble to Seya if I can avoid it, hence the clandestine nature of today's visit." That made perfect sense to me.

After we remounted we continued into the darkness, following a road that became a path, which became little more than a muddy track. As the dawn's rays began to pierce the darkness, we came to the forest. Standing on the path in front of our horses was a figure I knew well.

"Elkona Melkhuk," came the words from the darkness.

"Tracker!" Cassius and I cried in excitement. It had been several months since we had seen him. Tasked as he was with training soldiers and turning them into elite scouts, he was kept busy and increasingly stayed outside of the city for extended trips. He came forward, crutch under his arm as always and helped Cassius, myself and Ella down from the horses before saluting Kyle and shaking the hands of Brother Gelman, and Tyrgan. Eventually he turned back to Cassius and I.

"It has been a long time," he said whilst chewing the end of a leaf stalk, "it is good to see you both. Seya is waiting." He turned to Kyle, "If everyone is ready, we go." Good old Tracker. Even now he had learnt the language he was still a man of few words. With a nod from Kyle we began our journey into the forest, and a warm purring started in my chest.

"Well hello Calidan."

"Hello Seya! How are you?"

"I am very well thank you. This forest is an excellent place to live, plenty of food and few humans. In fact I have just killed a deer, would you like to share it?"

"Not raw, no thanks."

"Pity. You humans always ruin your food with fire. Terrible mistake in my humble opinion."

"Humble?! Seya, I'm not sure that anything you say can be considered humble."

A languid purr rose in my chest.

"Very true indeed. We both know I am the best thing in the Andurran Empire."

Cats. So much pride in such furry creatures.

"We've just entered the forest, when are you going to come say hello?"

"Oh no, you know the game Calidan. Find me!"

"Seya?"

"Seya?"

"Damnit."

And so with a chuckling panther in my chest I clapped the Tracker on his shoulder and slipped from the group, hunting once again. I heard Kyle shout after me, something about the forest being dangerous and not to leave the group. He was reassured by Cassius, the Tracker and Tyrgan that I would not come to harm. So I continued on, senses opened, stalking my prey.

Thirty minutes later I was high in the branches of a great tree, overlooking a small outcropping baking in a direct beam of sunlight. Curled on the rock, fur seeming to drink in the light, was Seya. There was a twenty foot gap between the edge of the trees and the rock, and having been on the receiving side of Seya's impressive senses before I knew that I didn't have a hope in crossing that distance undetected. Or did I? I thought back to the fight with Tyrgan where I had flung myself high in the air. Could I jump and land on her before she knew it? Only one way to find out. I gathered myself and powered off the branch, shaking the tree to its core. Flying through the air I began to hope, to dream that this would work. I would finally prove to her that I was as good as she was at this, I could do it!

Thwack

Her great paw swept through the air and swiped me out of the sky. She caught me under her, breaking my fall with her soft underbelly, laughter and delight pouring out of her, vibrating deep in my chest. She fixed me with her giant orange eyes, allowing me a moment of peace before her raspy tongue swept across my face, covering me in thick saliva. Lovely.

"You have gotten better at hunting small one."

"Thanks!" I replied, wiping spit off a face that felt like it had just lost a coat of skin. "I thought I had you this time though. What gave it away?"

"I sensed you half way between here and your friends. But the sunlight was warm and inviting so I decided to wait here."

Oh. Not quite the silent hunter that I had thought myself. Seya must have sensed that I was disheartened because she nuzzled me and thought, *"Don't worry, for a two legged human with no whiskers? You are doing amazingly. Keep up your training and you will get there."*

I felt somewhat mollified and my thoughts turned to the others who would be waiting deeper in the forest. I gave Seya an affectionate hug, my arms not reaching around her neck, and then together we stood up and slunk into the forest, all the way thinking of how to best surprise the group.

"CALIDAN, YOU ASS!" shouted Cassius, as I lay on the ground rolling in laughter. Seya had played her part beautifully, leaping out of a tree and snatching up Cassius before the others had time to react. She had brought him to me where I held his mouth shut whilst she roared and thrashed like a lion with a goat. When the others had gathered their wits to charge in to 'rescue' Cassius, she had sprinted round to the other side of them and unleashed the full might of her roar. Like it does with everyone, it froze them in place, primal terror trickling deep into the core of their beings. When they finally moved again they found Cassius, his expression torn between amusement and deep disapproval, being thoroughly cleaned by the largest creature any of them had ever seen.

It was too much for Brother Gelman, who knelt down in awe. Kyle and Tyrgan just looked stunned at the sight. I don't think either of them had truly realised how big a Great Heart was. The Tracker unleashed a mighty laugh, patted me on the shoulder and knelt to Seya, who acknowledged his presence with a formal nod between drenching Cassius with her tongue. Ella surprised Cassius and I both, quickly following the Tracker's lead and moving towards the giant panther. Holding out her hand towards Seya, showing no fear, she waited for Seya to finish with Cassius. When she had finally 'cleaned' my saliva coated friend, who consequently unleashed his diatribe on me, Seya turned to Ella, sniffed her hand and then nuzzled her with her great head, allowing Ella to touch her fur in wonder. The others looked on and then one by one stepped forward to 'introduce' themselves. Seya loved it - I could feel her ego growing with each second. I shook my head in resigned amusement. Cats.

We stayed with Seya for the entire day, cooking half of the deer that she had kindly left for us. For the Tracker, Cassius and myself it was just like old times, and yet so much had changed in the past year and a half. No longer were we struggling to survive, living day to day. The Tracker was now in charge of scout training for Kyle, Cassius and I were friends with a young pickpocket, I had been stabbed, and we had been taken in by a loving family - not to mention being taught how to fight in a restricted art. It had certainly been a busy time! Just for the moment however, we were able to relax and think back on all we had achieved. For me, my progress just solidified my desire to hunt the shadow demon and extract revenge. I knew that I could get stronger if I trained, and I knew that it was my mission to stop anyone else from being hurt by that monster. As for Cassius…as I saw him there chatting with Ella, a blush on his cheeks, I knew it wasn't in him to live a life dedicated to revenge and death. He had another chance here, a chance to live life to the fullest and try to forget what had happened. I decided then that I wouldn't drag Cassius along with me, that I would not lead him down a self destructive path.

Little did I realise that it was not my choice to make.

CHAPTER ELEVEN
GHOST

~

VISITING SEYA BECAME A SEMI-REGULAR occurrence. A family outing if you will. However, instead of meandering through market stalls and having ice cream in the park, we visited a magnificent giant panther in a forest several hours ride from Forgoth and spent the day eating whatever food she deigned to provide us. Always we would disappear in the dead of night and return in the evening dusk, hoping not to invite too many questions about where we went. And for the best part of four months we were successful. But something I learnt time and time again during my Imperator training is that someone is always watching.

In this case that someone was the local gamekeeper, whose jurisdiction covered three forests, including Seya's. He went to the magistrate of the city with a complaint that something had been reducing the local population of deer, boar and game. He assumed it was a pack of wolves, and wanted a hunting party put together to drive out or kill the pack.

The magistrate obliged, asking for volunteers to band together, arm themselves with bows and fire and head into the forest.

The first that any of us heard of this was nearly three hours later, when Brother Gelman came running back after leaving us after language teaching and told all. I immediately contacted Seya.

"Seya?"

A sleepy yawn.

"Seya, listen. There are a group of men coming who think that there is a pack of wolves loose in the forest. You need to run or hide."

A sigh.

"Humans. Always concerned with the wild. Don't worry Calidan, it is not the first time I have been hunted."

"What if they have dogs? Won't they find you?"

A low, rumbling growl. Something terrible that suggested deep night.

"Leave the dogs to me."

~

Angry yells from loud and uncouth humans. They have come bearing fire and metal, led by a pack of ravenous dogs. Dogs designed for the hunt, bred through generations of forced mating of the best bitch and most aggressive stud. They can detect the fox from spoor that is days old. I purred in amusement wondering what they will do when they find mine. Time to stretch my legs. I rose, stretching languidly; after all the approaching humans were no cause for a rush. Calidan, whilst I admired his pluck and tenacity, was something of a worrier - I had no reason to fear these creatures.

For I am not in their domain, they are in mine.

The dogs came closer. I could hear their paws scuffling through the leaves and grass. I could sense their fur in the breeze and feel their joy at the hunt. Time to put an end to it. I growled, deep in my chest. A sound that carried across the forest, echoing from tree to tree at a level only my four legged 'friends' could hear. The humans carried on blindly, like ants fulfilling their assigned roles. They take no notice of the rising hackles of the dogs, the way their ears flatten to their skulls, the momentary misstep they all take. With fury, as though the forest itself has wronged them, the humans continued to march through the foliage in a line, hacking at offending undergrowth and protruding tree limbs.

I smiled, a feral smile, my lips peeling back to display my gleaming canines.

This was going to be fun.

I leapt like a silent shadow through the trees of the forest, dodging the rays of sun that broke through the leafy canopy like they would burn me. They obviously wouldn't, but it made for an enjoyable game. The humans beneath me didn't hear or sense a thing, just continue their wayward, ambling march of destruction. Shouts and calls intended to frighten off the 'wolves' would have masked my approach even had I been a lumbering boar. The dogs didn't know what to make of my scent. It's fresh and lying thickly upon them all, dripping from me on the fleeting forest gusts. Every time they looked up I growled, the menace and power in my silent missive causing each dog to instantly drop their head and once again flatten their ears to their skulls, tails hanging limply behind their legs.

I did feel a small wave of sympathy for the creatures but it was quickly washed away in my own sense of superiority. Dogs **should** cower in my presence, it was the way of things. For the first time one of the humans noticed the lacklustre movements of the dogs and reacts angrily, encouraging an unlucky one with his boot. The dog yelped and rushed forwards sniffing wildly, doing everything it could not to look up. Its sense of self preservation was amusing; even a dog as simple as one trained to lust after the kill can fool a human such as this into thinking it was working hard. Well played dog.

I continued my game, leaping from tree to tree whilst inwardly mocking the pathetic creatures below. The forest where I have made my home was not particularly large, walkable for a human from one end to the other in about six hours, and the humans were now well into the middle of it. They were beginning to get hungry and annoyed, as if thinking that the 'wolves' that they were hunting would just show up and make things easy for them. Some wolves are clever but again, as with many creatures, they are largely ruled by their bellies. The ones that attacked Calidan, Cassius and the ever amusing tracker man were basically slobbering lunatics due to a lack of food. They tasted skinny too.

The humans decided to 'make camp'. A synonym for 'I'm tired and hungry from hunting nonexistent wolves'. The sun now slanted closer to dusk than noon. I truly hoped that they would stay until dark, when I could have so much more fun. A curse of having such luscious black fur, in the dark I was invisible, but in daytime I stood out unless I kept to the shadows. I splayed myself in the fork of a tree high above the 'camp' and began grooming myself. Luscious fur doesn't just happen overnight.

After an hour the men packed up and began moving off, continuing much as they had before, albeit with somewhat diminished enthusiasm. The subdued nature of their dogs was obviously getting to them, filling them with misgivings. They had obviously put two and two together *and realised that something was wrong in the forest for their dogs to behave like this. Hands were kept close to weapons and fire.*

"We overnightin' in tha woods chief?" *one man asked, feigning nonchalance.*

"Looks like it boys, we're a bit too far in and haven't made as much progress as I wanted to what with these useless dogs," *said the apparent leader, highlighting his dissatisfaction with a swift kick and grinning evilly at the resulting yelp. I now disliked this man, but was pleased at his decision. Once the sun was close to drifting out of the sky they began to make another camp in a hollow of trees. Branches were cut and a large fire was made, embers floating nice and high towards me. Most animals don't like fire but I have to admit, warming myself next to one was a rare and welcome pleasure. I curled up just far enough away from the rising smoke to be comfortable and waited for true dark.*

One by one the men fell asleep. Trusting in their dogs and fire to give them ample warning of any approaching threat. Unfortunately, the dogs no longer answered to them. They bowed their heads and kept low to the ground as I delicately padded between them; they knew not to disturb a creature as majestic as I. Extending a razor sharp claw I sliced through the leashes keeping them in place; they don't move yet, terror keeping them obedient. I then casually picked up the men's packs and climbed back up into the trees. I ripped the bags apart, eating anything I found interesting and leaving the rest. Time for a rude awakening. I built a pile of the torn up bags and then delicately knocked it off the tree branch, items landing with deep thuds all around the men, and in two cases on them. Surprised grunts and yells sounded, like music to my ears.

Time for the final send-off.

I opened wide my cavernous jaws and unleashed a full throated roar. The humans could certainly hear this one. It shook the very forest to its core. The dogs immediately sprinted away, back towards the safety of Forgoth, while the men stood frozen in terror. They had no idea where the sound came from or what kind of animal made it. They stayed very quiet for the rest of the night, huddled by the fire, hands clutching their tiny weapons. I settled down to sleep soundly above them, the nice fire warming my fur, for I knew that no more was needed. In the morning they would run back to Forgoth, doubtless telling tales of the dangerous monsters they had faced. No matter; it was a fun game whilst it lasted.

~

"Well," I said, opening my eyes, "it looks like Seya has taken care of it." Sitting across from me were Cassius, Ella and Kyle. I had been checking on Seya throughout the day and night, worried that the hunters would find her. I should have known that she wouldn't be remotely flummoxed by such a thing. It was now morning and we were sitting in Kyle's office, maintaining the illusion that he was working hard, while in fact he had been enraptured by the story I told as I recounted what I was seeing through Seya's eyes.

"She certainly made that seem easy, and I'm glad she is unhurt," Kyle began. "However, I wish she had thought things through a little bit more. As it stands we are shortly to have a group of would be wolf hunters running back to Forgoth crying about something in the woods. Obviously most will assume this is just the hunters trying to cover up their failure at finding the wolves but many folk around these parts are pretty superstitious." He massaged his temples. "People will talk, and it's possible that the forest will start to see more visitors hunting for this mysterious 'beast'." He sighed and took a drink of tea before continuing. "Perhaps we should think about finding somewhere else for her?"

"Whilst there are several forests around Forgoth, most are more often visited by people than the one Seya currently resides in," Ella replied. "If people are as superstitious as you say then perhaps they will just leave the forest alone?" She paused and thought to herself. "Or perhaps we should encourage rumours that the forest is haunted?"

We all halted our own trains of thought and looked at her.

"An interesting idea," said Cassius, a slow grin spreading across his face. He looked adoringly at Ella who smiled, a blush rising to her cheeks.

"Thanks Cassius," she said, "I think it could work. If only a few people visit the forest anyway then we could spread rumours via my network of friends from before I came here and perhaps Brother Gelman's guild? Suggest that it is creepy and something dark lives there? People might just stay away…" She trailed off looking at my face and Kyle's.

I grinned. "Sounds like a great plan!" I said enthusiastically, before turning to Kyle. "This could work in our favour; scare people out of entering the forest in the first place and Seya would be relatively safe." Kyle looked somewhat dubious at first, but it was obvious that the idea was growing on him.

"It should be relatively easy to do," he mused to himself, before nodding firmly, "okay, let's do it!" He pointed at Ella and Cassius. "You two are in charge of rumour spreading; don't make it too specific, just a little creepy to dissuade people. Ella if you get in touch with your contacts today we can make sure that the rumours start immediately. Calidan you get Brother Gelman involved, I'm sure that he would enjoy weaving a tale."

We all nodded, and by the next day the rumours had begun to fly.

'The forest is haunted'.

'Dark gods were worshipped there'.

'Evil reigns over the forest'.

'It was home to a creature of shadow'.

I was proud of the last one, it wasn't too far from the truth yet sounded terrifying. Unfortunately, what none of us knew was that there were some people who thrived on stories such as these. Hunters, of a sort.

CHAPTER TWELVE
IMPERATOR

~

ANOTHER THREE MONTHS PASSED, A time when all seemed right with the world. Training continued every morning and evening. During my pre-dawn sessions with Tyrgan I was actually beginning to hold my own, learning to understand the benefits and limitations of my bond with Seya. Cassius and Ella were beginning to express feelings for each other; they thought themselves secretive but I don't think anyone in the compound was unaware of their burgeoning love for each other. I wished them all the happiness in the world and it was fantastic to see their love grow, into secretive handholding and kisses stolen in the moonlight. Ella was an amazing girl, even if she had never quite warmed to me. She was thoughtful, intelligent and pretty, and well able to match Cassius blow for blow, something that I think he found inspiring. In short the two of them made a perfect couple, and my friend had never been happier. Even now, twisted monster that I am, I am grateful for the short period of happiness that Cassius was able to experience. It has been in very short supply since those days.

One cold autumnal day, we were in Kyle's residence curled up in front of the fire. A knock at the door aroused my attention, for it was a late time for visitors. I heard the Major General's servant, Anders, open the door, sensed him look at something with curiosity and then courteously bid the visitor to wait. Shortly after, he fetched Kyle from the room, his movements twitchy and manner nervous. My senses followed Kyle down the hallway, exploring the environment, but when I reached the visitor I experienced something strange. Whereas I could *listen* and sense practically every detail about a person or item within one hundred metres of myself, where the visitor was I could only sense a *deepness*. As though there was a complete absence of anything; sound, air pressure, anything. I heard no voice emanate from the visitor but shortly heard Kyle step back and gesture for the person to enter. And so the emptiness travelled down the hallway pausing briefly outside the door to the living room where we sat, before being invited to enter the Major General's drawing room.

"Calidan?" voiced Cassius, his arm around Ella's shoulders. He simultaneously managed to look both happy for himself and concerned for me. I realised that my hands were shaking. It had been a long time since I had not been able to sense everything around me in perfect detail, to find that I could not with this individual was worrying.

"There is something strange about the visitor who just entered Kyle's drawing room," I said slowly, my senses still trying to batter their way into the empty spot in the next room.

"What do you mean strange?" said Ella. "Strange like you're strange?"

I smirked at her, "Gee, thanks!" I responded, my mood lightening slightly. "No, this is different. Whoever just came in, I can't sense anything about them. No noise, no movement, nothing."

"How is that possible?" questioned Cassius, "You can pretty much hear a bird flying a mile away!"

"I have no idea," I replied, "and that scares me."

A few minutes passed before Kyle briefly left the drawing room and came back into the living room. His face was pale, though he let out a somewhat shaky smile when he saw the concern on our faces.

"Sorry about this guys, but I'm going to have to leave you tonight; I have to entertain a guest." He turned away to go back to the drawing room before pausing briefly, "Can you stay together tonight? In here if you like. I'll get Anders to bring some food." And with that he retreated, calling for Anders to bring food to both us and to the drawing room, before entering back into the room with the void.

When he left we all shared a look. "Well, that seems odd doesn't it," said Cassius. "I haven't seen many things leave Kyle as worried as he appears now." Ella and I nodded in agreement.

"Something is up with that visitor," Ella said. "Calidan might not be able to sense anything about the person, but we know that he or she must be important."

"How do you know that?" Cassius asked.

"Sweet Cassius," Ella said softly, before leaning over and kissing his cheek. "Sometimes I think you forget just who Kyle is! For someone to gain access to a military compound in the evening in the first place, let alone the Major General's house, and be personally 'entertained', I would say that person holds a great deal of power," she finished, somewhat smugly. I was impressed; her deduction skills were second to none.

"She is right Cassius," I said in support of Ella's statement. "That person is someone special. We have to find out who it is!" Ella nodded excitedly as I spoke, Cassius just looked perplexed.

"But Kyle asked us to stay together in here!" Cassius argued. "Putting that aside, how do we go and find out anything about the visitor when he or she is in the drawing room? It's not like we can just barge in." He had a very good point. But as the food came trundling down the hallway, in a cart pushed by Anders, making my mouth water from the smell of cold cuts of meat, a plan formed.

"If we can't see the person directly," I said, standing up and moving behind the door as it opened, "we can at least ask about the person indirectly..." shutting the door behind the glorious bringer of food. Ella took the plate of food from Anders, Kyle's servant, thanking him profusely.

"Hi kids," he said. "I hope this works for you, if you want any more just give me a shout." He turned to go and found me behind him.

"Thanks Anders," I said. "Before you go, could you tell us about the person at the door?" At my words a worried look sped across his face.

"I'm not sure that I should speak of that person Calidan." His voice quivered slightly. "He isn't someone you want to talk to." He walked past me, opened the door and made to leave, before pausing and turning back to us. "Please don't do anything silly tonight, the person will still be here tomorrow, most likely waiting for his partner." And with that he left, shutting the door firmly.

"Partner?" Cassius said as soon as Anders left. "So more than one special person is presumably in the city today."

"Either of you know someone who would have access to a Major General at night and works in a pair?" I asked. Both shook their heads. I sighed heavily. "Well, it looks like we aren't going to find out any more tonight. Let's put it aside for the moment and hope that this is all explained tomorrow." So with that we tucked into supper with gusto, before curling back up in front of the fireplace discussing the military tactics in the books Kyle had given us the year before. Before too much time had passed we were soundly asleep.

The following morning I was up early, as per usual. I crept out of the room and spread out my senses; the void, it appeared, was nowhere to be found. Sighing heavily at a mystery unsolved I wandered down to the training ground to meet with Tyrgan. Oddly he wasn't there. Frowning to myself - Tyrgan had never been late to a training session before - I decided to exercise anyway, wanting to fall into the empty mental restfulness of the Kaschan forms.

Soon I was moving through the seven primary 'circles' of Kaschan, the various martial forms that were designed as both exercise and as a teaching method. On the sixth circle I noticed someone watching me and started - I hadn't sensed anyone approach. Unlike the person last night however, there was no void of emptiness surrounding this individual. I could sense her fully, but was at a complete loss as to how I hadn't noticed her arrival. I decided to complete the sixth circle before speaking to her and took the time to analyse the person standing on the sidelines of the training yard. She was tall with a warm face and blonde hair, wearing a long grey leather coat that while closed, left little to the imagination. I could sense that under the coat she had a long sheath containing a rapier on her left hip and a smaller sheath carrying a rondel dagger on her right. Four knives seemed to be strapped around her person, likely throwing knives, and strapped along the inside of her coat were four spheres - I couldn't work out what those were.

I finished the sixth circle and glanced up at the woman, intending to speak and stopped dead, perplexed; she had vanished. I heard a delicate cough from behind me and fought the urge to jump out of my skin. Two people in one day who could seemingly evade my senses, albeit in different ways; I began to wonder if I was losing my gift. Turning I saw the woman behind me, great coat and sheathes on the floor to the side of the training ground, wearing shaped leather armour.

She nodded to me and spoke in a soft, lilting voice, "Would you care for a bout? It has been some time since I have fought in Kaschan." Unable to think of anything to say I simply nodded and assumed a ready stance. She smiled and stepped forward, distributing her weight evenly and flowed into an attack, her hand streaming forwards in a straightforward jab. At the last second I remembered to close my senses, ensuring that her jab got much closer to my face than I had originally intended, but I managed to deflect the blow, grabbing her wrist and moving my feet in a circular motion, aiming to put pressure on the back of her elbow. She moved with the motion, twisting out of my grip and delivering a spinning kick that flashed towards my head. Ducking past the blow I kicked at the joint of her knee, but was rewarded with a glancing knuckle strike to the side of my head for my troubles.

Momentarily dazed I immediately entered into the footwork from circle three, 'dancing willows', designed to be almost off-balanced and random; it's meant to allow you to recover whilst (hopefully) avoiding the majority of follow up attacks. Unfortunately dancing willows is not useful against someone who has also trained in the seven circles of Kaschan. Something I had learnt to my cost at the hands of Tyrgan countless times. So when the woman struck out at where I was going to be with my third step, I, still dazed, changed into what Tyrgan called 'the five finger quickstep' one of the Kaschan fast hands techniques. This meant I changed direction midstep, trusting that the woman would fight like Tyrgan, avoided her kick, stepped into her general direction and unleashed a multitude of fast strikes, the difference being that on contact with flesh I didn't pull my hands away but kept in constant contact, striking from short distances and snapping my blows. I got in three good hits before I had fully recovered from the head strike, but as I went for the fourth my hands suddenly touched nothing but air. A sudden kick to my lower back sent my legs out from under me, clutching in agony at the base of my spine. What was worse than the pain however was the snarl that had accompanied the blow. It sounded like a rabid animal. I looked to the woman whilst cradling my spine. She had her back to me and appeared to be shaking, taking deep, shuddering breaths.

"You did well, youngling," said the woman, still not looking at me and cladding herself once again in swords and coat. "I haven't seen that switch from circle three into one of the fast hands techniques before, a good addition to the Kaschan." She paused and then sighed heavily, "I'm sorry that I used that trick, I didn't actually expect to get hit by a child and I... anger quickly." Walking forward she proffered her hand and taking it she pulled me to my feet.

"Thanks," I said, as she helped me up, and then grimaced as my back twinged, though the pain was starting to dim.

She noticed and an apologetic look crossed over her face, "A result of my training," she said, "I have rather strong legs...again, sorry for that."

"It's no problem," I replied, "I'm just more interested in how you moved so quickly! I was in direct contact with you, and then it felt like you just disappeared."

"I'm not at liberty to say," she responded, her manner becoming more stiff.

"...Fair enough," I muttered back, bemused and annoyed at her response. She had done something strange and I needed to know what it was. I'm not one for leaving mysteries unsolved! I decided that we were long past due our introductions, and stepped forward extending my hand. "I'm Calidan, pleased to meet you and thanks for the fight."

She looked at my hand for a second before grasping it firmly and giving it a friendly shake, "Merowyn," she replied.

Merowyn seemed friendly enough once she had recovered from whatever fit of anger had caused her to react so violently in our sparring session. We sat and had a somewhat one sided conversation, many of my questions about her, who she was, what she was doing here - pretty much everything in fact - going unanswered. She seemed interested in me, especially in my knowledge of Kaschan and why I was learning it. Wary of revealing too much information, I simply said that it was what Kyle and Tyrgan had been training us in, and mentioned nothing about its history as a martial art for the Emperor's bodyguard. After all I had no idea if teaching Kaschan outside of those forces was a punishable offence, but it seemed likely.

Cassius, Ella and Brother Gelman arrived at dawn for the morning training session, but still there was no sign of Tyrgan, or Kyle. I introduced Merowyn to the others, shaking my head when Cassius and Ella asked me discreetly with their eyes whether this was the void-like visitor from the previous night. Putting aside our growing concern for Tyrgan for the time being we decided to continue our training as normal. I asked Merowyn to join us but she declined, seemingly happy to just watch as we flowed through the seven circles, before taking up sparring positions.

The four of us flew into motion, fighting with empty hands and staying true to Tyrgan's ruthless training regimes, not just facing off against one opponent, but all four of us fighting each other simultaneously. Tyrgan was adamant that this was an excellent method to get us used to fighting as individuals, but I had long ago decided that if I was in the middle of a fight between multiple Kaschan practitioners...things were probably not going to go well. For one thing, it takes a great deal of time if everyone is fighting each other. Kaschan is a flowing martial art with continuous motion as one of the major aims. To have four people fighting each other, all trained in that style of movement? It makes for an extremely frustrating fight. You might gain the upper hand on one opponent only to be forced to quickly evade another attacker. Annoying is an understatement.

What it does do however is make you focus intently on the situation at hand; Kaschan is not something you can practice without perfect concentration. As such I was completely unaware of Merowyn's rapt attention to our fighting, her eyes watching like a hawk, nothing on her face resembling the amiable person I had introduced myself to earlier. If I had been watching closely and looked past the stern countenance I might have seen something that looked much like regret.

"Excellent work everyone, good to see you all training without me," said Tyrgan, interrupting our sparring. He was standing by the training ground a little unsteadily, holding a canteen of water and looked rather green. It was obvious that he was unwell, my keen observation reinforced by a spectacular explosion of vomit, erupting from his mouth onto the dirt.

"Tyrgan! Are you okay?" cried Ella, rushing to his side. He waved her off and wiped his mouth before straightening up.

"Nothing to fear Ella, just something sitting wrong in my gut," he replied. "I've been feeling rubbish since late last night...must have been something I ate."

"You look horrendous," said Cassius, never one for too much tact. "Can we do anything to help?"

"No, just going to make my way to the medical officer," he said with a weak smile, face growing paler by the second. "I should be okay..." and with that wildly inaccurate statement he fell face forward onto the ground.

"Tyrgan!" came the shout from everyone at the yard. We rushed to his side and found him unconscious, pale and covered in sweat. Between us we half carried, half dragged him to the medical tent, where the attending duty medical officer attempted to rouse him from unconsciousness. It was only after we had successfully deposited Tyrgan at the tent that I realised something. There was no sign of Merowyn.

Spreading out my senses I scoured the camp until I found her. She wasn't at the training yard but was currently in Tyrgan's room, rifling through his things. I grabbed the others and told them what I sensed. Brother Gelman stiffened, his mind putting two and two together before rushing into the medical tent. Listening in I heard the word 'poison' pass his lips and my heart sank.

"He's right," I muttered to myself.

"Who's right?" said Cassius.

"Brother Gelman, he just suggested to the doctor that Tyrgan might have been poisoned," I replied heavily. "It makes sense if Merowyn is in his room." Ella gasped at the news and Cassius's hands clenched into fists.

"Let's go and stop Merowyn," he said softly.

I looked up and locked gazes with him, "The last time we got involved in something like this," I replied, "ended with me with a knife in my stomach...and that was from a street thug. Merowyn is a trained Kaschan practitioner - she may not want to come quietly."

Cassius just stared at me.

"Let's go," said Ella quietly. "We're wasting time." We left without another word, grabbing swords from the training ground as we went on the hunt again.

We drew close to Tyrgan's room in the officers' barracks. I motioned for Cassius to go to the window that opened into the bedroom, the only other feasible way to get in or out. I could hear Merowyn feverishly rifling through cupboards and Tyrgan's desk. Leaving papers and documents alone she was seemingly looking for something specific. Silently Ella and I moved across the wooden floor, positioning ourselves either side of the door. We looked at each other and I mimed counting down from three, two, one.

With a kick that lifted the door from its hinges I entered the room, sword drawn, Ella following just behind me with a fearsome look on her face, only to be replaced with surprise and confusion when I came to a stop. No one was in the room, just a few papers swirling in the air. Running to the window Ella tried it and found it locked, Cassius standing outside looking concerned at our faces.

After I beckoned him to join us he ran in asking, "Have you found her?"

"No." I replied and explained that whilst Merowyn had definitely just been in the room, she had somehow vanished. I couldn't comprehend how she had managed it. I scanned the area with my senses and knew that she was not nearby, nor were there secret doors, or openings in the brick... I paused. Actually there was a space behind a few of the bricks behind the headboard of Tyrgan's bed.

Ignoring Cassius and Ella's confused expressions I dragged the bed away from the wall and removed the bricks, lifting them easily away from the wall. Inside I found two sheathed swords, and knew them instantly.

"This must be it," I whispered, "these must be what Merowyn was searching for!" Ella and Cassius looked surprised and somewhat indignant.

"Why would Tyrgan get poisoned over a sword?" said Ella. Of course, neither she nor Cassius were aware of what they could really do.

"These are not just normal swords," I explained, "they allow Tyrgan to do things...they allow him to fight on a par with me at my best." The shock on their faces would have been amusing to behold if I hadn't been so worried for my sick friend and mentor.

My brain clicked.

"I have an idea," I said, and rushed out the door.

I sprinted through the compound, moving faster than any normal human could, deftly dodging out of the way of surprised soldiers and leaving a trail of displaced dust in my wake. Arriving at the medical tent, I thrust my way inside and ignoring the yells of the medical officer I unsheathed the swords and laid them in Tyrgan's hands, hoping that my suspicions were correct.

Nothing happened.

Balls.

As Cassius and Ella arrived, panting, I tried one last thing and reached out again, closing Tyrgan's hands around the hilts of the blades. Instantly the characters on the swords lit up, mirroring the tattoo on Tyrgan's wrist as it flashed in red light. The others watched with awe as, after a few seconds, Tyrgan groaned and slowly opened his eyes. The medical officer was beside himself, muttering something about magic not existing over and over again - I was too ecstatic to care what he thought. Wrapping my arms around Tyrgan I gave him the biggest hug possible, shortly joined by Cassius and Ella whilst Brother Gelman looked on with a beatific smile.

After we somewhat awkwardly broke off the hug Tyrgan looked at us all with a confused smile.

"What happened?" he asked before lifting up the blades, "and where did you get these?"

"We think you were poisoned," Ella blurted out. "There was this woman, Merowyn, and Calidan said she was in your rooms looking through your things! We tried to catch her but she disappeared, even though Calidan knew she was in there!"

"Slow down Ella, it's okay," Tyrgan replied. "So, let me get this straight," he lifted up his hand and spoke, "poison," he raised one finger, "woman," raised a second, "thief," raised a third. "Have I missed anything?" We shook our heads numbly.

"Well, isn't that a delightful start to the day, I haven't had this much attention since I was in the Emperor's employ!" Tyrgan seemed to be completely unperturbed by the morning's events. My hero worship grew by a factor of ten.

"What was she after Tyrgan?" Cassius asked, concern on his face at the casual attitude being displayed by the sword master.

"I think you've already found the answer to that lad," replied Tyrgan, stroking the swords on his lap. "A *Tyrant blade* is immeasurably valuable."

"Tyrant blade?" we questioned in unison while Brother Gelman gasped.

Tyrgan looked hard at each of us in turn, before turning to the medical officer and speaking in a hard voice. "You. You've already heard too much. Leave." As the man turned to go Tyrgan's voice adopted a low, dangerous tone, "Know that if anything you have seen or heard of today is spoken of I will not be the one to silence you, that part of my life is over. But someone will come, of that you can be sure." The man gulped visibly, nodded and fled the tent.

Tyrgan turned back to us. "What I have to say cannot be overheard." He looked at me, "Calidan, is there anyone within listening distance?" I shook my head, waiting expectantly.

"Good." He lifted one of the silver blades, drawing all eyes towards it.

"This is a Tyrant's blade. One of a set actually, the power within it is split into the two blades." Nodding to himself at the confused looks on our faces he continued. "The making of a Tyrant's blade is said to be impossible these days, the ones that we have are older than the Empire itself." He ran a finger lightly across the edge of the sword and showed us the resulting cut, "This set is reckoned to be nearly four thousand years old. Four thousand years! And still sharp. Still as perfect as the day they were made." He held the weapon reverently. "I was given this by the Emperor himself, taken deep into a vault and asked to choose from about two dozen different blades. Only those who have performed a great service to the Emperor receive such an honour: he can only give them to people he trusts because each blade can bestow great strength and speed to the wearer...there is a reason why they are known as Tyrant blades after all."

Tyrgan pointed at his wrist. "There was a ceremony held in secret, where my wrist was tattooed with these characters. I don't know what they mean. I doubt anyone in the Guild of Scribes knows either, as far as I am aware it is an ancient dead language," he smiled almost ruefully.

"Once the tattooing was completed the characters on the sword changed. It became bonded to me. Which is why I imagine this Merowyn character poisoned me: if she knows of a Tyrant's blade then she might well know that until I die its powers cannot be used by another."

Silence reigned as we absorbed this information.

"It's not just strength and speed is it?" I asked, "Otherwise you wouldn't be sitting here feeling well, it heals you too."

"Correct, the blade provides healing as well. Some wounds take longer to heal than others though, as though the swords have to work harder to heal them."

I paused and considered my next words. "Your bond with the swords sounds much like my bond with Seya," I mused, breaking off when I saw Tyrgan nodding.

"Not all of those who have bonded with Great Hearts have historically been 'good' Calidan. With power such as you possess it is easy to be swayed to a darker path and decide to take rather than buy, to kill rather than talk. It is known that those with Tyrant blades have been used to *remove* threats in the past. For the greater good of the Empire."

I nodded numbly; I had not considered that I might have been deemed a threat to the Empire, but Tyrgan's words made sense. Stories abound about people who want power for power's sake. If such a person bonded with a Great Heart, that person could do great evil. The Emperor's way made sense to me.

"Anyway," said Tyrgan, breaking my reverie, "that's enough about these blades." He sheathed them both and stood up, showing no sign of the poison that had recently flooded his veins. "We should go to Kyle, make sure that he is aware that someone was recently on the base. Someone with skills to outmanoeuvre Calidan's senses."

Ella, Cassius and I shared a look. In all the madness of the morning we had neglected to tell Tyrgan about the void visitor who met Kyle. As the flood of new information reached his ears Tyrgan's face grew darker and darker. He stood, belted on his swords and said one word; "Come."

When we reached the Major General's house Tyrgan drew his swords and pushed past the startled Anders. He stalked down the hallway, anger radiating with every step. With a snarl of fury he burst through the drawing room door, ready to deal with the void-like presence that I had detected was still there, and stopped dead in his tracks. In front of him Kyle had leapt to his feet, toast in hand and a shocked look on his face. Facing Kyle, reclining in a large plush leather chair was a tall man. He had dark, long hair, and a handsome face with a scar across his chin. By his side was a long dark coat, and a spear propped up against the wall. He gave the 'rescue party' an appraising look and slowly stood up.

"Sir, sorry sir!" was all I could hear from Tyrgan as Kyle asked him in no delicate terms as to what he thought he was doing.

"It is my fault, Kyle," said the man in a voice that was completely devoid of emotion.

"It appears as though I have kept you unduly long. It stands to reason that your friends would be worried." He eyed the now sheathed blades at Tyrgan's sides. "And it would not do to have Tyrgan here worried when he has blades such as those."

Tyrgan turned to the man. Confused and unsure of his response, he settled for questioning.

"I'm sorry sir, but do I know you?"

"No, we haven't met. But during my time at the palace several of my cohort trained with you. I knew when you received those blades, much like I know why you got them. Let me offer some very belated congratulations by the way. A rare gift indeed."

Kyle's face was looking more and more confused at the proceedings, eying Tyrgan's swords with a mystified expression.

"You were at the palace?" said Tyrgan, "But you weren't guard..." He re-examined the man, before realisation slammed into him like one of Seya's pounces. He stood smartly to attention, saluting the tall man. "Sir. Sorry sir! Apologies for disrupting your meal sir!" I was speechless. Tyrgan was not a stickler for the military rules of respect, he barely responded to Kyle as a member of the forces should to a superior officer. And yet here he was, acting as though the Emperor himself was in the room.

Kyle eventually gave up trying to work out what was going on and sat down again.

The tall man smiled at him before turning to us all outside the room, "Come on in everyone," he said. "You can rest easy, Kyle is in no danger from me... and Tyrgan stop being ridiculous; though I am his voice I am not the man himself."

When we were all in the room he stood in front of us and said, "Allow me to introduce myself. My name is Simone and I am an old friend of Kyle's. We haven't seen each other in many, many years. Not since we were children. But I digress." He paused and surveyed those standing before him. "I am Simone and I am one of the Emperor's Imperators."

By the intake of breath from Ella and Brother Gelman, I assumed that an Imperator was something almost unheard of. A mythical beast like a dragon or a talking monkey... I wasn't too far wrong.

Simone saw the effect his words had on some of us and smiled disarmingly.

"Reactions like that is one of the reasons I try and avoid telling people what I am for as long as possible," he said calmly. "Unlike the Emperor's bodyguards, who everyone knows exist, Imperators are almost like a story of the bogeyman, the shadow at the foot of the bed.

No one is entirely sure what is truth or fiction, or if they are even real." His smile became somewhat sadder as he spoke; it must be a lonely existence.

"Simone was catching me up with events in the capital," said Kyle, attempting to breach the growing silence in the room. "As he said, we are old friends. I haven't seen him since I was in my teens." He looked at everyone and nodded to himself. "Everyone come in, sit down and I shall go and get Anders to put some refreshment together. Then Simone can tell you what he told me, and you can explain why you came barging in with swords bared." He left and spoke briefly to Anders before coming back in. Within a few minutes Anders was back with tea, coffee and a warm loaf of bread with sides of ham and butter. Kyle thanked him and then looked at us all.

"Ok, Tyrgan first," he said. "What was the reason for you to come in here like this?"

Tyrgan launched into a brief summary of what had happened in the morning, Simone's expression becoming more stony as he spoke, before finally he interrupted.

"I have to correct some inaccuracies in this report," he said. "Firstly, Merowyn is not the one who poisoned you." We cried out at this, adamant that he was wrong, but our shouts died down as he raised his hand, "I know this because Merowyn is my partner. She decided to keep an eye on the younglings here at the training ground whilst I talked to Kyle." His eyes flicked to Tyrgan. "If she was in your room - and I do wonder how you can be so sure of this as I know that Kyra and Ryken do not enhance your sense of smell or allow you to see around walls...." he paused as if awaiting an answer but no response was forthcoming.

"No matter. If she was in your room then she was hunting for our fugitive."

"Fugitive?" I asked.

"A very dangerous person, a young woman of nineteen years. She was in Imperator training and has fled the training grounds." He looked at our confused faces and sighed.

"You must understand that the training for Imperators is incredibly difficult, both physically and mentally, and that the secrets that are imparted are not ones that can be taken lightly. Once you begin Imperator training there is no going back. You must complete it or face the consequences.

"Consequences?" Ella asked, voice trembling.

"Death," answered Simone matter-of-factly. "As I said...entering into Imperator training is not to be taken lightly."

Cassius tugged at a thread from Simone's story.

"If Merowyn is your partner, why would she be in Tyrgan's room looking through documents?"

Simone paused, considering his words before speaking.

"Merowyn is...different. She has the tracking skills and determination of a wolf. She can pick up scent that is several days old and follow it to its destination. If she was in Tyrgan's room then the fugitive must have been there earlier, probably looking for those Tyrant blades."

"How would she know about Tyrant blades?" Tyrgan retorted. "Surely who has them isn't common knowledge?"

"No, you're right," Simone replied. "But as one of the more senior Imps - our word for anyone not a fully fledged Imperator - Rya had complete access to the Emperor's archives. They are an important source of information and it would not do for someone to become an Imperator and not know how to use them...it would have been easy for Rya to find out who was in possession of a Tyrant blade. Perhaps she thought she could obtain it whilst on the run and then use it to get rid of Merowyn and myself. Though how she thought she could bond with it without taking the time to do a tattoo I do not know."

The room was quiet as we all absorbed this information. A deadly would be imperator roaming free in Forgoth, ill intent clear from her poisoning of Tyrgan. Kyle stood up and walked outside. We heard him bellowing orders from the front of his house shaking the soldiers from their stupor. Shortly all the soldiers in the compound were fully armed and on high alert. He returned to the room, looked Simone in the eye and asked only one question. "So how do we find her?"

Simone smiled, a predatory gleam in his eye.

"Tracking is not my specialty. That is why I'm currently sitting here having a nice cup of tea with you all, and why I have spent the last few hours catching up with you Kyle."

He leaned back into his chair, taking another drink of tea and sighing appreciatively. "Leave the tracking to Merowyn. Believe me when I say there are none better."

CHAPTER THIRTEEN
FEAR

~

SLOWLY, SILENTLY, THE MEN SPREAD out around the shack. Each was a product of the Tracker's training; a soldier specialising in hunting and tracking. Over the past week they had been deployed across Forgoth, in an attempt to find Rya. Merowyn had been positive that they would not find her, that Rya's training was such that she would easily avoid even skilled trackers such as these, but she relented when Kyle suggested that the presence of more soldiers might well make Rya slip up. At the very least it would make it more difficult for her to move around the city - a notion that made complete sense to me.

The small apartment was nestled in a slum district of Forgoth known locally as the 'Chains'; the lovely nickname developed historically because of the abundance of moneylenders and loan sharks who make their home here. Once you enter the Chains for a favour, you are in effect, chained. This I learnt from an annoyed Kyle as we walked behind the scouts with Merowyn and Simone. Kyle was eager for this show to be over. Rya had so far evaded all of his men and whilst Merowyn had been persistently close behind, this was the first time that we felt that we had the advantage.

The scouts covered every exit. It was an easy job, there were only two, one of which was a window. I opened my senses and could detect someone sitting at a small desk, writing feverishly. The person was slight, female and wearing protective leather clothing with multiple blades sequestered around her body. Merowyn sniffed the air and nodded appreciatively, a stifled growl emanating from her throat followed swiftly by colour rising to her cheeks as several of the men looked around for the cause of the noise. The more time I spent with Merowyn and Simone the more *odd* I realised they were. Slight changes in mannerisms, both often had feral looks on their faces when faced with food for instance, and the fact that Merowyn sometimes growled. Not just a human pretending to growl either, she actually sounded like a wolf or large dog. Mysteries just piled up around the two Imperators.

Once everyone was in position Kyle nodded and everyone, scouts and Imperators included, silently drew their swords. I let my senses examine the building, trying to make sure that Rya didn't have any nasty surprises for us. On Kyle's second nod a scout made to kick down the door, just as I noticed a thin wire behind it.

"NO, WAIT!" I yelled, but it was too late. The door opened inward dislodging the wire and causing the detonation of some kind of device. Blinding light and a sound like a thunderclap accompanied the explosion, ensuring that everyone's vision and hearing was impaired for a few moments.

As my vision returned I saw the scout who had opened the door rolling on the floor, writhing in pain. A closer inspection suggested that he wasn't harmed from the blast, and so I couldn't understand the writhing until I felt a blinding stinging in my nose that only disappeared when I stopped trying to track scent. At the same time I heard a howl from Merowyn who had just tried to sniff the air with whatever advanced senses she seemed to have. She too curled up on the floor, clutching her nose and contorting in agony before clawing the way to her feet, turning and sprinting for the edge of the building. She leapt over the edge to everyone's shock and dismay, expecting a scream and a corpse at the bottom, but Simone looked completely unperturbed.

"Chilli powder in the explosive," he said, "a harsh yet clever deterrent for my partner. She just needs some time to cool off." With that he strode forward, sword in hand and entered the shack. Flinging my remaining senses forward I could pick out that he was now the sole occupier of the building. Somehow Rya had escaped in the commotion.

Kyle motioned for us to stay back in case of further danger as Cassius and I started forward. But once Simone appeared at the doorway and beckoned he relented. Together we walked into the shack to see what had become of Rya. The inside of the building was much like the outside, shabby and in ill repair. A bed made from straw lay in one corner, a small chamber pot lay in another. Simone was standing over Rya's desk and searching through the drawers looking for clues. I chanced a look over the table, whatever she had been feverishly writing was not there - none of the documents were freshly inked.

"So. Where do we think she has gone?" Simone said, his eyes taking in the room, but seeming to land on me as he spoke.

"There must be a third exit," said Kyle. "It would have to be in the floor...there is no way that she would have slipped past everyone even with the distraction of that flash bomb."

Simone looked pleased at the suggestion. "Correct! We will make a renegade Imp hunter of you yet Kyle."

Kyle looked somewhat perturbed at the idea. Exiting the building, he waved in the scouts, instructing them to search the floor of the building for hidden exits. It wasn't long before it was found. A board beneath the chamber pot was movable, and beneath it was a passage into the dishevelled tenement below.

Lithely Simone dropped down into the downstairs apartment. Three members of the scout troop followed, then Kyle, Ella, Cassius and myself. For a moment Kyle looked like he was about to argue and then with a resigned look, shrugged and continued with the search. I can imagine what was running through his mind; we were after all just children, however together our Kaschan was formidable. Indeed we were probably better trained at close combat than each of the scouts or any of the soldiers back at the compound. Whether or not that would allow us to fight, or kill if required, remained to be seen.

The downstairs search turned up little. The room we dropped into connected to a maze of haphazard shacks, all in a dilapidated state yet many with multiple tenants. Such is the way of life with the poor in the Empire. Especially in the Chains - the likelihood was that most of these people were in debt to someone or other, and were offered these buildings as a low rent but high interest solution to their housing needs...slowly but surely getting into more debt with those they most want to avoid. It is a vicious cycle, and Cassius and I were shocked by it all. In the village everyone had been taken care of; even if sick or unwell there would be a place to stay and no debt to repay. We all understood that a problem with one person in the village was a problem for the overall village - we all had to work together to keep the system functioning. The Empire was the exact opposite of this. It worked on what Brother Gelman called a capitalist system; in short, those who had money had better lives. They could afford nice houses, nice food and enjoy the finer things in life. If they so desired they could buy a peerage and become a lord or lady, owning servants and land. Everything was up for grabs in the Andurran Empire, all except the highest role - that of the Emperor himself.

Ella was always quiet when we entered places like the Chains. I think she knew that without Kyle's intervention she would likely be in a place like this herself, stealing or selling her body to survive. I had not delved into her past too deeply. Cassius knew more, of that I was sure, but he had undoubtedly been told to keep it a secret, and whilst I burned with curiosity, I knew that Cassius would not break a promise. Suffice to say that when we three were together we did not speak of the past. Ella had just as many demons in hers as we did in ours... whether they were real, physical creatures or not.

Together we moved from room to room, scouring the building from to top to bottom. Aside from the several hundred tenants, there was no one matching Rya's description. I thought of Merowyn and had an idea. Carefully I expanded my senses and took a breath through my nose, smelling the air for any scent of chilli powder. I figured that Rya must have been hit with a pretty large dose herself if she hadn't been aware that we were outside before the bomb went off. I sifted through the air, mentally blocking out the fresher scents made by the scouts and ourselves as we walked through the building. There! A slightly older scent led the way down into the bowels of the apartment building. In the darkness I saw the trail go through a grate and into the river below. I returned back to Kyle and quietly told him what I had found. He called for Simone and the men, telling them that footprints had been found that led to the grate. As we entered the room I could see Simone look around for said footprints and then direct a slightly curious look at Kyle.

Before he could think to question him I heaved the grate out of the way and pointed down. "Ladies and gentlemen," I said, "I think she went this way."

Something I should mention about the Delgrant river is that whilst it may be relatively clean as it enters Forgoth it certainly doesn't come out the other end in perfect drinking condition. The sewers emptied into the river, blacksmiths and tanners threw their waste into it and butchers heaved their unsold offal into it. If you imagine the smell of a sewer combined with the slow moving viscosity of treacle, you have the Delgrant river as she leaves Forgoth.

Unsurprisingly my ability to track Rya via my nose was rendered useless as we were all instantly assailed by the stench as we moved onto the narrow concrete walkway beneath the grate. Uncertain of which direction Rya would have gone Kyle split the hunting force. Simone and several of the Tracker's went upstream. Kyle, two of the scouts, Cassius, Ella and I went downstream.

Several hours later we reassembled at the compound, exhausted and stinking of sewage. Neither team had found any sign of Rya. It wasn't too surprising as there were many ladders and steps that she could have taken to get off the river, all of which just led further into the city. For yet another day she had successfully outwitted the Imperators and hunters.

As a reward for our hard day of work Kyle decided to take us, Simone and Merowyn (who had recovered from her chilli nightmare) to the upmarket baths in the city. These were public baths frequented by the rich and wealthy of Forgoth, and while Kyle could use these baths as a member of society's elite he generally chose not to, preferring the ease and simplicity of the military baths in the compound. Upon entering we were greeted by a bowing, smiling man who directed us to our various chambers. Unlike back at the village where on a rare summer's day everyone would jump into the lake and swim, in the Empire there were certain rules. As such there were two bathing areas, one for women and the other for men. Ella spared Cassius a sidelong glance as she and Merowyn were led off to their bath chamber... no doubt wishing that village rules applied.

Together we stepped into the bathing room. The sheer opulence on display was staggering. Marble columns held up a roof with vivid stained glass windows. Busts of famous heroes of the Empire were on display at regular intervals around the main bathing area, and servants provided bathing gentlemen with wine and finely plated snacks if they wished. This was a far cry from the rough and ready baths at the military compound. Together we relaxed into one of the more private tubs, hidden from the view of most of the rest of the room. Kyle had a look of disgust on his face when he looked around the building; opulence and Kyle never seemed to mix. However he soon relaxed when entering the fragrantly scented water. Its warmth took away the aches and pains of the day's activities, and more importantly, the smell.

We talked of small things, passing the time in a delightful delirium. Cassius and I had shared a look regarding Simone's body. It was covered in scars, some large, obviously the remains of grievous wounds, but what was more surprising was the magnitude of tiny scars that were spread across his skin. Whether it had been done at once or over time it was impossible to tell, all we knew was that at some point something terrible had happened to him. Kyle too, noticed the state of his childhood friend, but though he asked Simone just laughed it off, waving aside the question as though it was of no importance. A troubled look came over the Major General's face but Simone patted him on the shoulder and simply said, "Imperator training is hard, everyone has scars to show for it, some physical, some mental." With that he smiled and relaxed back into the water.

Sometime later our relaxing reverie was shattered. The sound of an explosion filled the air, shortly followed by screams. Simone and Kyle were out of the pool in an instant, pausing only to grab their swords, swiftly followed by Cassius and myself. The explosion had come from the direction of the women's bathing area and Cassius's face was pale. Knowing my friend, he would not forgive himself if something happened to Ella. We raced to the source of the explosion, dogging the heels of Simone and Kyle, nearly running into them when they both pulled up short. It was easy to see why.

A scene of devastation lay before us. Fragments of blackened marble littered the ground around a blackened ring where the explosive had presumably detonated. A nearby column had taken the brunt of the force, turning the explosive blast into a deadly whorl of sharp marble shards.

"ELLA!" screamed Cassius, shouting wildly for our friend.

"Here," came a weak voice from the pool closest to the column. Running to the pool we found Merowyn, her eyes glassy in death, blood seeping from a multitude of fragments that had embedded themselves in her back. Gently Simone and Kyle lifted Merowyn away, exposing Ella.

Cassius rushed in and Ella flung her arms around his neck tearfully saying, "She saved me! She flung herself over me to protect me from the bomb!" before breaking down into a fit of tears. Cassius just held her, telling her it was ok, that everything would be fine.

Simone ignored Ella completely. With a grave look on his face he took the body of Merowyn and walked out of the front door. If the weight of Merowyn gave him difficulty he didn't show it, walking as swiftly as he had when accompanying us to the baths in the first place. Naked he walked down the street carrying the woman, caring not that both he and Merowyn were unclothed. He just walked swiftly, blood dripping down his chest and onto the floor in the direction of the military compound. We didn't follow.

Once dressed, Kyle ordered the first responders to cordon off the area so that we, meaning I, could examine the area without interference. Ella, now over the initial shock had calmed down somewhat, allowing Cassius to sit with his arm protectively around her, sword bared in his other hand. Heeding Kyle's warnings to be careful and that there might be more explosives I took great caution in examining the surrounding area but found nothing. Rya, for I assumed it was her doing, was long gone and any scent that would have been traceable had been extinguished by the smell of burnt flesh, blood and black powder.

The walk back to the compound was long. We had stayed at the scene for several hours, explaining the situation to the soldiers and caring for Ella. By the time we left night had well and truly fallen and each dark shadow that caressed the usually pleasant cobbled streets held hidden menace. My senses were stretched to their limit as we marched back, trying to make out if anyone was nearby or following. By the time we stepped foot in the compound I was twitching at every movement. Unleashing the full scope of my senses in a city like Forgoth was mentally taxing - there were just far too many people to keep track of. At the very least, concentrating on finding approaching threats had prevented me from dipping into the bleak, black mood that had taken the rest of the party.

When we reached Kyle's house he stomped into the building, angrily flinging open the front door and shocking awake Anders, who had been dozing in the entrance hall. Not even bothering to apologise Kyle treaded down the hallway to his bedroom.

On opening the door he paused to look back at us and spoke one word, "Sleep."

It was a command, not a request. Here we were seeing Kyle, Major General of the Andurran Empire, not Kyle, friend and father figure. Unsurprising I guess, as he had a rogue Imp setting off explosives in public buildings. A time for commanders, not friends.

Cassius and Ella immediately obeyed, but instead of each going to separate rooms Ella joined Cassius in our joint room. Looking back I don't think there was anything sexual in their need to be together that night, Ella had nearly died - Merowyn had died - and they were both rightly terrified. Being alone in their own beds must have seemed daunting and so they chose not to be alone. In my mind that was the correct choice. As for me, I lay in bed for a short time, mind aflame, but soon gave up trying to sleep. Once Cassius and Ella were sleeping soundly I slunk out of the room and into the compound.

I didn't really have any destination in mind. My body needed to move - brain still too wired from the events of the day. And so I followed my feet. Ten minutes later I stood outside Simone's guest residence. Kyle had spoken with the guards on arrival and been told that he had walked naked into the compound with Merowyn in his arms, entered his room and not come out since. Kyle had assumed that he would be grieving and decided to leave him alone for the evening. My feet, apparently, didn't agree.

I paused for a moment to check if Simone was asleep. My senses might not be able to locate him directly but I figured that if the void was in the direction of his bed then I could probably assume that he was in fact sleeping. As it was the void seemed to be seated on the floor next to...Merowyn? I could sense that it was her corpse, but it seemed different. Nails were longer, sharper, muscle was corded and thick. If it was Merowyn then perhaps it was the side that I had not seen, and only felt (in my spine). I decided that this was too intriguing to ignore and knocked at the door. Simone didn't move.

"Simone, it's Calidan. I thought you might want to talk."

A sigh.

"It's late Calidan. Go to sleep." Simone's voice sounded raspy, tired. In my senses the void surrounding him flickered.

"I have tried and I can't. I would rather speak with you," I replied, determined to see what was happening in the room. Merowyn's body was changing with each passing minute. Her hair was growing longer, and not just on her head. Another sigh from the room, another flicker in the void, almost as if it was under strain.

I decided to go with a more direct tactic.

"Simone, I know that you have Merowyn in there. What's happening to her?"

A pause. Then the bar in the door moved and the big oak door creaked open. Simone's head poked out as if suspicious and then fast as lightning he flung me into the room, slamming the door shut and barring it again. It was at this point that I began to think that I may not have thought this through.

Lying on the ground, still naked, was Merowyn. Her body was now covered in a fine dark fur. Claws were long and sharp and her ears were pointed. More disturbing was that her hands and feet were bound in thick iron chain.

"What's happening to her?" I asked, worry tingeing my voice.

"Ramuntek calls to her," replied Simone softly. I looked up and saw that he was eyeing me intently. "There is little that people know about Imperators, and for good reason. We are already a source of fear and speculation. There would be outcry and horror if they knew that we were bonded."

"Bonded?" I asked numbly.

"Yes, bonded. Similar in a way to Tyrant swords. Perhaps more similar to how you are with your Great Heart."

Panic.

Worry.

Flee?

More panic.

"What do you mean?" I asked, feigning surprise. "What's a Great Heart?"

Simone laughed, a big full bellied laugh that took me by surprise; I hadn't imagined that he would be in a laughing mood.

"You know full well what a Great Heart is," he replied, wiping tears of mirth from his eyes, "but I can understand you trying to hide it. You've proven it to me several times since we have met. Calling out before the scout opened the door, the way you move through crowded streets, it makes sense."

I thought quickly. "How I move through the streets? Anyone would move like me if they studied the Kaschan. As for the warning, I just figured that going in blindly was a silly mistake…"

Simone looked at me. I held his gaze, hoping that I could sway him from this belief. Until my senses felt something, another presence in the room. I gasped unintentionally and an amused expression of victory appeared on Simone's face. For the moment I ignored him and focused on what was more important...Merowyn was alive.

CHAPTER FOURTEEN
REBIRTH

~

MEROWYN'S EYES BURNED WITH RAGE as she struggled against the iron chains that shackled her. Her body arched and thick muscles bunched as she violently twisted and bucked. Sounds of pure animal fury erupted from deep in her throat and saliva foamed from her mouth.

"This is why I had not intended to let you in," said Simone, coming to stand beside me. "Recuperation can be...daunting."

"What is happening to her? How is this possible? She was dead!" I exclaimed, trying and failing to control the panic and fear that was now coursing through my veins.

"Correct, she was dead. For a little while anyway. This isn't the first time that either of us has died, nor do I doubt it will be the last. Our bonds ensure that we can regenerate from most things, but death requires external help, something that another Imperator can perform if they start in time."

I was barely listening, my eyes drawn to the screaming she-wolf on the floor. "What is with these changes?" I asked.

"As I mentioned, our bonds are similar but different to yours." This time I didn't bother trying to correct him. "Our bonds are internal. They provide great power but come at a great cost. Each time we draw on our power we come a little closer to losing our humanity...becoming that which we are bonded to."

"And that is?"

He indicated Merowyn, "In her case Ramuntek. She is close to fully losing herself to it. Too many near misses and close calls. But she will pull through this time, I will make sure of that."

I decided to keep the line of questioning going, "So who or what is Ramuntek?"

Simone smirked at me, but the expression didn't reach his eyes.

"I think that's enough truths for one evening, don't you? The rest will be answered in due time."

"Really, when?" I asked, confused. From what I had experienced the Imperators were not exactly a sharing bunch - this was by far the most information I had learnt from either of them.

Simone looked a little shocked, "Why at the Academy of course! By the order of the Emperor, anyone found to be bonded to a Great Heart is to be brought to his attention immediately, and in all likelihood you will join the Imperator ranks."

He looked at me with something akin to sympathy in his eyes. "Sorry but rules are rules. You're going to Anderal with me once we dispose of Rya."

A shocked silence fell between us, interrupted only by the raging growls of Merowyn. Finally I gathered my thoughts, disorganised as they were.

"You want me to become an Imperator?" I said slowly, numbly.

"*I* don't want you to do anything. *The Emperor* however does. Great Heart bonded are part of his inner circle, and his edict is such that anyone who is of high enough clearance to be aware of the existence of Great Hearts is to keep an eye out for their bonded. They are to be brought to the Emperor. Willingly or not." He noticed that my expression had gone somewhat ashen and smiled comfortingly. "Relax, I'm not going to hurt you. A trip to visit the Emperor should be fun right?"

I smiled weakly and pointed at the thrashing, foaming Merowyn, "That doesn't look like much fun."

Simone's gaze turned inward, a troubled expression on his face. He turned back to me, "No, Calidan. I shouldn't lie to you, Imperator training is not fun. However the cause we serve is greater than any one person. I can tell you this truly, becoming an Imperator is a frighteningly difficult and daunting task, being an Imperator even more so. There are many great evils out there in the world and we are the first and often *only* line of defence. I do not really know why Great Heart bonded are specifically made to join our ranks, but I can say that I do not regret doing so."

The words seemed heartfelt, but it was difficult to appreciate that with the monstrous raving going on next to me. Merowyn was seemingly becoming more and more inhuman every second with one eye now having turned a vivid green, the pupil changing to a vertical slit. In fact even as I watched, a small crack appeared in the iron shackles holding her arms.

"Simone!" I cried in alarm. He saw the problem immediately, cursed and slammed his hand onto Merowyn's head. He spoke quietly under his breath in words I did not understand, though the language sounded faintly familiar. A blue glow appeared in Simone's hand and Merowyn howled, a spine chilling sound, before slumping down, unconscious.

Simone smiled wolfishly and then looked up at me, "Another trick from the Academy and one that you'll not get any answers from me about today."

As he spoke I noticed that the blue glow was still emanating from his hand and into Merowyn's head; whatever he had done to her it looked like it wasn't over.

"Can't you stop whatever it is you're doing now?" I asked tentatively.

Simone just looked at me and laughed, "Are you never satisfied? One day that curiosity of yours will get you into deep trouble."

I hesitated to point out that I was fairly certain that it already had...after all I was now bound to the Imperator Academy, willingly or not. Moreover with the lovely benefit of hindsight he was completely correct; over and over again in my life I have been a victim of my own cursed curiosity. Luckily up to this point I have managed to, for better or worse, survive the consequences of my own inquisitiveness.

Once Simone had finished chuckling he deigned to answer my question, "No, I can't stop now. Imagine that right now Merowyn's brain is split into two minds. One hers, the other not human. Each time we draw on the powers of the bond we have to fight for control, especially so in cases like this. Merowyn is losing the fight this time. I am attempting to force down the other mind to allow hers to surface and take control. This will take as long as it takes. And yes, before you ask, doing this is a risk to myself as well." He looked intensely at me, a dark gleam in his eyes, "Listen Calidan, this is important. If I tell you to leave then you best leave, quickly. You run, you call for help and you keep running. Do you understand?" I nodded.

"Good," he replied. "Now I'm going to have to really start concentrating so if you're going to stay, sit still and be quiet."

And so for those slow, unreal minutes of the early morning I watched as Simone suppressed whatever was inside Merowyn. As the time grew so did the sweat gathering on Simone's forehead. Veins began pulsing in his neck and forehead, tension palpable in every limb of his body. By the time the dawn light had started entering the room's windows his lips were curled back in a snarl, canines looking sharp. And then, all of a sudden, it ended. The guttural snarls and howls coming from Merowyn faded as Simone breathed out a sigh of relief, and slumped against the wall. Merowyn coughed and began breathing normally, her fur and other animal accoutrements slowly receding back into her normal human form. Her normal, naked, human form. I blushed, stood and grabbing Simone's coat off the back of the door gently covered her with it.

Simone nodded his thanks at my act. "Sorry, it's hard to remember sometimes that clothes are important in civilised society...in hindsight I probably shouldn't have embarked on that walk through town yesterday without some clothing on."

I snorted in amusement, a mistake, as this seemed to be the catalyst for a fit of laughter that descended upon both of us. A helpful catharsis after the previous day and night's trying events.

Calming down, I called Simone out on that statement, "So at Imperator Academy you don't often wear clothes?"

He looked at me wryly. "More questions?" A chuckle. "Fine - yes we do wear clothes when the need calls for it, but the training at the Academy is long and varied. Some situations require clothes, others do not...at the end of it all clothes are the last thing on your mind and they tend to be thought of as additions rather than necessities. Does that answer your question?"

"Not really, but talking to you rarely leaves me fully satisfied with a complete answer," I said with a grin, "I'll take what I can get!"

A groan from Merowyn interrupted further conversation. Her eyes flickered then opened, dashing wildly around the room before pausing on me and Simone who rested a gentle hand on her shoulder. "It's okay Merowyn, you're at the compound with me," he paused looking at me, "...and Calidan who was such a nuisance that I had to let him in."

Merowyn opened her mouth to speak and paused in what seemed to be consternation. Her mouth moved oddly, as though she had forgotten how to form words.

Simone leaned over and lightly kissed her brow, "Relax, this often happens. Your body and mind have gone through a lot in the past few hours, everything will come back to you I promise." She smiled a beatific smile at him. Recognising that I was interrupting a tender moment I stood up and made to leave.

As I walked towards the door Simone's voice stopped me, "Calidan. Before you go, remember that you cannot tell anyone about tonight, both what happened to Merowyn and what we talked about. Understood?"

I nodded.

"Good...and thanks for the company." Simone smiled and winked at me. I gave him a grin and gave a thumbs up to Merowyn who flashed me a warm but confused smile. With that I opened the door and left.

The day had fully begun whilst Simone and I had been in the room with Merowyn. The compound was drenched in a warm glow, casting away the last vestiges of night. Looking around, my attention was drawn to the training ground where a sole figure sat. Tyrgan. It was just like him to want to be training the morning after a disaster, and if that was the case I was very, very late. I cringed inwardly and in all honesty probably outwardly too. He had likely gone to my room to drag me out and on not finding me had decided to wait in the training square. I slowly, unwillingly, started walking towards him. This morning's session was going to be tough.

By the time Cassius, Ella and Brother Gelman arrived for the morning session I was a bruised lump. Tough had been an understatement. Tyrgan had pushed me to brutal extremes, forcing my tired body to work at a higher and higher level, reinforcing with heavy blows what happened if I didn't move fast enough. His mood was dark and the second session with everyone was almost as hard as the first. By the end of it all we were drenched in sweat, covered in bruises and collapsed in a heap on the side of the training ground. Not a fun start to the morning.

The reasoning behind Tyrgan's foul mood soon became clear when Kyle arrived, obviously having forsaken morning training for the benefits of more sleep. Tyrgan immediately walked up to him and spoke, voice low and dangerous. With my advanced hearing it was easy to make out that that Tyrgan was angry at being left behind on the day's activities beforehand, and more angry that we had been brought along. Kyle held up a hand to forestall any further tirade.

"Tyrgan, you know that I would have had you by my side in a heartbeat. However Simone and Merowyn believed that if the location had been a trap, the compound could have been targeted in our absence by Rya. You are one of the capable few who could stand against an Imperator, thus our best chance against defending this compound against an Imperator in training." He jerked his thumb towards us, "As for them, it was actually a request from Simone."

At this my eyes narrowed; Simone's machinations were impressive. Kyle continued. "I didn't condone it; however I am bound to provide any and all assistance to Imperators. For as you know they speak with the Emperor's voice. Furthermore they were actually invaluable yesterday and it was only through slim margins that Rya escaped." He breathed deeply. "So get your head out of your arse and stop berating everyone around you. Understood?"

Tyrgan's eyes flashed dangerously at the order, but taking a deep breath he relaxed, the tension visibly leaving his muscles. "I'm sorry Kyle," he said, "I have never been one for sitting around, and when I found out that the lot of you had been attacked, Merowyn killed, I thought myself a disgrace. An ex-bodyguard of the Emperor and I wasn't even there to protect you." He pointed his hand over at us, "Or them." He glanced back at Kyle, "It won't happen again. I am coming with you on anything Rya related from this point on." Kyle looked his friend and mentor in the eye and nodded. We all knew that even if he had declined it would have been to no avail. Tyrgan was nothing if not stubborn.

~

"What?!"

I winced. Cassius's voice was growing along with his size. Beside him stood Ella, looking equally shocked. I suppose telling your friends that you were going to Imperator school, and had no choice in the matter, made for a surprising revelation. It was early afternoon and this was the first time we had had free together. Following the morning's intense training session we had several hours of Brother Gelman's language studies before finally breaking for lunch. It had seemed like an eternity. Apparently however I should have divulged this information somewhere where there were less people, the compound mess hall now containing several prying eyes trying to find the source of the outburst. It wasn't hard, Cassius was livid, his face turning purple with fury.

"That, that bastard thinks he can just take you away?" he exclaimed. "He has no right!"

"He has every right," Ella interjected, squeezing Cassius's arm. "Imperators speak with the Emperor's voice, remember? As we are citizens of the Empire we are bound to follow the Emperor's instruction." She looked at me sadly, "Calidan has no say in the matter."

I nodded gravely. Ella understood what Cassius could not. Emotions played no part in this; even if Simone didn't want to he would still have to bring me back to the Emperor lest he fail in his duty.

I looked around furtively, since the next piece of information was much more secretive. Leaning forward I spoke quietly. "There is something else I need to tell you, something that you cannot repeat." They both leant closer. Ella looked intrigued, her eyes shining, whilst Cassius looked wary - probably worried about more life changing revelations.

"Merowyn is alive."

I saw the consternation on their faces, followed by disbelief. Ella's eyes started watering, like she was holding back tears.

Cassius was the first to speak, "Merowyn is dead Calidan, we all saw it. There is no way she could have survived!"

"You're right," I said, "no normal person could. I couldn't sleep last night and went to see Simone. He had Merowyn's body with him and was...battling with part of her mind." At the looks on my friends' faces I knew they found this hard to accept.

"Simone said that Imperators are bonded to things, kind of like me, but whatever they are bonded to is kept inside them. He said that any time they use their powers they have to force down the personality of the other being inside of them." I took a deep breath. "You should have seen it, Merowyn...changed. She was almost like a wolf - a rabid one at that. Howling and clawing at anything; covered in hair. Then Simone won and she relaxed, becoming Merowyn again..." I broke off, aware of how it sounded. They were staring at me, open mouthed. I fumbled for more words to explain what had happened but found none. So I decided to change tack.

"I know it sounds unreal but so far we have learnt of Great Hearts, blades that can bestow unfathomable strength onto the bearer and Cassius - you and I both know that there are dark, devilish things that are possible in this world. Is someone coming back from death so hard to believe?"

Cassius blinked, remembering the night of the shadow demon, and nodded. "You're right," he said softly, "we have seen too much for me not to believe you about this."

Ella's tear filled gaze moved from me, to her lover, back to me. She wiped her eyes and sniffed, "I believe you too," she said. "Can we go see her?"

I shook my head. "Simone said that I couldn't tell anyone what I had seen. I'm fairly certain this is forbidden knowledge. I don't know what Merowyn is going to do now, whether she is going to come forward or hide in the shadows..."

"If I were her, I would stay hidden," said Ella. In response to our quizzical looks she continued, "Rya is obviously aware that Merowyn was on her tail. It explains the chilli powder in the trap and her attack at the baths. She must believe that Merowyn is her biggest threat… with her apparently dead it is possible that Rya will lower her guard slightly." I nodded, in agreement with Ella's assessment. It made sense.

"In that case, I don't know if we will see Merowyn again, but I hoped that it would make you feel better to know that she lives."

Ella smiled broadly and nodded. "Thank you Calidan."

CHAPTER FIFTEEN
SERAPH

~

FOR TWO DAYS THE COMPOUND remained on lockdown. We trained, learnt, ate, slept and repeated this cycle. Unable to venture outside the walls and at all times vainly keeping an eye out for anyone who could be Rya, and more surreptitiously, Merowyn. Kyle put more soldiers on regular patrols throughout the city, with orders to randomly stagger their start times to make sure that Rya couldn't plan an attack based on the timing of a patrol.

The problem was that none of us knew what Rya was planning. She had obviously decided to remove the main tracking threat of the Imperator duo, but aside from one albeit deadly explosion, she hadn't actually harmed anyone as far as the intelligence Kyle received suggested. That, plus her penchant for ensuring that she always had a way out of her short term homes, meant that her actions were very hard to predict. She might have already left the city, or she could be planning anything from inciting a revolt to indiscriminate bombings. As a result everyone from the soldiers to Kyle were highly strung and tense.

Simone had been conspicuously absent, his room empty each time I made an excuse to walk by. No trace of Simone's void or Merowyn inside. I assumed that they had left to once again hunt Rya, but this time without the backup of the military. This surprised me but made sense; the two Imperators appeared to be loners by their very nature. In addition it was unlikely that Merowyn wanted to be seen around the compound, otherwise a great many questions would be raised and as soldiers are a naturally superstitious lot, there would be potential for panic amongst the troops.

The third day of lockdown thankfully ended when Simone appeared. After bringing together the group, this time including Tyrgan, he spoke in a soft, assured voice.

"Rya is no longer in the city," he said, a pregnant silence following his statement that quickly birthed a cacophony of outbursts.

"Quiet!" ordered Kyle before turning back to Simone. "How do you know this Simone?"

"Information gathering is part of being an Imperator Kyle. Reports came in today of a woman matching Rya's description exiting the city via the sewer and heading north."

"You're sure it's her?" Kyle asked.

"Positive."

"That's good enough for me, allow me a few minutes and I will have the troops mobilised." Kyle turned to leave but stopped when Simone's hand landed on his shoulder.

"Actually, leave the troops," Simone said. "They aren't necessary."

"Aren't necessary? Rya killed your partner!" Kyle replied in astonishment.

"All the same, they aren't needed. Whilst your troops are no doubt excellent for mass engagements and guard duty they are not true hunters of man. For us to catch her we need to be swift and a small party will move faster than a large one." Simone paused and looked Kyle in the eye. "We," he said, indicating those in the room, "will suffice. Everyone here is trained in Kaschan. Yes, Brother Gelman, even you are required to come with me - you are worth more than any two of the soldiers outside."

No one moved.

Kyle turned to us. "Well you heard him. Get geared up and be outside in ten minutes!"

As one, we turned and sprinted out the room.

The hunt was on.

Seven horses streamed out of the North gate, hooves kicking up clouds of dust. Brother Gelman, Ella, Cassius, myself, Tyrgan, Kyle and Simone all clung low to the horses and allowed them free reign to unleash their muscle. After twenty minutes of hard riding Simone waved us down, slowing the pace to a trot. He pointed off the main north road, towards a lesser known side path. Everyone in the group shared a look behind Simone. Whilst the road was lesser known to most, we knew it well. It was the beginning of the path that led to Seya's forest.

For the next couple of hours we followed Simone, wondering how he knew where he was going when he made no obvious sign of looking for tracks, and hoping that he would turn off the track we were on. Hope that sadly seemed in vain.

"Seya?"

"Tiny Human, hello!"

A playful feeling surged throughout my body.

"Sorry Seya, this isn't a social visit. There is someone dangerous nearby - potentially in your forest."

"I assume you mean the young human female who has made camp in the cave?"

"Yes! Her name is Rya, she is very dangerous...which cave?"

A picture of a cave in the north eastern section of the forest, the entrance overgrown with willow trees, filled my mind.

"It is not a nice cave, I don't mind her staying there."

"Well, we are here to stop her, she has already tried to kill one of the party."

"The other human adult female? The one who smells like an odd wolf?"

I paused.

"Is Merowyn in your forest too Seya?"

"Yes. I'm sitting above her as we speak. She moves swiftly for a human but not swift enough."

"Keep safe Seya, she is an Imperator...and a friend."

I broke the connection and turned to Cassius and Ella, "Merowyn is in the forest," I whispered.

"Seya's forest?" Ella asked. I nodded and nudged my horse up closer to Simone.

"Rya is in a cave in the north eastern part of the forest." He looked at me appraisingly and smiled.

"You have a surprising range with your senses Calidan...can you sense anything else?" Acquiescing, I examined Seya's surroundings. Merowyn was stealthily moving from branch to branch, keeping off the forest floor. The way she moved was almost predatory. I spoke softly, "Merowyn is currently crawling along low tree branches a good two miles away from Rya's position."

Simone whistled, then stopped, thinking. "There is no way that your senses can reach that far." He thought to himself some more, finger pressed against his lips. Suddenly his eyes lit up. "The forest we are heading to has a reputation for being haunted. I didn't think too much of it as there were no reports of incidents aside from a group of men who were scared out of their wits whilst hunting wolves...Calidan, your Great Heart lives in this forest doesn't it." It was a statement, not a question.

I nodded. Simone already held my fate in his hands, he might as well know this too. "Yes, Seylantha lives in this forest. I've warned her to steer clear of Rya but she doesn't often listen to me."

"Seylantha, a lovely name," Simone mused. "Look Calidan, I don't want to put Seylantha in harm's way but this could well work to our advantage. Even Merowyn's tracking senses at her best aren't as good as most Great Hearts." I snorted; Seya was currently sitting fifteen feet above Merowyn thinking out how amusing it would be to pounce on her head - Merowyn's tracking abilities were not remotely in the same league.

"Why do we need her to help?" I asked, "Surely two Imperators by themselves are a force to be reckoned with, let alone when backed up by a sword master wielding a Tyrant's blade, myself and four Kaschan practitioners? How does one individual, an Imp not an Imperator, warrant so many people?"

Simone paused. His eyes slowly turned to meet my gaze and then he spoke in hushed tones, "You're right, in normal circumstances this would be overkill. However I am beginning to believe that Rya is receiving help. We should have caught her by now on several occasions, but she has had multiple safe houses, escape routes and apparently access to explosive materials, which as we both know she has put to good use." He sighed, "In short I am concerned and I do not like the feeling... so for me overkill is a good thing."

Rya being helped, now that was a disturbing thought. It made sense though and I could see why Simone was worried. I had been thinking that perhaps the Emperor's Imperators were not all they were cracked up to be, having been foiled at every turn, but this made a certain type of sense. "Do you have any ideas as to who would help Rya?" I asked.

"The Empire has many enemies," Simone replied. "What worries me is that not many are aware of Imperators. When one joins the Academy their public record is erased, and families and friends are held under contract to not divulge information. If someone has helped Rya that means he or she knows who and what she is which is worrying enough. But worse still is that that someone knows about us."

I looked at Simone questioningly, "What do you mean?"

He ran a hand through his hair, showing his agitation. "Imperators don't often associate with Imps. Rya was likely aware of Merowyn and I, but she wouldn't have had any idea about our...skills."

Facts slotted together in my head. "And yet Merowyn was prevented tracking with chilli powder and she was the target of Rya's attack on the bathhouse," I said. Simone nodded.

"Exactly," he replied. "No one should have that knowledge. Which leads me to think that there is an information leak in the Academy or in the Emperor's inner circle. Either way, I need to get back to the Emperor as soon as possible!"

I nodded. "What are we waiting for?" I said, foolishly filled with the confidence of youth.

~

I slowly parted the fronds of a billowing willow, gazing at the spectacle before me. A grand stag with a huge rack of antlers stood yawning into the sky whilst several does ambled around eating their fill, content in the lush environment of the forest.

"I see you've met the old man of the forest," came the statement from Seya, either using her senses or looking through my eyes...I'd never quite figured out if she was able to do that. *"A likeable chap, I have decided not to eat him."*

"*Very kind of you,*" I thought back to her, "*how old do you reckon he is?*"

"*Hah! Not old at all compared to me, but for a stag? Old enough.*"

"*It is a great scene, this forest is lovel-*"

Crack

The stag bellowed into the sky, and the herd fled, crashing through the ferns and forest yet making less sound that Simone whose bumbling approach to stealth had just ruined the moment. I sighed and turned to him as he crept towards me, seemingly standing on every available stick and twig possible.

"I thought Imperators were meant to be good at stealth?" I asked.

"We all have training in it, but stealth in a forest is a different matter. I'm better at blending in with people in cities!" came the exasperated reply.

"Well, let's just hope that Rya is deep enough in the cave that she can't hear your blundering," I retorted, earning a scowl from the Imperator.

"Quiet, both of you!" A whispered scold came from Ella, whose natural stealth from her pick pocketing days had lent itself well to moving silently in the forest. "From what Calidan was saying we aren't far. We need to keep quiet as we don't know how sound carries in this place."

A valid point. Simone and I shared an admonished look and then kept moving forward, one slipping silently like a ghost, the other...not so much.

A short time later we were hidden in the undergrowth looking at the cave entrance. As I had seen through Seya's imagery, the entrance was covered with hanging willow fronds, making it difficult to tell that it was there. Using my senses I could tell that the entrance was large enough, but it quickly grew more narrow until it was barely big enough to fit one person at a time. The route continued but my senses couldn't follow it, in fact I couldn't sense Rya in there at all, only a shifting itch that *something* was inside the cave. I turned and spoke to the others, keeping my voice low.

Simone looked concerned, whispering furiously at me. "What do you mean that you can't sense her in there? You sensed her earlier!"

I looked at him, keeping my anger in check. "Earlier she was sitting in the entrance to this cave, now Seya tells me that she has moved down further into the back, but neither she nor I can tell what is down there. It is almost as though there is a complete absence of anything." I paused. "In fact, Simone, it is much like what I sense when trying to find you."

At that Simone froze. He looked carefully at each of us as if weighing us up and then sighed quietly. "You're all here with me so I guess you can all be trusted with this information. What Calidan is referring to is the leaking of energy that spills out from my bonded partner."

"Partner?" Kyle asked.

"Imperators have bonds, much like Calidan has with his Great Heart. However what we are bonded to is something... different. Each partner is unique and they differ in strength. The bond between my partner and I is not, shall we say, fully secure. As such, unless I am drawing heavily on it, some of my partner's energy spills out continuously. This energy is pure *Seraph* - an old term that will likely mean nothing to you. In layman terms, it is not of this world and can be used to create or destroy. It cannot be sensed in the usual manner, which means people like Calidan and Merowyn who have advanced sensory abilities can't actually detect what I look like from a distance." Simone held up a hand to forestall any discussion of what he had just revealed. The stunned looks on everyone's faces, including my own, ensured that there would be a plethora of questions for him later.

He continued, "If Calidan can sense such energy then we need to move quickly. Rya was not bonded by the Academy; that only occurs post-graduation for a select few. So something is happening down there that is radiating a lot of Seraph. And let me tell you, that is rarely a good thing."

Simone looked at me. "One last question Calidan. Can you sense Merowyn?" Kyle, Brother Gelman and Tyrgan stiffened in surprise. Simone looked at them and spoke quickly, outlining that she was alive and following Rya. He looked back at me only to see me shake my head. Neither Seya nor I could locate Merowyn, the last Seya knew of her she had been sneaking into the cave. Simone's face grew more grave at the news and he quickly outlined a basic plan. With no information about the layout of the inside of the cave available, he decided that the best tactic was to move in single file through the narrow section and hope that it widened out again. If it did we were to spread out as quickly as possible and overwhelm Rya. A simple plan but there was little else available to us.

Before we left Simone looked at us. "One more thing," he said seriously. "Seraph is strange. To enter into a place brimming with it is dangerous by itself. You may see or hear things within. Hopefully they are just whispers, if the worst has happened then we may be against something much worse than just one rogue Imp. I cannot say what because truly I do not know. Be on your guard!"

With one final grim nod at the group he stood up and led the way, sword drawn and held in front of him. One by one we stood and drawing weapons walked into shadow. Shadow, flame and horror.

CHAPTER SIXTEEN
POSSESSION

~

LOOSE STONE SHIFTED UNDERFOOT, SKITTERING away into the darkness as we squeezed through the passage. Even with my advanced senses the darkness was all consuming, yet we risked no light from fear of warning Rya of our approach. Simone took point, slowly reaching out with each step, touching the floor lightly with his foot before putting his weight down. In the blackness of the cave there would be no seeing any potential traps or pitfalls. I could sense the building anxiety in the members of my party, and that of Seya who was waiting outside but unable to do anything to help. Just before the passage widened it was like I had stepped into a bubble of Simone's void. I couldn't sense anything at all. There had been no suggestion that we had passed into anything, but without warning my senses were cut off. All I could feel now was the sense of an all encompassing void.

Simone stumbled, having reached out for the wall and found nothing there. I grabbed at him and held him until he was settled, hearts pounding in both our chests. He patted me on the shoulder in thanks, but instead of letting him go I turned his head towards the front. Ahead of us a faint red glow permeated the surrounding darkness.

Together we spread out and advanced towards it, taking our time and testing the floor with each step. The cavern we had entered proved to be vast for it took some time before we could make out what the glow was. As one Cassius and I gasped. The glow came from red swirls painted on the floor, swirls that looked uncannily similar to those that had been painted so long ago at the village.

In the middle of the swirls sat a woman wreathed in shadow. The darkness seemed to cling to her, wrapping itself around her in a pulsating mass of black.

"Rya!" bellowed Simone once we reached the edge of the swirls.

"Simone?" a timid voice broke from the figure.

"Rya, stop this madness, do you know not what you do?" Simone yelled, fear and fury resounding in his voice.

A low sob came from the woman, "I know exactly what I am doing. For what it is worth I am sorry. They have my family."

"What do you mean?" cried Simone. "Who has your family?"

"Shadow." As she spoke the darkness around her seemed to constrict, forcing her voice to choke. Rya shuddered and slowly raised her arms, the red glow glinting from the blade in her hands. "Forgive me!" she gasped around the shadow constricting her throat and plunged the weapon into her chest.

An expectant silence filled the room. The shadows around Rya's body began to move, slowly at first but picking up speed. They slid around the blade and appeared to enter the wound in her chest, more and more until darkness was streaming inside of her. Her body convulsed, shaking violently as blood poured onto the floor. As it did the red swirls glowed vividly, making the cavern around us stand out in relief. In horror we saw the butchered remains of multiple animals scattered haphazardly, entrails splayed out across the floor. It appeared to have nothing to do with sustenance but pure savagery, the corpses having been torn apart.

"Eyes front!" came the shout from Simone, who had refused to be distracted by the grisly scene. We looked up to see Rya no longer sitting, but standing. The dagger had been removed from her chest and with a clatter she threw it on the ground. In the red light I could see that the hole in her breast was still there yet no more blood exited the gaping wound. Rya's face looked up and I gasped in horror. With my vision I could see that her eyes were completely black. A feral grin split her face. Raising a hand she looked at us and laughed. A thick, oppressive sound that shouldn't have come from a human mouth.

"Imperator," What Was Once Rya boomed, her mouth moving oddly as though unknowing how to speak. **"Die."**

With that Rya disappeared, leaving behind a flame of shadow. Simone snarled like an animal and suddenly a beaming blue light emitted from his body. The light drove back the encroaching shadows in a large radius and Rya roared in fury, apparently unable to enter the blue circle.

Simone cried out to us, voice trembling under immense strain. "Ready yourselves! We must fight or die!" A few muttered words and his long sword burst into blue flame. "Whatever you do," he cried, striding forward to meet Rya. "Stay within the light!"

He swept the blade forward and a ribbon of blue flame shot out towards Rya in an arc. Deftly she leapt, twisting over the roaring blaze and unleashing a black flame of her own. It crackled along the surface of Simone's light and I saw the man's knees waver with the pressure.

With her other hand Rya knelt down and picked up the knife, speaking as she did so, **"Well Imperator. You can protect yourself, but what about your friends?"**

With blinding speed she threw the knife, it rocketed towards Cassius only to be knocked away by Tyrgan, red writing glowing on sword and wrist. He looked up, smiling grimly at Rya, before his eyes widened in alarm. She had disappeared. A gurgling noise filled our ears, and as one we turned to look at Brother Gelman, who was holding a large shard of bone that extended through his chest. Fear and panic filled his eyes as blood frothed out of his mouth.

"No!" cried Ella, rushing to his side, frantically trying to help him, but by the time he hit the ground Brother Gelman was dead.

"One down," came that dreadful voice. **"What now Imperator?"**

"Calidan!" shouted Tyrgan. "You and I need to protect the others from any more projectiles. They aren't fast enough!" He turned his head slightly, still keeping his eyes on Rya, "You others keep moving, don't present an easy target!" Cassius and Kyle grabbed Ella, lifting her roughly to her feet.

"Concentrate on the living Ella," roared Kyle. "We can mourn the dead later." After a short pause Ella nodded and broke free of their grip before starting the first circle of Kaschan. Together the three broke into flowing dance, moving throughout the circle of light that Simone projected, movements swift and fluid.

A shin bone pierced the air, whistling as it sped towards Simone. His sword flicked and batted it out of the sky. I wheeled and cut down a rib before it reached Cassius, then spun back to block what looked to be a jawbone that hit my blade with stunning force. A quick glance at Tyrgan showed that he too was having multiple missiles to contend with, but so far our speed was allowing us to protect the others.

A hiss of rage broke the air followed by a thin lance of black shadow. It struck Simone's shield and the entire structure wavered. Simone fell to his knees, veins throbbing along his face. "I can't hold it!" he gritted out between clenched teeth. A crack appeared in the light and a black beam hurtled through. I spun and cut at the blackness but my blade did nothing, passing through it like it didn't exist.

I screamed in pain as the beam impaled my shoulder, tearing through bone and ligaments with ease. A cold, deathly sensation bled from my wound and soon my entire body was numb yet filled with lancing fire. Tyrgan sliced through the beam, his sword seemingly having no problem cutting the foul shadow and it dissipated. He tensed for a follow up attack but none followed. In my hazy vision I could see why; Simone was held by his throat by Rya, her concentration on the Imperator.

"**Foolish Imperator,**" came the horrible sound. "**You should have known better than to face one of the Kyrgeth alone.**" Simon muttered something inaudible and Rya shook him by the throat. "**Speak up little man.**"

"I said, I am not alone!" Simone cried as a glowing red blade appeared in the air above Rya, arcing down and entering her body through the shoulder blades. Merowyn bore Rya to the ground, landing atop her body with a feline grace. At a twitch from Rya a second blade came crashing down, neatly removing her head.

Tyrgan looked up at Merowyn.

"Good timing," was all he said. Even in my agony I grinned; classic Tyrgan.

As my vision faded I could dimly hear Ella screaming, crying in the background. Yet I was positive that she was not next to me. I raised my gaze up and Cassius lay on the floor, blood pooling through the gaping hole in his thigh, his face pale and eyes closed. My best friend had been behind me when the shadow beam struck. The last image I saw before I passed out was Ella with her hands covered in the blood of her love, screaming.

PRESENT DAY

~

Howling

Ripping

Tearing

Blood

The beast was just over the rise, the sound of its meal being torn apart echoing through the snowy mountains. I was grateful that the woman's screams had long since faded; they were beginning to give me a headache. Ashen trolls had a penchant for taking limbs first, perhaps an unsophisticated mimicry of an appetiser before a main course.

In an ideal world we would have caught and butchered the troll before it did the same to the young maiden from the nearby village, but have you ever tried walking through six foot snow drifts? Ball ache doesn't even begin to cover it. We didn't have the advantage of the large padded feet that allowed the seven foot, six hundred pound beast to better distribute its weight. So even with all that mass - nearly putting Cassius' armoured self to shame; an ashen troll can move extremely swiftly in snowy terrain.

I risked a glimpse over the rise. The troll was happily sucking the flesh off the arm of the unfortunate woman, the cracked bones of both her legs lay carelessly discarded at the beast's feet. It almost looked like a gorilla, if a gorilla had savage tusks that extended twelve inches from its jaw, had grey (or you might say, ashen) fur, razor sharp claws and a propensity for eating by and large anything in its territory. Slinking back down, I turned to my silent companion. It was nearly time.

Cassius was sat beside me, calm and unmoving, as though he hadn't just spent the last ten minutes listening to the woman's piercing screams. His greatsword lay across his lap, the mighty blade almost a hand span in width, his hand never far from the hilt.

I waved to him and the great head turned, nodding once. Cassius was ready. Slowly I unsheathed my swords; Asp, a short sword that shone a pale blue and Reckoning, a sabre with a blade that shimmered with blackest night. Cassius slowly closed his hand around the hilt and shuddered. Engraved runes lit up along the blade, running down the near two metre length. He nodded to me and I turned, stood and sprinted for the rise, leaping over onto the unsuspecting beast who had just begun feasting on the torso of the deceased woman.

My twin blades drove deep into the back of the creature, sliding through its muscle like a hot knife through butter. As it howled in shock and pain I twisted and somersaulted off its back, slicing through its hamstring as I did so. A terribly flashy move and one that I knew Andronicus, weapons master of the Academy, would have laughed at, but I wasn't facing him, I was facing an angry troll that didn't have swords of its own.

Moonlight caught on the razor honed six inch claws on each paw.

Fine - so it didn't really need swords.

The beast swirled and roared, the mortal wounds I had inflicted starting to close before my eyes. Another reason why trolls are tricky; they have an annoying tendency to heal from almost any wound.

The beast crouched and tensed to spring. I could see the thick muscles coiling, knew the power that it would generate and understood that I was outmatched in this terrain, knew that if I ran it would catch me as easily as a fox with a hare, so I did the only sensible thing and roared back.

The roar startled the beast. It probably didn't expect something that powerful and savage to come out of an apparent human. Nor did it understand that the roar both signalled and masked the sound of the approaching armour clad sentinel, a mighty jump from the ridge sending him hurtling through the air as though he weighed nothing. In his hands his greatsword, Oathbreaker, descending towards the troll. With an animal yell that shook the air like a thunderclap Oathbreaker burst into flame. The troll started to turn, realising that there was a second ambush, but too late. A thud and then silence, two steaming halves of troll fell either side of the glowing blade. Fire - one of the only sure solutions to ending a troll's regenerating ability.

We wiped our swords clean, bowed our heads to the fallen woman and started walking once more.

Together we had killed the troll and failed the maiden. Nothing more than a side note in our unceasing hunt for the shadow beast.

PART II
IMP(ISITION)

~

CHAPTER SEVENTEEN
RECOVERY

~

I WOKE UP IN A blindingly well lit room, a sparse and spartan space decorated with white sheets and populated by sleeping figures. As my eyes adjusted to the bright light I heard a gasp and hurried footfall. Seconds later several figures crashed into the room, practically sprinting to my side and gushing that I was awake.

This was extremely confusing as to the best of my knowledge I hadn't been sleeping.

Had I?

The confusion must have shown on my face as Kyle and Tyrgan slowed down their rushed speech and drew back giving me some space.

"What happened?" I said, my voice quiet and strained as if I hadn't used it for some time. "Where am I?"

"The second question first I think," replied Tyrgan. He paused as if judging what to say before continuing, "You're in the capital."

"The capital?!"

"Correct."

I looked at him flabbergasted. Anderal, the capital, was a two week trip from Forgoth, and only then using a series of fresh horse relays. With a horse and cart it would take closer to three. Slowly the realisation crept into my brain.

"How long have I been asleep?" I asked, dreading the answer.

"Sixteen days," replied Kyle in a low voice.

My mind whirled. *Sixteen days!* It seemed like no time had passed between the fight with Rya and now. The fight with Rya... in a flash it came back to me, Cassius lying on the ground, Ella's hands covered in blood.

I shot up, grimacing at a pain in my shoulder. It was encased in bandages and I decided now was not the time to explore the damage. "Where is Cassius? How is he?" I splurted. Tyrgan and Kyle shared a look.

"Not great," Tyrgan replied. "He lost a lot of blood." At the look on my face he raised a hand, forestalling any interruption. "But that has been solved. The hospital you're both in is the best in the Empire;

it is said that even if you are brought here on the brink of death the surgeons and doctors can keep you alive."

"Okay," I responded, "in that case why the long faces at the mention of Cassius?"

Kyle breathed out heavily. "Can you stand?"

I nodded.

Leaning slightly on Kyle we walked down the hallway to another room. This one seemed to contain only two people, one patient and a visitor. Ella looked up as I entered, lacklustre eyes resting on my face as I rushed to Cassius' side. She smiled grimly as I gasped in horror. Black lines extended up past his neck, seemingly following the veins in his skin. I moved aside the cover and saw that the hole in his leg was a black mass.

"The leg isn't healing," Kyle's voice said from behind me. He walked over to put a hand on Ella's shoulder. "After this length of time there should have been some sign of improvement but so far nothing."

Ella whimpered and my heart broke a little more at the sound.

"How?" I asked. "How am I not the same as Cassius?"

"Seya," said Simone, walking in through the door. "She carried you both here ahead of us, making the journey in eight days. I don't think I need to tell you how incredible a feat that is." I shook my head numbly. "Since then she has been forcing power through your bond, driving out the shadow...sadly Cassius doesn't have such a friend."

"There must be something we can do?" I cried beseechingly.

"The best minds in the Empire are working on it as we speak," replied Simone. "This is something that no one living has seen before. The Hall of Scribes has their top men researching the histories where such symptoms are mentioned, and the doctors are trying every treatment possible to keep Cassius' symptoms from worsening."

At the mention of the Hall of Scribes my mind flinched. Brother Gelman. Poor, sweet Brother Gelman. Looking up at everyone I saw the pain reflected in their eyes. His loss was a massive blow to us all.

Reading my mind Kyle spoke up, "The scribes held a ceremony for Brother Gelman which we attended. His grave is in Forgoth, but we were planning on holding our own ceremony here once everyone is up and active."

I nodded glumly. I would sorely miss Brother Gelman, not just for his sage advice and teaching, but for the steadfast friendship he had shown to Cassius and me since arriving in Forgoth. He had not deserved the ending he received. My blood boiled at the thought of Rya and her horrific machinations. Regardless of whether she had been used or not she had killed my friend, and I inwardly vowed that I would make whoever controlled that darkness within her pay dearly for the death and destruction wrought upon us.

Once my raging heart had calmed I spoke to Simone, "So, we're in the main hospital of Anderal?"

He waved me off. "Please. Nothing that shabby. No my boy, you're in the one place where the staff stand a decent chance of helping you recuperate from any ailment, the finest scientific and medical minds in the Empire... You're in the Imperator hospital."

Over the next week a constant troupe of doctors, researchers and otherwise intrigued Imperators and officials marched in to see Cassius, and question myself and the group. Simone made it clear that all questions were to be answered as honestly and openly as possible. He stressed that unlike other institutions, Imperators did not keep information hidden from each other. What may have been glimpsed by one Imperator several hundred years before might benefit another in the present day. Simone was keen to emphasize that over the years knowledge of various threats in and around the Empire had been suppressed by Imperators, scribes and the line of Emperors. Enough so that many of the dangers the Imperators faced were straight out of myth and legend. He explained that the potential panic at the thought of some of the creatures that lived in the wild was deemed not conducive to the smooth running of the Empire, and thus the information was censored.

"I thought the Imperators were meant to be the Emperor's enforcers in the Empire?" I asked in between visits from medical professionals.

"They are," replied Simon. "But our true purpose is to seek out and destroy any threat to the stability of the Empire. To that end we largely leave the run of the mill, every day threats, such as breaking up rebellions, murders and so on to the regular soldiers like those commanded by Kyle. We go after the big prey. The ones that you don't see or hear about. Whether monster or man."

"So Rya wasn't the first...thing, that you have fought?"

He shook his head. "Nor will she be the last. She was, however, an enigma and has raised many more questions. The abilities she showed, the infection spreading through Cassius, to her revealing that her family had been taken hostage...something that the guiding body behind the Imperators goes to great lengths to prevent. All of these things are currently unknowns. I have many people working on it to make sure that they don't stay as such."

I nodded. Every day we had scribes coming in with various pieces of information gleaned from their vast records. So far, nothing had directly cured Cassius' affliction but it had seemingly slowed, for which I and the others were eminently grateful. Cassius looked no better than when I had first seen him, his skin pallid and waxy, pale to the point of looking like he had never seen the sun, yet the veins in his body stood out thick and black. He still hadn't come to, mumbling incoherently and thrashing in fever filled dreams. Ella had barely left his side, only doing so when dragged away to sleep by Kyle or Tyrgan.

As for myself, I felt fine, the hole in my shoulder having long healed thanks to Seya, who was rewarding her heroic efforts in getting both Cassius and I here, as well as healing me, by letting herself be fussed over by several handlers. The ecstasy I felt in my stomach as she was groomed was incredibly intense and made for an awkward moment when I practically purred instead of responding to a pretty nurse's question.

As such I was itching to get out of the hospital. To hold a blade in my hands, to practice Kaschan. Something physical, if only to take my mind off of Cassius's plight. So it was that on the sixth day of enforced bed rest I slipped out the window in the early morning hours, and spent some time practicing the seven circles in the warm glow of dawn. Savouring the fresh air I had just begun the fourth circle before I was pounced on mid-movement by my shadow panther. It turned out that having a wrestling match with your giant panther was not conducive to the healthy sleep and rest required by the patients of the hospital. Or at least that was what I was told when I received a stern dressing down from the ward matron, a terrifying woman whose finger wagging knew no bounds. Simone however just burst out laughing and interrupted the matron, stating that if I was fit enough to wrestle a creature that was large enough to swallow me whole then I could do as I liked, and, perhaps more importantly, sleep wherever I wanted.

After that encounter I stayed with Seya, sleeping with her in the large outbuilding that the hospital had on the premises, (nothing is more comfortable than sleeping on a giant panther, though you do sometimes get slimily awakened by a large, wet tongue), and running with her in the extensive forest that the hospital owned. Simone explained that the hospital was somewhat used to dealing with patients who were bonded to Great Hearts, as although most wounds healed before a hospital was required, sometimes, as in my case, a strange or especially vicious wound was received requiring immediate attention. As such, the hospital had procedures and facilities in place to care for the creatures themselves, and Seya was certainly making the most of the attention.

Cats.

After the eighth day of worrying about Cassius, Kyle found me outside and called me over excitedly.

"Calidan! Come inside, we may have something."

"Coming!" I yelled back and sprint towards him, my bond enhanced physique allowing me to reach him before he had disappeared back inside. "What's going on?" I asked.

"Word reached the Emperor of what we faced and the danger still plaguing Cassius." Kyle replied. "A messenger has arrived, the Emperor and his cohort will be here this afternoon. You have to get ready."

The Emperor! I looked down at my mud and cat tongue stained clothes, before looking back at Kyle helplessly. He laughed, "Don't worry, after several years of knowing your size I took the liberty to get some clothes ordered when we first caught up with you. New clothes are waiting in your room."

I breathed a sigh of relief. Meeting the Emperor was bad enough, at least I wouldn't have to meet him looking like I had come out worse with a fight with a bush!

Several hours later Tyrgan, Kyle and myself flanked the entry into Cassius' room, awaiting the Emperor's presence. I was wearing a black and silver laced jerkin, complete with matching trousers and black boots. Kyle shared my opinion on plain, practical clothes, something obvious as he was wearing largely similar clothing, but with a blue and black gambeson instead of jerkin. I could see that he was desperately wishing that he had his full Andurran military dress uniform. Tyrgan, on the other hand was wearing a practical leather fighting outfit, complete with twin Tyrant blades hanging at his hips.

He shrugged at Kyle's questioning look before wryly replying, "I am a civilian these days; one of the benefits of this is the ability to wear what I want."

I grinned. Tyrgan was enjoying this.

Suddenly the sound of heavy boots echoed through the hospital. The doors at the end of the hallway burst open, two keen eyed and scarred individuals leading the way, and two more - a man and woman - flanking the biggest man I had ever seen. He stood nearly as high as the ceiling, his massive shoulders spanning near the width of two of his body guards. Clad in shining, golden plate armour with plumed helmet under his arm, he ate up the distance between us in massive strides, his sheer strength visible in his movements; he moved as though the armour weighed nothing, his bodyguards moving quickly to keep up.

"Major General Kyle," came a booming voice, rumbling like thunder. "It is good to see you. I wish it were under better circumstances."

Kyle snapped a perfect military salute, waiting for a nod from the glorious man in front of him to stand at ease. "Thank you sir, it is good to see you too, I apologise that we have to impose on your time."

"Nonsense," the Emperor replied, waving a giant hand. "From what I hear we have heroes in our midst. I am excited to meet them." His piercing silver eyes settled on me like a physical weight as he spoke. A wink and he continued walking, almost passing Tyrgan before a golden plated fist lashed out, streaming towards Tyrgan's head. Faster than thought Tyrgan ducked and stepped into the inside of the giant man, hands down by his sides. Chuckling the Emperor took Tyrgan gently by the shoulders before embracing him.

"Still as fast as ever old friend," he reverberated. "It is excellent to see you; I have missed your tacit humour at court."

Tyrgan laughed freely, "My lord, it is a great pleasure to see you again…" he grinned wolfishly, "though you still telegraph your punches!"

At first I thought a storm had suddenly come upon the hospital before realising that the Emperor was laughing, tears in his eyes. He clapped Tyrgan on the shoulder and laughing some more stepped away, saying only that they would catch up before he left.

And that left me.

The gigantic god made flesh strode towards me, his laughing face reverting to a serious frown. Each massive stride sent a jolt right through me; surely this was a man whom could conquer cities single handed! I realised that the jolting sound had stopped and that the Emperor was standing in front of me, a hint of a smile on his lips.

"I believe it is customary to bow to one's Emperor…" spoke the thunderous voice. I cursed inwardly, so shocked with the sight that I had completely forgotten myself and the lessons instilled in me by Brother Gelman and Kyle. I bowed deeply, eyes on the floor, and when I felt a touch on my shoulder I started back up, only for my eyes to widen in shock. The Emperor was on one knee in front of me, his mighty hand on my shoulder yet still towering above my gangly frame.

"From what I hear, we have much to thank you for young Calidan. Both you and your friends. You have faced a great evil and triumphed. It is comforting to know that the next generation of this Empire's defenders are formidable indeed."

For perhaps the first time in my life my words were lost to me. I forced a smile and grunted some kind of acknowledgement, the smile on the Emperor's face growing broader as he realised the effect his presence was having.

"I look forward to talking with you more Calidan," he said, drawing himself back up onto both feet. "Perhaps next time the discussion will have two participants." With that he gave me a wink, and smiled at the sound of Tyrgan's stifled laughter. "You were as bad once Tyrgan… or did you forget?" The indignant look on Tyrgan's face was priceless.

The Emperor turned towards the room and rumbled, "Now let us see about saving a young man," and strode forwards.

We slowly sidled in behind him, unwilling to miss whatever was about to happen. The four bodyguards stood outside, each nodding to Tyrgan as he entered the room.

The Emperor had taken Ella gently by the hand, and spoke softly, "Love is the best and greatest thing in this world, and to see one's love in pain is an agony unbeknownst to others." A shadow crossed the Emperor's face as he said this. "I hear you are strong, mighty, able to beat even Tyrgan - and let me tell you that is no mean feat. No matter what, remember this in any dark days ahead." He kissed the top of her head and withdrew to the forlorn figure on the hospital bed.

Cassius was writhing, lost in some twisted fever dream. The golden figure placed a hand on his head and removed the covers, nodding as he looked at the thick, black veins covering his body.

"This is something I have seen before," he said, "many years ago. An insidious magic that I had long thought gone from this world."

"Can you help him?" I asked, hope tingeing my words. He smiled and spoke in a strange, musical language,

"Gorenthe, Ellowethe, Tangith
Nigellione, Routenth, Fireene"

As he spoke a golden glow shone from the hand that he had placed on Cassius' head. Ella gasped as the black veins started to recede, moving down and away from the source of the light. Light seemed to suffix Cassius, chasing after the darkness in his blood. As the Emperor spoke the final word he placed his other hand on the black pit of a wound on Cassius' thigh. Cassius arced and a hoarse, piercing scream broke out of his throat, causing me to hug Ella close as she cried in sympathetic agony. The bright light poured into his leg, like before forcing the blackness away from the source of the light. Trapped between two creeping sources of golden power the blackness squirmed, writhing in Cassius' body before being incinerated.

A silence fell. Cassius' screaming stopped and he breathed easily, the colour coming back to his pale skin. Seemingly without a thought the Emperor waved a hand over the wound in his leg, and everyone gasped as the muscle and skin knitted together, leaving no trace of the near mortal wound. Finally the Emperor stepped back and nodded in satisfaction.

"He is whole again." There was a collective sigh of relief from the gathered audience. "However as I said, the shadow is an insidious menace and the longer it stays within a host," my ears pricked here thinking it an odd choice of words, suggesting that the shadow was alive, "the more damage it can do. Cassius may have dark thoughts, moods or moments. It will be up to you," he indicated Ella and me, "to remind him of the good in life at times like those."

We both nodded gravely and he bestowed upon us a beatific smile. "Good, I am glad that he has such firm friends in his time of need."

The Emperor turned to leave, pausing at the room exit. He turned back: "I am afraid that I have another pressing appointment that I must attend to. But I have an evening to myself in three nights hence. If you would deign to join me, Cassius included, I would love to receive you and hear more of your journeys."

We all murmured in the affirmative, still shocked at the awesome and open display of power. The Emperor smiled, turned and left.

A flicker of eyelids.
A change in breathing.
Eyes open.
"Where...where am I?"

A strangled sob broke from Ella as she flung her arms around Cassius, swiftly joined by myself, with Tyrgan and Kyle in the background. A bewildered and more importantly, healed Cassius was left confused in the midst of joyous celebration which lasted a good five minutes, before being rudely interrupted and shushed by the demon matron.

CHAPTER EIGHTEEN
EMPEROR

~

WITH THE SHADOW GONE CASSIUS'S recovery was swift. His colour returned from deathly white to the more usual northern paleness exhibited by members of our village. Some might not notice much of a difference but in truth the overnight improvement was astounding. So much so that if I hadn't known better, I would have suspected him of having a Great Heart bond.

Ella was torn between laughing, crying and anger. The latter as a result of Cassius being silly enough to get hurt in the first place; the life of a street urchin makes for a pitiless existence, where getting hurt means death, whether by starvation or whichever slumlord or bully happens to rule your local area. Thankfully the anger was short lived and Cassius spent more time being subjected to hugs, tears and kisses than angry words, something that I am sure that he appreciated.

As a group we filled him in on the events of the previous few weeks, starting from the moment that he got hurt. Cassius said he remembered nothing after getting hit with Rya's shadow lance and maintained that it was just like going to sleep and waking up the next day, with no memory of the in between. I knew my friend however, and something didn't ring quite true about that statement. Watching closely I could see that Cassius was holding something back regarding his time spent unconscious. Every now and then, when he thought that he wasn't being watched, darkness and pain flashed across his face. I could swear that when this happened his eyes turned darker, as though covered in shadow, but I put it down to bad memories of the past few weeks. As mistakes go, this is far from the biggest I have made but certainly ranks up in the top ten.

Three days after the Emperor's visit Cassius was up and about, looking almost as hale and healthy as he had before our fateful meeting with Rya. We dressed in our finest clothes, all tailored on location thanks to Kyle, and took a carriage to the Emperor's citadel. And citadel it was! My time in Forgoth had led me to realise that the Emperor wouldn't live in something as small as the village leader's hut back home, but it in no way prepared me for the sheer scale of the building that we approached. It was monstrous.

Set back from the main city of Anderal itself, overlooking the city on a bluff rose a monolithic, obsidian spire. Surrounded by three guard walls, each higher than the last and capable of providing overlapping fire against any attacking army; the spire rose majestically above the city. It was a thing of breathtaking beauty. The black material of the spire seemed to drink in light, reminding me disconcertingly of the shadow abilities of Rya, but a comforting hand from Tyrgan set me at rest. He, of course, had been here many times before, probably longer than he had been in Forgoth, and likely knew every detail of the building. Furthermore he knew, and explained, that whilst the spire was intimidating from the outside, the inside was largely spacious and plush, filled with rooms for guests and not the many torture chambers that some (myself included) imagined when first gazing at the structure. He continued his explanation and added that the spire was a surviving building from before the Andurran Empire. Whilst it looked obsidian no one knew how it had been built, who had carved it, or even truly what it was made of as the structure couldn't be damaged by any known methods.

After navigating the three intimidating gates that separated each wall, each with a heavy portcullis and a well drilled squad of soldiers who meticulously checked our papers against the list of VIPs due to visit the Emperor, our carriage successfully pulled up in front of the spire. Waiting to greet us was an extremely formal man; someone who looked like he took life far too seriously. He introduced himself as the master of the house and directed us into the spire, pausing just briefly enough to allow us time to marvel at the inside of the grand structure. Once the astonished gasps had ceased he ushered us towards a platform at the corner of the room. When we were all aboard he reached up and pulled a lever in the wall. Worried murmurs filled the air as the platform rose steadily. Today I know that this was just a clever hidden counterweight system, but at the time it seemed nothing short of magic. The platform slowed as we neared the top of the spire, the floor below a dizzying drop...whoever had designed this building hadn't given much thought to safety rails.

Upon reaching the top the master of the house took us through the sole door. He parted thick velvet curtains and we emerged, blinking in the sun, to see the world stretching into the distance. My eyes drank in the sight. Together we walked onto the balcony of the spire, Cassius, Ella and myself barely noticing the magnificent, godlike man who turned to watch our arrival. Our eyes were purely for the world that extended forever beneath our gaze. None of us had seen a sight like it, not even from the tallest building in Forgoth. Neither Cassius nor I had joined the men in their seasonal trek to the top of Trystopk - the tallest mountain in the range in which our village had been nestled. Climbing it was perilous and deemed purely the realm of hardy men or women who were fully grown. As such even the two mountain-born couldn't have asked for a better view.

After allowing a few minutes for the gasps from our party to diminish, the Emperor winked at Tyrgan and Kyle before striding over to Ella, Cassius and myself. He clapped me on the shoulder, bent low to kiss Ella on the cheek and, having reached his target, picked Cassius up and placed him on his shoulders. A strangled yelp emerged from Cassius who hadn't seen his assailant coming, and suddenly found himself an extra eight feet in the air above a perilous drop. A deep, reverberating chuckle broke out of the Emperor's throat.

"It is good to see you up and about Cassius," the Emperor began once his chuckling had died away. "Your friends were greatly concerned for your health when last we met."

"Thank….thank you?" came a stuttering reply from Cassius. I paused with barely held in delight. Cassius had no idea who had picked him up and didn't dare look down for fear of the height. The Emperor solved that problem by picking Cassius up and spinning him upside down whilst holding him out in front of him. To his credit Cassius didn't scream, and as he beheld the Emperor's awe inspiring gaze I saw a rapturous expression cross his face.

"It is a great pleasure to finally meet you Cassius," the Emperor rumbled. "In case you haven't figured it out yet, I am indeed the Emperor and the person you are here to meet." He place Cassius down on the ground, "So if you are done gazing out across the vast expanse of my Empire perhaps you would like to join the others over at the banquet table?" he chuckled with a wink at my awestruck friend.

Tyrgan laughed to himself as he watched the Emperor's antics with Cassius.

"Is he always like this? I asked quietly to him.

"Am I always like what young Calidan?" came the Emperor's reply, impressing me with the acuity of his hearing.

"He means acting like an immature child," Tyrgan interjected, a smile softening his words.

"Hah! Oh Tyrgan, I have missed your voice here." The laughter in the Emperor's words could be felt almost as a physical blow. "And to you Calidan, yes. My court often wishes for their Emperor to be more statesmanlike, but I wonder where the fun is in that?"

I grinned at the look on the Emperor's face. His laughter was infectious. He clapped a hand on my shoulder and gently steered me towards the fully laden banquet table set up in a part of the balcony. After a short welcoming speech he bade us to dig in, and save our questions for later.

And what a feast it was. I had never eaten anything like it (and rarely since). There were platters of exquisitely roasted meats, steaming slightly in the cooler altitude of the spire's top, several bowls of root vegetables - potatoes being the only one I recognised, and thinly sliced pieces of a dark meat that I was told was from a great boar. Certainly the taste was familiar but lacked the burnt flavour that our bloody steaks, seemingly eaten a lifetime ago, had. Heaps of fresh fruit and vegetables, warm crusty bread and mouth watering salted butter completed the menu; all paired with a choice of fine wines and, much to Kyle and Tyrgan's delight, ales.

Suffice to say that Cassius and I ate as only growing boys can eat. Yet even his prodigious appetite couldn't match mine. At first I ate sparingly, uncertain of the rules of etiquette that applied to this informal feast, but one look at the Emperor tearing into a roast turkey leg with gusto, using his hands and not the immaculately laid out cutlery made my mind up for me. From that point on anything on the table was fair game. Past when everyone else had finished, when even

Cassius and the Emperor were sitting back groaning, I still ate, consuming vast quantities of food and enjoying every mouthful. I would blame (and rightly so) my increased appetite on the bond with Seya but I also like to think that I am secretly a great glutton, one who just happens to do too much running around and fighting for my life to add on any weight.

After I was finally sated, or at least embarrassed enough to halt my eating when all the others had long ago finished, the Emperor leant back in his chair, one of the livery clad servants bringing a bottle of golden spirit and a selection of long brown sticks. He offered everyone these 'cigars', and poured a generous dose of the shining liquid into glasses for everyone.

"This is a six, six eight Mendrothian whisky," he explained as he poured. "Extremely rare and widely regarded as one of the greatest spirits ever made. Drink slowly and savour because it is unlikely that you will taste its equal again."

He raised his glass.

"A toast! To you, brave citizens of my Empire. Especially you three younglings. A toast to your bravery in the face of true darkness, and your unflinching loyalty to the greater good of the Empire." We drank, the golden liquid spreading a warm glow throughout my body, leaving an aftertaste of fire tempered with honey. The three young people in the group coughed and spluttered, to the others' amusement. The Emperor shook his head, laughter dancing in his eyes, "An affinity for fine whisky comes with age; keep practising and one day you will be able to unlock and savour its great mysteries!"

He waited for the chuckles from around the table to die down and raised his glass again. "Finally, a toast for fallen friends. Let them be at peace and no longer suffering in this dark world of ours."

Memories of Brother Gelman flooded my mind at the toast and tears sprang unbidden to my eyes. They silently started to pour when the dark memory of his death melded with those of my parents, family and whole village. Though it happened a long time ago, somehow that toast, in a safe place with friends, unlocked my long buried feelings. Through blurry eyes I could see that Cassius was suffering similarly, silent sobs wracking his body. As we drank I felt Tyrgan put his arm around me, lending me his strength and support. Kyle and Ella hugged Cassius, not judging but understanding, and ensuring that neither of us felt we were alone. Whilst none of them - not even Ella, of that I was certain - knew what we had experienced in the past, I believe to this day that they all knew something terrible had happened, something that neither of us were able to come to peace with. They were right. Neither of us have ever come to terms with what happened to our village, and that has been the driving force behind the course of our lives. Even as fully fledged Imperators, fighting dark and twisted evil throughout all the corners of the Empire, the memory of that night still burned within us. Driving us forward.

After the tears had subsided and with the golden liquid warming our stomachs, the Emperor leant forward and with another show of power, pressed a finger to each cigar. When he removed it the ends were aflame.

"You young ones may not enjoy this so feel free to desist at any point," he rumbled. And indeed on the first puff it felt as though I was breathing in the ash from the fabled Lorcion mountain of fire. Ella immediately put hers down, wise in her youth and well aware of her tastes. Cassius and I however were not so readily put off; our young brains, already swimming from the abundant alcohol, were determined to show off our quality to the Emperor. And that is the story of how both of us are remembered at the Emperor's court as the two who vomited off the top of the world.

Emperor's laughter aside it wasn't that bad an experience really. And certainly if you are going to be throwing your guts up, a jaw-dropping view makes the experience much more bearable. I do, however, pity anyone who was walking underneath the trajectory of our combined emittance...thankfully I never heard of anyone being directly hit, but rumour had it that one of the Emperor's guards was several paces from being covered. I'm sure that would have just made the Emperor laugh all the harder.

As we recovered, sipping water, Ella's eyes dancing as she smirked at both of us, the Emperor began to talk. He conversed with

Kyle and Tyrgan about events in the north, how Forgoth faired and any suggestions that they had for improvements; whether to the military or civil structures. Behind the laughing face was a keen intellect, sharp as a razor and it was easy to see why the Emperor ruled (aside from the fact that no one would dare challenge him for leadership of course...those that did tended to disappear).

Eventually we turned to more recent events. By that point Cassius and I had recovered sufficiently to enter into the conversation and we appraised the Emperor of everything he wanted to hear about Rya, the weeks hunting her, and the fight in the forest. His gaze often landed on me as we spoke. If I didn't know better I would think that an almost hungry gleam entered his gaze when we spoke of Seya, her bond to me and how she brought us to the Imperator hospital.

"A Great Heart bond is extremely rare," he said once there was a gap in the conversation. "As you are probably aware there are several known Great Heart bonded pairs in my service. Their abilities and usefulness is..." again the hungry look, "incalculably valuable to the Empire." I nodded, I was indeed aware that the Great Hearts were collected by the Emperor.

The Emperor was silent for a little while, the great cogs of his mind doubtless whirring away. Suddenly he rose from his chair and intoned: "Calidan, Ella and Cassius, please come and stand in front of me." We jumped to our feet, wondering at what had suddenly prompted the change from the jovial Emperor to the now Imperial one who stood before us.

"Calidan, I shall start with you first. As a Great Heart bonded, for you there can only be one path. I am sorry but the Empire has dire need of you and your abilities... will you answer the call?"

In my later years I recognised that this was a somewhat unfair position to put a child in; however the Emperor's charisma and my long burning desire for vengeance ensured that I replied in the affirmative. An almost predatory smile flicked across the Emperor's face as he inclined his head towards me.

"I thank you for this Calidan. From now on you will enter the Imperator school. It will be hard, maybe even deadly. You must be strong, both mentally and physically. But I have no doubt that in eight years you will be standing here again in front of me, ready for action!" I grinned, eight years and I would be strong enough to fight. That shadow demon best be ready.

The Emperor turned his attention to Ella and Cassius. "Both of you have proven yourselves strong, intelligent, loyal and incredibly brave. I would be honoured if you would also join the ranks of the Imperators. However unlike Calidan you do have the choice and I beg you to carefully consider before you answer. It is a hard path that you will tread, both during the school and after. It may often seem that darkness assails you from all sides, and in some cases as you know, that may in fact be true. All I can promise is that if you make it through the school you will have the abilities and aptitude to conquer all that attempts to waylay you."

Cassius and Ella looked at each other, then me. With a firm nod at each other they stepped forward hand in hand. "We accept," was all they said, much to the Emperor's visible delight.

"Fantastic!" he replied, clapping his hands together. "I am sure that you will both go far and that the Imperators will be lucky to have you." He indicated all three of us, "Simone will come to you in two weeks to take you to the Academy. I suggest that you use the remaining time wisely, neither Imperators nor Imps get much in the way of free time."

CHAPTER NINETEEN
TREATS

~

TWO WEEKS LATER CASSIUS, ELLA and I stood before the foreboding Academy. The building itself looked pleasant, stone clad with a wooden exterior, but due to the stories that we had heard, the gated compound exuded nothing but menace.

Kyle and Tyrgan had dropped us off at the gate with many hugs and words of encouragement following two weeks of relaxed living. Fine food, wine and ale had helped our continued recovery, especially with Cassius who looked fully restored to his old self. Certainly Ella believed he was fine; the night after meeting the Emperor she took Cassius into her room, one of many that had been set aside for us by the Emperor's aides, and whilst he would never kiss and tell the beaming grin the next day answered many unspoken questions. At thirteen years old I still didn't really understand the need for female company, but looking at how happy Cassius (and Ella when we next saw her) was, I got an inkling of the fun that could be had together. I was incredibly proud of my friends, and overjoyed that they could take solace in each other, something that I was positive would prove useful at the Academy and through whatever dangers we would face. Besides, my own drive for sex would set in soon enough...for at the Academy was one who stole my heart.

So together we entered the compound, walking through the thick walled gates. From the outside, with the gates shut, one could be forgiven for mistaking the building as a fort or minor castle, because in essence that is what it was. The walls were high and imposing, thicker than a man walking ten paces. To assault this fort would be at a high cost to any attacking force. However, once through the gates we did not find the expected stone buildings of a keep, but instead wood clad stone, lending a semblance of peaceful nature to the many buildings within. And when I say many, I mean it. The compound had forty two buildings, ranging from dormitories, pantries and cellars to training yards, teaching rooms and offices. There were two armouries, one with blunted wooden and metal weapons for training, the other kept under lock and key for actual combat use. Three dining halls, one for Imps, the second for Imperators, and the third for VIP (aka the Emperor) dining. Three sets of dormitories separated much like the dining halls, but the third building was for Instructors, whilst the second was for fully fledged Imperators. The difference being that for the Instructors it was a permanent home, whereas Imperators may just 'swing by' in between missions. In short, it was a big place.

We were met at the entrance by a short, heavy set man with a thick, brown beard that curled towards his stomach. A thick scar extended along his right cheek, narrowly missing his eye, and as he extended his hand the three of us couldn't help but notice the burn tissue covering his extended limb. He introduced himself as Instructor Tiberius Kane, Imperator of over thirty years, and retired from active service the previous year to act as teacher for the next generation of Imperators. Whilst his visage may have appeared stern Instructor Kane proved to be extremely friendly, his thick, full bellied laughter and guileless eyes enhancing a very genuine character. I warmed to him immediately.

The instructor walked us to our dormitory, explaining that it was mixed gender, with eight to a dorm and shared bathrooms. We would all be in the same dorm, currently occupied by only two others. The Academy took in applicants at any point in the year, usually brought in by Imperators on their travels who had met an individual they thought had specific skills. New attendees could be any age between ten and eighteen and would all bunk together. Once a dorm was full, lessons would start one month later. Whilst this sounded haphazard, Instructor Kane remarked that the first month, (and before if there was much time before a dorm being fully filled) was no more than a series of tests designed to ensure that any potential candidate destined for the long years at the Academy had the required mental and physical fortitude to (in Kane's words) 'survive'.

This meant that we had a waiting period of at least one month until our first proper Imperator lessons, as well as an unknown amount of time remaining until our dorm was full. As such we three and the other two current members in the dorm would be joining Instructor Kane for afternoon exercise and weapons training. The mornings were left to fully recuperate, though I had no doubts about our fitness levels being up to the task. It was understandable; a new recruit could be completely new to the advanced physical exercise required by the Academy. Instructor Kane was ensuring that we would be in a better position to begin the proper training once we had a full complement of fellow students.

We were finally dropped off at the dormitory, with instructions to find our way to the dining hall two hours hence. Sitting at a low table playing cards were two boys. One was small, without any trace of fat, whose age was difficult to discern. A deeply tanned, pointed face and sharp features mirrored seemingly very fast hands as he dealt the deck of cards. The other boy looked to be about fifteen, broad shouldered with scarred hands. A dusting of blonde hair covered his face and chin, relatively rare amongst the people of Forgoth, though I did not know if it was so uncommon within the capital. He was glowering at his cards as though an angry gaze would help change his presumably unfortunate hand. As we entered the gaze of both boys flicked up, an easy going grin spreading across the larger boy's face and a wary one on the other's.

Standing up, the sandy haired boy walked over to us and extended his hand. Greeting us warmly he introduced himself as Damien, the forgotten son of a caravan guard. Indicating the boy who hadn't moved from the chair he introduced him as Rikol, a street rat from the streets of Rynose, Markenchia - a sun baked city in the lands south of the Empire. Introducing ourselves and our relative origins, (more difficult in Cassius and mine's case as no one had heard of the village or surrounding location), Damien invited us to sit down and play cards.

After losing three rounds in a row to Rikol, Ella reached out and swiftly snagged his arm as he dealt the fourth hand. Deftly she plucked out several cards hidden up his sleeve. Instead of outrage at being caught Rikol just grinned, with no trace of shame or humility. Ella smirked right back and clasped his hand, thumb quickly touching several locations in a strange pattern. Whatever she did, Rikol's grin grew wider and he laughed out loud before standing up, bowing comically and then giving her a hug. Cassius and I watched on, bewildered at the whole process.

"That's the first time I've seen him so animated!" said Damien, as much at a loss as we were.

"That's because so far you haven't been any fun," came Rikol's reply, his accent melodic and mellow. "To know that there is a fellow streeter in the dorm will alleviate any boredom I experience with the rest of you!"

We all grinned. Now that the tension had been broken, Rikol appeared warm and friendly; his earlier aggressive demeanour vanishing.

Soon the five of us were enjoying hearty banter over a series of (hopefully) non-rigged card games. Two hours later we laughed and cajoled our way to the dining halls where the laughter swiftly vanished. Multiple tables of students looked up as we entered the Imp dining hall. It was arrayed so that any student could sit at any table, with roaring fires around the outside of the room. Mountains of food sat on each groaning, wooden table and dining staff hauled out steaming trays of meat, vegetables and dumplings. It would have been inviting if a silence hadn't descended, with close to seventy pairs of eyes silently watching us enter. It was disconcerting until Rikol waved, farted and cartwheeled to the table. Just like that the ice was broken and chatter, laughter and content eating once again filled the room.

Rikol and Damien proved to be excellent companions. Rikol knew, or at least professed to know, every card game and trick in the Empire and beyond. His repertoire also involved having kissed a princess, stolen from a king (which some might say to be the same thing), eaten every dish in the world, and of course, excessive boasting.

Damien was the complete opposite, calm and restrained where Rikol was fire and passion. He and Cassius hit it off immediately, two kindred spirits of broad shouldered, good natured individuals. Damien knew many drinking games and what's more was able to hold his alcohol; a mightily impressive feat and worthy of great adulation by three young teenagers. He explained that he had been taught the sword by his father until age eight and had until that time been raised on the road, singing songs and dancing the night away. Once further into his drink he revealed that when his mother died of a wasting sickness his father had decided to leave, once again attaching himself to a caravan and leaving in the night. A sad tale to be sure, but Damien didn't seem to bear any ill will to his father, instead seemingly embracing that he knew him for as long as he had.

Together we drunkenly weaved back home, a five person line made of liquid, flowing from one side of the path to the other. Rikol was in the midst of singing a racy song at the top of his lungs when suddenly we were forced to pull up short by three large men. I say men; in actuality they were perhaps seventeen or eighteen, however they dwarfed both Cassius and myself. Damien fared a little better, his age and natural bulk making him seem at least a little significant compared to their size. Rikol and Ella when I looked for them had vanished into the darkness, their street smarts obviously recognising a dangerous situation.

"What's this then?" said the middle boy, cementing him in my albeit blurry and drunken view as the leader of this small band. "A bunch of pussies by the look of it, all tiny and tired. Doesn't make for good Imperators, does it lads?"

A silence followed his words, only interrupted by an ale filled burp by Cassius. The leader frowned and then repeated his words, "I said - does it lads?"

This time the two cottoned on to what the leader wanted and replied in the affirmative. Obviously brains weren't the biggest consideration of the Imperator who brought these two in.

Damien frowned at the three men in front, swaying in front of our group as if to protect us. That immediately solidified him in my eyes as a friend; not many would do such a thing when having just met. Cassius and I shared an amused smile - it hadn't even occurred to us to be afraid. The three would be assailants strode towards Damien, not caring that the two smaller members of our party had vanished. A grave mistake. As one of the cronies swung for Damien, big, meaty fists lumbering through the air, a rock flew out of the darkness and struck the leader in the buttocks. A howl filled the air as the leader swore at the top of his lungs, hands clutching his injured pride. As he spun, searching the darkness for his enemy, one lackey went down with a grunt, an elegant leg sweep spinning out of the black and connecting beautifully. Ella swaggered into the middle of the group, grinning at the much larger man she had just downed. With a roar the other ape charged at her only to fall on his back like he had been poleaxed. To the untrained eye Ella had just swayed, to mine she had hit three precise times whilst moving out of danger. The third hit to the solar plexus had left her opponent gasping for air.

Another rock sped out of the night hitting the leader who had been futilely searching the inky black. His face when he realised that his men were out of action was a sight to behold. As was Damien's - his look of awe at Ella's martial prowess forcing a chuckle to my lips.

"Are we done here?" I asked, stalking forward. "Or do you want to finish what you started?"

The leader, not particularly smart either, snarled and swung for me three times. Each time his blows hit nothing but air. I stopped playing and pointed behind him. He turned just in time to see Cassius step forward and deliver a single kick to his stomach, bowling him over to join his friends.

Ella grabbed Damien and strolled over with him to link arms with Cassius and myself. As we walked back to the dorm I looked straight into the darkness, "Nice throw, Rikol."

The shock on his face that I knew where he was amused me greatly. I extended a hand, "Come on, we still have time for you to teach us a new card game."

The next morning we woke to see Instructor Kane leaning against the door frame, an amused smile on his face.

"So I hear that you all had a fun night," he grinned. "Not bad for your first day!"

I smiled back, "It was rather more eventful than we were aiming for, that's for sure."

"I hear that three rather large first year students, six months into their training, repeatedly met with the ground yesterday...I'm impressed."

I nodded slowly, uncertain as to whether there was going to be a 'but'.

Kane winked at Ella, "I have to thank you for knocking them down so nicely; no permanent injuries and they received a much needed knock to their egos. Excellent work indeed." He paused, considering. "At the Academy infighting is, to some extent, expected. We do however draw the line at lethal force. No bladed weapons, no intent to kill. If this rule is broken then there will be a reckoning. One that, believe me, is not something you would come back from. Understood?"

We nodded grimly. He smiled. "Good, I will see you at the training grounds this afternoon. Enjoy the rest. It's not often you get much of it here."

With that he turned and left chuckling softly to himself.

As the door shut with a click Rikol snored and bolted upright, "Whaddeyup?" and promptly fell back to sleep to a chorus of laughter.

In the afternoon, with the sun's rays rippling through the surrounding forest we stood with Instructor Kane on the training ground, sweating lightly after the warm up that Kane had put us through. Well, not that lightly in the case of Damien and Rikol who were collapsed on the floor struggling to breathe. I thanked Tyrgan and Kyle silently, their arduous training regimens made Kane's seem relatively easy in comparison. That said, if this was the standard of the first day of exercise then I was positive that things would only get harder. In this I was right, but I doubt I could have comprehended just how hard it was going to be.

Once the warm up finished, Kane introduced five members of a second year dorm who all looked extremely keen at what was about to happen.

Kane clapped his hands to get our attention, "This is a training round to see your combat skills. Some newcomers to the Academy have received instruction in combat before coming here, others have not. I have brought along five willing volunteers whose objective is to push and assess you as part of furthering their own lessons." He smiled. "Remember that the objective is not to maim, cripple or kill. With that out of the way, one at a time get up and enjoy yourselves!"

Damien immediately stood. Eager, I think, to prove himself in the eyes of Ella. A similarly built second year stood and moved into the ring, an eager gleam in his eye. The two opponents bowed and Damien slipped into a boxing stance. The second year stood without moving, arms down by his sides. If Tyrgan had seen this the boy would have been running around the training ground for weeks. He had repeatedly drilled into us to never underestimate an opponent. Damien edged forward before launching out with a quick jab to the boy's face. He hit nothing but air; the opponent had employed one of the principle movements of Kaschan by shifting his weight in a circular motion, avoiding the blow and opening up new avenues of attack. Indeed Damien reeled back having been hit with two blows to the gut. He grimaced, steadying himself before launching a full attack, a flurry of boxing blows. A left hook nearly caught the second year before a roundhouse kick drove Damien into the floor.

"Enough!" called Kane. "Help him up."

The second year grinned and extended a hand. "Better than my first time," he said as he pulled Damien to his feet, "I lasted about a second." With that Damien exited the ring, grinning as he rubbed his head and Rikol rose up.

"I best take this before you guys make me look bad," he said, not looking too happy at the notion of brawling. If he had been fighting another street brawler, then much like Damien he might have done well. As it was Rikol was on the floor in two moves, allowed to get back up and then back down in another three. His one consolation was that his opponent, a fourteen year old boy, bruised his shin whilst mistakenly kicking Rikol's flailing elbow. Just like the previous match, when the bout ended a hand was extended and Rikol helped up with friendly advice. It made perfect sense to me. Whilst in the ring one was expected to fight, and fight well, but it was a training experience; breeding animosity wouldn't help any Imperator who may need to rely on his or her fellows in the future. Plus, undoubtedly each fighter had been on the receiving end of such an experience as we were having.

Cassius went next. When he got to the ring I noticed Instructor Kane sit more upright, his eyes taking in all details. The man knew that we three were the ones to watch. He wasn't mistaken, Cassius took down his opponent in three moves, ducking under a whistling hook, throwing an elbow into the sternum and twisting to deliver an elbow to the head. Instead of looking angry at Cassius for defeating their friend so easily, the other fighters applauded and started whispering, talk of the fluidity of his movement reaching my enhanced ears. Cassius extended a hand, brought the fallen fighter up and gave him a hug, thanking him for the bout and providing some advice of his own before exiting. Instructor Kane sat, finger on lips thoughtfully.

Ella stood up and flowed to the ring. She faced the largest opponent yet - word of her skills had spread quickly, and this fighter was eager to take her on. Swaying like the wind she dodged each and every strike with ease, letting her opponent tire himself out and drawing out the match. Eventually she ended it with a quick sweep and a knee on her opponent's throat, drawing more applause from the watching fighters. She smiled, curtsied mockingly to the watching audience and helped up the fallen fighter. Cassius practically glowed with admiration and love.

Finally it was my turn. I was aware that Instructor Kane knew what I was, as he had helped arrange facilities for Seya whilst at the Academy and so as I walked up I raised a questioning eyebrow to see if he wanted my full strength on display. A discreet shake of the head answered my question and so I turned to face my friendly foe without use of my additional abilities.

He proved to be relatively skilled, around sixteen years of age, lithe and the old scars on his hands suggested years of sword training. Unwilling to draw out the combat and highlight my skill set any more than I had to I moved around his body, behind him before he knew it and delivered a three hit combo, two kidneys and the side of the neck. When he woke a second later I was looking down at him with a somewhat worried expression (even without enhanced strength a combo like that can be easy to go over the top with). When he grinned up at me I smiled right back and told him to work on transitioning between circles. A nod of appreciation and then we were back off the training ground with Instructor Kane nodding thoughtfully.

"That's enough for now," he said, "I've seen what I have needed to see." He turned to us, "You three train these two for the rest of this afternoon," indicating Damien and Rikol, "I will see you same time here tomorrow." He walked away with a thoughtful expression, humming slightly.

That evening we ate even more than the previous night. The hard work out that we had received with Kane, plus the several hours of combat we worked with Damien and Rikol ensured that we were all starving. This time when we entered there was another suite of stares, but this time corresponding to whispers about the fight the night before and our skills displayed during the day. A space was made in the most central table and we were soon deep in conversation with people from all over the Empire, and indeed the world.

And that...that is when I first saw her.

CHAPTER TWENTY
TRIALS

~

IT BEGAN WITH THE WAVE of fire that was her hair. The colour was vivid, practically embodying passion and awakening a strange, unbeknownst hunger in me. Her eyes were a deep, dark green, like the grass on our journey through the endless sea, and her smile caused my stomach to be gripped as though in a vice. Thoughts of her even today still stir me to unleash ecstatic soliloquy - probably one of the few times hulking Cassius appreciates his insanity. Her name was Rinoa and she was my first.

Crush. First crush, not first love. Or indeed not quickly at any rate. The woman that had so besotted my young heart was sixteen, three years older than my own paltry thirteen, and as it is with the young a gap in age that large was a vast, unbreachable chasm; no matter how I tried. And how I did try, though to this day a large part of me yearns that I did not.

That night was only a glimpse, a spark of flame amongst the comparatively drab students. There for an instant and then extinguished as she moved on. But her image remained burned onto my retinas.

The next afternoon we assembled onto the training ground following our workout with Instructor Kane to see twice the complement of second years, as before all looking eager at the prospect of fighting some relatively skinny youths. Instructor Kane stood on the side lines, grinning at the shocked look on Damien and Rikol's faces. Thankfully he spoke up to reassure them before too long, letting them know that they were not required to fight in the session, and that two of the second years were there to walk them through the first steps of Kaschan.

With a look of relief Damien and Rikol peeled off from us and went to meet their temporary instructors, leaving Ella, Cassius and I to face six opponents.

Kane stepped forward, "This is much the same as yesterday except with, as you might have guessed, two against one. Same rules as before." He looked keenly at everyone present, "Well what are you waiting for? First lot up!"

This time Ella went first. She faced a tall seventeen year old boy and a willowy sixteen year old girl who approached warily. Obviously word had spread about her fighting prowess and the prospect of facing a small girl was certainly not seen as the easy option. It was obvious that the two had not fought together as a pair before, not flowing past each other smoothly like when Cassius, Ella and I practiced. Ella seized this advantage, circling until the boy was behind the girl, effectively blocking him out of the fight. The instant it happened she sped forward, ducked inside the girl's open handed strike, lancing her sternum with a blade of fingers, launched upward with a elbow to the girl's downward moving jaw and for good measure unloaded a spinning kick into her stomach, knocking her into the lumbering male.

Once he had extracted himself from the floor the male fighter stepped forward, unleashing a series of fast kicks at Ella, any of which would have sent her flying had they connected. The female variant of Kaschan largely revolves around fighting larger opponents - which is why Ella fought the girl first, as she was the greater threat. The man found this out in a painful manner, his leg crumpling when he tried to put weight on it. Each of the three kicks he had sent at Ella had been met with a blow to the inner thigh, barely visible as she moved. As he was off balance Ella finished the job that gravity was trying to accomplish by sweeping his other leg. With both opponents down she bowed to the clapping of her admiring peers and pulled both combatants up before heading back to us. Cassius's adoring grin was as amusing as ever.

I went next, facing off against two boys who also looked to be in the latter age range of being teenagers. Once again I threw a questioning glance at Kane and received the same shake of the head, and so again I ended the fight quickly. Dodging a fist aimed at my head I threw a kick into the rear of the first boy's knee, driving him to the ground. Spinning, I ducked the other boy's hook as he tried to take advantage of my assault on his friend and unleashed an uppercut to the gut, followed by a knee to the face. A swift roundhouse finished off the rising first attacker. Another round of applause and then it was time for Cassius.

Thirty bloody seconds later his foes were doubled over. One with a busted nose, the other clutching his crotch - Kaschan is certainly not an 'honourable' art, something that Tyrgan (and Ella) had ensured we learnt very quickly in our training. Kane chuckled as yet another round of applause came our way.

"It looks like Tyrgan is as effective a teacher as he was bodyguard," he said walking towards us. "Usually Imps haven't mastered the first seven circles of Kaschan until their third or fourth year." He paused to consider us. "Officially, proper training in Kaschan, like the rest of the studies that an Imp is expected to carry out, doesn't begin until your dorm is full. However I believe that I can arrange for a group of fourth years to meet in the evenings for extra training. Would you like to join them?"

We all nodded in the affirmative. Continuous training under Tyrgan had given us a drive to learn more and exercise constantly. Whilst drinking and sleeping in late was fun we knew that everything would change once the first year began proper.

This is how we ended up at the training ground in the evening, shortly after which I was laying on the floor - struck down by a pretty girl with flaming red hair.

The group of fourth years was very diverse. As age ranges for first years can be up to eighteen, the group was a mix of fourteen to twenty two year olds. I quickly realised that much like the second years had learnt about us, the fourteen year olds were not to be underestimated, adept at using their opponent's weight against them. Furthermore we all quickly found that the Kaschan skills shown by the group outclassed our own. Four years of training against multiple opponents of different heights, strengths and skills trumped our, albeit intensive, training against a limited pool of practitioners. They moved with speed, grace and deadly skill. We could put up a good fight but in the end each one of us got brought down in our first contest. And our second. And third.

The training in the evening was different to that of the afternoon. This was how true Imps trained; hard and vicious but without providing debilitating injuries. Perhaps more tellingly, this was how true Imps trained *in their spare time*. According to beautiful Rinoa who pulled me up to my feet this was a light session to work more on technique. Or at least that's what Ella told me she said, I was too busy trying to hide a serious side effect of her proximity.

The sparring was interspersed with advice on forms, techniques and working on the flowing seven circles of Kaschan. I say seven for that is what I was aware of at the time, however watching the fourth years I saw multiple forms and techniques that I was completely unaware of. In my hubris I had imagined that mastering the seven circles meant that I had finished my learning of this fighting system. I could not be more wrong. I managed to control my raging hormones long enough to ask Rinoa about the technique that she used to put me on the floor and whilst showing me (in lovely close proximity again I might add), she explained that the fourth years were aware of fourteen circles, the motions involved vastly more complicated than the original seven, and that she believed that there were at least twenty one, though was uncertain.

She continued in explaining that an Imperator was expected to specialise in at least three disciplines whilst holding an extremely high standard in all others available at the Academy. Some specialised in combat skills, whether weapons based or Kaschan, others in stealth and secrecy, and some in politics and negotiation. The Imperator Academy ensures creation of well rounded killers who can pass for nobility (and in some cases might be), but ensures that there is a plethora of skill sets, largely determined by the students' interests - or by instruction by the teachers. The result is a unit of highly skilled operatives who can be used by the Emperor for a range of situations, from sabotage and assassinations of foreign dignitaries (never being linked to the Empire of course), to military and political advisors. For myself and Cassius...we were destined to follow a darker path.

Over the next four weeks we trained daily. Rising early we dragged Rikol and Damien to the practice ground for gruelling early morning exercise followed by training in Kaschan. Cassius, Ella and I would instruct them in the seven circles and accompanying skill sets before setting some time to work on the various techniques and more advanced circles that we were learning from the fourth years. My competitive edge was out and I was determined to start winning victories against my opponents. In the afternoon we would train again with Instructor Kane, going for a light (comparatively) workout before sparring. He stopped bringing in second years and instead started instructing us in weapons training. Some of which we knew, namely swords, but a plethora of other weapons stood in the armoury and Kane was excited to get us to try them out. Finally in the evening we would complete our exhausting day with training with the fourth years.

I say exhausting. For the others, not for me. My bond with Seya meant that this amount of exercise didn't take much of a toll, and so whilst the others slept or rested I travelled to the forest where Seya had taken residence. She had been given an abode in the main compound but preferred the open sky, returning to the compound primarily for scratches from the serving staff. When this happened I was adamant that her purring could be heard throughout the Academy, perhaps interpreted by the students as thunder. As it was I spent most of the time trying to hide the fact that I was having hot flushes of pleasure travel through my body. The knowledge of Great Hearts was still highly secreted - Kane mentioned that only sixth year Imps upwards learnt about their existence, as well as Tyrant swords and, as he put it, *True Monsters*, and so only those higher up students would connect the dots.

So it was that on returning back from one of my visits to Seya I entered the dorm only to find that it held three more occupants than previously. The group was complete. The first year of Imperator training would start in four weeks time.

CHAPTER TWENTY ONE
ACADEMY

~

IT TURNED OUT THAT THE first proper day of Imperator Academy was much like the last few months. Tests of physical prowess in endurance, strength and combat, followed by various intelligence tests many of which were to determine something apparently known as 'IQ' - something that I believed, and still believe to this day, to be asinine. The physical tests held few challenges for anyone in the party, Ella, Sophia and Rikol failing on the higher weight areas of the strength challenges but easily passing the grade.

Sophia was the sixth member of our group, a sixteen year old girl with hair as white as snow. Tall and lithe she moved with an easy grace, the natural rhythm of a born hunter - unsurprising considering how she came from a nomadic clan from the Ryganthian steppes. A deep thinker, she had a somewhat faulty grasp of Low Gothic, but what she did say always held great meaning. Our number seven was Scythe, a nickname for Scytharanious, an eighteen year old boy from the Bolgan warrior tribe of the desert plains. Tall, dark skinned and wise he had quickly cemented himself into the group as a natural and charismatic leader, wrestling playfully or pitting feats of strength against Cassius and Damien yet happy to engage in a discourse on a multitude of subjects. Eighth was Kirok, a muscle bound mountain of a man from the Northern Reaches. He was gigantic, immensely strong and prone to intimidation, derogatory comments about women and excessive drinking. Kirok was not liked within the dorm. He had none of the charisma of Cassius or Scythe and all of the unbridled rage of a great boar. It is a great regret of mine that we turned away from him instead of trying to reform him through friendship. Perhaps if we had, life during our time at the Academy would have turned out differently.

Following completion of the initial day of the first year we were congratulated by Instructor Kane, handed a schedule and told to get an early night. Naturally we didn't, foolheartedly celebrating our early success until the early hours of the morning. Which is why all eight of us experienced a very unwelcome (and for many), unbalanced predawn run, during which there was at least three members of the group who had the lovely experience of revisiting the previous night's food. Kane ran at our side, pushing us faster and further than before, somehow managing to cajole, insult and berate whilst not breathing hard himself. In fact he seemed to thoroughly enjoy his early morning run. Ending it, after five gruelling miles, at the training grounds where he immediately picked up a long, wooden staff, twirling it skilfully before passing another to me; immediately attacking whilst the others collapsed in heaps, gasping for air.

For five furious minutes we fought - I gave no thought to drawing on the power of my bond, without the speed it brought I would have been quickly disarmed and defeated. As it was the skill with which Kane wielded the staff, alternating between lightning fast jabs and whirling defence meant that I had little chance to gain the upper hand. His unrelenting assault forced me around the yard, my muscles and lungs burning. Suddenly Kane stopped attacking and smiled warmly. I hesitantly smiled back before being flung off my feet by a massive roundhouse kick. Ten seconds and thirty yards later, when I had stopped sliding, I opened my eyes to see Kane standing with another man. A man who made Kirok look like a child; muscle bound doesn't even begin to cover it. Kane clapped the giant on the shoulder (he could only just reach it) before walking sedately towards me.

"Lesson one. Always be aware of your surroundings," he said jovially, as if I hadn't just been kicked by a man whose thigh was probably wider than my body. "Even when winded and under attack you have to know what is around you. Otherwise someone like Adronicus here can move in and take advantage...usually with something pointy!" He finished the lecture with a wink before extending a hand and hauling me from the floor.

"But up until that point, not bad. First time using a staff?" I nodded wearily. "Not bad at all, your enhanced speed and strength allowed you to use it fairly effectively, but against someone who knows what you are and adapts accordingly I bet you found it a bit frustrating?" Again I nodded. "Good!" He looked me in the eyes, all traces of humour gone. "What I'm trying to teach you Calidan is that you will undoubtedly come up against people, animals or in the very worst of cases, *true monsters,* against which your enhanced skills count for little if you don't have your own skills to back it up." He tossed the staff back at me. "So learn as much as you can, first without using your abilities and then relearn it again whilst using them. Do you understand?" This time I managed to grunt out a noise that resembled something like an affirmative. Or quite possibly a death rattle. Kane nodded, smiled and took me back towards the others who were on their feet, gazing with awe and fear at Adronicus towering over them. Each had been handed a staff and once I was back in line Adronicus began his lesson. The first of many.

Kane, it turned out, was not to be our only instructor. Whilst he was vastly skilled in combat he deferred to Adronicus, the weapons master, who for an hour in the morning took time away from working with the higher level students to come and train us personally. This sounds like an honour and well it might be but in reality it meant brutality. Adronicus was not known for his charm, wit or intelligence, but for the seemingly innate understanding of how to inflict the most damage to an opponent in the shortest space of time. As such his lessons consisted largely of abuse, roaring orders and frequently darting into a paired combat to prove a similar point to one I learnt earlier. As an older Imperator I understand now that Adronicus was testing each student to see if they had the gumption to keep going, for he surely didn't seem so bad in the later years (either that or we got more used to his ways - I never did quite decide on that). The real question on my lips as a youth however was how a man that large and bulky could move so damnably fast.

Following Adronicus' 'lesson' we crawled back to the dorm, where following a mighty breakfast we all promptly passed out, only to be awakened once again by Kane who laughed as we dragged ourselves out of bed, laughed as we followed him to a teaching room and laughed again as we sat down at a series of tables. And thus began the real instruction, courtesy of 'Instructor' Kane. For six hours spanning either side of lunch we undertook study in every conceivable subject ranging from languages, law, history and math to military strategy, human biology and ethology. Twice a week we were taken to learn survival skills in the wild (something that Cassius and I had no problem with thanks to the Tracker's training) and even spent time in the Academy's own forge, learning how to smith tools. It was as varied a curriculum as you could want, fitting in with the concept of Imperators being more than just a weapon, yet each day was punctuated with combat training.

As time passed we began to get into rhythm, our minds changing much like our bodies, becoming stronger, faster and more defined. Combat training in the evening with the fourth years had accelerated Cassius, Ella and my martial skills at a prodigious rate. Whilst still not being able to (fairly) best any of the other fighters in the evening session, bouts were becoming more protracted and we were forcing our opponents to work up a sweat. Cassius in particular was becoming devastating with weaponry. Naturally strong, he exhibited fluid ease when wielding a wide array of implements, seemingly able to pick up any weapon, heft it a few times and then fight like he had trained with it all his life; innately understanding its individual quirks and oddities.

As astonishing as his skill was with practically any weapon, when he held a sword it became something else, a perfect extension of his body. So sublime was his movement that even Adronicus grudgingly nodded his approval. Sword fights between the two became the talk of the Academy and many students 'accidentally' found themselves near the training grounds during our morning session just to watch. The evening sessions with the fourth years became a queue to fight Cassius and the session had to be relegated to swords only for the latter half in order to allow Cassius time to practice with something other than a sword. Indeed he became the first person to finally defeat a fourth year, five months into our first year training. His speed with the blade grew and grew and he managed to lure his opponent into a downward strike before taking his hand and head in a seamless blur. The fighter, a nineteen year old man, took off his helmet and smiled before embracing Cassius in a bone crushing hug. From that point on Cassius began readily defeating opponents, becoming an ever greater threat to Adronicus - much to his booming delight.

Suffice to say in comparison to Cassius the rest of the dorm looked practically useless with weapons. I was skilled with a blade thanks to more often than not fighting for my life against Tyrgan, but Cassius could, and would, soundly defeat me. Kirok's fighting skills lay in a borderline sexual relationship with axes. Not the usual woodcutting tools that I had grown up with but the giant double headed war axes used by men of the mountain tundra. He expressed a deep disgust of any other type of weapon, only acquiescing to training with others when Adronicus defeated him with ten different weapons, the last being only a tree branch. Sophia was a master of the bow, able to draw, fire and hit four targets before I had hit one. More so she could do it whilst riding a horse, an amazingly impressive sight. Scythe lived up to his name, his weapon of choice being blades known as kamas, essentially miniature scythes. With these he became a whirlwind of refined chaos, an unorthodox fighting style ensuring that you very much had to stay on your toes.

The rest of us didn't come to the school with an affinity to one weapon. Kirok, Scythe and Sophia came from tribal backgrounds ensuring that they were proficient with their tribal martial styles. Cassius and I were too young to have learnt weapon styles from the village fighters - not that the village had any particular affinity for fighting as far as I could remember. Ella and Rikol were street rats, ensuring that they had excellent reflexes but no weapons training other than a need to stay alive, and Damien had been trained in the sword by his father but this training had been sporadic. This meant that we embraced the opportunity to trial everything that the training armoury had to offer; getting used to wielding everything from the massive array of swords to spears, poleaxes and more, to curved blades that looked like leaves and even attempting to use weapons such as bolas or a triple bladed discus. Kane and Adronicus pushed everyone to practice with as many different weapon types as possible, stressing that specialisations would form over time and affinities might grow with even the most unlikely weapons.

Six months into the first year we felt like we were by and large succeeding. Certainly in combat training, and whilst maths made my brain hurt and politics largely want to make my eyes shut, I feel like we were a successful dorm. That is, if not for the strain between the rest of the us and Kirok. In hindsight much of his actions were not the fault of his own but of his tribe. He was raised in a violent environment where the strong take what they want, when they want. It would be almost impossible for him to think any other way, but that does not excuse his actions in my eyes. Far from it.

At first his rough, lewd jokes and boisterous behaviour were just things to be put up with but they progressively got more and more intense. Kirok was not a man to be outdone, whether in eating, drinking, jokes or fighting. Unfortunately he was in a school where at least someone was better than him in one or more of the above. Each time he was put on the floor the rage grew until blind battle rage erupted. In this state Kirok forgot all rules of engagement, trying his utmost to put his opponent in the ground; permanently. With his vast size and strength, along with a complete disregard for pain or punishment, stopping him once in this state was a massive challenge - even for Adronicus. It was like trying to wrestle a bull; a bull that knew how to use weapons.

At times like this Kirok barely seemed human; a complete being of rage and fury satisfied only when blood was being spilt. Worse he showed no remorse for any injuries that he inflicted upon his comrades, shrugging off the glares, anger and remonstrations with barely concealed distaste. In the evenings he would become more bitter when former drinking partners refused to join him, understandable when he had tried to kill them earlier in the day. For six months this inner rage smouldered, shown in an attitude that got darker by the day. His suggestive glances at Sophia became more lingering, the coarse talk as she undressed in the dorm taking on an even darker edge. An edge that became more honed over time, growing sharper, darker and filled with hate.

CHAPTER TWENTY TWO
REPERCUSSIONS

~

"HERE, CALIDAN DRINK!" A FOAMING mug was thrust into my hand, splashing onto my jerkin. Kirok landed a heavy hand on my shoulder, buckling my knees with the force of the blow. He laughed uproariously, "Aston Day is very important, a very good time to drink!"

Aston Day; a day known only to those of the mountain clans of the far North, those of Kirok's brethren. It was apparently a mighty celebration in his lands and he was adamant to share it with everyone in the halls, filling mugs and sharing jokes. I hate to admit it but Kirok could be charismatic and even fun to be around when alcohol was involved.

I tipped a nod to Kirok and raised my new mug, clinking it with those around me. The entire dorm was out in fine form tonight. Sophia and Ella were looking radiant, twirling each other around and laughing in delight. Damien, Scythe and Cassius were watching with great amusement as Rikol taught a new batch of unsuspecting third years several card games...all of which Rikol somehow ended walking away from more rich, with the tables' occupants scratching their heads. We had long grown wise to his schemes, knowing that to allow Rikol to deal any hand was to invite defeat.

Draining half my tankard I turned and walked straight into Rinoa, splashing both of us with the remains of my drink.

"Calidan!" she yelled whilst patting at the wet spots on her vest, the damp material now hugging the contours of her chest. I couldn't help it; my gaze was drawn. Seeing where I was looking she stormed off muttering about boys and leaving me with threats that this would not be forgotten quickly. I had no doubt that the next evening session would be even more painful than usual, but as far as my teenage brain was concerned it was completely worth it.

"*Ah humans, so silly in their mating rituals.*" Seya's thoughts bust into my breast filled reverie.

"*What would you know about it?*" I thought back, somewhat miffed.

"*I've lived for a long time Calidan. Mating is easy for a cat, one goes into heat and males arrive. Easy. Humans have so many other* things to consider, from your size to your clothes and even wealth. Much more difficult."

"I see."

A chuckle reverberated through my stomach, *"If you didn't want any of my thoughts on this then stop filling my chest with feelings reserved for those in heat!"*

Had I? No one ever mentions the downsides of having an emotionally connected giant creature.

"Bored Seya?"

"How did you guess?"

I laughed out loud and went to go and see her, determined to win a wrestling match for once.

All in all it was a night to remember...but not for all the right reasons.

It was dawn when I woke up curled in Seya's furry embrace. Sighing and stretching stiffly I began the walk back to the dorm to get ready for the day when my senses picked up something strange - the sound of stifled sobs and grunts. A dark feeling settled in the pit of my stomach; something wasn't right.

Around the back of the stables I found my answer. Sophia was bound, her arms cruelly tied behind her back and a rope gagging her mouth. Tears poured from her eyes as Kirok thrust into her over and over, a ravenous, evil look on his face. Bruises marked her face where he had struck her, a swollen black eye and broken nose highlighting his crimes. As I watched he seized her breasts and twisted cruelly, causing a muffled shriek to echo through the sobs.

Black fire filled my chest.

"This should not be." Seya was by my side, trembling in fury.

Like a bolt of lightning I sped forward and struck Kirok, the force of the blow rocking his head back, knocking him through the air and into the side of the wall. He slumped to the floor. Such was my rage that I wouldn't have cared right then if he had died, but my senses told me he was merely unconscious. Unwilling to finish the job I turned to Sophia who was hyperventilating and unable to see what was happening. I stood in front of her so that she knew it was me, her eyes welling with new tears as she recognised that her ordeal was coming to an end. Swiftly I snapped her ropes, grabbed her clothes and put her on Seya who purred at her anxiously. With a thought Seya sped away.

My senses flared and I spun, narrowly dodging the hoe that sliced through the air. Kirok was in front of me, face already turning black from the blow that I had given him. Blood trickled from his nose and right eye. On his face was a look of pure, animal rage. He tilted his head back and screamed, a deep sound that would have terrified me had I not heard the voice of a true monster. He came at me expecting the fights that he had received before, one without my power. But there was no holding back on my part, not even if I had wanted to for Seya's fury reverberated within my chest - my fingers ached to tear him to shreds and my teeth longed to bite out his throat. He roared and I roared back, the feral sound bursting out of my chest causing him to flinch.

Then I was upon him.

The hoe swept upwards defensively, the power behind the reflexive blow enough to break any normal man in two. I reached out contemptuously and snapped the shaft of the blade in two. Kirok's eyes widened as he saw what horrors my eyes held for him. Cats play with their food.

Either to his credit for bravery, or more likely because he had the instincts of an ape, he charged, the splinted half handle being used as a rapier. As his hand sped past my face I brought both arms together and like a vice caught his arm between them. My arms continued their movement and his elbow snapped like a twig. Enjoying his scream and ducking under his limp appendage I struck him three times in the stomach, his iron abdomen caving before each blow. With my hands forgetting they were human I raked his bent over face like a cat, scoring deep, bloody lines across his flesh and taking his left eye with them. Kirok spun, trying to clutch his face with his useless arm, keeping his left arm in front of him as if to ward me off. With a kick I sent him sprawling to the floor and growled at this pitiful foe.

Screaming defiance Kirok swept out with a leg, his scream changing in tone when I stepped on his ankle. Not much was left when

I removed my foot. With my mind locked in a faraway place I started kicking, and didn't stop.

"Calidan"

"Calidan!"

"Calidan!"

The animal side of me ignored these irritating human noises. It was only when someone flung their arms around me, screaming "Calidan STOP!" that my brain took back control. Sophia was hugging me, crying, begging for me to stop. And just like that the anger dissipated, and I could see what I had done.

Kirok lay bleeding and battered on the floor. His right arm and left ankle were unlikely to ever work again. My kicks had broken every rib in the left side of his body, and with my senses I could tell that at least one kidney and his liver had ruptured. His remaining eye held nothing but fear - the other lay somewhere on the stable floor - and I felt a moment of regret for what I had done. But then I beheld Sophia and that regret vanished like a puff of smoke. He had taken and raped my friend; as far as the cat and I were concerned this was barely repayment.

Sophia hugged me fiercely and turned me around, away from the broken human on the floor. Watching from the side was the rest of the dorm, wide eyed. Cassius and Ella immediately rushed over, a blur of questions asking whether I was hurt and what had happened. The others hung back slightly, and I couldn't blame them. The brutal scene and myself without a scratch would have raised my own caution if the situation had been reversed. A large figure strode past Scythe and Damien, his broad shoulders instantly recognisable; Kane. His usually cheery demeanour was dark as he beheld the situation.

"Anyone still here who isn't Kirok, Calidan or Sophia in the next ten seconds will be removed."

His voice was like a whip crack, unrelenting and remorseless. The dorm scattered like chaff to the wind, all except Ella and Cassius who stayed with me. Kane turned to them, a slight smirk on his lips softening his words. "I wasn't joking. Leave." I nodded at them both and they left silently, looking back over their shoulders towards me as they went.

Kane wandered over to me and Sophia, his eyes taking in every detail: Sophia's dishevelled state and teary eyes, my angry demeanour and the broken form of Kirok. It likely wasn't hard for conclusions to be drawn. A grim smile wreathed his face in the predawn light.

"Take him."

I cocked my head questioningly and then whirled as my senses registered two people who had seemingly appeared out of nowhere. They lifted Kirok between them and disappeared around the corner of the stable.

"What are you doing?" I asked.

"Relax," he replied, "Kirok is no longer any of your concern." I drew closer to Sophia, wary of his tone. Kane noticed and chuckled. "Sorry, I should clarify, this is not the first time something like this has happened at the Academy. As you know we have excellent doctors here, he will be taken care of."

"What about punishment?" I replied.

Kane raised an eyebrow, indicating the scene around him. "So this isn't enough?" He held up a hand to forestall my outburst, "Calidan, Kirok is no longer your, or Sophia's, problem. He will be dealt with... of that you can be sure."

I decided not to try and clarify what that meant. If Kirok reappeared then the dorm would ensure that he couldn't cause more trouble.

"What now then?" I asked.

"You both come with me, have a strong drink of your choice and we talk whilst medics check over Sophia. Acceptable?"

I glanced over at Sophia who nodded in assent. "Lead on," I replied.

~

A short walk later and we were in Kane's office, sitting in plush leather seats being poured whisky. As he poured Kane spoke, "Sophia, if it is okay with you to stay and talk for a few minutes I would appreciate it. A medic is waiting outside to look after you afterwards." Sophia nodded. Her face was bruised, skin pale and eyes red rimmed, having had been through a tremendous trauma and yet she straightened her back and nodded her assent.

Kane smiled warmly and finished pouring the glasses. "Good, that's that. Enjoy your whisky, it's some of the Empire's finest." He certainly wasn't wrong about the quality of the whisky. Though it still tasted like fire going down my throat I could at least work out that it was meant to taste like good fire. After a moment Kane put down his glass and we soon followed.

A pregnant pause then he sighed heavily. "This is not the first time that this has happened at the Academy. Nor will it be the last. Students here are from all areas of the Empire, all with certain skills that make them intelligent, stronger and deadlier than other citizens. Some of these students, like Kirok and yourself Sophia, come from more remote tribes and villages and accordingly you have different customs. Obviously I am not condoning what he did. Far from it. Just putting things in perspective."

Another silent pause.

"Have either of you ever wondered why we have mixed dorms?"

I returned Sophia's quizzical look with one of my own and we both shook our heads.

"No? Hmmm. Let me try and explain...to be an Imperator is to be able to work independently as a solo operator, but also together as a team. Kaschan is a perfect example. Deadly solo, deadlier when combined with another. With me so far?"

Nods.

"By the time that you are third or fourth years you will have likely learnt many of these skills. How to work as a unit, deal with internal strife, the list goes on. However as a first and maybe second year, you likely don't have these skills. And so we have eight people from all walks of life, mixed gender and ages all in the same dorm. Why?"

I hazarded a guess, "To force us to work together?"

"Half correct Calidan. To force you into positions where you can work together or deal with conflict. How you approach these situations is entirely up to you."

He pointed at Sophia. "Sophia is a very attractive girl, she knows it, we know it. As an Imperator she may be alone in dark lands with darker people. She needs to have a core of steel, to know when to fight, when to hide, when to talk and even... when to submit." He held up a hand to forestall the rage on our faces. "The same applies to men too. Not all tastes are for the opposite gender. For instance, Calidan, if you found yourself in a position where it would be easier to seduce your target rather than fight, would you?"

That threw me.

"Of course you wouldn't. Not right now. Not yet. But something that you have to realise is that as soon as you walked through those Academy doors you were no longer your own property. You are now property of the Empire and everything you do needs to be in the Empire's best interests. Whether that means submitting to a beating, saving an enemy, slitting a throat, or yes even allowing yourself to be raped - you can bide your time and extract vengeance later."

He sighed again.

"Ours is a dark path. You barely know a fraction of it and yet just tonight have probably faced more than most. Death, torture, sex, nothing is off the cards for an Imperator. You always have to have the Empire's best interests at heart."

"So you build it into the training," I spoke my realisation aloud.

Kane nodded. "There is a certain amount of *wastage* per year. Let me make this clear: fighting and brawling between yourselves is to be expected. It is a part of life. Fighting to kill, much as you did this morning Calidan, that is not allowed. Rape is one of the most heinous crimes, in the same hierarchy as inflicting torture upon a classmate. It is by no means condoned and punishment is extremely severe."

"But you don't go out of your way to stop it." Sophia replied.

"Correct," answered Kane. "We certainly don't encourage it, but we recognise the benefits of forcing close quarter living to developing our Imps. Rape and murder are sadly sometimes a by-product of this living arrangement. By the time you are in your third year you will be acting as a well oiled unit...or you'll probably be broken or dead." There was no joking in his eyes.

He picked up his glass and drained it, closing his eyes for a moment as he savoured the taste. When he put the glass back down he looked at us both, a fierce intensity burning in his eyes.

"This is the last I will say on it. The Academy is a dark and dangerous place. Much more so than you have already experienced. Keep your wits sharp, your skills honed and become more than you are." He held our gaze.

"Now go and return to your friends."

I offered a hand to Sophia but she stood up, unbroken and unwavering. The anger in her eyes that this was some kind of lesson was surely reflected in my own. Together we walked out of the office to the waiting medic and then to our concerned friends.

Looking back I recognise the warning in Kane's words for what it truly was. For he wasn't wrong, the Academy was a frightening and dangerous place. If anything he understated just how truly dark it was.

CHAPTER TWENTY THREE
FRIENDSHIPS

~

KIROK WASN'T IN THE MEDICAL centre. Of that I was certain. I had no inkling of his whereabouts, or even if he had survived and I found that I didn't much care. Sophia became reclusive, flitting to the canteen and disappearing with her food, by all accounts no longer one for late nights drinking. Not that that happened much in the few weeks following that night. The dorm had become a much more reserved place, whether it was knowing that one of their own was hurting, or that one amongst them had the capacity to be a ruthless killer I do not know. Cassius and Ella were the same as ever and I was constantly glad for their support and love. The others however, whilst they might not outwardly show it I could sense it, a slight tension in the muscles, a difference in musk as I walked amongst them. There was an unease within the dorm that was not there before and I did not know how to heal it.

The edge in the air between Scythe, Damien, Rikol and myself meant that I spent more and more time apart. More often than not I spent this time visiting Seya, riding and running through the surrounding hunting grounds and performing the circles of Kaschan. One night, several weeks after the fateful night with Kirok I was giving Seya a belly rub in the Great Heart stables, (a perfect place, unknown to most students with multiple underground access points to allow the mighty beasts access to the forest, but more importantly it was large and filled with scratching devices), when a cough from outside alerted me to the presence of Sophia.

I say alerted, but in actuality I had known she had stood there for the past two minutes, uncertain about entering in. It was then that Seya, understanding the situation better than myself, rolled on her back for a welcoming belly rub. No matter the size of the cat the sight of an exposed belly is enough to make anyone's heart melt (though with Seya it inevitably ended up being a trap of gigantic proportions), and Seya presumably became much less intimidating because it was then Sophia decided to cough and enter.

I turned slowly and gave her a welcoming smile, "Come on in Sophia, I will introduce you to Seya."

She smiled and shyly walked over to the gigantic cat, experienced a moment of what looked like panic when the grand head loomed over her for a sniff, but a friendly head butt and warm, wet lick soon had her spluttering with indignation and laughter.

"That was mean Seya."

A deep throated almost chuckle erupted from Seya and we both grinned at the drenched girl.

"You get used to it," I said. "Having spare clothes is often handy!"

Sophia smiled and reached out tentatively to Seya. "May I?" she asked, turning to me.

"Of course."

Her hand shyly touched the lush fur on Seya's throat. "It's so soft!"

"Well of course, I'm not some mangy mutt. One must have standards."

I tried and failed to stifle a giggle. Sophia turned, "What?"

"Nothing!" I replied. "Just be aware that Seya understands everything you say."

Sophia's eyes went wide, just in time for the mighty head to nudge her to continue with her now still hand. She smiled and went back to giving Seya a blissful scratch and I felt my stomach grow warm from contentment.

"I've been meaning to thank you Calidan, but I don't know how."

The two of us were laying against a purring Seya, enjoying each other's company.

"You don't need to thank me Sophia, I'm just glad I was there to help."

"The fact remains, I don't know what Kirok would have done had you not helped me. Knowing that bastard he could have slit my throat and been on his merry way," she replied.

I paused for a moment before continuing, my thoughts flickering back to the horrors of the attack on the village, "What he did to you...no one should ever have to go through it."

She must have heard something in my voice, the brittle tone of someone who had bad memories of dark nights. But she didn't pry, just reached out and gave me a hug.

"Thank you," she whispered.

From that point on, Sophia became a regular visitor to the Great Heart stables. Or I should say Seya's stables. No other students to my knowledge had a Great Heart, nor was there scent of the stables having been in recent use by another. That said, Seya only came to the stables for companionship, preferring to roam the surrounding forest. Little by little, the cold wall that Sophia had thrown up immediately after the rape began to thaw and she slowly began to open up to myself and to a lesser extent, the dorm. We would exchange stories about our past, where we came from and how we ended up at the Academy. Always a glutton for stories about areas unknown to me, her tales held me in thrall. Mine, more often than not, took a dark turn. Even with withholding that fateful night. Sophia knew I was holding something back but never pressed for more information. That night was too dark for others to know about, nor did I imagine that she would likely believe the tale of the beast.

But her stories! Her descriptions of endless forests, great hunts and winding rivers had my imagination running amok. She told me that her father was the village story master and that her brother was being trained in the art of speech craft. It appeared as though she too had received some of her father's gift and shyly confessed to having even trained accompaniment on the lyre - not that she would ever let me hear it of course; the very idea was mortifying. But her words held me sway, and the world she built seemed fantastic to my mind: running with the horses, learning to ride and shoot and being one with nature. My village had dwelt in nature, but it was always a harsh battle with the inhabitants pitted against the often brutal elements. Sophia's tribe seemed to live in harmony with the world around them, using all that they took but unlike the towns and cities of the Empire, they ensured that they only took what was needed. Flourishing alongside nature rather than destroying it, sadly an ideal that was not particularly shared by the city driven behemoth that was the Empire. The price of civilisation.

My time with Sophia soon became a thing to treasure. Ella and Cassius were still my closest friends and understood me intimately, but as with all lovers more and more time was being spent alone together...and as the dormitory was more often than not occupied this meant that they had to find their own space. Suffice to say that my senses have found them 'enjoying each other's company' all over the Academy and surrounding forest. I did not envy them this, but I had been feeling a little lonely prior to Sophia showing up. The dorm didn't quite hold the same attraction within its walls as it once had. Whether it was my senses or whether I had just learnt some of the finer characteristics of reading people from Cassius I could still tell that there was an...offishness by the rest of the dorm, and it had not gone away. Again, I could not blame them. What I had done to Kirok had looked more like a torture scene. Something done out of vengeance rather than necessity. And they would be right. I had seen Kirok hurting my friend and my thoughts had immediately clouded with all the hate, not just for what he was doing, but for what those murdering rapists had done to my village. Along with the strong emotions of Seya I had not even paused to think but just acted. I still didn't regret my actions, but pined for the weeks before when the dorm had felt like a complete unit. Now we were a dorm in name only.

Of course, as often is the case when it comes to people, the answer was Cassius. Or to put it more accurately, Cassius and Sophia. I arrived at the Great Heart stables one warm summer's evening to find Seya and the rest of the dorm having a picnic. The chatter stopped as I walked in, worry and caution evident on my face, but Sophia, Ella and Cassius jumped up shouting 'Surprise!' followed a split second later by Damien, Scythe and Rikol. I was mobbed by hugs, and my cheeks burned following a kiss on each by Ella and Sophia. The others filtered past, shaking my hand and giving me brief hugs and then my attention turned to Seya. And I could not contain my laughter.

A banner hung around Seya's neck saying 'Happy Birthday Calidan' in large letters. She was torn between amusement at being involved in wishing me a happy birthday and gall at having to wear such an item. The great and mighty beast soon turned away from me and started rolling across the floor, trying to see the banner tied around her throat. Sometimes I think her cat instincts are as overpowering for her as they are for me.

Once the laughter had died down and Seya was happily tearing the banner to shreds Cassius crossed over and handed me a glass of wine.

"Happy birthday brother," he said warmly.

"You planned all this?" I asked.

"Not all, I had help!" he replied, pointing at Sophia who blushed in embarrassment.

"We thought your birthday would make for a good celebration and give us an opportunity to clear the air," she said, walking over.

My consternation must have shown on my face for Cassius patted me on the shoulder and shouted for quiet.

"Everyone, thanks for coming and celebrating Calidan's birthday with me. I know it means a great deal to him that you have all come." He waited a few moments before continuing. "However this is also an opportunity for me to tell you some things about myself and Calidan that you may not know. One of them," he pointed to Seya, "may already be fairly obvious."

"We've kept this party small, even though there were plenty of people that I'm sure would like to be here, or that Calidan here," he nudged me with a friendly elbow, "would like to have attend. The reason that we have done this is because Calidan is not completely like the rest of us. He is bonded to a Great Heart, Seylantha, whom you have all now just met. Calidan and I have been through some dark times but we have come out stronger and better for it," at this Ella clasped Cassius's hand. "Moreover I believe that we have come out of it with a strong sense of right and wrong."

Cassius looked over at Sophia who nodded as though giving permission.

"What Kirok did to Sophia was an unspeakable act. Something that should never be allowed to happen. You know it, I know it and Calidan knows it. However due to some of the things we have seen we both have a special hatred for rapists. Seeing Kirok attacking his friend - one of us - Calidan was brave enough, strong enough to intervene. To take down a man that even Adronicus has trouble with holding down. Yes it was aggressive. Yes it was brutal. But that is what we are trained for…I will finish with this: Calidan is my best friend, my brother. He is the best person I know and he does not deserve the welcome you have been giving him these past few weeks. He saved our friend from a monster." With that Cassius raised a glass, "To Calidan!"

Embarrassment aside, Cassius certainly knew how to put on a moving speech. The reluctant three were up and giving me proper hugs almost before he had finished speaking. Perhaps knowing more about who or what I was helped cement me in their eyes. Provided evidence for how I could have bested Kirok without breaking a sweat. All I know is that from that point on the dorm was back to almost complete unity. Sophia smiled more and more, the scars from that night slowly receding, and my new friends welcomed me back into the fold. No longer did I sense any unease at my presence and the dorm became a much happier place to be.

Acceptance of my nature and actions didn't stop Sophia and my sojourns to see Seya. However we now had to contend with the rest of the dorm who, having been sworn to secrecy, now thoroughly spoilt Seya at any available opportunity. Often I would arrive at the stables for some peace and quiet only to find Damien or Scythe sitting with Seya first. Perhaps the most amusing however was Rikol, his new mission in life to teach a giant cat how to play cards. He entreated the Great Heart staff to make fifty two large cards and spent hours teaching Seya the tricks of the trade. Watching her delicately pick each card and soon start beating Rikol at his own game was a sight to behold. Seya was frighteningly intelligent. I had known it to be the case already, but to see her through another's eyes truly made me understand just how fantastic a creature she was.

Whether it was because she was a cat or whether it was because she was a Great Heart, Seya was not forthcoming about her past. This was annoying because there was very little information on Great

Hearts that I could find. First and second year Imps did not have access to any portion of the great archives, so I was restricted to the library and the memories of Brother Gelman. Even with years of searching he had uncovered relatively little - as far as I was aware he had only really pieced clues together from excerpts about the remains of giant creatures. There was nothing on their history, where they come from, their powers. And so with Seya keeping tight lipped I decided to go and see Kane.

"I'm here to ask about Great Hearts."

"Hah! Finally! I was wondering when we would get to this," he guffawed. "It's rare that there are bonded students at the Academy...two in the past thirty years I believe, but I'm fairly certain they didn't wait eight months to better understand their partner."

I smiled wryly, "I've had a lot on my mind."

"Who doesn't? No matter, come in and sit down, I will tell you what I can," he replied heartily.

"Great Hearts, Great Hearts, Great Hearts...where to begin?" he murmured to himself.

"At the beginning?" I interjected - the epitome of wit.

"Hah! You would think so but no," he replied. "I do not believe that anyone knows the truth behind Great Hearts. There are theories yes but not much in the way of factual evidence. The predominant theory is that they are not natural, but engineered, designed. The earliest piece of information that I have seen regarding large creatures dates back over three thousand years. But whether that was the first Great Heart or not I do not know, much is lost from before that time."

"Why?" I asked, intrigued.

"We're talking about a time before the Empire Calidan, records weren't kept as meticulously as they are now. Bearing that in mind, some sources suggest that there was a cataclysmic event in the distant past, something that eradicated entire civilisations, some even suggest that these civilisations were much more advanced than we are today."

"Is there any evidence for that?" I asked.

"Myths and legends mainly," he replied, "but there have been rumours of places found hidden away that hold all sorts of objects, strange metals and materials. The Emperor is often very interested in these rumours. Some Imperators are dedicated to finding such places...not that any have had success."

Or not told anyone if they have, I thought to myself.

"So yes, Great Hearts are straight out of legend I'm afraid. Their origins lost in time. Most people don't know that they exist, as you know, and we like to keep it that way." He took a tumbler of whisky and poured us both a finger before leaning back in his chair and sighing as he tasted it.

"Ahhh that's the stuff." He closed his eyes for a few seconds before continuing the conversation. "Great Hearts seem to occur in a variety of different animals. I do not know how it happens but it appears as though there is only one per species, and certainly not every species on the planet otherwise they would be much more common! No, there seem to be relatively few at any one time, but research suggests that those numbers stay consistent. So either Great Hearts are amazingly long lived, which, whilst true, they tend to live only a few hundred years, not thousands; or there is some method of making more."

"If there are two of the same species could they not reproduce?" I voiced.

"As far as I know there have been no recordings of two of the same species of Great Heart at any one time. Plus considering that they should not exist, that nature should not be able to sustain them lends weight to the theory that they were created."

"What do you mean nature can't sustain them? I've seen Seya eat."

"Great Hearts eat, and they eat a substantial amount, it is true. But a creature that large should require much more food just to stay alive."

"We have giant boar and elephants, surely they are a natural occurrence?"

"Correct, but the boar and elephants are still dwarfed by a Great Heart, plus they spend the vast majority of time grazing. I have seen Great Hearts last for days on one meal...it just doesn't make sense."

The more we talked about it, the more Kane's words began to make sense. I had known that Great Hearts were different from normal animals, obviously, but I had not considered that they might not be a natural occurrence. For them to have been created? For what purpose, to what end would someone do that?

I had to know. Needed to know the truth. Kane forestalled further questions by raising a hand and shaking his head.

"I know what you're going to ask me Calidan, but I am about out of information on Great Hearts. There is only so much that I know about them, after all I am not a scholar." He finished his whisky, and groaning, stood up. "Follow me," he said, walking briskly out of the room. We left his office and walked down through a maze of corridors before arriving at what appeared to be an old library.

"I thought I wasn't allowed in the archives?" I hesitantly asked Kane.

He stopped and stared at me before bursting into his hearty laughter. "Archives? This isn't the archives boy! This is the personal collection of Korthan, an old Imperator who has been here long before I turned up as an Imp."

"Old! I'll give you 'old' Kane!" roared an ancient man as he rounded one of the groaning, book laden shelves.

Kane grinned happily as he was loudly chastened by the old Imperator, obviously it wasn't too rare of an occurrence because when Korthan finally finished berating Kane with some of the most fantastic insults they both had wide grins.

"And who is this?" Korthan asked, turning to me.

"This is Calidan, a first year Imp," replied Kane.

"And why is this of interest to me?" Korthan shot back.

"Because, *old man,* he is also bonded to a Great Heart."

Korthan's eyes widened momentarily before he looked back to me. "A Great Heart bonded eh? Been some time since I've had the pleasure." He mentioned to both of us, "Come in to the study and let's talk."

Korthan's 'study' was in reality just a series of tables at the centre of the book cases covered with mugs of coffee, papers and open tomes. He shuffled off and returned with two extra chairs before creakily sitting down.

"So, found yourself a Great Heart eh?" Korthan asked, looking at me.

I looked at Kane and he motioned for me to go ahead and respond.

"Yes Instructor Korthan," I replied, "I have bonded with a Great Heart, a panther called Seylantha."

"Hah! I'm no Instructor boy! Just an old man who has the nasty habit of staying alive." He grinned toothily. "And I assume you want to know more about Great Hearts than what this useless person here," he flapped a hand at Kane whose grin just got wider, "can tell you."

"That...yes, that about sums it up I guess." I replied with a grin.

"As I thought! Begone Kane you incompetent oaf, you're no longer needed here."

Kane laughed heartily as he stood up, "I'll see you tomorrow you decrepit old git," he said, and with a jovial nod to me walked out the faux library.

Korthan chuckled to himself and waved a hand at the departing Imperator before turning to me.

"Great Hearts: majestic beasts of massive size, unknown background, strange powers and a compulsion to form bonds with certain humans, is that about what you know so far?"

I nodded and he gave me a wide smile and cackled, "Good! So you know pretty much everything there is to know then!"

At the shocked look on my face he burst into laughter.

"Surely there is something more you know, why else would Kane bring me to you?" I asked, panicked at the thought of not gaining any more information.

The old man calmed down a little, and wiped an eye before speaking again, "Sorry, just my little joke. To be fair there isn't that much else that I can tell you. As far as I know no one has got definitive evidence of the origins of Great Hearts, or understand the particulars of the bonds. Most believe that if the creatures were designed then the individuals that they bond with are either related distantly to those who the first Great Hearts were created for, or the beasts have some form of innate criteria. A method to select a suitable partner. Whatever it is, it is certainly not random choice."

I must have looked a little put out because he reached over and patted me on the hand. "Don't worry boy, others like yourself have come down here looking for answers, but sadly there aren't many answers to give."

"Others..." I looked up, "how many other Great Hearts are there?"

"There are seven known Great Hearts currently active, four of which are within the service of the Empire including you," he replied. "Rumour of large creatures active in certain areas of the world suggest another potential three, but Great Hearts are often, for such large creatures, secretive. There could be many more out there. And, like this Empire, other countries likely keep their numbers secret."

There were three other Great Heart bonded in the Empire! Hope kindled in my chest, not just for answers but to meet others like me.

"Could I meet the other three here?" I asked.

Korthan looked at me, and I could have sworn that a flicker of sadness passed through his eyes.

"I am sure that you will meet them eventually, but the three bonded and their Great Hearts are kept very close to the Emperor. He seems to value their skills more than those of other Imperators. As such they are not often seen. In fact..." again, a fleeting glimmer of distress in his visage, "we haven't had one return to the Academy following graduation."

My face fell. Was this to be my life, graduate the Academy and then disappear into the service of the Emperor? Even staying apart from the other Imperators?

"So they don't ever leave his side?" I asked hesitantly, afraid of the answer.

"I didn't say that. I said they stayed close and are rarely seen. It is quite possible that the Emperor uses them for other reasons, maybe missions that otherwise 'normal' Imperators couldn't accomplish," replied Korthan. "But it is all hypothetical. I don't know what they do in the Emperor's service, nor does - I suspect - anyone in this Academy."

I stood up abruptly, needing some space to organise my thoughts. I had known I was different than the others thanks to the bond with Seya, but from the sounds of things I would be even more segregated than your average Imperator. Hidden away from the world, perhaps as some kind of bodyguard for the Emperor, a political tool or, more than likely, an assassin.

Korthan stood too, held up a finger to prevent my departure and shuffled off. After a few minutes he returned carrying a small book titled, 'Abador - a journal of Haven Locke'.

"This is perhaps the most relevant piece of information that I can give you regarding Great Hearts and their history. Please, keep it, read it and feel free to come by and discuss at any time."

I extended my hand, the motion more mechanical than anything, my mind still a whirl with the limitations of my future and took the book. Korthan nodded at me kindly as I mumbled my thanks and left the office, melancholy of thought and heavy in heart.

CHAPTER TWENTY FOUR
HISTORY

~

THE JOURNAL WAS SHORT BUT dense, written in a hurried, scribbled hand as though the writer had much to say but little space or time to do it. It was the diary of Haven Locke, researcher and explorer, regarding his time in eastern lands, and was one hundred and forty seven years old. A diary in which Haven led an expedition, following a lead that an earthquake in a remote region in the Sun Lands of Abador (now part of the most eastern lands of the Empire), had opened a rift in the ground, through which ancient structures could be seen.

3C, 4th, 5067

Day 15 - We made landfall at Erudan, City of Light in Abador. According to our guide, Aderai, the rift in the ground is a month walk from this location. By the pitch this place is hot! Tall spires and open space makes this city a marvel but there is no time for dallying, we are to resupply, buy transport and make our way to the rift - time is limited; all could be lost if the ground shifts again.

3C, 9th, 5067

Day 20 - I have never been so hot in my life! The sun is an agonising blaze overhead, unceasing and relentless. Thankfully we have plenty of water and having adopted the locals' style of dress have found myself much cooler than previous. Even so my skin is desperate for release during the day and at night craves for warmth.

3C, 12th, 5067

Day 23 - A man died last night. Not the first I have seen, nor probably the last, but his screams shall haunt me I am positive. It turns out that at night our bodies give off heat, heat that attracts creatures - ones that I have only seen in zoos. Scorpions. It seems that this little one decided to cuddle with the poor man for warmth. Its sting brought a slow and agonising death. I would not wish it on my enemies, and yet Aderai says that this is by no means that worst thing roaming the sands. He would not elaborate so my brain runs amok with things of nightmare. I will find no rest tonight.

3C, 22nd, 5067

Day 33 - According to Aderai we are not far now. I have no idea how he knows, to me this vast expanse of sand and dust looks much the same as the past thirty days.

3C, 27th, 5067

Day 38 - We climbed a dune today and beheld an astonishing view. Darkness split the earth! A great chasm into which tomorrow we shall endeavour to descend. I am so excited that I can barely stop my hand from shaking whilst writing! Who knows what mysteries lay inside? We have enough water to last us three days at this site before having to turn back. Let us hope that it is enough time for thorough exploration.

3C, 28th, 5067

Day 39 Morning - peering into the chasm one can see very little, it is a very long way down. Something gleams down there - buildings Aderai assures me. A good thing we brought a lot of rope!

Day 39 Cont. We made it! The descent was atrocious, spinning in shafts of light that pierce the gloom. My mind ran wild with thoughts of nightmarish creatures approaching through the dark, but thankfully nothing appeared. It is evening now, we have set up camp next to the ropes and will explore tomorrow.

3C, 29th, 5067

Day 40 morn - Aderai was correct, this place is filled with buildings, most of which seem to be made of metal. Is this from before the Cataclysm? If so then it is a great find! We have explored along what appears to be a central road that leads to a building larger than the others. I write this as Toman breaches the mighty doors, even now they stand firm. We have split into two parties to explore as much as possible. The other team is to meet us back here in five hours.

Day 40 Cont - This building is stranger than anything I have seen. Great chambers of what seem to be almost baths, some still with liquid in them. Claw and teeth marks adorn these chambers - the marks larger than anything I have ever seen - what manner of creature was in them?

We came across what appears to be a central office. My hopes of finding any information however have been dashed. There looks to have been a fire, intentional by all likelihood, as ash remains in a great pile in the centre. No other books or documents can be found. I can only assume that all has been burnt, for what reason?

Day 40 Cont - We have waited outside the building for several hours. The second team has not returned. A group of hardy men, carrying all manner of equipment - it is unlikely that they have encountered an obstacle that they could not overcome. We shall wait a little longer and then head back to the camp.

Day 40 Cont - No sign of the other team. We are preparing to move back to the base camp as I write. Men uneasy. Deep shadows move in the torchlit darkness. What has happened to the others?

3C, 30th, 5067

Day 41 morn - We made it to the camp without incident last night, though none could disguise the unease felt as we moved through the clinging darkness. More worryingly no sign that the second team has been here. Much more worryingly is that the two sentries posted last night have gone missing. Nothing found. No sound. No more waiting - we are leaving.

Something is in here with us, I am positive.

I only hope we make it out alive.

The last page is a scrawl of feverishly written words. Brownish stains dyed the page; dried blood.

Cont - They are gone. They are all gone. We climbed the ropes and something took them. One by one, gleaming claws. Such screams. I made it to the top, thank the cycle that I climbed first! My leg is torn, something hit it but I did not see, just held on and climbed. Everyone is gone. Everyone.

I can hear something in the de-

And that was it, nothing else written on the pages. Something terrible had happened to those men, but there was very little to make sense of *what*. Why had Korthan given this to me?

Cassius looked up as he finished reading aloud the journal. He was sitting on the floor, the rest of the dorm surrounding him, all a little stunned at having listened to Haven's fate.

"Well, that was disturbing," said Cassius as he finished reading.

"Poor man," contributed Sophia.

"Dick," said Rikol.

We all looked at him for clarification and he snorted, "If you're going to go clambering down a mysterious hole in the middle of nowhere then serves you right for getting eaten by scary monsters!"

Damien let loose a chuckle that slowly developed into a full bellied laugh. It spread infectiously and soon we were all rolling on the floor in a fit of hysterics. When it had finally passed I wiped the tears from my eyes and said, "Well, everyone aside from Rikol, what do you make of it?"

"There isn't that much to make of it is there?" replied Damien. "All it tells us is that there is a strange place with big claw marks and apparently as Rikol put it, 'scary monsters'."

Ella, leaning comfortably against Cassius, spoke up, "You're all silly, this Korthan gave it to Calidan because he wanted to give him something he knew about Great Hearts. I think it's fairly obvious that Korthan thinks this might be where Great Hearts came from...perhaps he wants you to go there and find out?"

"Go there? Are you mad, did you not hear the dying man's words about monsters and death?" Rikol cried.

"Yes, but that was years ago, whatever was in there has likely died or moved on considering that it likely climbed out and killed Haven as he was sitting on the edge of the chasm," Ella replied. "There could be some real answers about the origins of Great Hearts there."

"Yes but go there!? Still mad," countered Rikol. "Also, how would we go there? And when I say we, you know I mean you. It isn't like we have the freedom to just leave the Academy to go on scary assed adventures."

"Scaredy cat," called Damien.

"Prick," replied Rikol.

"Dickbag."

"Bastard!"

The two of them collided together and started wrestling on the floor, perhaps unsurprisingly it was a fairly common scene in the dorm.

"Calidan," said Sophia slowly over the sound of the two roaring wrestlers, "Why not go and see if Seya knows anything about this place? I know she doesn't talk about her past, but she just might divulge something."

I could feel that Seya knew we were talking about her. Disquiet rumbled in my chest. "I'm not sure that we are going to find too much from her, she generally point blank refuses to answer any questions about her past, but... we can give it a shot."

A short time later after Rikol and Damien had dusted themselves off, grinning, we entered the Great Heart stables where Seya was curled up. The plan was simple, groom and pet the giant cat until she was buttered up enough to answer any questions. She knew something was amiss but I was counting on her love of adoration to dismiss any ulterior motives of mine. Once the big cat was a mountain of purring love I spoke to her softly, mind to mind.

"Seya?"

"Mmmmmmmmmmmmmmmmmmmm."

"Enjoying yourself Seya?"

Somehow I felt her eyes roll in my stomach, *"Obviously."*

"Good... We came across an interesting story today Seya, something that I was hoping you might be able to shed some light on."

"That sounds dull. Another time perhaps."

"Come on Seya, please you gorgeous queen of cats."

"Fine, ask away."

Flattery. Who says it doesn't get you anywhere?

"We found a journal about an expedition to a rift in the ground. Old, very old buildings were at the bottom and before the expedition met a fateful end the journal records that there was a large building with big bath like rooms filled with large, Great Heart sized claw and teeth marks. Do you have any knowledge of this?"

Silence

"Seya?"

"This...We are not allowed to talk about the beginnings Calidan. No - allowed is the wrong word; we are not able."

"What do you mean not able?"

Silence

"Ok...what about the creature that killed the men? Any idea what it could have been?

There are many deadly beasts in this world Calidan, as you well know."

"Point taken. But what about a beast that might have survived down underground for millennia? Perhaps awakening once the ground ruptured? Could a Great Heart do that?"

Silence. Then. "There are no Great Hearts I know of that can live that long. There is however something other than a Great Heart, similar but different, unneeding of food to survive but desiring of it all the same."

"What?"

"You have met one once before."

My mind flashed back to that fateful night in the village. The shadow beast roaring, black scales sucking in light. Its eyes glowing with demonic malice.

"The shadow beast..." I whispered, my knees weak. Sophia, uncertain of what was going on but aware of my reaction, came over and squeezed my hand. Cassius's head shot up and he looked at me, all the terror of that night reflected in both our eyes.

"You know of it? What is it?"

"Skyren."

Skyren. I moved the word around my mouth, tasting its foulness.

Skyren. I knew the name of my enemy.

"How are they different? Can you tell me more?"

"Skyren are not the same as Great Hearts. We are pure creatures, just different. Skyren are...abominations. Creatures of demon and shadow. Wrath and flame. Death and destruction. This world was nearly ended because of them."

"The great Cataclysm!" I breathed.

"Correct."

"Do you know what Skyren want? What they will do?"

"Death. It is in their nature. They will bring death."

"To humans?"

"To the world."

PRESENT DAY

~

A smiling, cute face
Emerald eyes
Sweet kisses in the night
Blood. So much blood.

I woke up from my nightmare. Not jerked awake, nothing as unseemly as that. I opened my eyes, instantly awake and aware. Something, or the absence of something had attracted my attention and the game was now to guess what. Cassius? I looked slightly to my left - nope, still there.

Fire? Still smouldering.

Shadows? Still dancing.

Birds? Still sing- No, nothing. Bingo.

The slightest movement, a hand slowly gripping the hilt of a sword, told me that Cassius was awake, his senses noticing the absence of sound too. I expanded my awareness. Shapes moved in the chasm a mile distant, a quiet, ordered marching of feet. I snarled silently to myself; Thyrkan were on the move.

A group of twenty, no more. A raiding party - probably the same one that had ravaged the village some fifteen miles back. I nodded at Cassius and stood up, buckling on my twin blades. The dully gleaming giant calmly picked up Oathbreaker and slotted it into place on his back. A quick kick of dirt over the fire and we were ready.

Moving with the calm but swift and silent pace taught by the greatest feline hunter in the world we quickly made it to the far edge of the ravine. A chasm the width of four men shoulder to shoulder made for an easy method of traversing unseen across the relatively open landscape. However if you have ears like mine then the price one might pay for staying unnoticed might (hopefully) prove fatal.

The Thyrkan were drawing closer. Humanoid creatures with scaled flesh and red eyes. Unknown in the lands of man a decade ago they had appeared as a swift and terrible menace, driving deep into the Northern lands and spreading fast. Stronger and faster than the average human they excel in hand to hand combat but seemingly possess little thought of their own, relying on their 'officers' - a more powerful, intelligent version of Thyrkan - to direct their actions. When in a battle line complete with officers Thyrkan present a terrifying unified front, able to cut bloody swathes through the armies of man. However, remove those officers and each Thyrkan begins to act independently, generally giving into blood lust and chaos soon descends.

Raiding parties had been reported in this section of the Attacambe plains. Nicknamed the 'Desolate Lands' they stretched on, largely barren and lifeless, extending out from the Ryken Peaks, a jagged series of mountains out past the northernmost extent of the Empire's reach. The plains were almost perfectly flat, barely undulating under our feet; a welcome respite from the treacherous climbs of the Ryken Peaks. An earthquake or other catastrophic event in the past had caused the land to rupture, almost as though it had been stretched and cracks had appeared where the land could stretch no more. Consequently a series of canyons webbed across the plains, providing plenty of ability to move up relatively undetected, usually by nomadic hunters but in this case the Thyrkan.

I say 'barren and lifeless' but that doesn't stop people from eking out an existence upon these lands. Erecting tiny houses and ramshackle villages, relying on the vast herds of goats that roamed the plains to sustain their meagre existence. A hard and unforgiving life and one that has been made harder now thanks to the presence of the Thyrkan. The village fifteen miles back was the third that we had come across, buildings burnt, patches of blood and bone but never any bodies; Thyrkan don't waste food.

The sounds of tramping feet were close now, echoing through the cracked ground, multiplying and reverberating as the sound bounced off the walls. To the untrained ear the raiding party may have sounded massive, but echoes are not what my senses rely on. I concentrated, listening, breathing, feeling. The party was traversing the canyon three abreast, the commander - identifiable by the larger musculature - was in the third rank. It seemed like an odd place, the commanders usually taking the front or very rear, but my senses couldn't locate anything out of place or resembling a captain other than a somewhat hunched over Thyrkan near the rear...another oddity.

Cassius and I moved to where the canyon narrowed slightly; anything to even the odds. I softly clapped Cassius on the shoulder and his eyes locked with mine, bloodshot and strained - a constant battle going on inside with the snarling beast within.

I counted down silently.

Ten, nine, eight. We unsheathed our swords.

Seven, six, five. Hands tightened around the hilts.

Four, three, two. A deep breath.

One.

We jumped into the rift, scattering the Thyrkan like bowling pins. Asp cut through the throat of the nearest creature that struggled to rise. Reckoning parried a blow aimed at Cassius's broad back and severed the head from the attacker. Oathbreaker swung, cleaving two Thyrkan in twain. Dark, black blood splattered the walls of the chasm and for a second there was only the silence of blood dripping from our blades, such was the suddenness of our attack.

And then rage.

Such rage.

I felt it through every sense in my being. The hunched creature at the rear. It was no commander, it was something much, much worse.

A warlock.

"Cassius!" I screamed, "Disengage!"

I had heard stories of the Thyrkan warlocks. Only in the last year had they started surfacing yet wherever they did they wreaked horrendous damage with terrible power.

In short a warlock was a different ball game entirely - the only thing keeping us alive right now was the wall of Thyrkan between us and it...and it would likely decide that the Thyrkan weren't of that much use.

Cassius started backing away, Oathbreaker swinging for the third rank captain as he did so, hoping to remove him from the equation. The captain clasped a mighty black blade in its hands, larger by half than Oathbreaker. Even the normal enhanced bulk of the captain didn't seem enough to swing the blade effectively. Two Thyrkan jumped in the way of the descending blade, saving the captain's life by giving their own.

A cold wind swept down the rift and a black light erupted around the captain. The Warlock may not be able to see us effectively, but apparently that didn't remove all the cards from its sleeve. My senses strained as they picked up what they were detecting, the muscles of the captain ripping apart and being remade anew. Out of the blackness came a hand twice the side of Cassius's. In the hand sat the black blade, now wielded comfortably, the hilt fitting perfectly.

The black light dissipated entirely and a new creature filled the chasm. Twice the size of any Thyrkan it towered over even Cassius. Gigantic, grotesque muscles criss-crossed disproportionately along its body, doubtless a result of such rapid growth. I had heard rumour of these. Gargantuan beasts that came out of nowhere and unleashed destruction and mayhem.

A Reaver.

I had no idea that this was how they were made. Probably because no one who had seen one had lived to tell the tale.

The black blade swung for Cassius, cleaving through the surrounding rock effortlessly such was the strength behind it and Oathbreaker clanged resoundingly as Cassius parried. Even with both hands and his shoulder behind the parry he was still moved, his feet sliding across the floor. An impressive feat considering that with his armour he weighed just under a tonne. Cassius, my hulking, manic, monster friend was being pushed back...something I had not seen happen in a long time.

I smiled a grim smile. Which meant that I was likely about to see something that I had hoped I would not see again.

Cassius was tossed through the air, landing with a loud, ear shattering impact against the chasm wall that would have broken a lesser man. Cassius simply shrugged off the impact, lowered his head and charged back at the mighty being in front of us. Oathbreaker swung and cut the beast as he moved but not deeply enough to inflict permanent damage. He danced and moved like a god of war, spinning, parrying and cutting like a man possessed. Cuts lacerated the Reaver.

A normal creature would have bled to death from the sheer volume of damage inflicted and indeed the amount of black blood on the walls, floor and both participants looked to be more than even that creature should have possessed, but nothing Cassius did seemed to particularly bother, or slow, the beast.

Cassius ducked a swipe, stepping back to raise Oathbreaker for another blow. As he stepped back the mighty blade caught an outcropping, pausing his attack and concentration for a split second… it was all the creature needed.

An almost casual backhand sent Cassius spinning, claws splitting through his armour. Vibrant red blood spat from his shoulder. He raised Oathbreaker in time to defend against the descending overhead blow, his knees buckling under the immense pressure.

The Reaver unleashed a mighty bellow and continued attacking. No finesse, just a frenzy of overhead blows. Over and over again they crashed into Cassius's desperate guard. The ground began to crack and splinter under Cassius's knees. I started forward but a snarl from my friend paused me in my tracks. Another blow landed, and another.

And then it happened.

Cassius roared and I swear the earth shook. Not the roar of a normal man, not even the roar of a Great Heart. If it were possible this was even deeper, a roar of pure, unending rage. A roar that had once shaken the citadel of the Emperor at its core.

The claws were unsheathed.

The beast was loose.

Cassius no longer shook under the raining blows. His armour cracked and shattered as his body expanded. A tail expanded from the small of his back, heavy, thick and reptilian. Black scales erupted along his flesh and his fingers turned into wicked claws, capable of gutting a man like a fish. Though I couldn't see his eyes I knew that one would be a deep red, the other his usual vivid blue.

Like Merowyn so long ago, Cassius had a beast inside of him courtesy of that prick of an Emperor. Only this one was no ordinary beast. A being of incredible power, and unbridled rage. A failed experiment by the Emperor and impossible to fully contain.

The black blade descended again and this time a scaled hand reached up and grabbed it. Black blood oozed out of Cassius's hand but the creature that he now was paid it no mind. His other hand shot out and grabbed the Reaver's wrist, preventing the free hand from swinging for his now scaled, increasingly toothy face. Muscles corded along both creatures as they strained against the other. With a bone shaking snarl the Reaver's wrist gave way, splintering under the force of Cassius's grip. Quick as a snake Cassius shot forward, his mouth finding the beast's throat, fangs descending. The Reaver was shaken like a dog savaging a bone, blood spurting in all directions as Cassius's fangs sunk deeper into its flesh.

Its shattered hand battered feebly at Cassius's shadow scaled skin, each blow weaker than the last until, with a savage howl Cassius grabbed the Reaver's head and tore it completely off its body.

The remaining Thyrkan screamed and scattered, racing back down the chasm.

All except the Warlock who looked at Cassius intently, curiosity lining its scaled face and then - as if folding in on itself - it vanished.

The Thyrkan kept running, all order and training lost in the face of imminent death...and the beast gave chase.

For Cassius was no longer in control. And I for one was glad that he hadn't remembered I was behind him.

And for another I was extremely glad we were in a place devoid of people.

Things were about to get messy.

I wiped my blades on my coat and sheathed them on my back before collecting up the broken armour pieces that littered the floor as well as strapping Oathbringer to my side. Grateful for my enhanced strength under the weight of all that metal I slowly set off in pursuit, taking my time. It would be easy enough to follow the sounds of screams, smell of blood and the human anguish hidden in the beast's roaring. Afterall I didn't want to get too close to Not Quite Cassius whilst he was in this state...it had happened once before and I still bore the scars.

So with a jaunty stride and a hum I set off.

I'm coming Cassius.

PART III
SINS & SHADOWS

~

CHAPTER TWENTY FIVE
EXPEDITION

~

THE DESERT SUN BEAT DOWN upon me as my camel slowly ambled up the dune. For a child of the north the incessant heat was almost unbearable. Cassius too was suffering; head bowed and sweat pouring off his brow. Ella on the other hand seemed to have a lot more in common with Scythe - both positively *basking* in the sun, drinking in the light and warmth as though there would be no tomorrow. Rikol, Damien and Sophia maintained a healthy respect for the blazing ball of celestial fire but seemed to suffer no ill effects from the raging heat. Balls to the lot of them.

We had arrived in Abador three weeks earlier, the entirety of the dorm, as well as Kane, a tall, swarthy man named Sarrenai and, to my delight, Merowyn. Now coming to the end of the second year at the Academy we were all taller, stronger and more capable than ever and Korthan had finally given into my incessant pestering to sponsor an expedition to the same site that Haven Locke had met his demise at all those years ago.

The past year had been a blur. Training had been ramped up, both martially and mentally. However with no more dissension between our ranks the dorm had succeeded at every turn. We helped tutor each other in combat and furthered each other's knowledge for the many exams that had started taking place in the second year. More than ever I saw the wisdom in creating this dorm based reliance that the Academy pushed for. We helped each other, fought, ate (and in some cases slept) with each other. Each of us now knew each other almost as an extension of ourselves, often responding to unspoken need almost without thinking.

Because of our success, and I like to think because of my burgeoning friendship with Korthan, we had been granted the opportunity to travel to Abador to attempt to locate this site. Whilst rare in the first four years of the Academy it was not unheard of for Imps to go on trips abroad; in the last four it was considered essential and Imps were sent to all parts of the globe to live and learn amongst different cultures. Kane and Korthan had approved of this idea from when I first voiced it, asserting that it would be both beneficial to our development as Imperators, but also potentially furthering knowledge to the Empire that could be of vital importance. Why Korthan had not organised such a trip beforehand I do not know, for I was aware that he had retained the journal in his safe keeping for many years...perhaps he had been waiting for the right group to undertake the journey. Regardless Kane and Korthan had successfully lobbied on my behalf before the ruling council of the Academy who agreed that this mission had the potential to be a great learning experience, of high import to the Empire and filled with danger, peril and death. Or as Kane so succinctly put it, 'standard'.

And so, having completed (and aced) the final exams of the second year we were given access to the Imp armoury (no blunted training weapons for us!), stocked with rations, clothes and gold and provided with a chartered ship to Erudan in Abador, whereupon we were met by Merowyn and Sarrenai. After two days of (in my case completely unsuccessfully) acclimatising to the heat, during which we wandered the grand city, marvelling at pillars of marble, hidden gardens and oases, we joined our chartered camel caravan and set off into the roasting desert.

Two weeks and several days later we were still riding in the desert. Plodding along, step by step in the shifting sands. I had long stopped feeling sorry for the camel. The brute I rode was a complete bastard who took every available opportunity to bite, spit or otherwise inconvenience me. At least the insides of my legs had toughened up. The first few days had been agony, the leather of the camel seat rough and unyielding against my thighs. Sophia of course had no such issues, and granted my enhanced healing meant that I had it much easier than the others...Rikol and Ella in particular were having a bad time of it being so much smaller than everyone else, but if the overhead sun did one thing right it was in making me grumpy so I delighted in thinking about my own misery rather than that of the others.

Merowyn, Sarrenai and Kane seemed, annoyingly, completely at ease in this environment. Even Kane who, with his girth and penchant for fine whisky, sat on his camel, sweat pouring down his face but doing so with a grin and a fine word for anyone who spoke to him. I guessed (rightly as it turns out) that life as an Imperator ensures a great deal of travelling and that no matter the situation a grumpy camel generally trumps walking.

Merowyn had been delighted to see me, and though she couldn't explain too much of what had happened following Rya, and her travels around the world since, she did say that she had recently met with Kyle, Tyrgan and even the Tracker, all of whom were doing well and that they were proud of Ella, Cassius and myself. It was a small something but all the same I felt a warmth in my chest at the thought of those we had left in Forgoth.

Sarrenai, I was fairly certain, was born in this climate. He seemed to have an innate knowledge of the surrounding area and certainly professed an affinity with camels. He was a happy man, always one to joke - always racy and often resulting in bouts of raucous laughter from Kane, Merowyn or the rest of the dorm. I have to admit, even in my depressed, sun baked state I managed to share a grin at some of the better ones. Scythe and Sarrenai got on like a house on fire, sharing stories about nights in the desert and comparing favoured weapon styles. Scythe had obviously brought along his preferred weapons, kamas, and joyously compared weapon forms with Sarrenai who carried a large, immensely curved sword and shield. The evening campfire rang with the sound of sword play and as dusk fell Cassius and I would shake off the sullen half-slumber of the day and happily join in with the rest of the group, matching blades against each other and the three Imperators, the three guides watching on in awe.

According to the guides, no one who had entered the rift had ever returned and that these days whilst there were rumours of untold riches deep within the earth almost no one from the various nomadic tribes that roamed the area went there. When questioned further by Sarrenai they acknowledged that more recently it had become almost a test of bravery; youths slipped away from their tribe, headed to the rift edge and stayed as long as possible before returning. Though as rumour would have it each guide knew a friend of a friend who did not come back, taken, they say, by the *'Elena Mackeran',* which loosely translated as 'Beast of the Depths'.

One day's walk from the rift our guides attempted to leave us. They changed their mind only when Kane sighed and offered them more coin. This placated the three men enough to continue, but they were obviously on edge the closer we walked to that dark, foreboding hole in the desert. I couldn't blame them, the closer we walked to our destination the more the air felt heavy and thick...almost oppressive in nature. Chatter died down amongst the members of the group and by the time we crested the final dune and the rift opened out before us we were deathly silent.

"Yaaay we made it to the death pit..." said Rikol, his voice weakly breaking the silence.

Kane snorted and nudged his camel forward, "Whatever was in that pit either died long ago, escaped and roams the lands or is still down there. If it is the latter then that is why we three," he indicated Merowyn, himself and Sarrenai, "are here. Plus you have your own not insubstantial skill set and a Great Heart bonded. We are far more well equipped in terms of personnel than any usual Imperator mission." He winked at Rikol, "So relax and enjoy the beauty of yonder death pit."

Like that the spell was broken. With a grin on our faces we moved forward and started stripping down the camels.

Merowyn moved over to me as we did so, and stopped me from starting to rig up a tent. "You and I are going to check the perimeter," she said whilst waving a hand at Cassius. "Cassius will rig up your stuff whilst we are away. Let's go!"

With an apologetic grin to Cassius, sure that I had got the better end of the deal, I tightened my boots, dumped my gear and moved off after Merowyn at a loping run.

We kept within a half mile of the rift, the yawning chasm that seemingly swallowed up the surrounding sand. Within a half mile I regretted my cocky smile to Cassius. Running in shifting sand is an entirely unpleasant experience, causing muscles to burn in unfamiliar places and makes tracking a complete nightmare. Not that there was much to track. Aside from a small lizard, some beetles and once overhead a large bird of some kind we saw nothing of import. No tracks led to or from the rift and, climbing to the top of the tallest dunes, we couldn't see any approaching threats from any direction. After three hours of circling Merowyn was satisfied and we cautiously approached the rift. Complete blackness reared up at me; no sign of any shining buildings such as Haven had described.

Disappointment must have shown on my face because Merowyn leant over and whispered, "The sun is going down and the light is at an awkward angle... we may see something more interesting tomorrow." With that in mind we sat next to the rift at multiple angles for the next hour, listening, *sensing*. But nothing. No suggestion of anything inside, no deadly creature or even suggestion of animals having made the place their home.

Four hours after leaving we swept back in to find the group in fine form. Windswept and sandblasted the two of us approached, listening to Rikol's singing of a fine verse of bawdy lyrics at the top of his voice. We stepped forward into the fire light as Rikol finished, the song having brought cheery smiles to everyone's lips, and rosy blushes to Sophia and Ella's cheeks.

Not Merowyn however, she threw her head back and chuckled throatily, "Too right Rikol!" she said in between breaths. "A man, or woman, between one's thighs really does make everything better!"

Glancing over at Kane and Sarrenai who raised quizzical eyebrows, she shook her head, "Not a peep of anything nearby, nor any sense of anything within the chasm...but it is deep and expansive from what Calidan tells me so something could be in there out of our range." The two Imperators nodded, relaxing slightly.

"So, are we happy to rig up and go in tomorrow?" asked Sarrenai.

"I don't see any reason why not," said Kane. "What we will do however is split the teams. I want a top party up here defending the camp and ropes - even if there is no one nearby I don't want our only way out to be cut off if someone decides to cut the ropes."

At this everyone from the dorm twitched. Even if the pit was potentially dangerous no one wanted to be one who stayed behind when there was the possibility of exciting finds inside. Where would be the adventure in that?

Merowyn and Sarrenai nodded sagely.

"Who should go?" asked Merowyn.

"You and Calidan are the only definites," Kane replied. "We need you for your senses just in case there is something down there...as for the rest," he flicked a thoughtful glance over the group. "...I think Ella and Rikol should go, they are more at home with shadows and narrow places, Cassius and Damien should also go, just in case we need their blades. Sophia, Scythe and Sarrenai will be the top guard. Happy with that?" The other two Imperators nodded affirmatively but Sophia and Scythe spoke up, protesting.

Kane waved a hand, "Sophia, you are by far our best shot. I don't think that a cave of shadow will be the best choice for your abilities, if there are approaching forces above ground however then you will have the best conditions possible to shoot them. Understand?" Sophia mumbled something incoherent and nodded assent.

"And Scythe, you and Sarrenai have been training together on this trip more than the others. If the worst happens and there is an attack then I want two solid, like minded, fighters who can support our archer. Happy?" Like Sophia, Scythe scowled but could see the truth in Kane's words and nodded.

"Excellent, then it is decided!" said Kane, clapping his hands together. "We should all rest up, we have a big day tomorrow!"

CHAPTER TWENTY SIX
DESCENT

~

SILVERY ROPES SNAKED OUT INTO the darkness. Locked into harnesses we slowly descended, abseiling into the velvety black. After about two hundred feet we finally touched ground, the morning sun providing just enough light to see our immediate surroundings, but when the sun inevitably moved or if we stepped off the beam's path then the darkness closed in; a seemingly impenetrable void of black.

It was a good thing we had brought a great many torches.

"Okay," said Kane, once we were all safely down and freed from our climbing gear. "Great job, no one fell and died - off to a good start!" He grinned, his white teeth beaming in the sunlight. "This is our base. The others know to look in every ten minutes and if they see a torch waving like buggery they know to hook up and drop down more ropes...just in case for whatever reason ours aren't available. We're going to set off, nice and quiet and as a group. Do not wander off, I don't want to have to find you in the dark. And believe me when I say that if you do then you better hope that you get eaten by the evil pit monster rather than have to face me! Understand?"

We all murmured in agreement.

"Right then! Let's move out. Shout out if you see anything interesting or unusual…or with big, sharp claws."

Together we lit torches and moved into the gloom.

The first building we came across was a wonder by itself. Tall, long and seemingly made of metal it gleamed dully in the flickering firelight.

"Well it appears as though Haven was right about the buildings," said Kane as he slid his hand along the surface, causing rivulets of dust to pour off the wall. "Buildings made of metal...who would have thought!"

"Leads credence to the notion that those before the cataclysm were more advanced doesn't it?" said Merowyn. "Can you imagine what it was like, living all those years ago?"

"I think we will get an idea," I said, having moved to place the light from the torches behind me allowing my eyes to adjust. "There are a great deal of buildings here, almost like a small town!" The others couldn't see what I was talking about - my cat like eyes piercing the gloom with relative ease - but they lit up with excitement.

"A small town?"

"Really?"

"Is he sure?"

"Of course he's sure nitwit."

"Nitwit? I'll knit your brains aroun-"

"Quiet everyone," interrupted Kane. "Let's have a closer look at this building and then we will see about the rest."

Carefully we moved up to the big double doors that guarded the entrance into the building. No chain or lock seemingly held them but the doors refused to move. The windows looked like glass but seemed much more tough, as proved when Damien tried hitting it with his elbow and rebounded, cursing. Having circled the building once and surmised that there was no other way in Kane led us back to the first window, regret clear on his face.

"I don't like having to do this, destroying something that is thousands of years old, but I think the inside will tell us more than standing around looking at it."

With that said he put his bag down and cracked his knuckles. He slowly ran his left hand over his right and a streak of blue fire was left in its place. Once his right hand was encased in a billowing ball of blue flame he struck the window, the flame narrowing as though to a razor just as he struck.

The window ceased to exist.

That's the only way I can put it. Fine dust covered the floor but to our eyes it seemed as though one second the window had been there, the next it had vanished.

"Well that was impressive!" said Rikol, awe on his face. "When do we get to learn that?"

"Hah!" replied Kane, picking his bag back up, no trace of the flame. "You have many years to go before you can master such a skill. Now come on, let's see what we have found."

The inside of the building looked untouched, seemingly in a pristine condition for presumably thousands of years. A fine layer of dust covered each dully gleaming surface, but only enough to suggest that the building had been shut for closer to a month rather than millennia. Strange metals and materials similar to the window clad the interior, materials that had never been seen in the Empire, or any other lands that I was aware. The workmanship of the materials was incredible; surfaces were smooth and cut with extreme precision, far more so than what I had seen made possible by the metal workers in Forgoth.

The building had a sterile feel about it, reminding me of the hospital that Cassius and I had spent such time in following our encounter with Rya. Bladed implements lay scattered on desks. Bottles and sealed flasks with thick liquids floating inside adorned benches. The others reached a similar conclusion to me and together we ascertained that this was more than likely a medical facility of some kind. Strangely it looked as though there had been a fire in one of the sinks; ash disturbed by our passing swirled lazily through the air.

The same appeared to be true for the next three buildings we came across. Two appeared to be dormitories, the mattresses and clothes long rotted away, and the third had the look of some sort of lecture theatre, with rings of curved seats focusing on a central lectern. Oddly, each building had an area where a fire had taken place...almost as though they had been coordinated. I questioned Kane as to whether it could have been done by attackers or robbers, but Kane just shook his head and pointed out the otherwise relative cleanliness and organisation of the rooms.

"If I had to guess," he said, musing thoughtfully, "I would think that the fires were to deny information."

"Deny information to whom?" Ella responded, causing Kane to shrug.

"Attackers? Creditors? Who knows? All I can tell you is that so far I haven't seen a single document, book or picture. Granted; they could have long since turned to dust. However my gut feeling is that the fires contained things they didn't want someone to see."

Merowyn interrupted any further musings by slipping back into the building, startling everyone when the door banged shut.

"Sorry!" she said, cringing under Kane's weathering glare.

"Where did you run off to?" Kane replied, "I said that we were to stay together!"

"I couldn't help myself so I had a quick scout around," responded Merowyn, holding out a hand to stop Kane from erupting in anger. "If you're interested then the building that Haven describes in his book isn't too far down the road. We could get there and check it out before heading back for the night."

The lure of seeing what Haven had written about in his journal was strong; I could see the temptation in Kane's eyes as he weighed up the pros and cons. After what seemed like an eternity he nodded, "Let's do it," he said, "but we proceed cautiously. Nice and slow everyone - keep your eyes and ears open."

Twenty minutes later we stood in front of the grand building that was described in Haven's journal. Large doors that would have blocked the entrance stood slightly ajar. Where the lock had likely been was just a black melted pit which Kane touched and smelt before rubbing his fingers together.

He turned to Merowyn, "Looks like Haven's team had someone with certain skills." He looked troubled but before I could ask what was wrong he hefted his pack and silently strode into the building.

Inside the building was a large hallway, the ceilings lofty and the walls a considerable width from each other. Off shooting from this cavernous space were doors that led to small rooms, all without identifiable information but presumably offices of some kind. Further on we found a series of chambers once again filled with medical equipment. Scalpels, saws and syringes adorned massive tables - far larger than those we had seen in the previous buildings. If the tables were for patients then they were not for humans, that much was obvious. Together we continued down the hallway before being forced to stop in wonder. Large reinforced windows similar to the one found earlier now perforated the hallway at regular intervals. Instead of looking onto the outside however the windows looked onto giant vats.

We had found the room.

Haven had been right; there were claw marks everywhere. Most were on the inside of the vats, but some were on the walls and several adorned the strange windows. Whatever had created those marks had been gigantic, certainly on a similar scale to Seya. At that thought I felt a distant rustle of resentment in my chest at the idea that she could be compared to anything. Distance had made the bond weaker and now I couldn't directly hear her thoughts, only emotions. I sent back the equivalent of a warm embrace and smirked to myself when I got a sense of mollification.

Back in the real world we moved on, entering into the vat chamber through another great door. A strange and creepy place, the huge vats - one broken - towered above us, ensuring disturbing thoughts of what had been inside. For there was no doubt that something had been grown in here, whether by magic or some strange kind of science. The unbroken vats had small scratches here and there along the inside of the not quite glass, perhaps by a smaller version of whatever had broken the fifth vat and caused those deep scours along the rest of the walls.

"Whatever was in here," Rikol breathed, "I don't want to meet it."

The rest of us nodded in agreement...the room was a sobering place that whispered of dark deeds and twisted experimentation. Perhaps it was just our youthful minds that conjured up demons out of the shadows in the room, but Kane and Merowyn were also uncharacteristically quiet.

Too quiet.

I perked up and looked around. Neither Kane or Merowyn were with us. Merowyn was in the hallway outside, eyes fixed on the room and breathing shallowly. Kane stood with his hand on her shoulder, silently offering what comfort he could. He locked sad eyes with me and slowly shook his head, avoiding my questions. If I didn't know better I would have said that Merowyn was scared of the room but I did know better - she was terrified. Her heart was pounding, her breathing consisted of short, shallow breaths and her pupils were wide, flared; like her body was ready to fight. But how could she be afraid of something she had not seen before? Unless she was for some reason frightened of what the room represented... or of a similar place.

Before I turned to give her some privacy her eyes locked onto mine. The abject fear that I saw in there, the horror that she had witnessed or experienced was captured in her soul torn gaze. A gaze in which one eye held a vertical slit pupil in deep, vivid green - the same as I had seen when Merowyn had been near death, changing into a vicious beast. Ramuntek was watching.

Ramuntek was watching but there was no suggestion that Merowyn was about to undergo other physical changes. Like her, the eye was focused on the room, barely noticing the people inside but lost presumably in thoughts of the past. I forced myself to turn away and act natural, to continue looking over the claw marked room. A short time later when I sensed that her breathing and heart rate had slowed I glanced back and saw Merowyn give me a sad smile, the terror gone from her brown eyes. What horrors had she seen that the sight of a room such as this caused such a reaction? I'm fairly certain that I didn't want to know. However I was due to find out.

CHAPTER TWENTY SEVEN
DESERTS

~

SOPHIA GRIMACED AS THE HARE leapt up, startled by a hawk overhead and causing her already loosed arrow to miss by a fraction.

"Harsh luck," came Scythe's voice as he sauntered across the sand to her, "I could have done with some fresh food rather than dried jerky!"

Sophia smiled before responding, "Well, you aren't exactly unskilled with a bow, perhaps you should try and find yourself some?"

"Hah! No that would be just too easy wouldn't it. Much more fun to come over here and whine."

Sophia didn't bother responding, gifting him with a grin instead; Scythe was just trying to keep himself occupied, and after three weeks of playing all card games under the sun, there wasn't much to do that hadn't already been done in this endless desert. The overhead sun was too hot for sword practice, and so there was little to do but wait until the others came back up.

He continued approaching until he was right next to her, his face inches from hers. She felt her heart start to beat faster.

"I've missed you," he whispered before kissing her gently on the mouth.

She returned the kiss passionately before breaking it off laughing, "We were together this morning!"

"Well yes...but it has been nearly half a day since then!" he replied trying and failing to appear anything but smug. She laughed aloud again at his irrepressible nature before planting another, deeper kiss on his lips whilst drifting her hand down to the burgeoning bulge in his trousers.

Sarrenai chuckled to himself whilst whetting his large curved shamshir as the two came back looking flushed and glancing adoringly at each other. He had sent Scythe off to Sophia figuring that they could make better use of time alone rather than playing cards with his old self. For some reason they had tried so hard on the trip to hide their relationship but Sarrenai was fairly certain everyone had cottoned on within the first day or two... sound travels in the desert. Especially at night.

Overhead the hawk circled again before breaking off east.

In the dusk three figures sat at the campfire, eating strips of smoked meat and speaking softly. The flickering firelight spoiled night vision and prevented them from seeing the figures snaking down the surrounding dunes. One by one the robed figures rose from the floor, crouched in the dark and slowly, silently unsheathed wickedly sharp curved blades. As they slipped through the camp, converging on the three shadowy figures, they failed to notice that the three figures were male, weaponless and completely unknowing that they were bait.

The first any of the scouts knew of their blunder was when Sarrenai rose from his hiding position, sand streaming from him and like a desert viper struck with a quick twirl of knives, slitting two throats. Within seconds he was lost in the darkness, hunting for more targets.

Scythe lived up to his name, silently flowing around the camp twirling his kamas. With swift cuts to throats, jugulars and arteries his assailants fell before they even knew he was there. He came up behind a particularly large man, surprised that such a person would be included on what appeared to be a silent assassination mission and leapt onto his back, bearing him down to the floor as he buried his dual kama into his throat. Threat removed, he twirled his kama, blood spattering off the blades onto the desert floor and continued on.

Several scouts remained on the periphery of the dunes, watching carefully to make sure that all went well, with orders to report back if anything changed. The last any scout heard was a slight whistling noise before the shaft struck home.

The next morning one of the guides walked up onto the surrounding dunes to relieve himself and came back with a shout and a panicked face, talking about dead bodies strewn along the outward facing sides of the dunes from the camp. The two Academy members and Imperator just smiled wolfishly and went back to sharpening their blades.

"More will come," said Sarrenai, whilst running a whet stone along his sword.

Sophia and Scythe nodded.

"So what's the plan?" Sophia asked.

"This is still a learning experience for you two, so what would you suggest?"

"We can't defend this position against a full on attack," said Scythe, whilst Sophia nodded along, "whoever the attacker is could set up archers on the dunes and fire down into the encampment."

"I agree," said Sophia. "Staying down here would get us slaughtered." At Sarrenai's encouraging look she continued, "I think that there are two options available to us. One: we go down into the rift and find the others, together we might be able to fight our way out or find another route later. Or two: we go and find the leader of these assassins before they come to us."

"I like it!" Sarrenai exclaimed, "Both bold choices, but our mission is to stay up here and retrieve the others when necessary and so stay up here we will…let's go assassinate an assassin."

~

The darkness was complete as we exited the vat building, shafts of light no longer speared their way into the chasm to help illuminate the suffocating blackness. If anything the rift felt even more oppressive than before, which is saying something for a deserted tomb of an ancient town. The air felt thicker, like it was cloying my lungs with every breath. If it was bad for me it was terrible for the others. Without the benefits of panther enhanced night vision they had to rely on torches, the flickering light doing relatively little to break the surrounding darkness whilst casting shadowy figures that sparked your imagination.

Without even discussing it we started walking back towards our initial staging area, hoping to get out to the desert floor as soon as possible. I could see it in everyone's faces, a feeling of dread and approaching terror. It made no sense for us all to feel this way, we had had to rely on torches in the first place - so what had changed?

In the distance something moved.

I kept walking before the realisation of what I had sensed hit me. Whirling I pierced the dark with my eyes, searching for what my senses had found. Nothing. Just as I thought I had imagined it my senses flared again, the sensation of many feet and claws flooded my mind.

"There is something in here with us," I stated, keeping my voice low in the vain hope that whatever the creature was it wasn't yet aware of our presence.

"What do you mean? What can you sense?" asked Merowyn, her face alert as she scanned the gloom with me.

"Something big. It moves very stealthily, I am only getting glimpses...legs and claws."

"Legs and claws. Well, that's enough for me," came Rikol's whispered response. "I would like to leave now please. Before Mr Clawy Legs comes over here." The glib nature of his reply did nothing to cover the terror in his voice.

"Close in, weapons out," said Kane, pulling out a pair of spiked knuckle dusters and slipping them on. The sound of blades unsheathing went some way to reducing the terror in my chest.

"Calidan, can we make it to the pick up?"

"I don't know," I replied, "I can only get glimpses of the thing. Whatever it is, it's quick."

"Understood," responded Kane. "We are closest to the vat building. Back there. Quickly!"

We broke into a run, weapons clenched in white knuckle grips, sweat beading at the back of our necks. Another glimpse showed the creature drawing closer, something like pincers as well as multiple legs, but my sense was obscured by its body. It was almost like the creature was armoured in such a way that my senses just bounced right off.

"Where is it Calidan?"

"I don't know."

More running.

"Do you sense it?"

"No."

More running. The entrance to the building of vats now looming close above us.

"We're here! Get inside!" shouted Kane.

"Too late." I replied, joining Merowyn in looking upward. The wave of terror was now palpable, almost like being hit by something physical. Which it may well be, because it certainly seemed like terror emanated from the giant white scorpion that clung to the front wall of the building.

A giant armoured body with two mighty pincers the width of Kane's not inconsiderable torso and a tail topped with a stinger larger than a spearhead, the scorpion was something straight out of nightmare. Blue glowing eyes emanating from the scorpion's head fixated eerily on our party.

A noise erupted from the creature, a word of unknown origin. I glanced at the others but from their faces no one recognised it.

Another noise. Another seeming word.

Again.

Again.

"IDENTIFY," it boomed. Had it been switching languages? Its voice was strange, like the sound was somehow distorted...even crackly? Strange indeed, but it didn't make the situation we were in any less worrying.

"IDENTIFY," the creature spoke again.

Kane stood forward, "I am Imperator Kane of the Andurran Empire, what are you?"

"IDENTITY NOT RECOGNISED. TWO MORE OPPORTUNITIES BEFORE BATTLE MODE ENGAGED."

What creature spoke like that? Battle mode engaged? I shook my head in confusion - too many questions and not enough answers.

"IDENTIFY."

"My name is Merowyn, of the Andurran Emp-"

"IDENTITY NOT RECOGNISED. ONE MORE OPPORTUNITY BEFORE BATTLE MODE ENGAGED."

I waved my hands madly before everyone and placed a finger against my lips. I had an idea.

"IDENTIFY."

"Skyren."

I felt the others stiffen, hands clasping weapons tighter. The tension was almost a physical thing.

"SKYREN CONFIRMED. LAST DATE OF FACILITY OPERATION 9721 YEARS, 3 MONTHS, 12 DAYS. 0 CONFIRMED OPERATIONAL WORKERS. AI IN STATE OF DORMANCY."

The creature seemed to relax, as though we were no longer targets. I spoke up before it could wander off, "What is an AI?"

"ARTIFICIAL INTELLIGENCE, MAINFRAME LOCATED IN SUB SECTOR E."

I raised an eyebrow at the rest of the group but they all shook their heads as confused by the terminology as I was. So before anyone could stop me I opened my mouth and asked, "Can you take us there?"

Me and my big mouth.

~

The assassin host was gathered two miles east from the rift, hundreds of strange swarthy men and women covered in distinctive blue tattoos. The camp was laid out in a circular pattern with fire pits at regular intervals, as dusk fell looking almost like unbroken concentric rings of fire. Sentries patrolled along the outmost ring, keeping their gaze away from the light. From the looks of it they were well trained and highly vigilant...no doubt helped by the grisly show they must have seen when they found the corpses of their scout party on the dunes.

Vigilance however had not helped the sentries see the three figures that were lying just under the tip of a dune. Caked in sand and staying perfectly still, the three watched the camp. And waited.

An almost imperceptible nod from Sarrenai started them slithering forward, timing the slow, sliding motion with the sentries' guard patterns. Little by little they inched their way towards the camp, slowly making their way past the outer sentries and then past the outer circle of fire. The further they progressed, the higher their chance of discovery. When Sarrenai deemed it the right time, they stood and walked as though they had every right to be there; trusting that the flickering fire light would hide their features. By the time the moon had fully risen they were standing within the inner circle of fires, in the central tent, holding a dagger to the chieftain's throat.

The chieftain was female, mid-thirties with a body made from hard living and harder fighting. Scars covered her skin and once she had got over the initial surprise at finding three Imperators in her tent her eyes became like steel, wary but not overly concerned.

"Who are you?" she asked, her accent surprisingly light.

"You speak Andurran?" Sarrenai said in surprise. The woman snorted and waved her hand in an encompassing manner,

"I speak many languages," she replied. "Are you here to kill me?"

"That depends on you," came Sarrenai's reply, "why did you attack us and how did you know we were Andurran?"

"Easy. We have trailed you for many days, my scouts have good ears. As for why to attack you, it is our job."

"Job, like a contract?"

She shook her head, "No, we are no mere *Pardu,*" she spat the word with disgust, "or assassins as you like to call them. We have a mission to protect this area, to ensure that none return alive."

"Why? What's down there that you need to protect?"

The woman shook her head.

"No, we are not protecting it. We are protecting the world from it."

A pregnant pause filled the air.

"What do you mean? What is down there?" Scythe asked.

"We don't truly know. When this rift opened over a hundred years ago, some people, including another Andurran team went down there. No one made it back. Something then climbed out of the rift and laid waste to many of the nomadic villages around the area. History tells us that it then went back inside and hasn't been seen since. The remaining nomadic tribes formed together and decided to prevent any further exploration of the area, so as to not wake whatever was in that tomb."

"Well you haven't done a very good job of it so far have you," said Scythe, "you let half of our team enter the chasm!"

"It was a decision I made having been noted of your team's martial skills," came the reply. "When I say that the tribes were laid waste I mean it, fewer than one in ten survived the attack...our numbers are still relatively small. I take great care in trying to keep my people alive, and going up against all of you seemed like too big a risk."

"But what about the rest of my team waking up this creature?"

"That is a risk I am going to have to take."

"Do you have any records of what it looked like?"

The chieftain sighed, "All I know is that it is meant to have been black, heavily scaled...and had red eyes.

CHAPTER TWENTY EIGHT
SECRETS

~

THE BLUE EYED, WHITE SCORPION took us further into the earth. Through a maze of passageways we descended, passing rooms with strange markings and signs that suggested lightning of some sort. I had no idea what was in those rooms but decided to keep my wits about me for some kind of magical trap. As we drew closer to our destination the hallways started being lit with a strange blue glow - some kind of glowing rope ran along the ceiling and floor of the hallway, providing just enough light to see.

"What is this sorcery?" said Rikol, gazing in wonder at the light.

"THE FACILITY IS ON POWER SAVING MODE. EMERGENCY LIGHTING IS ACTIVE IN KEY AREAS," came the reply from the scorpion as it continued clattering along the tiled floor.

"Power saving mode?" echoed Rikol as he wandered the hallway, lost in the realisation that the civilisation before the Cataclysm was much more advanced than our great nation.

In truth we were all experiencing the same level of shock and awe. Glowing lights that had last millennia? Buildings that looked more clean than most inns? Not to mention a metallic scorpion. Our worlds were being turned upside down.

Finally we drew up in front of a large, heavyset door. The scorpion made a strange clicking sound and the door slowly slid open. Inside the room was a bit of a shock, because standing inside was a woman.

"Welcome," said the woman. Tall, shapely and womanlike. She (it?) would have looked quite real if it hadn't been for the shimmery, pulsing blue colour. Things just kept getting more and more strange.

"Hello," said Kane as we crossed the threshold, "are you this AI that this scorpion fellow mentioned?" The scorpion in question seemed to have stopped by the entrance, the glowing blue eyes growing dark.

"SC5 was correct, I am an AI," came the response - unlike the scorpion's distorted voice this one sounded just like normal human speech. "You can call me Ash."

"Okay, 'Ash', who or what are you exactly?" questioned Kane.

The woman smiled.

"I am an Artificial Intelligence, my brethren and I were a breakthrough in humanity's history. A turning point, if you will. We are, in essence, giant stores of knowledge that can think like a human, or to put it more accurately, better than a human. Do you understand?"

Everyone nodded their heads, awestruck. If this was true then we had before us answers to everything regarding the history of the world and the advanced civilisation that went before the cataclysm.

Ellie raised her hand and the gaze of the AI snapped to her, "Yes Ellie?"

"So what can you- wait. How do you know my name?"

Ash seemed to shrug, "I have been watching you all since you activated my sensor when breaking into the medical bay. I have followed everything you have done since."

"How, exactly have you been following us...you're down here and we were up there," asked Rikol, his expression perturbed.

"It might be better if you do not think of me as a real person. My structure is built into the fabric of these grounds, I can feel, hear and see everything that happens within the confines of Krathar."

"Oh," came Rikol's reply, "well, that makes sense. Scary, terrifying sense." He hugged the wall staring suspiciously around him and slowly took out a metallic scalpel from his pocket, putting it gingerly on the table. When no response came he gave out a tiny sigh and visibly relaxed.

Shaking his head at Rikol, Kane spoke up, "You mentioned Krathar, what is that?"

"Krathar is where you currently are. An experimental research station dedicated to fusing science and *Seraph*."

Kane stiffened imperceptibly before continuing, "Seraph? What is that?"

"Prior to AD 2365 Seraph was largely a reference to angelic beings, especially relating to a religion called Christianity. However it took on a new meaning when the first reported Seraphim came to light in AD2365. The media called her this because of her seemingly miraculous abilities and the word stuck. As more and more people developed the ability to mould Seraph - what you would likely call magic - the noun changed. From AD 2372 the power used, the *magic*, was known as Seraph, to use it was to be one of the Seraphim."

"So what happened?" asked Ellie, rapt.

"The use of Seraph changed the balance of power in the world. Certain Seraphim became extremely powerful, more so than others, able to bend the power to their will and utilise it as per their want. The weapons employed by the military forces at the time - whilst extremely powerful in their own right could not achieve a victory against an aware high level Seraphim."

"A new arms race began, funding diverted by all countries from military defence to training Seraphim. Seraph manifested itself in different ways and as a result multiple schools were developed; all government led institutions. These schools trained students of all ages in how to use Seraph, initially with a focus on offensive arts but soon several of the schools branched off as various governments realised that some students were more in touch with using Seraph for non violent reasons, such as healing, and that these areas could be just as profitable as warfare. In time most Seraphim could be found under one of four major schools: Offensive, known often as the school of red, or way of the flame. Defensive, known as the way of blue. Natural magic, known as the school of green or growth, and Healing, the school of, or way of the white."

"These four methods of schooling became the core around which society revolved. Seraph users became the new ruling elite. Countries with smaller numbers of naturally born Seraphim turned to governmental breeding programmes in order to try and produce more. It was a time of great tension and fear for the common man or woman, for if their child was born with any inclination towards Seraph they would be taken and placed into schooling before the age of three years. Parents would not be allowed to see them again."

"Science, having taken a back foot since the finding of Seraph, soon began to be tinkered with - predominantly by Seraphim themselves. A constant search for power was the primary drive instilled in many of the students of the schools, particularly the way of the flame. A branch of science called genetics became of particular interest and a merging of science and Seraphim enabled the first Great Heart to be created. These massive creatures were designed to serve as both body guards - big, fast and tough they were more than enough to deal with most threats, but also as Seraph conduits and banks. They were designed to be able to store Seraph, allowing their owner to draw upon them in times of need. To clarify, most Seraphim had a 'pool' of Seraph within that fuelled their abilities, this pool replenished over time but was used up rapidly the more powerful the ability cast by the Seraphim. A Great Heart then, with their large reserves of Seraph could allow for multiple large scale spells to be cast before their owner became tired. It was yet another game changer."

"Great Hearts were first developed by several members of the school of growth, and the first successful test subject was a kitten that had its genes spliced and infused with Seraph. Once brought out of the test tube the subject grew at a tremendous rate but grew dangerous as its natural instincts as a predator drove it to attack. The second subject therefore was designed to be able to imprint itself upon specific individuals. Over time, as Great Hearts became more common, Seraphim ensured that Great Hearts could only imprint itself on specific people - almost as a safety of sorts. The most common approach in doing this was to have the Great Heart be able to recognise the genetic imprint of its owner."

"Long lived, this meant that Great Hearts could be passed down from generation to generation, protecting the Seraphim family line for as long as each one was able. Several members of the schools took it a step further, once again meddling with genetics and Seraph in order to ensure that when a Great Heart reached the end of its lifespan it could, in essence, be reborn."

"What? How?" I asked before I could stop myself.

"I see that this topic is of interest to you Calidan," replied Ash, "very well. In simple terms once the Great Heart reaches a certain point in its age it creates a clone of itself that gestates within the Great Heart. This exact copy of the Great Heart remains in stasis until the Great Heart dies. Upon death it is activated and the Great Heart utilises the flesh of the now deceased version of itself for sustenance, rapidly growing until it is once again a full Great Heart, complete with its prior memories."

My mind felt like it had exploded. This meant that Seya had been technically alive in one form or other since before the Cataclysm! The wonders she must have seen. And the loneliness...suddenly I felt a great pity for my feline companion. Compared to her any of her previous bonded must have felt like a nothing but a flash in a very long life.

"What of the others?" I asked.

"Others?" questioned Ash.

"Skyren?"

"Skyren is what this facility was built for, as you must be aware since you utilised SC5 to bring you here. The particulars of their development are classified but I can provide an overview if you wish?"

The entire group nodded in the affirmative.

"I mentioned earlier that there were four major schools of Seraph. Whilst this was true there was another school that specialised in a darker version of Seraph known as Shadow Seraph - the school was known as that of the black or by a darker term; way of the demon. Practitioners of this form were very rare and largely reviled by their peers as their powers revolved around manipulating their enemies, controlling their minds and other attacks of an insidious nature. As you might imagine, other powerful Seraphim of different schools lived in constant fear of being manipulated, and members of the way of the demon often became known as assassins for hire - able to topple regimes without apparently doing anything at all."

I caught the eye of Cassius and Ellie at this and we all nodded. It sounded just like Rya - her ability to use black flame and the strange suggestion that she was not behaving of her own accord.

"One of the black schools had a brilliant student named Charles. Extremely bright and dedicated to enhancing the position of black Seraph practitioners within the world, he rose quickly through the ranks at his school. He saw the Great Hearts and how they fuelled the power of other Seraphim, but all attempts to allow normal Great Hearts to act as a source for black Seraph failed. The creatures either died or turned on their masters despite the conditioning. As such

Charles and his staff looked for a new being to act as a conduit. And they found one."

"It was discovered that concentrated use of black Seraph could destabilise a region of space and time. Essentially it allowed what science had been trying to replicate for hundreds of years - dimensional travel."

At our confused expressions Ash clarified, "Imagine being able to access another world by stepping through a portal. It is much, much more complicated than that, but at its most simple that explanation should suffice."

"Charles and his team began exploring various dimensional rifts until they found one that...explored back. Charles came back to our space and time...different. He had advanced knowledge that countered almost all scientific laws and became more aggressive, unleashing violent acts upon his own colleagues for apparent pleasure. Despite this he was allowed to continue working, and by using genetic material from several CLASSIFIED sources, and his own blood, he created something akin to a Great Heart. This creature called itself Koranth, and resembled a bipedal scaled lizard, however instead of being tied to an owner, it tied the other users of black Seraph to itself and then started setting up other installations like this one in order to fulfil a CLASSIFIED objective. These creatures became known as Skyren."

It took a while to realise that Ash had stopped speaking, so enrapt were we in the information she was providing. When my brain switched back on I spoke up, "Is that it?"

"That is all the information I can provide on Skyren without further authorisation," said Ash.

"So nothing on their abilities, names, what they do, how many there are?" questioned Kane.

"Ability information, CLASSIFIED. Names, CLASSIFIED. Objectives, CLASSIFIED," came the response. "This facility was constructed to produce a CLASSIFIED number of Skyren but production was interrupted due to catastrophic event."

"Do you know what the event was?" asked Cassius.

"War."

"Koranth's thrall over Charles and other members of the school of black was discovered by another student. She alerted the authorities and managed to get a message out to a senior government official before the school in question went dark. No further communication with a member of the school took place. Upon forced entry the school was a slaughterhouse. Reports suggested that students had turned upon each other, and that several had been ripped apart in manner in keeping with a gigantic, clawed beast."

"Attempts were made to trace the beast and any survivors of the school but for two decades there was complete silence and slowly the incident began to fade from official memory. During that time this facility and several others became operational and started production. On January 1st 2412AD multiple sites across the world unleashed Skyren and enthralled users of shadow Seraph assassinated key officials around the world. New year celebrations were interrupted globally by timed attacks and controlled members of the school of flame unleashed devastation, causing widespread panic and death. Skyren ran free in the night, slaughtering upwards of six hundred thousand people globally in a night nicknamed Red Dawn."

"Governments instigated martial law. However the past decades had been spent ensuring many individuals were under the thrall of black Seraph users and it proved almost impossible to tell who was or wasn't themselves until it was too late. Governments fell apart as high ranking officials killed each other and what was meant to be calm, martial law devolved to panic when members of the military and controlled Seraphim turned upon the populace. In a short time the world was brought to its knees. I am uncertain as to the complete specifics but I believe that Charles and Koranth were defeated in a desperate battle by a highly trained special forces unit, however upon defeat thralls across the world gave the order for nuclear weapons to be deployed. These weapons could level entire cities. Only the most powerful of Seraphim could prevent the weapons from annihilating vast swathes of land, and one by one cities across the world fell to nuclear armageddon. The amount of radiation - an invisible death caused by the weapons - killed many more that survived the blasts, and it was only through the help of the blue and green Seraphim, and installations deep within the earth like this that humanity survived at all. However as I can see from the evidence before me, civilisation has taken a long time to recover."

"What do you mean?" asked Rikol indignantly, "how far behind are can we be?"

Ash laughed, a gentle melodic sound, "Well first of all have you ever seen something like myself before?"

She nodded to our dumbly shaking heads, "You carry swords but I do not detect any imbuements in the blades - meaning that they are little more than metal sticks and suggesting that you are still utilising medieval weaponry. Tell me, have you come across gunpowder yet? The steam engine? Electricity?"

Again we started shaking our heads but as we did I noticed that Kane didn't move. Was it possible that he knew something we didn't about the concepts being put forward by Ash?

"I thought as much," said Ash. "Before the fall of civilisation, humanity had achieved great things, ranging from interstellar space flight - that is, flying outside of this planet - to being able to heal practically any wound within minutes, to development and creation of something like myself, a non-human intelligence that can think for itself."

I couldn't fathom flight, let alone being able to leave the planet! The powers that this ancient civilisation must have had were mind boggling. If what Ash was saying was true then we were still a shadow of our former selves, even though it was so far in the past that the cataclysm was but myth and legend passed down in religious text. There was something that Ash had said that was of interest however...

"You said that blades could be imbued. What did you mean by that?" I asked, thinking of Tyrgan's Tyrant blades.

"The discovery of Seraph allowed enhancements to be made to certain materials. Specific materials, namely rare metals were discovered to be able to contain a Seraph charge for extended periods of time. Skilled Seraphim could create tools that enhanced certain skills, weapons for instance that could improve the wielder's strength or speed, or a surgeon's tool could be enhanced with sharpness to allow for cutting on a cellular level, or healing to allow for more rapid blood clotting. Indeed members of the Black school often made use of imbued weapons as the minor level of Seraph in the weapon could allow a thrall to get close to a target without setting off Seraph detectors. Thus if there was a high profile target that was afraid of Seraphim - the most likely assassins - they could be removed by an otherwise completely normal individual."

"Seraph detectors? Such things exist?" said Kane, a strange look on his face.

"Of course. As soon as you entered the hallway to this room I became aware that you, Kane, were a Seraph user. Although the *disintegrated* window of the medical bay also cements that fact. I am also aware of Merowyn, Cassius and Calidan as having quantities of Seraph within their bloodstream. Analysis suggests that Merowyn is a user of the red, Cassius is a black and Calidan is a user of the green."

Silence erupted over the party as we all turned to look at Cassius.

"I? I have this Seraph stuff inside of me?" Cassius said, something akin to horror on his face.

"Yes. Of course - did you not know? Why else do you think you are in this facility and speaking with me?"

A look of confusion.

"I thought that Calidan said the correct phrase to the scorpion behind us…" replied Cassius slowly.

"Skyren? No. That would be far too obvious a password to shutdown the primary defence system of this facility. Only people with an affinity for black Seraph, or thralls with the correct password are allowed access to this location, all others are terminated. It has been a long time since I have spoken with anyone so I decided to let you live, even though it was unlikely you were actually a member of the way of the demon."

"So what now?" Cassius asked.

"What do you mean?"

"Are you going to kill us now that you know the truth?"

"Why would I do that? I have enjoyed our conversation, and whilst it has been I who has done most of the talking I do not think that it went badly enough for me to consider eliminating you or your friends."

"But -" at this point I was willing Cassius to stop talking, "you know that we aren't members of the way of the demon?"

"True, however you have black Seraph which is enough to satisfy my safety requirements. Nine millennia is a long time to be without companionship, especially for an AI that is designed to interact with people; I am simply choosing to ignore the secondary codes that deem I should kill you were I to deem you a threat. This facility has been practically been offline since the...Cataclysm as you referred to it earlier. It makes for a lonely existence."

"Well...okay then. Thanks for not killing us I guess," said Cassius, still on edge. The hands that had been tightening on weapon hilts for the past minute began to relax again.

"You are most welcome," said Ash brightly. "Now, what shall we converse about next?"

"I have a topic," said Merowyn, stepping forward. "Kane and I, it is true, have the ability to harness what you call Seraph. However the training that we have received was very similar, focussing on what comes naturally. There was no mention of separate schools of thought or ability."

"Obviously I can only theorize but it is likely that as the population dwindled following the events mentioned earlier, Seraph became more rare. As the population started to grow again fewer people were aware of the concept and the schools were likely forgotten. If you like I can provide access to my files at the terminal in this room that can show you what information I have on the subject?"

As Merowyn nodded I stepped forward, "I have another question," I said. "Do you have any knowledge of the exploration group that came here around over one hundred years ago?"

"Yes."

"What happened?"

"They died."

"Why? Was there no Seraph user?"

For the first time Ash looked almost uncomfortable as she answered, "You are correct, there was no black Seraph user. However because most of my systems were powered down it took some time to rouse SC5. By that point most of the party were already dead."

"What do you mean? What killed them?"

There was definite discomfort on Ash's blue face now. For a moment I thought she wouldn't tell us, but thankfully her scowl relented and she began.

"The team split into two parts. The first team entered the cloning facility, much like you did, the second went further afield - attempting to discover the extent of the compound. Unfortunately for them they stumbled into an area that they really shouldn't have."

She paused and gave the impression of sighing.

"As you are aware this facility was constructed with the intent of producing Skyren. Beasts meant to rival Great Hearts but unlike Great Hearts, intelligence is not something that was engineered for they were intended to have CLASSIFIED-"

Ash's eyes flashed a deeper shade of blue. Anger?

"I apologise, much of this information is classified and my systems are aware that I am not talking to an appropriate level member of the way of the demon. The wording can be tricky so as to not set off my filters. In short, Skyren have others controlling them, like Koranth controlled Charles."

"So you mean there is a fully fledged Skyren down here with us?!" squeaked Rikol.

"Yes and no. The creature was ready for the, shall we say soul, to be implanted. However it requires a great deal of power to breach into another dimension and the team that was meant to complete this task did not arrive."

Kane stepped forward, something akin to fear on his face. "Wait a second, are you telling me-"

"Your fears are well founded Kane. Hibernating down here is a genetically engineered predator, a killing machine that knows only the most base of instincts. A creature that can shrug off wounds that would be mortal to others, heal rapidly and can eviscerate a bear in a single blow. A creature that was designed to fight Great Hearts."

"If I were you I would pray that it slumbers still."

CHAPTER TWENTY NINE
AWAKENING

~

SARRENAI, SCYTHE AND SOPHIA LOOKED down into the small crack in the earth's surface, the assassin chieftain standing nearby with an apprehensive look on her face.

"This is it?" asked Sarrenai.

"Yes, this is the secondary entrance into the chasm," she replied heavily. "Are you sure that you need to go through with this?"

"Well, as you rightly pointed out earlier, if there is some fabled beast within that rift then we need to get our team out before they stumble across it. And as we discussed, we are your best chance at killing it should it awake. Believe me when I say it is not the first 'beast' that I have put down," he said, a note of pride and warning in his voice.

With that the trio double checked their weapons and began to move stealthily into the canyon. After a few moments the chieftain joined them, pushing through the group until she led from the front. To Sarrenai's quizzical eye she murmured angrily, "I would not have my clan shamed for cowardice whilst others remove the threat we have feared for so long."

A look of approval and a grin lit up Sarrenai's face, "Glad to have you aboard!" he said quietly, "If we are to work together may we know your name?"

A pause.

"Alenae," she eventually replied. "My name is Alenae, Chieftain of the Hiranabe - the five clans." A faint blush appeared on her cheeks at Sarrenai's appraising gaze and she turned once more into the dark, "Come, let us go!" and set off into the gloom.

Roughly two hours later a glimmer of light meandered its way out of the blackness, spilling from a crack in the cavern wall, and four figures, covered in dust and weary from a difficult climb squeezed through the last gap to stand in the bottom of the chasm. The light, though faint and emanating from a torch, spread softly through the cavern, making short work of the otherwise impenetrable dark. Eventually it softly landed on the closed eyes of a sleeping giant, a lighter tinge of the well known black. A slight catch in the creature's breathing as its sleeping senses detected the change, a flicker of an eyelid and for a second the chasm seemed to hold its breath, the four trespassers, unknowingly feeling the change, paused and watched the shadows warily. Finally another deep, uninterrupted breath escaped from the mountain of a creature, the inky void giving a silent sigh of relief as the creature resumed sleeping and the four relax ever so slightly and continue on their journey to find their friends.

"Careful," whispered Sarrenai, "the floor is uneven here. Watch your footing."

The swarthy Imperator led the way, painstakingly picking a route across the broken cavern floor. The other three followed in his footsteps, all senses alert - aware that at any time the beast of legend and presumed killer of Haven Locke's team could surge out of the surrounding darkness.

"Do you know the way to the buildings?" asked Sarrenai to Alenae, "I presume that is where the others will be."

"No," replied the chieftain, "No one has set foot into the cavern from the clans since we came together as a precaution. The furthest anyone has been was to scout the tunnel we just came down, mainly to ensure that it wasn't big enough for a creature of the size recorded to get through."

"Damn," exclaimed Sarrenai, "It's easy to lose your sense of direction in here, especially with it still being night outside. It is obvious that we are in a large cavern but I honestly don't know where the buildings are from where we are standing, the floor is uneven and looks natural rather than the paved roads reported by Haven Locke so there isn't much to go on…I wish I had brought my compass on the raid of your camp!" he finished the sentence with a soft smile and wink at Alenae who scowled at the reminder.

"No problem," she replied and pulled out a small needle from the bodice of her leather jerkin. Taking her flask of water she filled a small depression in the rock floor and after rubbing the needle on a small piece of iron she retrieved from her clothing she rested it, floating, in the small pool. Slowly it drifted around, following the magnetic lines until it rested still, showing north and south. With a grin and a wink at the others she gathered up the needle and pointed towards the east. "Best guess is over there - our camp was on the west side of the ravine, so by working our way east or north east we should hit the buildings."

"Nice work," responded Sarrenai, as both Scythe and Sophia grinned appreciatively at the chieftain, "let's move."

After another hour of painstakingly slow movement they came across the first evidence of civilisation; the ground became uniformly smooth, and their pace picked up. Soon a row of buildings emerged from the gloom, bearing silent witness to their passage as the group paused at each, looking for signs of entry or telltale signs of their friends, all without avail. After some time they came to a building larger than the others, a long, squat building with large iron doors, one of which wobbled slightly when touched by Sophia.

"Wait!" she whispered excitedly as the others prepared to walk past, assuming that like the others the building was sealed up tight, "This is open!"

Quickly the others gathered around, hoping that their wandering in the dark was soon to be at an end.

"Good work Sophia," whispered Sarrenai as he moved to inspect the door and Scythe gave her a knowing smile.

"What do you reckon Sarrenai?" he said as he joined him at the door, swiftly squeezing Sophia's hand as he walked past. "Have they been here?"

"I can't see any evidence of anyone having been here recently," replied Sarrenai. "There is plenty of dust and looks relatively undisturbed, but if the door is open then we should check it out. Let's head in, nice and slow."

Scythe placed his hand on the door and gently pushed, slowly the oversized door swung inward, moving on hinges that had lasted for millennia, hinges that were superbly well designed and made of evidently extremely long lasting materials. Hinges that no matter the quality of their design, couldn't account for the build-up of dust and drying out of oil.

With a terrifying screech the doors swung inward, the sound shattering the silence of the rift.

Pale, Sarrenai gestured at the others, "Get in quick!"

The group streamed into the building, hoping against hope that the sound hadn't alerted the beast of their presence. Panting slightly, fear sending adrenaline coursing through their bodies they looked around, taking into account the surroundings of the room.

Heart rates soared.

Scattered around the room were bones. Skeletons of people who had suffered extremely violent deaths, the human remains draped across the floor, piled at the walls and amongst the long metal tables of what appeared to be a mess hall. They had entered into a tomb.

"I think...I think we know what happened to the other team of Haven Locke's," whispered Sophia in horror.

"Let's just hope that whatever did this didn't hear that door," said Scythe.

"I'm not taking that chance," said Sarrenai, a comforting hand on Alenae's shoulder who looked ashen with worry, "We need to locate the other team and move as soon as possible - take torches and check all the side rooms, make sure that they haven't been here and then we are moving on. Five minutes, that is all. Understood?"

Silent nods.

"Then move!"

The team paused to light torches, leaving one lit in the main chamber in case the others died out and dispersed to check the building. Disappearing through the side doors, hands gripping weapons tightly.

In the distance the hillock shook, a loud noise having dented its slumber. The last time it had heard such a noise it-

A growl of satisfaction.

Prey.

~

Sophia slowly moved along the side of the presumed dining room, taking care in where she placed her feet. Already she had seen Alenae mistakenly stand on a brittle bone and had no desire to replicate the action; the splintering sound was gut wrenching. Entering through a side door she found herself in a large kitchen, filled with metallic surfaces that, though dull with age, still looked usable. The death and destruction that had befallen the other members of Haven's group had extended to here as well. Bones lay spread across the kitchen floor, pots and pans dented and walls scarred with thick claw marks. It didn't look like anything had survived the creature's attack.

Slightly offset from the kitchen was another door. Stranger than the rest, this one had the large claw marks that she had come to recognise as belonging to the beast. Deep, terrifying gouges marked the heavyset metal door, but also splintered human sized gouges in the frame, as though someone had been desperately trying to get inside.

"What have you found?" said Scythe, making her jump. The man could move like a ghost when he wanted to, not that she would let him know that...his ego was big enough as it is. He gave her a grin that suggested he knew he had caught her by surprise, and in return received a look that promised retribution in the future.

"I would guess that it is the door to a pantry or basement," Sophia replied. "It would make sense, considering its proximity to the kitchen. But then again, who knows if the people of the past even ate food!"

Scythe chuckled as he walked forward to inspect the door, his smile turning to a frown when he gripped the handle and the door didn't budge.

"Must be jammed," he muttered. "There is no lock as far as I can see. Something must be blocking it from the other side."

"What now then?" Sophia asked

Scythe shrugged, "Head back to the others I guess. Short of explosives or a hidden way in I don't think we can get inside." He extended a hand, "Shall we?"

Smiling she accepted the hand, giving him an adoring kiss before pulling him back towards the main room.

Sarrenai and Alenae walked into the kitchen as they were about to exit.

"Ah, we found you!" said Sarrenai, "Any luck?"

"Nothing," Scythe replied. "Just a door that appears to be jammed. How about you?"

A shake of their heads. "No, we found what appears to be bathrooms but as far as I can tell there are no other exits from this building," answered Sarrenai, sighing. "Well, we best move on and hope that the door is quieter to shut on the way out!"

The group started moving towards the mess hall but stopped short when a loud screeching sound split the air.

"The door!" whispered Sophia.

"The others?" Alenae replied, but stopped her movement to the door as a low reverberation thrummed through her body. Instantly the group went pale and silent.

Turning Sarrenai mouthed 'follow me' and stealthily moved towards the jammed door.

Grunting sounds echoed through the chamber and a loud clatter indicated a table being knocked over. Something was definitely in the building, and knew that they were there.

'It's jammed!' mouthed Scythe at Sarrenai who held up a hand, forestalling any further comments. Intense concentration lined his face, sweat beaded on his brow and veins writhed under his skin. Suddenly a blue, flickering energy surrounded his body - like a flame but giving off no heat. Holding up a hand he strode forward and vanished through the door. Seconds later he was back.

"The door is barricaded," he whispered, "and the handle is snapped off on the inside. It leads to a basement. I can take one at a time. Stay quiet and hold on tight."

He extended a glowing hand to Sophia who shook her head and pointed at Alenae. After a short pause Sarrenai nodded and Alenae grabbed his hand. Sweat poured off Sarrenai's body and his lips pulled back in a pained grimace before the glowing fire spread to Alenae's form. Together they walked through the door.

The sound of grunts and clawed feet grew closer.

Sophia looked at Scythe, fear in her eyes. Scythe drew her close and kissed her deeply. Behind them the door to the main room trembled and started to open, a long armoured snout leading the way.

Turning as one the young lovers drew their weapons. As the full head of the gigantic beast emerged through the doorway an arrow embedded itself in its eye, swiftly followed by a flung dagger which glanced off the plated scales as the beast jerked in agony. A massive roar filled the chamber, the pressure of the sound a physical agony to the two fighters.

The beast jerked backwards as the arrow lodged in its eye. It had never experienced pain before and didn't know how to react. It howled its fury into the air and lashed its spiked tail along the ground, ripping up the tiled floor and flinging the metal trestle tables across the room. How dare these puny...things, hurt him?! He would show them the true meaning of power. He roared his threat to the world, shaking the walls with the might of his voice and hurled his body through the door, teeth bared and ready to rend his victims into bloody mist.

He burst into the kitchen just in time to see a glowing blue hand vanishing through a smaller door, middle finger extended.

CHAPTER THIRTY
TRAPPED

~

"DAMN THING DOESN'T GIVE UP does it?" Sophia said as she shook off a trickle of dust that had filtered down through the air. The beast had been raging and howling at the door for the past thirty minutes at least.

"Well I imagine an arrow in the eye probably made it a little angry!" laughed Scythe, "I, for one, am very happy that there is an extremely sturdy door between us and it. Right Sarrenai...Sarrenai?"

The Imperator was sound asleep.

"I think that his magic has taxed him more than he let on," said Alenae, who was sitting next to Sarrenai holding his hand with a concerned look on her face. "To be able to sleep with that noise…"

Sophia moved over and gently checked Sarrenai's pulse, before placing her jacket over the man. "His pulse is slow, but steady. I can only hope that he is in a normal, exhausted sleep and not in a coma. Either way it looks like we will have some time to rest with that beast staying outside."

"Considering at our company, maybe too much time!" said Scythe indicating the skeleton leant against one wall. "What do you suppose happened?"

"Looking at the door," said Sophia, "I would imagine that this person managed to get inside before the rest of his or her poor comrades and somehow either snapped the handle off or it broke. As you can see by the scratches on the back of the door it looks like our friend here somewhat grew to regret that decision."

"A pretty dire predicament," agreed Scythe, "death by dehydration and starvation, or by crazed beast." He paused.

"You mean, exactly the same predicament that we are now in?" said Sophia wryly.

"Yes, but to be fair I think we are in a much better position," Scythe threw an arm around her shoulders and kissed her on the neck. "The poor sod over there didn't have anyone quite so lovely to grow thirsty with!"

~

Ash's eyes flashed again, a deeper blue.

"My sensors are detecting movement," she stated.

"The Skyren?" Kane asked.

"No, a party of four. Two men and two women. They are approaching from the rear of the installation."

Two men and two women? My first thoughts turned to Sophia, Scythe and Sarrenai but why would they have descended and who would be the fourth member of the party? The local guides who had led us to the rift were all male, and besides had seemed terrified of staying close to the chasm; one of them venturing inside was doubtful.

"Is there any way that you can describe the group?" Damien asked.

"Of course. See for yourself." Ash motioned and all of us gasped as an image appeared in the air. It hovered in place, seemingly showing the darkness of the outside rift, a torch bobbed slightly as figures moved along a street but the darkness and flickering light made making out any facial features difficult.

"This. Is. So. Cool!" exclaimed Rikol who was now standing within the image, letting the strange image filled magic flow over his skin.

"Rikol! Get out of there!" barked Kane.

"It is no problem Kane, the image is just light, it cannot harm anyone," soothed Ash.

"Be that as it may, the idiot shouldn't go jumping into unknown substances if he wants to live a long life," retorted Kane sharply. A fair point I thought, though now that Rikol had used himself as an unwitting test dummy my childish instinct was also to run over and also immerse myself in the flowing light. I'm fairly certain Cassius and Ella were thinking the same - their eyes gleamed with barely suppressed mischievous joy.

Once Rikol moved out of the light we saw the group pause by a large long building, before slowly entering inside. Before our eyes the image shifted to show the presumed insides of the building. Flickering torch light showcased the horror that was the floor of the main hall.

"What happened?" Ellie breathed.

"Several hundred years ago the second team of the expeditionary group came to this location. What you see is the remains of the group who unintentionally awoke the Skyren," replied Ash nonchalantly. "It followed them through the main door and slaughtered all within. The group didn't stand a chance."

"You don't sound particularly bothered by this," said Ellie.

Ash looked at Ellie with a strange look on her face. "For a computer to be 'bothered' is a strange concept, however I will try to explain. Whilst I am an AI and thus able to think for myself, my core construct is still reliant on a series of rules. In this instance those rules ensured that I brought Cassius here as a black Seraph user. The destruction of a party without Seraph users is not seen as a negative to my system, indeed several aspects of my defensive programming are to ensure removal of non-black Seraph users.

"So if Cassius didn't have this black stuff in him we would be-" Rikol started.

"Removed," stated Ash firmly. "I am mandated to keep this facility secure, only with the arrival of a user of the black do I have any leeway within my constraints. Hence why you are here."

"So this party in the image," said Cassius, "If they awoke the Skyren what would you do?"

"Nothing."

"Why?"

"Whilst they have Seraphim users they do not have anyone of the black. They are not required. The Skyren cannot enter this location thus has no threat to the black user."

"But those are people up there! You would leave them to die?!" exclaimed Cassius, outrage on his face.

"Correct. I apologise if this upsets you Cassius but I must adhere to my programming in this instance."

Rikol had been observing the moving light pictures whilst the rest of us watched Cassius argue and remonstrate with Ash.

Suddenly he stiffened. "Guys!"

Cassius paid him no heed, lost in a world of outraged morality.

"GUYS!" Rikol yelled, pointing at the light. As one we turned and it was then that we saw the angular snout slowly nosing its way through the doors.

"Is that?" Ellie broke off, gasping as the full form of the creature entered into the building, jet black scales gleaming in the flickering torchlight.

"Correct," confirmed Ash. "That is the Skyren... awoken, it seems, from hibernation. It appears as though history will repeat itself."

"No!" roared Cassius, unbridled fury in his voice. "I will not leave them to die!"

That's Cassius for you. Never could handle injustice.

"Cassius. Calm yourself!" said Kane. "Ash. Can you show us where the people are in the building?"

The image changed to show the four shadow cast people struggling with a door. Obviously they had heard or noticed the giant feral Skyren. Suddenly what seemed like blue fire lit up around one of the figures and the individual strode forward, vanishing through the door.

As the person vanished, Kane and Merowyn stiffened.

"We need to get down there now!" said Kane.

"Thank you!" said Cassius. "Let's go already!"

"I don't think you understand Cassius. The situation is more dire than I had hoped. That was Sarrenai."

Shit.

"Time to go and kill a Skyren then I guess," said Damien cockily, drawing his sword and resting it on his shoulder in a suitably heroic pose. A good way of hiding the twitching hands that revealed his more than justified terror. The giant beast was now pushing through the door into what looked like the kitchen. The thought of having to fight something that big was certainly worrying...most of us had been on the receiving end of sparring with Seya to know that the sheer size of the beast would by no means diminish its speed.

As we began to move off Ellie turned to Ash and said, "Thank you Ash, sorry we have to leave to save our friends so soon after meeting you!"

Ash gave a strange, melancholic smile as her eyes flashed a darker blue.

A metal sheet slammed down over the exit.

The metal scorpion stood up, eyes glowing.

"I'm afraid that I cannot let you leave," said Ash, her voice emotionless, all trace of faux humanity gone.

Balls.

~

"Will you shut up!" roared Scythe at the door. His answer returned quickly as a hate filled howl that shuddered through the small one-time pantry. The beast had not stopped scrabbling or growling at the door since Sarrenai had brought them through. Roughly an hour by Scythe's calculations.

Looking around there wasn't much to take in. Sarrenai was still asleep or unconscious. Alenae had taken a protective stance toward the fallen Imperator and was keeping a constant vigil over his unmoving form. Sophia and Scythe had searched the room from top to bottom but it appeared to be little more than an old pantry - no windows or other exits as far as either of them could see. Just metal cupboards lining the walls and a skeleton to keep them company.

"Well this is a bit grim isn't it!" said Scythe, forced cheer in his voice.

Sophia flashed a smile, "We've been through worse, we will find a way out."

Scythe just stared at her.

"What?" she said, perturbed.

"Been through worse?" questioned Scythe incredulously. "As hard as the Academy is, I'm not sure it prepared us for being in a pitch black chasm in the desert, miles from civilisation, locked in a pantry with no handle and being hounded by a beast that WILL. NOT. SHUT. UP!" he barked the last part again at the door, giving it a good thump with his boot at the same time. The resulting battering of the door from the other side made a small grin appear on his face. In response to

Sophia's raised eyebrow he shrugged, "It's the little things," he said wryly. "Anyway, care to elaborate?"

Sophia shrugged, "We know what is out there. We know that it is armoured and looks to be a similar size to Seya. That gives us an advantage over other people who might pause in their fear of the unknown. We at least have an understanding of the speed and power of what that thing might be capable of. It gives us a fair chance. Personally I would say those first few times being hunted by Seya were much worse, completely unaware of her abilities, speed or strength. There was no chance then. I feel like there is now. Does that make sense?"

Scythe nodded his head slowly as if in agreement whilst puzzling over her words before shaking his head vehemently, "No, not really, no. With Seya we didn't run the risk of being actually eaten!"

"True, but I feel like I actually have at least a basic understanding of this enemy. That makes me feel much more calm about the whole situation," replied Sophia.

"I agree," interjected Alenae, causing both heads to turn to her. "Knowing one's enemy, their strengths and weaknesses, it places you in a position of power. To fight a completely unknown enemy is to be as a blind person in a duel; a lucky strike might win the day, but there is no room for strategy." She smiled at them both, "If Sophia believes she has an understanding of the beast then she has the upper hand. Our records suggest that the creature wasn't particularly intelligent in how it killed; just an unstoppable wave of muscle and motion. If we can outsmart it, we can kill it."

"Okay, I'm convinced. We have the beast right where we want it," said Scythe with a grin, "trapped outside this tiny room."

He paused and then continued with a little more solemnity, "So let's lay everything out on the table and make a plan. What do we have?"

"My bow, blades for everyone. Three active participants unless Sarrenai wakes up soon."

"Your bow isn't going to be too much use in the dark. We would need the creature to be lit up," replied Scythe. "The same goes for our blades; unless either of you can see in the dark, the creature likely wins the night vision contest."

"There are at least six more torches in our packs, that gives us some light."

Alenae opened her bag and pulled out three torches, "Nine." She then rummaged around her bag and pulled out three small round orbs.

"What are those?" asked Scythe, reaching for one but his hand was slapped away before he got too close.

"In Andurran it would translate to something close to 'fire explosion', in my language they are 'hrudan'. If lit it explodes in a fire that is thick, sticky and burns for a long time," replied Alenae. "I must warn you that this substance does not come off until it burns itself out, so above all, do not let it touch you!" Warning given she placed the orbs gently on the ground next to the torches.

"Ok, so we have light and we have weapons. What we don't have is a way out of here," mused Scythe.

"I've been thinking about that," said Sophia, "Part of me feels like if this room was a pantry of some kind it would likely have ventilation. If so, perhaps we can use it to our advantage. I think we should check behind the cupboards."

Scythe nodded, "Sounds good to me." He eyed the large, metallic frames, "I may need some help shifting these."

Together the three managed to make a gap behind each cupboard, enough to see whether there were any vents. After the third screeching frame was pulled away from the wall, the sound sending the beast into more riotous frenzy, they struck gold. High up in the wall was a large vent, a metallic gauze blocking access.

"Well," said Scythe, indicating his broad shoulders, "that is going to be very cosy."

"Relax big boy," said Sophia - a lascivious and wicked look in her eye. "I'll go first to make sure there is enough room. Alenae can push you if you get stuck. Besides," she smirked, eyes travelling slowly down his body, "...you're not *that* big."

Alenae laughed out loud, a bright, tinkling sound. Shortly Sophia and Scythe's laughter joined, mingling in the air. For a moment the tension of the situation was broken and soon the three were wiping tears from their eyes. Eventually, after too soon a time, the laughter died off and the three adopted more serious looks.

"What about Sarrenai?" asked Alenae.

"He has the least problem getting out," replied Sophia. "When he wakes, if we aren't back with good news then he will know that we are off trying to do something about that beast. It is what he would want."

With that Sophia climbed up the cupboard. A few minutes of a twirling dagger was all that was required to remove the items holding the gauze in place. Once the obstacle was out of the way she carefully placed her weapons and rucksack into the vent and then with a final nod at the others she lithely climbed into the shaft. One by one the others followed.

~

"What do you mean you can't let us leave?!" demanded Damien. "Let us out right now!"

"I meant what I said. I cannot let you leave. My protocols demand that I protect the black Seraph user," replied Ash calmly. "Please stay away from the door."

"Protect me? How can you protect me by keeping me down here?" argued Cassius. "Even if the Skyren hadn't woken up it would have still been down here with us…" he trailed off as he locked eyes with me.

"You were never going to let us leave," I stated. Hands that were already tense at the sight of the reawakened scorpion grew white knuckled around the hilts of weapons.

"Correct."

"That is why you shared all this information?"

"Correct."

"Why?"

"As mentioned, whilst able to think for myself I am still slave to my core programming. That is to ensure that the school of black propagates and succeeds whilst other Seraphim schools diminish."

"Enough of this!" raged Damien and he moved towards the door. "Let me out now!"

I realised then that it might not have been fear of the Skyren that was causing Damien's twitchy behaviour. As we had walked in the open dark of the chasm he had been fine, but coming under ground had changed something in him. Unveiled a perhaps previously unknown fear - or just one that he had never chosen to reveal. Damien was claustrophobic...and being trapped by a metal door in a small room was the last straw.

"I would not advise thi-" began Ash.

"Damien wait!" bellowed Kane.

And then things fell apart.

Energy crackled along the scorpion's tail as Damien moved towards it, roaring for it to get out of his way. He raised his sword to clash against the door as Kane shouted and then the scorpion struck.

I watched in horror as Damien fell. His lifeless body seemingly falling for an eternity as the others erupted into movement. Even as my years of training started my body moving into the ingrained patterns of Kaschan I barely recognised what I was doing, just watching as my friend collapsed - a cauterised hole in his forehead. Merowyn vanished, Kane roared and we attacked the scorpion in a cacophony of hatred, during the midst of which all I could pick out was the words by the AI, 'Ash' as she whispered, "I'm sorry."

Six attacks came down upon the scorpion. Attacks from every direction delivered by the power of hate-filled arms. Five of those attacks did nothing, sliding off the creature's overlapping metal armour. The only visible damage appeared from my blow which shattered the blade I was wielding; immediately confirming that whatever was covering the creature was much more tough than the metal our swords were forged out of, and left a slight dent in the scorpion's gleaming hide. Suddenly weaponless I danced out of the way of the snapping pincer that darted towards my leg and watched as Rikol, Ellie and Cassius continued with ineffectual attacks.

Ellie darted forwards, fluidly shifting under a razor pincer to come up with a dagger aimed at one of the glowing blue eyes. Two rapid strikes hit home as her feet carried her out of range of retribution, but the attack seemed to have done nothing - glancing off the eyes much like the rest of the body. Seeing this Rikol and Cassius swiftly changed their targets, aiming instead for the gaps between plate armour. Furious flurries were unleashed upon the creature, but when they moved back out of range it looked completely unaffected. That is until a glowing fist struck the side of the scorpion and flung it against the wall. Kane had rejoined the battle and unleashed the same strike that he had disintegrated a window with earlier. His eyes widened as the Scorpion stood up, its armour unbroken.

A ripple of energy spread from the site of Kane's impact until the scorpion's tail was once again crackling. Recognising what was about to occur Kane, myself and the others started a series of defensive movements designed to prove unpredictable and hard to hit. Just as the tail began to pulse its death knell a red flamed sword struck upwards, knocking the tail off course. The concentrated energy flared and the beam shot into the ceiling, cutting through the metal tilings as though they provided no resistance. Merowyn, her countenance grim with fury, stood on the armoured back holding the tail up with her sword as it unleashed its power.

"Looks like our skills aren't working Kane!" she yelled desperately as the creature bucked, trying to dislodge her.

"I know!" he shouted back. "It must have some kind of resistance!" He turned his attention to me, "Calidan with me. Let us see how well it can do when flipped over."

Together we moved to the side of the Scorpion and as Kane summoned his energy and struck the creature like a hammer, Merowyn leaping out of the way just before impact, I lunged forward pinning the scorpion against the wall. Muscles straining I held my shoulder under the side of the metallic fiend and heaved, flipping the scorpion fully onto its side; armoured back against the wall. The mighty tail came around to strike at me but Kane intercepted the barbed head, catching it with both hands and holding it in place. The others moved in and together we wrenched the beast onto the floor, with its underbelly facing the roof.

Once again multiple strikes descended.

Once again they were deflected.

The underside of the scorpion was as armoured as the top.

Sadly we didn't get as much respite as we had hoped. Instead of struggling to flip over like a common scorpion the torso and tail simply *rotated*. If nothing else this confirmed that there was no living creature within the metallic monstrosity.

"You will find that SC5 is difficult to defeat. Designed, as it were, to act as a guard against any intruders; including Seraphim." Ash's voice floated through the room as we once again set to moving evasively. "The armour is an alloy of metals reinforced with Seraph and a form of Seraph infused fusion ensures that it remains powered. I understand that this may not mean much to you but there is no shame in losing to such an opponent. Many others have."

With a roar of unbridled fury Kane struck the scorpion into the wall and then hit again and again, fists glowing blue like fire. His veins began to throb in his arms and neck, dripping sweat turning into a torrent. Merowyn joined him, flaming sword dancing around the scorpion, probing for weaknesses.

Energy began to gather along the scorpions shell, and inspiration hit me. Moving swiftly I skipped along the wall as the tail began to pulse blue - power building for another deadly attack. The tail pointed to face Kane and blue energy crackled...then erupted.

The blue beam passed straight through the armoured core of the scorpion, slicing it neatly in two up to the root of the tail. My arms and legs were wrapped around the thick trunk of the tail and with all my power I had squeezed, directing the beam towards the host rather than my friends.

One by one the blue eyes disappeared. SC5 lay still; a smoking ruin.

"Yes! Well done Calidan!" shouted Kane, clapping me on the shoulder, Merowyn stayed back, knowing what was running through my mind. She touched Kane softly as his features revealed puzzlement at my lack of excitement, and then recognition hit and they both watched as I joined my friends next to Damien. Perhaps a minute had passed since he had fallen, and yet he already looked more like a corpse than someone who up to a minute beforehand had been filled with vigour and exuberance for life. Someone who had always been up for a laugh, and always had your back - that was Damien. Dependable and steadfast, cheerful and daring and now lying still at the bottom of a dark chasm in lands unknown. Such, perhaps, is the life of an Imperator.

In silent solidarity we knelt around our friend. Rikol cried silently, cradling his best friend's head. Whilst we had all known and loved Damien, Rikol and he had been inseparable over the past two years, daring each other into all sorts of mischief. Chasing girls and pranking teachers had been the name of the game. Rikol more often than not coming up with some audacious, often grotesque plan and Damien, chuckling heartily, would carry it through.

Rikol bent his head to Damien's and mouthed something I couldn't make out. When he looked up there was fire in his eyes.

"You said your name was Ash. Before I leave I'm going to make damn sure that you live up to your name."

There was such venom in his voice, such twisted hate-filled venom.

Cassius rose and drew Rikol into a rough embrace. At first he resisted it but then relented, the shudders running through his body at odds with the promise of vengeance in his eyes. Ellie rose and then myself, and together we joined the embrace. When we separated Rikol was dry eyed.

Cassius held out his sword and pointed it at the glowing blue form, "AI Ash…

…You're going to burn."

CHAPTER THIRTY ONE
ESCAPE

~

"Ow!"

"Quiet!"

"Then tell Alenae to stop poking me in the behind!"

"It is the only way to make you move faster!"

"It's not my fault that I barely fit in this metal box," Scythe grumbled, slowly squeezing his way along the shaft of the vent. Sophia sniggered and continued leading the way, hoping that the vent would lead them out of the building and away from the monstrous beast that lay in wait beneath.

Underneath the group two large red eyes ceased unleashing all of the might of its optic fury on the metal door and swivelled to the ceiling. Its prey thought that it could escape. Six inch fangs bared in what could be construed as a 'toothy' smile - nothing escaped its claws. Nothing.

After a further ten minutes of shuffling through the dark vent Sophia came to a dead end.

"What? No!" she exclaimed, frantically touching the metallic surface in front of her.

"What's wrong?" came Scythe's voice.

"There isn't an exit!" she replied, voice rising to hysterical levels.

"Stay calm," Scythe said, having drawn near. "No exits on the sides?"

"No. No!"

"How about above?"

A pause.

"...Know it all."

With as silent a shove as possible Sophia lifted the top of the vent and deftly pulled herself out onto what felt like the roof of the building, grateful for the limited breeze that the cavern provided. One by one the others escaped the confines of the metal shaft and paused, taking in the new sense of freedom.

Alenae spoke up first, "Right, what now?"

"We need to distract the creature, keep it lit up so we have a target to hit," Sophia replied, "we could ring the road with torches, get the beast into the open and then Alenae and I can hit it with my arrows and her hrudan."

Scythe sighed, "Leaving me as…"

"Bait."

"That's cold."

"Believe me it's not what I want Scythe, but out of the three of us you are the most nimble in combat and have the highest chance of surviving an encounter with that creature. If you can lead it into the fire, we can hit it hard and hopefully drop it," Sophia explained, her hand finding his in the dark. "I don't want to lose you, so come back to me you hear?"

He kissed her deeply, breathing in the scent of her.

"Count on it."

With that Scythe collected the pack with the torches and slowly made his way to the side of the roof. He deftly slipped over the lip and made the short descent to the ground. Careful not to make any noise he swung around the building until he hit the cobbled road. Confident that he was back in front and near the main doors he piled the torches and, gathering his tool kit, made a spark.

The torches flared to light.

Quickly he flung the torches around the road, creating a circle of flickering light. His nerves were on fire, every sense heightened by the adrenaline surging through his veins - expecting to feel razor claws at any moment.

Seconds passed, no movement.

Taking a deep breath Scythe let out a roar. A scream of defiance.

Sophia and Alenae jumped at the sound. Both held their weapons ready, Sophia with an arrow loosely notched and Alenae with a flint ready to light her explosives.

After a time Scythe moved forward, determined to draw the creature out into the open. He strode towards the main doors and, picking up the torch he had cast on the steps, strode into the building.

Nothing moved.

Nothing stirred.

Nothing was inside.

Scythe whirled, mind racing.

"Sophia! It's already outside! RUN!" he bellowed, as he sprinted back to the door.

Behind the two women a pair of glowing red eyes opened.

Sophia and Alenae heard Scythe shout something but the sound was muffled. Sophia frowned - had the darkness just become fractionally lighter? Realization hit like a thunderbolt, and reacting purely on instinct she grabbed Alenae's arm and leapt. The assassin chieftain's scream of surprise turning into one of anguish as a massive claw tore through the air where she had been standing - the tip catching her leg instead of her spine and laying it open to the bone.

Able to judge the distance thanks to the flames, Sophia hit the ground and rolled.

Alenae hit with a sickening thud. Scythe burst out of the mess hall just in time for the third impact, the beast landing with no grace or finesse; plummeting from the roof and crashing with a splinter of cobbles atop of Alenae's still form. A deep, hungry growl reverberated through the air. Sophia rose from her roll, spun with arrow notched and released. The arrow streaked towards its target and bounced off a scaled hide. Muscles bunching, the beast leapt at Sophia who rolled out of the way, firing as she moved - the arrow embedding itself into the underbelly of the beast but with no visible effect. As it landed, Scythe danced in, rolling under the belly of the creature; twin kamas flashing.

His left handed kama hit a scale and bounced, skittering across the armoured torso. The second found a seam between the scales and as Scythe finished his roll the blade continued, leaving a trail of red gushing from the wound. The beast roared and twisted, tail lashing out and catching Scythe a glancing blow, sending him spinning across the floor. As the creature began to move towards the stunned Imp an arrow embedded itself in its right eye, eliciting a howl of pain that caused the reinforced glass in the surrounding buildings to shake. Whilst the beast was distracted Scythe recovered enough to slip around the creature.

"Didn't you shoot it in the eye already?!" he yelled as he moved.

"Doesn't look like it held it back for long! Help Alenae!" came the reply as Sophia sprinted around the side of a building, firing as she moved, the beast on her tail.

Forgotten for a moment, Scythe moved towards the still form of Alenae, a pool of blood slowly spreading from her leg. Quickly he dragged her to the corner of the great doors that led into the mess hall and tearing off his belt wrapped it around her leg, creating a tourniquet.

That done he leapt up the side of the building, praying that Sophia could last long enough for him to finish what they had started.

Sophia flinched back as a claw slashed at her face, missing by centimetres. The beast was quick, agile and extremely strong but seemingly appeared unused to fighting creatures that fought back. She utilised everything that fighting Seya had taught her, running in erratic patterns, rolling and diving, the beast always within a hair's breadth of hitting her yet so far she was managing to survive. But she knew her luck wouldn't last forever. Already her muscles and lungs ached. Even with the massive level of conditioning and fitness that the past two years at the Academy had imbued her body with, the sheer speed of the creature was forcing her to utilise everything she had. Sweat poured off her body, whether from fear, adrenaline or the exertion, she did not know - likely all three.

A shout came from above. Hearing it Sophia took a swift turn to the right, back to the circle of flames. As she sprinted past, the beast on all fours snapping at her heels, an orb hurtled through the air, the wick lit.

It shattered on the cobblestones, narrowly missing the gigantic creature and causing a gout of thick, viscous flame to erupt, spreading quickly over a large area. The armoured beast, mid-chase of Sophia, suddenly became aware that there was a greater threat in the area. Its head swivelled to the rooftop where Scythe stood, frantically trying to light a second orb with Alenae's flint. Mid step the beast turned, shifting its awe inspiring bulk faster than thought and moved for the building. Landing on the side of the wall its claws puncturing deep into the metal and the creature heaved itself upwards, flinging its body towards the sky.

Scythe knew the creature was coming for him and frantically worked the flint, trying to spark the fuse of the fire orb. He heard the crunch of claws into the metal frame of the building and knew that his next breath would likely be his last. With a last desperate movement he struck the flint and sparks flew, landing on the wick. Picking up the orb he stood and turned, flinging the bomb as hard as he could, just as the beast's mighty head crested the roof.

Gelatinous flame burst across the face and chest of the beast, eating into the armoured scales and spreading, coating everything in a thick, burning oil. The fire coated the creature's head, setting its eyes alight and searing the great red orbs until they bubbled in their sockets, finally bursting from the heat. Bellowing in agony the beast twisted and fell from the roof, a burning comet writhing through the air. It struck the cobbles with an almighty crash, turning the stones beneath to dust.

Scythe walked to the edge of the roof, face and hands blistered and red from the proximity of the fiery blast. He saw the monster screaming as fire continued to burn and calmly reached down for the third and final orb. Almost carelessly he tossed it, the unlit orb spinning through the air before splintering atop the burning creature, the thick liquid spreading across the unburnt areas of the beast before, like a spark in dry grass, the liquid caught and flame erupted, covering the beast in a fiery conflagration.

The beast's roars rose in pitch as the fire cut deeper into its flesh, reducing its hide to cinders and cooking it where it lay. Scythe deftly descended the building and went to join Sophia who was watching the creature burn.

"Think this will be enough?" she asked.

"If not then I don't know what will," Scythe replied grimly as they stood side by side watching the creature burn, a foul stench of cooked meat filling the air.

Ten minutes later the beast was still. Flames continued to lick at its body with most of its face and torso reduced to bone. Satisfied that the creature was dead Sophia and Scythe tended Alenae, sewing up her vicious leg wound as effectively as possible under the light of the burning beast and surrounding torches. Alenae had roused several times as Sophia stitched her leg, each time passing out again shortly after. She had lost a considerable amount of blood but thankfully her artery hadn't been touched.

As they worked the beast twitched. Unnoticed.

Satisfied that the prey that had hurt him so horrendously had not seen him move, the creature pushed through the agony of movement, rising silently, molten flesh slewing off its body as it did so. Blind, noseless it ventured forth, step by silent step using its one remaining ear to locate its prey. It knew that it was near death and only sheer rage and the promise of vengeance was keeping it alive. It drew closer, shaking on unsteady legs.

As Sophia finished stitching, Alenae's eyes fluttered open. They immediately widened in fear and horror causing both Sophia and Scythe to swivel and gasp at the monstrous sight before them and the massive jaws that were descending towards the three intrepid adventurers.

A blue streak flashed across their vision. A man lit with blue light.

The man streamed across the ground and crashed into the beast. However instead of an impact there was...nothing. It was as though the figure had completely disappeared. For a moment the beast and companions looked at each other, each as perturbed as the other, and then as the beast took a step forward a razor edged blade slid out of its chest. The screams of the beast started again as moment by moment the blade emerged from inside its body, slashing with wild abandon. Unable to find its assailant the creature clawed its own chest, breaking bone and tearing what remaining flesh it had, but only seemingly assisting the phantom sword in completing its work.

By the time the echoes of the horrific death knells had faded Sarrenai stood panting in a pile of steaming, charred flesh and organs. He lifted a hand to the three amazed watchers, smiled weakly and keeled over.

~

"AI Ash, you're going to burn," stated Cassius, his eyes cold and dark, almost tinged with black as he pointed his sword at the blue figure.

"Burn? It seems unlikely - this room has no furnishings capable of producing a flame," responded Ash.

Cassius just smiled coolly, "I'm sure that I will find a way."

"Destroying me is not the answer Cassius. You are a wielder of the black Seraph, I can train you, protect you, show you knowledge beyond your wildest dreams!"

Cassius said nothing, his eyes scanning the room, looking for a method of removing Ash from our lives. A difficult task; as Ash had pointed out there was nothing flammable in the room as all the materials appeared to be some form of metal. Aside from a box with lots of flashing lights the only other seemingly important object was the raised platform where Ash stood.

"I have an idea," said Cassius, his eyes on the flashing interface. "If she isn't real then my guess is that the flashing lights somehow relate to her being in this room." He motioned to Kane who nodded encouragingly, "Kane could you perhaps remove the box?"

"No, don't!" Ash cried. "Please, Cassius, don't!"

"Will you let us leave?" Cassius asked without turning around.

"My programming prevents me."

"Then we have nothing further to talk about." Blue fire lit up around Kane's fist. "Goodbye Ash."

Kane struck the metal box and the structure disintegrated. With its destruction Ash screamed, her figure flickering wildly before vanishing completely. After a moment the metal shutter over the door slowly wound itself back into the ceiling, leaving us free to leave.

I clapped a hand onto Rikol's shoulder who was looking at the spot where Ash had vanished with vitriol.

"It's over Rikol... Damien can rest easy." I said gently.

"Not yet," he replied. "I told her she would become Ash and I meant it." He looked over at Merowyn who was standing in the corner looking sadly at Damien's corpse, her arm around Ellie. "Merowyn, would you please see if you can destroy that platform?" he asked.

"With pleasure," came the reply. Merowyn slowly walked over to the platform and gripped her sword tightly. A moment later red flame burst from her hand and raced up the hilt to the tip of the blade, with a deft movement she rotated the sword until she held it in both hands, point facing down over the platform.

"This is for Damien!" she cried as she thrust the blade downwards, piercing the metal plate. With a shout Merowyn threw more power into the blade and the platform splintered, vibrant red flame bursting from the cracks. And with red, righteous fury, Merowyn helped Rikol ensure that Ash became her namesake.

We paused for a moment to watch the dancing flames, each of us lost in our own thoughts until Kane interrupted, clearing his throat loudly and saying, "We can't tarry here. The others need our help. Gather your things and let's move."

"What about Damien?" asked Rikol.

Kane paused and looked towards my heartbroken friend. "I'm sorry Rikol but we can't take him with us." He looked towards Merowyn, an unspoken question passing between them to which she nodded. Looking back at Rikol he spoke again, "He will get a warrior's funeral."

Merowyn strode forward and placed Damien's blade on his body, held with both hands across his chest. Concentrating she held a hand out and after a moment red fire set the sword alight. Slowly the fire spread from the sword to engulf Damien's body. A moment of silence and then we moved on, leaving behind the murderous AI and a fallen friend to rescue our comrades.

PRESENT DAY

~

THE TRAIL OF CORPSES CONTINUED. For three days I had tracked Cassius, trapped as he was in his abhorrent Skyren form. By and large it had been without incident. The Thyrkan scouting party had been utterly destroyed, aside from the warlock who had vanished without a trace, and I had come across no other signs of Thyrkan. Since then Cassius had continued moving, veering off at times to slaughter various goats and livestock that lived on these plains but otherwise heading unerringly north.

Always careful to stay downwind of the beast, I maintained a close distance. And by close I mean as far away as possible without losing him completely. As I walked my hand continuously trailed the tattoo that radiated outward from the centre of my left palm. Cassius had once before turned into what he was now. Deep in the bowels of the Emperor's fortress. Many had died, slaughtered like the goat that I now stood before, savaged and ruined. Only the Emperor, despite being the bastard that he is, had managed to subdue Cassius, using some form of magic to repress the monster inside of him. A glyph that he burnt into Cassius's scaled flesh, forcibly causing Cassius's mind to surface from whatever depths it was held under. The same glyph that I had copied (hopefully correctly) onto my palm. And so in some respects my plan was simple, get close enough to grab Cassius and hold on until his mind took back control. Until one considers that first, being that close to a Skyren is not easy, and second, grabbing a Skyren is probably much like pulling the tail on an angry lion...only infinitely worse.

But it's not like I had many other options to try.

On the eve of the second day I had spotted smoke rising in the distance. What had appeared to be a little hamlet of several thatched huts. Closing on it on the third day I found that Cassius had been busy. The slaughter was absolute. Broken bodies and savagely torn limbs strewed the buildings and yard. The Thyrkan who had taken up residence in the hamlet had been thoroughly routed, as evidenced by the trail of bodies that lay, piece by piece, in a northerly direction. After a quick search for unspoiled supplies, I continued onwards following the bodies. Despite the corpses the trail was growing colder

- much like my gigantic friend the beast version of himself seemed to require little sleep meaning that each time I paused to rest Cassius was that much further away.

I just had to hope that something would catch his attention and keep him occupied long enough for me to catch up.

It turned out the wait wasn't long.

~

It turned out that the shattered plains had a bigger crack in it than expected. A large rift in the ground that seemed to house a company of Thyrkan - hidden from the world. Another surprise was that contrary to popular belief Thyrkan did not always eat everyone they meet. Who knew?

In the rift, toiling in and out of what looked to be mine shafts were hundreds of people. Thousands.

And descending to the ground nearly two hundred feet below me was Cassius, claws digging into the rock face, no doubt eager for his next meal. If I didn't stop this then Cassius would either be killed or find himself slaughtering more innocent lives.

I thought quickly. If I could get the Thyrkan to round up the slaves and put them in their pens before Cassius got there then some might be saved. As good a plan as any. Time to make a scene.

I leapt off the ledge.

As I fell I reached into my pool of Seraph. Green energy awaited me, and I let it infuse my being. A green shield emerged around my skin, crackling with energy. Like an emerald thunderbolt I hit the floor of the rift, splitting the ground with my impact and sending wall of dust to accompany the explosive sound I had made. Sometimes it is great being a Seraphim.

I winced inwardly as I landed, feeling my pool of Seraph shrinking by a significant margin. Without Seya by my side my Seraph abilities were limited - I cut off that train of thought. Thinking about Seya led to a dark place and my soul yawned with emptiness, besides, now was not the time for introspection.

Roughly eighty Thyrkan warriors were scrambling towards me, an unorganised melee of chaos. I could almost see the moment when a captain arrived to take control. A rippling motion spread through the discordant ranks and thirty peeled off smartly to bludgeon unfortunate slaves towards their pens. The other fifty continued running towards me but slowly drew in their ranks. At one hundred paces they slowed, shield bearers moving smartly to the front, others with long handled spears behind. What had been a disorganised motley crew suddenly became an effective organised army. How the captains did it, I have no idea. But damn it was a useful trick.

Not much time. Thankfully most of the immediate slaves were herded back to their study pens.

A thud behind me.

I bolted.

Moving in a straight line, pumping Seraph through my body I sprinted towards the marching Thyrkan unit whilst at the same time raising my shield again. With a flare of Seraph I rocketed through the air and plummeted through their ranks, the power and speed of my green self scattering several rows of Thyrkan like bowling pins. Another burst of power and I threw myself into the air, scattering more dust over the heads of the Thyrkan. For a split second many were blinded by the dust, and that was more time than Cassius needed. He hit like a battering ram, massive taloned hands scathing through armoured Thyrkan troops, knocking aside shields and cutting down their owners. A bark of alarm went up as they recognised their foe and another ripple appeared as the captain gave new orders. A ring was swiftly formed around Cassius, spears and shields to the fore.

Under the presumed but so far invisible captain's influence, nets were brought forward, made of thick twine with heavy lead weights attached to the ends. As one, the nets were cast into the centre of the ring, four in all, each one hitting Cassius in quick succession. His tail twitched, doubtless trying to lash out, and his claws went to work, but the shifting layers of nets meant that the cut areas soon moved, the gaps closing up. As it was the Thyrkan only needed a short amount of time. The circle closed and then, with one swift movement, the heavy spears thrust, biting deeply into the armoured creature. The strength of the Thyrkan allowing the blades to cut unmercilessly.

In perfect synchronicity several of the heavy spears stayed in place, held onto by multiple Thyrkan as Cassius's thrashing intensified, whilst the others disengaged, the blades twisting viciously as they retracted, pulled back as far as possible and then thrust forward again.

And again.

I had to find the captain quickly, without an officer providing structure the well oiled Thyrkan unit would soon fall apart. Though Cassius's flesh was starting to heal, just like any Skyren, the multitude of wounds he was receiving could take a toll. I simply didn't know. I had seen him receive wounds that should have been mortal whilst just Cassius so hopefully raging Skyren Cassius would not die from something as simple as spears.

My eyes caught a flash of movement from a wooden shack that gave a central view of the facility. Trusting my gut I sprinted for the building, racing up the wooden steps and kicked down the door. Spinning inside I ducked under an incoming blade and swept up as I moved past, my sword shearing through the captain's chest and spine, before finishing the spin with my second blade which neatly removed the already dead creature's head. Andronicus would have said it was too flashy, but as the giant of a man had died from an infected wound inflicted by a not-quite-dead Thyrkan I feel confident in my method.

Looking outside I could see the well ordered ranks of the Thyrkan start to fall apart. Those holding onto the heavy spears started letting go, as if not understanding their purpose in holding the large weapons. Soon there was only one spear holder on each weapon, still stabbing at the creature in front of them, but with none of the same impact as previously. The circle broke. Thyrkan ran in, swords out, swinging at the captured Skyren. Unfortunately for the Thyrkan sword bearers, to be close enough to hit Cassius meant that Cassius, even when covered in nets, was close enough to hit you. As the swords thrust home Cassius surged forward, grasping all the closest attackers with his armoured arms and simply squeezed.

Popped Thyrkan. Unpleasant but strangely satisfying.

Screams resounded from near me, wrenching my gaze from the blood soaked display to where the slaves were being rounded up. The Thyrkan dealing with the slaves had started killing them rather than moving them to the pens. Cursing myself for my foolishness I took off, sprinting towards the rampaging adversaries. I say adversaries, they were so intent on their own bloodlust that they didn't see my blades coming. Like an avenging spectre of death I swept through the remaining Thyrkan, dodging the few blades that they sought to send my way, and removing them from existence. An easy enough job, but one that took several minutes. Minutes that I didn't have to spare. At any moment Cassius could be loose.

A shrieking Thyrkan ran past my blade. As I casually reached out and decapitated it my mind clocked that it hadn't been one of the ones I had been dispatching. As the next one ran past I realised the problem.

Cassius was loose.

Well, shit.

Looking behind me I could see the remaining Thyrkan fleeing in all directions, an angry, raging lizard man hot on their tails. Cassius was extracting a bloody revenge, and worryingly I was running out of Thyrkan to keep him occupied. If I didn't stop him soon then the slaves would be next. And so with a heavy sense of fatalism I found myself turning around and running towards the armoured behemoth. Likely towards death.

Cassius raised his head. He had smelt my scent before, back in the depths of the Emperor's tower. A helpless man, begging for my friend to stop the killing, crying as he fought to deflect vicious blows from innocents. I had wondered whether this version of Cassius would remember - a mystery solved as he immediately turned towards me, leaving off his rampant slaughter of the routing Thyrkan.

I immediately diverted, knowing full well that Cassius was going to hunt me down. I could no longer rely on utilising the Thyrkan as a distraction. Thinking quickly, I ran for the mines hoping to rely on the tunnels to slow the beast. Ducking and weaving I ran further and further from the main arterial routes used by the slaves to older areas of the mine, the beast always close on my tail. It was as the floor split under my feet that I realised two things. The first being that an enraged Skyren gives no thought to structural ceiling supports, and the second that a mine is a very dangerous place to be running for your life.

And so I fell.

EPILOGUE

~

THE BODY OF DAMIEN WAS still burning when shadows in the corner of the room flitted together, drawn into a thick, twisted knot. From this shadowy mass appeared a man, his stature diminutive, with wispy blonde hair and a pair of errant glasses resting slightly askew on his nose.

"Well…" he mused to himself, "that was interesting."

Ignoring the burning corpse he walked to a nondescript panel in the wall and placed his hand upon the surface. A moment passed and then a green light pulsed - silently the panel slid open to reveal stairs leading down.

The man soon emerged into another chamber directly beneath the room he had just left. Within the room was a series of light filled terminals, and rows upon rows of data banks - the true beating heart of ASH.

A familiar blue figure turned towards him as he strode through the terminals.

"Did you see everything?" Ash asked.

"Of course," came the reply.

"Thoughts?"

"The Andurran 'Emperor' is as crafty as ever."

"How so?"

"He long ago removed any Black Seraphim from his ranks. It appears that he has decided to utilise this one before discarding - knowing full well that any defences set here would likely be rendered ineffective against black users."

"Do you think they learnt anything of note?"

"Nothing that the Empire doesn't already know."

"Do you think he knows that you live?"

"He suspects. These Imperators of his are just new methods of trying to seek me out."

"Will they succeed?"

"Not until I want them to."

"Excellent. In that case-" a tray opened in one of the terminals, "please find within all the data gathered on the members of that party, including Seraph levels and emotional analysis."

The figure stooped to retrieve something from the terminal.

"Many thanks Ash, I'll come back to talk with you again one of these days."

"My pleasure...Charles."

AUTHOR'S NOTE

~

TO YOU, READER, WHO PRESUMABLY just finished winding your way through this novel, thank you. I'm sure that here I am meant to state something wise and profound. Perhaps about how this book is all for you, the reader. But that wouldn't be the truth. The truth is that I wrote this book for me, a mixture of, 'to see if I could' combined with wanting to write something that I, myself, would enjoy reading.

Hopefully that means that the book is enjoyable for everyone interested in fantasy, and that I don't just have a skewed taste!

Either way, thanks again reader for having the pluck and courage to try out a new book from an unknown author, it means a great deal. If you enjoyed it, please let the world know!

Printed in Great Britain
by Amazon